Tales of the NAVIGATORS

✷ Strange Space™ Short Stories ✷

Volume 1

KATIE SILVERWINGS

Memphis, TN

PEPTALK PRODUCTIONS, LLC

Publisher's Cataloging-in-Publication Data
provided by Five Rainbows Cataloging Services

Names: Silverwings, Katie, 1991- author.
Title: Tales of the navigators : Strange Space short stories / Katie Silverwings.
Description: Memphis, TN : PepTalk Productions, 2024. | Series: Strange Space tales of the navigators, vol. 1.
Identifiers: LCCN 2024906077 (print) | ISBN 978-1-959922-21-6 (paperback) | ISBN 978-1-959922-22-3 (hardcover) | ISBN 978-1-959922-23-0 (ebook) | ISBN 978-1-959922-24-7 (audiobook)
Subjects: LCSH: Outer space--Fiction. | Friendship--Fiction. | Family--Fiction. | Individual differences--Fiction. | Science fiction. | Short stories. | BISAC: FICTION / Science Fiction / Action & Adventure. | FICTION / Friendship, | FICTION / Short Stories (single author) | GSAFD: Science fiction. | Short stories.
Classification: LCC PS3619.I58 T35 2024 (print) | LCC PS3619.I58 (ebook) | DDC 813/.6--dc23.

Published by PepTalk Productions, LLC 2024
Memphis, Tennessee, USA
www.PepTalkProductionsLLC.com

To my family, my friends, and the wonderful folks of the Strange Space™ Fan Club who've made it possible for all these stories to see the light of day.

Books by Katie Silverwings

FEATHERED FRIENDSHIP
✦ A Strange Space™ Novella ✦

CELADON
✦ A Strange Space™ Novel ✦

HOW OCEAN MERLANI STOLE THEIR NAVIGATOR
✦ A Strange Space™ Novel ✦

WARMTH AND DARKNESS
✦ A Strange Space™ Novella ✦

THE GARDEN IN THE DARKNESS
✦ A Strange Space™ Novel ✦

TALES OF THE NAVIGATORS: VOLUME 1
✦ Strange Space™ Short Stories ✦

ON THE SUBJECT OF KITTENS AND MITTENS
✦ A Strange Space™ Novella ✦

The printing of this edition of *Tales of the Navigators: Volume 1* was made possible through the generous support of the members of the Strange Space™ Fan Club, including:

Astral Navigator

Sharon T. Hinton

Space Adventurer (1 Year)

Tabitha

Thank you so much to all of my Fan Club members and supporters! I couldn't do this without you.

To find out more about the Strange Space™ Fan Club and join for free, visit:

www.KatieSilverwings.com/Fan-Club

Contents

The First Contact Era

The Novan War Era

The Post-War Era

CONTENTS

APPENDIX

Tales of the NAVIGATORS

★ Strange Space™ Short Stories ★

Volume 1

KATIE SILVERWINGS

FOREWORD

When the characters of the *Strange Space™* universe first introduced themselves, it was in the form of a novel bearing that name. My writing process, though, is one of discovery; I'm seldom the sort to outline something, write all of it, and then move on. I sit down with a general idea and start typing, and sooner or later the characters guide me to the story they actually want to tell. If I get stuck along the way, I ask one of the characters a question about themself and their world and write a short story to answer it. Sometimes, they drop hints about other moments in their lives in passing that turn out to be far more important by the time I get to the end of the final draft.

In the case of *Strange Space™*, I made the ultimately fortunate mistake of asking a certain grouchy old Navigator who appears in its first chapter just *who* the Florivan was who could put up with him. He introduced me to Celadon Toreval, and I have had a near-endless list of stories to write ever since.

Some of those first short stories I wrote to figure out the workings of this universe have gone on to be published as full-length novels. Ten of the others are presented here in this first volume of *Tales of the Navigators*.

Each of these stories offers a new perspective on the characters of the *Strange Space™* universe and the world they inhabit. I am so pleased to be sharing them with you!

–Katie Silverwings

TIMELINE OF *STRANGE SPACE*™ *ADVENTURES*

The following timeline lists all of the published *Strange Space*™ *Adventures* and Short Stories in roughly chronological order. Where stories feature major time skips, they have been placed based on the earliest events of that story.

Short Stories marked with *[1] can be found in *Tales of the Navigators: Volume 1.*

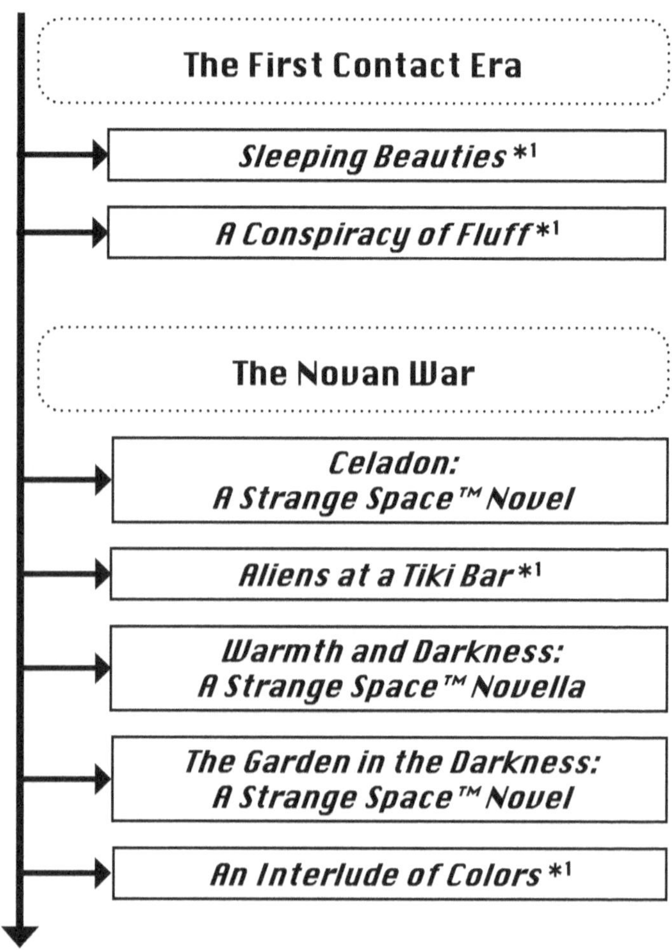

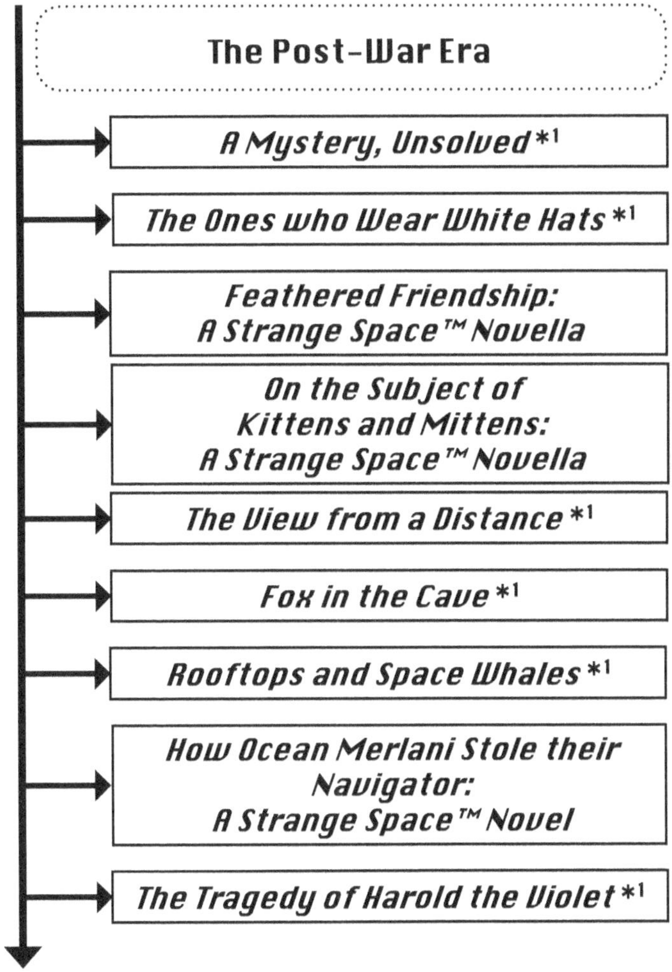

The Post-War Era

A Mystery, Unsolved *[1]

The Ones who Wear White Hats *[1]

Feathered Friendship:
A Strange Space™ Novella

On the Subject of
Kittens and Mittens:
A Strange Space™ Novella

The View from a Distance *[1]

Fox in the Cave *[1]

Rooftops and Space Whales *[1]

How Ocean Merlani Stole their
Navigator:
A Strange Space™ Novel

The Tragedy of Harold the Violet *[1]

The First Contact Era

Sleeping Beauties

✦ A Strange Space™ Short Story ✦

*To all the curious humans, explorers, and artisans who seek
to make the world resemble our fondest dreams.*

Space is big; everyone knows this.

The distance between planets is wide, and the distance between *stars* even more so.

With the laws of physics being what they are, even eight hundred years on from the colonization of Mars, the swiftest ships humanity has ever built cannot travel further than the edge of Sol's planetary system without taking decades or more to get there. Likewise, messages between Earth and her five extra-solar colonies are constrained to the speed of light itself. No method yet known to humanity can break that galactic speed limit, although generations of brilliant people have set their collective genius towards finding a means of doing so.

One particular chain of messages between Earth's Sol Coalition Scientific Directorate and the colony at Luyten's Star is a prime example of the limits of keeping in touch over the vastness of space.

The first message in the chain is one which creates great excitement both when it is broadcasted from Luyten's Star and precisely twelve years and one hundred and thirty-five days later when the signal finally reaches Earth. This message announces to all who might be listening that on the grand occasion of the colony's fifty year anniversary, the noted explorer Dr. Hereford Travis has announced he will be mounting an expedition to the nearby twin-star system of Procyon for the purpose of establishing a research base on one of its planets. Long range analysis has shown this particular exoplanet to be promisingly Earth-like. The expedition takes as its inspiration the efforts already underway by the celebrated pioneers of the Proxima Centauri colony, who had relatively recently completed construction of full satellite colonies on several planets between Alpha and Beta Centauri.

By the time the congratulatory message from Earth regarding Dr. Travis' expedition has reached Luyten's Star, the construction of LSS *Hulthemia* is already complete. It's quite a small starship when compared to the bulk of USS *North* or any of her generation-ship sisters who had carried colonists from Earth, but *Hulthemia* is far more advanced and doesn't have nearly so long a journey to make. Procyon is only a single light year away from Luyten's Star, after all, and with the small vessel's state-of-the-art engines and solar sails, the journey there has been projected to last just over twenty Earth-standard years. This will still be a lengthy voyage, but that too has been taken into account: the eleven members of *Hulthemia*'s crew will be traveling in cryogenic sleep, to awaken only when the ship has reached Procyon's heliopause boundary.

Dr. Travis' cordial response to the Sol Coalition Scientific Directorate is sent directly from *Hulthemia* after the ship has left orbit. On the amused recommendation of the mission's primary astrophysicist, the message includes a reminder that the Directorate will need to forward all future correspondence to the outpost on Procyon c which the team will be in the midst of building by the time word of their grand send-off from the North City Spaceport reaches Earth.

This message also includes video greetings from each of *Hulthemia*'s crew members as they climb into their comfortably small cryogenic stasis pods and Dr. Travis activates the system to seal them in and induce the deep hibernation state which will protect them from age and illness as the ship makes the long, lonely journey.

The sleeping explorers do not know precisely *what* they'll find, but the best data their long-range telescopes and scans have been able to compile has told them that the planet they have their eye on is capable of supporting Earth-type life. Nothing has ever been observed which would indicate sapient life forms with any level of technology in the system, but there is clearly life of *some* kind there waiting for them to study. Obtaining more precise information than that would be past the limits of humanity's present technology, even if the explorers' own home star hadn't recently been experiencing solar storms which interfere with the data collection just as much as the interaction of the solar wind from Procyon's two stars with the galactic cosmic rays has.

Still, enough data has been gathered for the colony's leadership to have agreed to send Dr. Travis and his crew forth. Humans are by nature a curious species, after all. Now that Luyten's Star's settled worlds have developed to a point where they can possibly send explorers onward, it's only natural that they'd do so.

It is, therefore, only with the greatest ceremony and appropriate words of optimistic pride in his ship and his team that Dr. Travis bids farewell to Luyten's Star at the end of his historic message to the rest of humanity. The message sent, he performs one last check of the vital signs of each of his crew members and confirms that the ship's autopilot is functioning correctly. That done, he is ready to climb into his own cryosleep pod.

As the seal on the translucent dome of the lid activates and the cryogenic stasis systems activate, Dr. Travis closes his eyes and relaxes, secure in the knowledge that he and his team will wake to a new world of discovery; the first of a new generation of interstellar explorers and pioneers.

"Eldest! Pardon the interruption, but I *must* speak with you."

"One moment, dear—Amaril? Why don't you take your practice sphere down to the Youngest's office and get their opinion on it while you wait for me? There's a good kitten—Now, what is it, Ireven? You usually let me know when you're coming to visit."

"I usually have more warning, Eldest, and usually things are of a less urgent nature."

"Oh, *urgent*, is it? I was wondering why you seemed so agitated. What is your urgent news, then?"

"One of our scouts has just sent a report of an encounter with a small ship."

"Have they, now, Ireven? What sort of a ship?"

"Alien, but not from any of the peoples we have come near before. It seems to be sailing on stellar winds alone."

"And what of the ship's crew?"

"Our scout's scans confirmed life signs, but the ship hasn't sent any signals indicating they're aware of our scout's presence. The periodic broadcasts our scout detected which led them to the ship seem to be automated and aimed towards the Near Red Star. We believe that is the ship's origin point. At its current speed, it is projected to pass directly through our system between twelve and fifteen solar orbit cycles from now."

"I see. The Near Red Star, you say?"

"Yes, Eldest."

"In that case, you will take one of our vessels out yourself to investigate further... and be prepared to greet these aliens, if they show themselves to be friendly."

"*Greet* them, Eldest? The Council's policy has always been that our vessels remain hidden—or at the very least, to dip into the Strange to avoid being noticed by aliens for more than a moment."

"I *am* aware of our policies, Ireven. The last Beacon to shine in our navigation spheres was traveling to the Near Red Star's system. I would not be surprised if these aliens are associated with him. If they are, they will certainly be worth our attention and greetings."

"...Yes, Eldest."

"I expect you to keep in contact over the relay-radio so the Council can be aware of the situation as it unfolds—and I would ask that you take my apprentice with you to observe on my behalf."

"Eldest? Are you certain? Amaril is little more than a *kitten*, and a survivor-smallest at that—and I know you have been training them, but they are still—"

"My apprentice is young, yes, but I believe they are ready. It would be good for them to take a turn jumping stars, if they are to one day be among those tasked with keeping them for our people. And while it may be true that they are extraordinarily sensitive even considering their circumstances... I would not be surprised if that turns to your benefit in the end. Trust me, Ireven."

"...As you wish, Eldest."

Dr. Travis is more than proud of the crew he ultimately assembles for the *Hulthemia* expedition. Each one of his volunteers is precisely the sort of cross-disciplinary expert needed to pull the expedition off and prove that a second, larger team should be sent to join them. Dr. Travis himself is, of course, a fully qualified medical doctor in addition to his hard-earned expertise in cartography and xenobiology. The rest of his team are similarly versatile. The doubling and mixing of specialties is valuable, too, when it comes to making the most of the limited space of the ship and the resources it could carry along.

They are all, without a doubt, the finest minds the Luyten's Star colony could spare for this first exploration voyage to their nearest neighbor in space.

They are also, all of them, the sorts of people who didn't have many close family ties to leave behind, or who were willing to volunteer for a potentially one-way mission anyway.

Along with her ten brilliant scientist-explorers, *Hulthemia* carries one young woman with an entirely different set of skills. This eleventh member of the team is less of an engineer and more of a *maker*. It will be her task to take care of the planned outpost once it's been built so the rest of the crew can focus on their own duties—and to find ways to create anything the researchers might require to survive and do their work that *Hulthemia* has not had the foresight to bring along.

This young woman is a different sort of brilliant, and the direct descendant of a similar specialist who'd been one of several carried in an early version of the cryosleep pods on the generation ship which brought the colonists to Luyten's Star. The skills her ancestor had as a metalsmith and fabricator were considered invaluable to the eventual building of the colony, but impossible to adequately pass on to the next generation in the environment of a starship; thus he and those like him traveled as precious sleeping cargo rather than passengers. They were the only ones among *North*'s founding colonists who had themselves lived on Earth. The rest were part of the third generation to live out their lives in space.

As the direct descendant of those craftspeople and builders as well as a highly skilled member of their professional lineage, it is only natural that she volunteered to be the one of her sort to join *Hulthemia*'s team of scientists and explorers.

Her name is Henrietta Rose Lin.

She bears her clan's traditional title as an *Artisan* with pride, even though her position with the expedition is on the merits of her practical skills rather than her artistic abilities.

Deep in the induced coma of cryosleep, her mind is occupied with dreams so vast and varied that there's little chance she'll ever remember more than glimmers of them when the day comes for her to finally awaken.

"You have a report for me, Ireven?" asks the voice over the relay-radio.

"It seems the crew is unresponsive or incapacitated, Eldest,and their ship is sailing on its own, without their input. What life signs we can read are very faint, in any case, although their automated signals seem to still be broadcasting regularly. What we've translated of their broadcasts to the Near Red Star indicates that we were correct in that being their origin point, and that they were originally coming to visit our Sanctuary rather than passing through our system as our projections show they will."

"But there are signs of life within, yes?"

"Yes, Eldest; the ship seems to have been severely damaged, though. Now that we are alongside them, we can see that their solar sails are torn and that they had maneuvering engines at one time, but these have ceased to operate some time ago. We believe the ship may have damage inside, too, but we are waiting for your decision before making a plan to board and investigate further. As near as we can tell from looking in through their viewports, the crew are all in torpor within some form of hibernation chamber."

"Good. Take all appropriate precautions to protect yourselves, but you have my blessing to board the alien craft. Learn all that you can from our sleeping strangers without waking them. When will their ship reach us?"

"If we can set them back on course, approximately twelve solar orbit cycles, Eldest—assuming their propulsion systems are repairable. They seem to have been moving at the limits of their technology before those were damaged. I believe their ship is small enough that we could try to carry it with us through the Strange and bring them home sooner, if that was the Council's desire."

"I see... Continue your investigation before you consider doing that, Ireven. Their craft may not be sound for travel by our means... and in any case it's best not to rush things. We've waited this long to meet our new friends, we can be patient for a while longer."

"Yes, Eldest."

When *Hulthemia* first launches, the expedition is hailed as one of the great triumphs of humanity. There are celebrations throughout the colonized worlds of Luyten's Star, and for a long time after the ship has departed, it is still a regular topic of conversation.

How brave the explorers must be, the colonists say, to leave everything behind for the sake of scientific progress!

What wonders will they see and broadcast back?

And then, just a bit more than six weeks after the ship begins its journey, a series of unexpected and violent coronal mass ejections from Luyten's Star itself cast their storm of radiation and solar wind out in all directions.

The colony's astrophysicists later determine that this months-long flare storm was likely a once-in-a-millennium event, but that knowledge does little to change the fact that the flares have damaged or outright destroyed a majority of the electronic equipment on every one of the system's settlements. Only a small outpost built deep in the caverns of one of the major moons orbiting the star's more distant gas giant is shielded enough to escape the effects of the flares.

It takes decades for the surviving colonists at Luyten's Star to fully rebuild and reconnect their collection of settled worlds—long enough that the abrupt end to broadcasts sent to its sister colonies and Earth will make the rest of humanity assume that the colony has been destroyed altogether.

In the meantime, *Hulthemia* is all but forgotten. Some of the citizens of the Luyten's Star colony still hold out hope that somewhere, the ship is still safely on its way to Procyon; most believe it has to have been destroyed entirely by the flare storm. Either way, there is nothing the colonists can do but regret that they will never know what happened to this crew of brilliant people.

The only consolation to those who knew the members of *Hulthemia*'s crew personally is that the bold explorers would have all been in cryosleep when the storm hit them. They wouldn't have suffered as their systems failed, only slipped away from an endless dream without ever feeling a thing.

"Eldest, we've successfully boarded the alien vessel. It seems we were right about them making their journey in hibernation chambers. We've managed to tap into what's left of their computer system without disturbing the surviving sleepers."

"Surviving sleepers, Ireven? How many aliens are there?"

"It appears that the damage to the vessel was more extensive than it appeared from outside. Aside from their guidance system and a central database we haven't been able to access, their main computer system has failed entirely. Several of the ship's other separate systems are severely damaged, including their life support—we've found six of the aliens in the chambers beyond help already, and I have concerns about how long the other five will continue to have power. From what Taril and I have determined, their hibernation chambers have back-up power cells separate from the ship's mains, but some of these have begun to fail as well."

"Do you believe you can carry out repairs for them without endangering the survivors?"

"Yes, Eldest. It will take us some time to learn their full language and systems, but their technology seems simple enough. Taril is already working on tracing the power flow to their hibernation chambers."

"Good. Do what you can for them; if needed, we will send a second team to assist you."

"Thank you, Eldest. I've transferred all the information we've gathered already for the Council's assessment."

"There seems to be something else on your mind, Ireven?"

"I... have a small concern about your apprentice, Eldest. It might be best someone came to retrieve them."

"Oh? What concerns you?"

"They've become quite interested in one of the sleepers... we've all sensed an impression of some kind of unique brain activity from the aliens, even though they're in something resembling torpor—but Amaril claims they can feel more than that from this particular one."

"I see... very well, put my apprentice on the relay. I'd like to speak to them."

"Yes, Eldest—Amaril! Come away from there, kitten. The Eldest wants words with you."

"I'm here, Eldest!"

"Ireven tells me you have been studying one of the aliens?"

"I have, Eldest! They are such curious creatures—I found one of them that feels like they could be a Beacon, like the ones you told me you could see in the navigation spheres and call to through the Strange when you were young."

"Is that so, Amaril? Why do you say this?"

"They're *bright*, Eldest! I've been sitting with them while Ireven and Taril were investigating the rest of the ship, because they said I shouldn't touch anything or get in their way... I don't know what it is that these aliens' minds do, but this one is stronger than the others. I can feel all of these *images* floating around the edges of them, and I think if I sit with them long enough I might be able to understand them, even—or slip into whatever it is these creatures experience in their sleep and actually communicate with them! It's hard to explain, but they feel like the edges of the Strange, almost—I'm sorry, Eldest, I'm not sure any of that makes sense..."

"I see... I would be interested to see what you can learn, if your sensitivity lends towards communicating with them. Tell me, Amaril, what do you think of these aliens, aside from the one you're so taken with?"

"They're... well, *odd-looking*, Eldest—I know you told me what the last Beacon had looked like, when you saw them in your visions, and these look like that for the most part—but in person they're so... colorful! And odd! And it's neat how they seem to be mostly shaped like us, even though they don't have tails or the right number of arms or eyes, and they all look so different from each other... but I like them! They're not too scarily different from us—not like the other aliens you've told me about, anyway—and they're explorers! Like you and the other Elders say *we* were before we came to the Sanctuary."

"I've seen the images Ireven sent of them... you're right, though, there's a good chance they're the people of the Beacons. If they are, then we have waited a very long time to finally meet them... do what you can to investigate your theory, Amaril. I will be interested to see what you find, if you can make contact."

"Yes, Eldest! Thank you!"

"Just be careful, kitten, will you? You may try to investigate this phenomena of the aliens' sleep, but I expect you to still follow Ireven's instructions too."

"Yes, Eldest, I understand."

Henrietta Rose Lin finds herself standing in a field of ripe grain, the golden waves rustling around her as if caught by a soft breeze. The breeze catches her hair too, tossing it lightly as a similar wave of shoulder-length woody brown and plum locks that is far too eager to escape from the bandana she wears to keep it out of the way while she's working.

The sun is warm on her tawny-pale face, the sky above cloudless and brilliantly blue in the light of the sun and its smaller twin. It's a bit strange, having a second sun—and such a bright yellow-white light from the larger one.

This isn't home, her memory tells her—home only has one reddish sun in the sky.

At the same time, this place feels familiar, as if she's been here before and forgotten somehow when and how she came to see it.

She runs her hand along the heads of the golden grain that grows up almost to her waist. Her touch sends another wave of motion through the dry stalks, joining onto the rolling rhythm created by the breeze. She's seen fields like this before, around the farm the older generations of her mother's family kept on the outskirts of the North City agricultural district.

This place, though, is calm and quiet, and without the sight of the house or the distant towers of the city on the horizon that would be there if this was her home.

She takes a deep breath of the sweet, clean air and sighs it out. She appreciates the breeze, at least. She can't remember why, but she feels like she's been somewhere small and stale for ages, until she found herself in this place.

Another rustling in the distance draws her attention. She sees streaks of blue and silver between the stalks as it comes closer.

"Hello?" Henrietta Rose asks, confused but unafraid. "Who's there?"

"*Hello?*" a voice echoes back in the breeze, over-toned with the sound of faraway wind-chimes.

A small creature, something like a six-legged, silver-furred cat in her eyes, slips out from the stalks of grain into the clear spot near her feet. It's an odd sort of cat, though, with a much longer tail with a defined tuft at the end of the tip and shades of midnight blue inside its large tufted ears. A third eye opens in the center of its forehead to look up at her as it comes to sit on a large stone she hadn't noticed was beside her.

"I must be dreaming," she says. "*You're* certainly not one of grandmother's barn cats."

Henrietta Rose reaches out a hand towards the creature. It looks at her curiously and allows her to stroke its soft fur. All three of the golden eyes close contentedly at her touch.

"*Dreaming?*" the wind-chime voice on the wind asks, even as the creature is purring lightly and allowing her to continue petting its head as if it were just an ordinary cat.

"Yes," she says, her memories starting to un-fog themselves a bit. "I must still be dreaming. My great-grandfather told stories about dreams like this, when I was little, from when he was in cryo-transit from Earth—even down to the field and the paired suns. I'm still in my pod on *Hulthemia*, only dreaming I'm somewhere else."

"*Would you like to see more?*" asks the voice on the wind.

The not-quite-a-cat places one of its six silver-tufted paws up on her arm as an invitation.

"Of course," she says, smiling at the creature. If this is a dream, then she has nothing to fear. It's only some wondrous thing from the depths of her imagination that's come to keep her company. "Which way do I go?"

"*Whichever way you wish,*" says the voice on the wind.

"You must live here," Henrietta Rose says to the creature on a whim, "why don't you lead the way and show me around?"

The creature dips its head as if it understands and hops down off the rock, gesturing happily with its long tufted tail for her to follow.

"*What news of the alien ship, Ireven?*"

"We believe we've made the last of the necessary repairs to prevent any further injury to the five sleeping aliens. Taril and I are still working to recover their other systems."

"*Good. And you will be setting their vessel back on its course to reach us?*"

"Yes. It will still take them at least ten more solar orbit cycles to make the journey, though, given how far off-course they were. We can't be sure if the repairs will hold that long, considering what a dreadful state their vessel was in when we found them."

"*I see. And your recommendation?*"

"I have two, Eldest. First would be for us to take their ship in tow when we return home—although I'm not certain it's structurally sound enough to survive jumping through the Strange even for a short distance."

"That seems too great a risk to the aliens. And your second option?"

"Second would be for us to watch over them. I'd recommend keeping one of our vessels on a rotation sailing alongside them for the duration of their journey to make sure that all remains well. That will also give us time to learn more from their databases about their species and find the proper way to awaken them when they arrive... and have us close at hand if our repairs fail and we need to take further steps to assure their safety."

"It would be a great benefit to us all if we have time to prepare to greet our new friends properly. I will discuss all of this with the full Council, but my inclination is towards your second option."

"Understood, Eldest."

"And how is my apprentice?"

"When we can get them to come out of their meditations long enough to tell us what they've learned? They're well, and surprisingly helpful. Amaril has absorbed a good enough grasp of the alien language now that they've been able to begin translating the ship's databases for us. They've acquired a set of computer access codes for us, as well, which is making our work far easier."

"Excellent."

"I am still concerned for them, Eldest—they seem to have formed a rather strong imprint on this alien they're communicating with."

"You fear for their safety?"

"It's more I'm concerned for what will happen when we leave the alien ship to return home—and what will happen when the aliens eventually awaken."

"I understand... please, Ireven, leave those concerns with me. I was aware of the possibility when I allowed them to engage with the sleeping Beacon in the first place."

"...Yes, Eldest."

From a dream of wandering through her childhood home looking for a misplaced shoe, Henrietta Rose turns around and finds herself abruptly standing in the grain field again, looking up at the two alien suns that chase each other across the cloudless sky.

She smiles and raises her face to the breeze—this time there's a faint scent of blooming flowers carried across from the next hill over. She wonders what sort of flower they are, and whether they're one of the ones she's been shown before or something new her companion has yet to take her to see.

She doesn't know anymore how many times they've met her in the field now, or how much of the wonders of this strange dream world she's still waiting to explore. All she knows is that when she finds herself here, she remembers she's dreaming; in this place, everything feels *real* in a way even the most vivid dreams she's ever had didn't.

"Hello, Henrietta Rose!" calls her companion in the voice made of wind-chimes.

"Hello, Midnight!" she calls back, walking over to the stone where they always meet her.

The creature she's named for the deep blue color they always have in their tufted ears and elsewhere on their body manifests out of the waves of grain in a streak of blue and silver motion. They're a lot less house-cat looking this time—more like a sleek six-legged tiger with the signature tuft at the end of their incredibly long prehensile tail. Midnight's form often changes when they come to meet her in the grain field; sometimes they're the catlike creature she first met, other times something more like a lemur or flying squirrel or something else small that can ride on her shoulder. Always, though, the ears and tail and the third golden eye in the center of their forehead are the same. Likewise, they always have the extra pair of limbs.

She wonders, sometimes, what they really look like when they're not here with her—if they have a single form that's true at all, and if they exist anywhere outside of where she knows them—but in all their wanderings together, Midnight has never given her a reason to ask that question. The most they've ever said in passing is that her mind suggested an appropriate form when the two of them first met and they tend to play with their appearance from there because they're not too old to remember how nice it is to be soft-furred and easy to carry around.

Somehow, she's been content with that answer.

Henrietta Rose holds out her hand to give Midnight some gentle scratches behind their ears when she reaches them. They purr happily and give her a nuzzle in return with the whiskers they're wearing as part of this form. That's another thing that never changes about her companion: they always like having their ears petted, just like the cats she knew back home did.

"Where are you taking me today?" she asks, now that the two of them have exchanged their usual greetings.

"Is it my turn again already?"

"Yes, remember? I showed you my memories of North City's Artisan neighborhood last time."

"That's right! My turn to lead it is, then. Where would you like to go?"

"Oh… anywhere, really. You always know the best places."

Midnight's laugh is even more bell-like than the rest of their voice. They hop down from the rock and stretch dramatically, then gesture with one of their frontmost paws. "I do know somewhere nice by the sea beyond the mountains."

"That sounds wonderful! I've always liked the seaside—even if back home the sea is full of critters that think people make for good snacks."

"Don't worry, Henrietta Rose. When I've been to this place before, all of the things that lived there sort of kept to themselves. I'd love to see what your seaside is like sometime, though."

"Well, that sounds nice. I'll have to try to imagine my seaside for you next time—this is only a dream, after all, so the critters can't hurt us like they would in the real world."

"I'll look forward to that. Climb on, then! I took the tiger shape for fun since you'd shown me that mural of what one looks like when we were walking through the fountain courtyards in the Artisan Neighborhood, but it'll be pretty useful for taking you where I want to go."

"You know, when I was a kid, I always liked to imagine what it'd be like to ride a tiger…" She laughs and climbs up onto her companion's back, holding on tight to the fur of their silver-ruffed neck as they begin running through the field and then leap up into the clear air of the sky. They take her across the wide world around the field, flying in the way that dreams allow in leaps and bounds with the wind rushing all around them.

Henrietta Rose knows full well that all of this is a dream. Still, sometimes she wonders what part of her mind her companion has come from; at the same time, she seldom wonders this for long. Just enjoying the marvelous places Midnight has to show her and sharing pieces of her life with them is enough to keep her in the present moment and far from thoughts of what must be going on in the waking world she's left behind.

"I don't understand it, Eldest. Their ship has been in orbit of our Sanctuary for weeks and there's still no sign of the aliens waking from their stasis."

"It is concerning, Ireven... Is it possible that the system responsible for waking the sleepers has failed too?"

"I... suppose it is. We must have missed something when we did all of the reprogramming last month so that their ship could come into orbit here safely. It could be that our initial repairs to their hibernation system weren't enough."

"Very well, then. Take your team back up to their ship and do what you must to ensure that our visitors will awaken. We are all eager to meet our new friends."

"Do you like it, Henrietta Rose?"

"It's *wonderful!*"

Henrietta Rose is floating with her companion in a sea of stars, just above a shining planet all in shades of black and amber and greenish-blue. They'd said they were going to show her something special this time, since it had been so long since they'd last seen her—and they were right. She could never have imagined something like this, even in her fondest dreams.

Midnight has been quieter than usual ever since they found her in the field. They've taken the same catlike form that they had the first time they appeared, and now that they've revealed their surprise they seem content to snuggle close against her while the two of them drift weightless among the stars.

"Is our field down there somewhere, Midnight?" she asks, straining to see if she can spot it.

"I think so. Somewhere on that southern continent, just near where the river folds around the jungles. But not entirely—our field is part of *your* home too, remember? You showed me how it blends into the ones from your family's farm."

"I remember."

In many of the wanderings the two friends have taken, Henrietta Rose has been the one to lead the way and show Midnight all the places she's ever been back home and everything she could remember of the feel of the places and the people she'd known. Most of the time, though, she's asked Midnight to lead—there's no shortage of wonderful things to see when they choose the path of the wandering. There's been a limit for both of them, though;

her places are only as she remembers them and can imagine them, and the people only like faint images unless she concentrates hard on a specific memory of talking to them. Midnight's places have been empty of people altogether, even though many of the things they've shown her must have been made by *someone*—although she's never thought to ask them why that is.

For the first time now, looking out at the stars and the planet below, she wonders if there's really more to her companion than just a dream and her longing to have someone like them as a friend. She volunteered for the mission she's on in part because she *didn't* have many close people to leave behind. She isn't the sort of human who's ever felt an inherent attraction to anyone or a need to find a romantic partner, after all, and the people in her extended family she'd been closest to were already old when she was a child. None of them had lived long enough to see her leave for the stars.

Henrietta Rose had always wondered what it might be like to have a best friend and companion, though. She's never been able to find even a *casual* friend who didn't ultimately either want to see her as a romantic prospect or leave her behind when they were at a point in their life to form a family.

Midnight is the dearest person she's ever known and the closest thing she's ever found to the sort of friend she's always wanted. When she wanders with them, she doesn't have to worry about the potential for one-sided desires or inclinations, either. Midnight is like *her*; they said as much during one of their first conversations, when she tried to explain to them why so many of the people she was trying to tell them about were in romantic pairs and that she had, in fact, had two parents instead of one. Midnight had acted like they'd never heard of such things before at all, and simply said that they liked having a friend to go wandering with.

Henrietta Rose likes having such a friend too, even if they *are* an odd sort of a creature who might not really exist.

She's spent countless hours enjoying their company now, and told and shown Midnight so much about her life, but she realizes now there's a lot she doesn't understand about them. The idea that they might be real somewhere is tantalizing.

"This planet is your home, isn't it?" she asks, looking down at the shining sphere and wondering just how much of it Midnight has already shown her.

"It is! I've been waiting forever for it to be time for you to see this—and I can't wait to show the best parts of it to you for real someday..." There's a sadness in their voice she's never heard before.

"What's wrong, Midnight?"

"I'm not sure you'll remember any of this, Henrietta Rose. *I* will, but you're not the same as me. We're trying to wake all of you up now, but you've been sleeping for so long... I can feel it clearly that you might forget." Midnight sighs, their ears and tail drooping as well. "And it's selfish of me, but I'm afraid you won't want to be friends like we are here if you *do* forget."

"Well... if I do, you'll have to remind me. I'm not letting my best friend go so easily." She gives her companion a reassuring scratch behind their ears, hugging them closer to her as the two of them continue to float in the empty space between stars and planets. There's a part of her still that thinks she's crazy, that this is just all an elaborate cryosleep dream and there's no way her friend is real—but more of her is elated at the prospect of waking up to find that they're waiting for her somewhere.

"I *will* miss sharing this with you, though. I don't know if I'd ever be able to come into your dreams like this again when you're not being held asleep so deeply."

"I think I will too—but hey, we'll have a whole new adventure in the real world."

Midnight purrs so loudly she can *feel* the joy coming off of them. "We will," they say, "I promise."

"I'll hold you to that." Henrietta Rose smiles back, then after a moment tilts her head curiously. "You said you were trying to wake us up?"

"Yes," Midnight begins, "and we need your help again to do that..."

When Dr. Travis emerges from his glass-domed cryosleep pod, the ship's computer assistant voice greets him cheerfully.

"Good morning, Captain Travis! Manual override activation of cryosleep wake cycle on pod one is now complete. Today's date is 2693.348. Time relative to the twenty-four hour Earth standard cycle and North City is 09:45. Total flight duration: 48.62 standard years."

As can be expected of a man who's spent nearly fifty years in cryogenic stasis, there is a delay of several minutes between when Dr. Travis hears the computer assistant read out these statistics and the moment when he actually processes what it's just admitted to him. "What the—that can't be right—Computer directive: Repeat last audio report?"

The computer assistant obliges. Dr. Travis can hardly believe what it's telling him.

"That shouldn't be possible." He scrambles to his feet, muttering incredulous curses under his breath. "It was supposed to be *twenty* years—Computer directive: What's the ship's status? And the crew? Where are we? And who authorized the manual override to wake me?"

The computer assistant is programmed to answer directive questions in the order they've been asked. To that end, it rattles off the answers one after the other before Dr. Travis can stop it and ask for clarification on any one point.

"Ship status: damaged, operational within minimum requirements for maintaining ship-wide life support and cryosleep pods. Crew status: Alert! Pods three through eight have failed due to power loss of unknown cause and show no life signs. Ship location: Orbit of Procyon c has been established. Response to query: Manual emergency override activation of cryosleep pod one wake cycle was authorized with Artisan Lin's access credentials."

"Miss Lin? Why? *How?*"

As the computer assistant is not programed to listen or answer questions unless the correct indicator phrase is said first, it has no response to this.

Dr. Travis looks around. The young Artisan is in the last pod on the other side of the room, still showing all the lights to indicate that she has not yet been awakened at all.

"Computer directive: begin wake cycles on all operational cryosleep pods, starting with pod eleven."

"*Error: Automatic wake cycle activation cannot be completed.*"

"...You're really not going to make anything easy for me, are you?" Dr. Travis asks, going over to check on cryosleep pod eleven himself and activate the manual override to awaken its occupant.

The ship's computer assistant has no response. Instead, it offers a new dimension to Dr. Travis' mystery. "*Notice: A message has arrived for you, Captain Travis; would you like to listen to it now?*"

"A message? From home?" Dr. Travis looks up from re-checking the young Artisan's vital signs as the cryosleep pod begins to slowly bring her out of hibernation. "Computer directive: identify and play message."

"*Sender identity: A friend, unnamed, using a digitized audio signal transmission and standard message inter-code protocols.*"

"Friend? What friend?" Dr. Travis' eyes widen.

The computer assistant doesn't identify his interruption and continues speaking over the top of him. "*Begin message playback:*"

A recorded voice replaces that of the computer assistant, one which is not stilted and robotic, but lyrical and gentle with an after-tone like wind chimes on a soft breeze. It is at once ageless and wisened—and undeniably *alien* even though it speaks in Human Standard language with a practiced ease.

"*Good morning, sleepers! I greet you as the Eldest among my people's Council of Elders. We look forward to welcoming your arrival. Our people have long awaited yours; we trust that we will begin as friends. We apologize that we did not encounter your vessel in time to save the lives of your lost companions, but we have done all in our power to ensure that those of you who awaken have arrived safely. Please accept the repairs we have made to your vessel as a sign of our good will towards you. When you are ready, you may call us on the radio frequency we have programmed into your vessel's computer and we will guide you to a safe landing on our Sanctuary Planet. Our Council of Elders has prepared a celebration in your honor and lodgings for your stay among us. Welcome to Procyon."*

Dr. Travis is, for perhaps the first time in his life, at a total loss for words.

Henrietta Rose Lin awakens from a fleeting dream and does not, at first, recognize where she is. By the time she's sat up in her cryosleep pod and listened to the near-frantic litany of questions Dr. Travis has for her, she's shaken off most of the fogginess of her long hibernation—and with it, most of the memories of the strange and wonderful dreams that have been her world.

She has no immediate answers for *Hulthemia*'s Captain of why her access credentials are on record as being used to wake him—nor, for that matter, why the computer records show a series of other system reboots, re-programmings, and course corrections which have been made in her name and seem to have been the reason the ship has safely arrived at its destination. She also can't tell him anything about who the 'friend' might have been who's sent the message he has the ship's computer assistant replay for her.

She does, though, experience a profound sense of familiarity when she hears the alien voice. Something about it stirs up memories of dreams and fields of golden grain, but it's all so faraway that she can't tell Dr. Travis anything more than that.

She finds a single rose-like blossom of some alien plant with black leaves and pale blue petals is sitting beside her pod when she first climbs out of it—although there's no indication of who left it there or why. This is yet another thing she can't explain when Dr. Travis asks her about it, although the alien flower captivates *Hulthemia*'s surviving botanist, Dr. Olsen, when they emerge from their own pod.

All she can say as she stares out the viewport at the planet below and the amber and black forms of its continents and the shining blue-green oceans is that she feels like she's seen this before, somewhere in a dream.

In this, the day when two alien species encounter each other for the first time on terms of friendship and curiosity, space is about to become just a little bit smaller than it was before.

✶ The End ✶

CHARACTERS APPEARING IN *SLEEPING BEAUTIES*

The following list of characters is divided by species and arranged in order of their appearance in the narrative. Only characters with significant "speaking roles" have been detailed here. All others present are listed as a group for the reader's reference; characters who are mentioned but do not appear are not included.

Florivans

THE ELDEST

They/them. Eldest of the Florivan Council of Elders. Mentor to **Midnight Amaril**.

MIDNIGHT AMARIL

They/them. A former survivor-smallest kitten. The apprentice of **The Eldest**.

IREVEN

They/them. Captain of a Florivan scout ship.

TARIL

They/them. Engineer of a Florivan scout ship.

Humans

DR. HEREFORD TRAVIS

He/him. Captain, LSS *Hulthemia*.

HENRIETTA ROSE LIN

She/her. An Artisan (metalsmith) of the ESS *North* lineage. Crew member, LSS *Hulthemia*.

DR. FLEUR OLSON

They/them. Botanist, LSS *Hulthemia*.

A Conspiracy of Fluff

★ A Strange Space™ Short Story ★

For Sharon T. Hinton, my wonderfully supportive Astral Navigator from the Strange Space™ Fan Club who requested this story about the kittenhood of Celadon Toreval.

Monica Malarius was, even in her own opinion, a lucky woman.

She'd been among the fortunate few in the first generation of Astral Navigators, for example. Granted, Monica and her Florivan counterpart were the *final* apprentices trained by the legendary Midnight Amaril and Henrietta Rose Lin, but they were still counted among the special pairs who were the first to guide the Sol Coalition's starships through the Quantum Space shortcuts which allowed modern space travel to be possible.

Monica knew all too well how fortunate she'd been. Even now, getting to the point of becoming a *prospective* Navigator was a fiercely competitive business. In Monica's day, it had been even more so, with hundreds of highly skilled applicants from each of the Sol Coalition's star systems trying their hardest to prove themselves worthy of being reviewed by the selection committee. Only a dozen or so each year were ever offered the opportunity to attend basic training. Then as now, in the Astral Navigation business, it all came down to whether or not one of the Florivans training to become a Quantum Space Drive Engineer clicked with any given Navigator candidate.

Luck had been on Monica's side back then, as she'd come to the conclusion that she'd have to go back to Earth and satisfy herself with a career studying stars from a distance rather than traveling them. Good fortune had crossed her path with that of a plucky young Florivan by the name of Indigo Taivin, and her life had never been the same. Who could have guessed that a misplaced sock could have such far-reaching effects?

All these years later, Monica was still delighted to call Indigo Taivin her best friend and lifelong companion. They made quite the striking pair, or so she'd often been told: her a tall, well-muscled human with deep blue eyes and blonde hair that was starting to show a streak or two of white; them a Florivan who barely stood as tall as her shoulder, the dark blue skin under their species' characteristic silver stripes a perfect reflection of their public name.

Monica and Indigo balanced each other out in more than appearance, and had been together long enough now that she couldn't imagine life any other way. Monica had never been the sort of person who was drawn to other folks in a physical or romantic sense, nor who'd ever desired any sort of intimate relationship by human social standards.

Being the counterpart of a genderless, asexual alien whose culture was centered around close friendships and kinship bonds instead suited her just fine.

Even if she and Indi *had* needed to retire from active starship service less than ten years after completing their training, that too was a stroke of luck in Monica's accounting. Indi's youngest sibling, Woad Tivree, was one of those rare Florivans who developed into a reproductive individual of the species. It was remarkable, according to Indi. A thing to celebrate, for sure, but also one that meant they needed to move back to the Florivan Sanctuary planet in the Procyon system so they could be there for Woad and their kittens, since there were no other members of their family line left.

Monica never thought twice about going with them. Woad had felt like her own little sibling ever since she first met Indi and they introduced her to the then-kitten their late parent had left behind. Becoming part of their household had always felt natural, for Monica. Living among Indi's people and helping their family grow was a grand adventure.

Several decades and a dozen kittens later, that little family had grown considerably. The youngest two of Woad's offspring would be starting their apprenticeships on a working starship soon, just like the ones most of their older siblings served on now. Monica, for her part, was content in her life as an Astral Navigator turned baker.

She was still the only human who lived at Sanctuary full-time, of course. Most of the humans affiliated with Florivans closely enough to spend much time on their homeworld, after all, were Navigators. They might stay a week or two when their ships were in port, but they weren't permanent residents. Monica, though, had made her home here. She was part of City-on-the-River's community now, and she liked it that way.

Monica had the good fortune, too, to be the only person on the entire planet who had a permit from the Council of Elders to keep and serve coffee. Her Florivan friends might like the smell, but the stuff was deadly poisonous to them and had to be handled with care. That trusted position meant that whatever humans did come to visit, she was likely to meet and hear news of the rest of the spacefaring community. Loneliness was never a problem for her, because of that, nor was disconnection from the wider world of her own species.

Today, though, offered the best stroke of luck Monica had experienced in quite a while.

It all started just as her days usually did: helping Indi and Woad get their long silver hair into just the right sort of braids to keep the baker's out of the way and the Elder's arranged to support their traditional beaded headdress and veils; letting the siblings braid her own blonde locks in whatever way suited them for the day; toasting up fresh bread to go with the assortment of fruit and roasted forest nuts for their pleasant family breakfast; coming downstairs into the bakery with Indi to get the buns and pastries they'd left rising overnight into the oven. Then, making sure that all of the culinary herbs in the pots along the wide front windows were properly watered and plucking what she'd need for baking later. A quick check of the breads and treats on display in the glass-domed stasis cabinets while Indi fluffed up the cushions in the cozy sitting area and made sure the whole of the place was clean and presentable, and they were ready to open the doors and welcome in their usual parade of folks seeking tasty baked goods and cheerful conversation.

Monica had loved the bakery ever since she first set foot in it. It reminded her of one she'd often visited as a child back on Earth—but with a distinctly Florivan spin on the necessary architecture for baking and sharing of things baked. It was a cozy place, with the bakery proper in the back and a big room in the front for guests to view the selection of breads and treats and then sit and enjoy them. A beaded curtain separated the two areas. The walls of the public room were draped with long, flowing tapestries showing scenes of the stars and the planet's different biospheres, all in brilliant colors which matched the soft, plush piles of cushions on the window-benches and at the various seating areas.

Indi had even converted one corner of the front display cabinets and long countertop so that Monica could have a safe, contained place to roast, brew, and serve coffee to their human visitors. Most days, lately, she only had the two Coalition Ambassadors in to share her coffee, but even when she was only brewing enough for herself, it was her second-favorite part of the place. Her favorite, of course, was the back workroom, where she and Indi had all the tools they needed to bake whatever they liked, including the big brick-fronted oven Indi's distant ancestor had built the whole place around. It took a touch of work and know-how to get that oven to do exactly what they wanted, especially since it was partially wood-fired, but there was a charm and character to it that the higher-tech appliances Monica had grown up with didn't have.

Dough kneaded, oven filled, and other morning tasks done, Monica was now busy folding her near-endless supply of bakery towels and napkins fresh from the wash. All of these were either creamy white or Woad's signature brilliant red. The white matched Monica's long pocketed apron, and the red was the same as her sleeveless tunic and knee-length trousers. She wore the household's colors just like Indi did, more out of long habit than anything. Florivan-styled clothing was *comfortable*, above all else, and between the ambient warmth of the big oven in the back and City-on-the-River's upland jungle climate, it was far preferable to the starship uniforms she'd worn in her youth. Being marked visually as part of the family had always pleased her too—and the fact that Woad had chosen her favorite color for their robes and insignias didn't hurt.

Monica was about halfway through her pile of towels and napkins when she heard a familiar little squeak from the floor beside her chair. She didn't have to look down to know that it was one of the many Florivan kittens who came through the bakery on a daily basis—although she didn't know which of the many Elders who had business in the nearby Council House the little darling would belong to. Kittens came and went as they pleased, in this part of City-on-the-River, and often visited the bakery if they became bored with whatever their parent was doing. Someone usually came to claim them sooner or later, and if not, Indi or Woad would know who to return lost kittens to at the end of the day.

"Hello, dear," Monica said without looking down. "Would you like to help me fold these napkins?"

Within moments, the kitten had scampered up to the table and was sitting in front of her amidst the stacks of neatly folded linen.

"Squeak?" the kitten asked.

"Oh! It's you, little Toreval!" Monica laughed, offering her hand to the kitten for a cuddle.

Most Florivan kittens looked pretty much the same: four arms, a prehensile tail nearly longer than their entire body, tufted catlike ears, and three brightly golden eyes on their otherwise human-like face, all neatly wrapped in the soft layer of silver fur that the adults of their species lacked. This one was less than a month out of their foster parent's pouch, still about the size of a small chipmunk. They were also distinctively *fluffy* enough that there was no mistaking them for any other kitten on the planet.

Among all the many kittens of various ages Monica had met and cared for during her time living at Procyon, *none* had ever been as brilliantly fluffy as little Toreval. They were adorable, even more than kittens always were. They had so much fluff and length to their fur that at times it was hard to tell just where one body part stopped and another began. Little Toreval was more of a ball of fluff with a face and tail, really. Their limbs were more or less defined depending on the humidity and whether their two foster littermates had found any success in helping them tame the fluff on a given day.

Little Toreval smiled and let out a chipper squeak, waving their incredibly soft and fluffy tail as they snuggled up to Monica's hand. They were an affectionate kitten, too, unless one upset their littermates. Monica had seen the wound on Coalition Ambassador Wexler's hand from the time this fluffy little overprotective scamp had bitten him. *That* had been little Toreval's first act upon opening their eyes—an odd introduction to the world for a Florivan if ever there was one, considering the pacifist nature of the species. In little Toreval's defense, at the time they'd mistaken the Ambassador for a predatory animal about to devour their foster littermate, Laryven. Laryven being a rather dramatic little kitten about being picked up unexpectedly hadn't helped that impression.

Kittens didn't normally do things like bite unless their survival instincts were triggered, of course, but it was clear that little Toreval was a touch more protective of the people they considered family even than the average kitten.

"Oh, you're such a sweet little thing, Toreval." Monica giggled and obliged the ball of fluff with a gentle scratch behind their ears. "I've never seen you all alone, before, though... did you misplace Laryven and Liret?"

Little Toreval's three eyes were firmly locked onto Monica's. They squeaked softly in reply. Of course, without Indi around to translate, she had no way of knowing for sure what the kitten was saying, but the tone gave the impression of a shrug.

"Ah, well, I'm sure they'll turn up soon... and when I'm done folding all of this, we can take you back up to the Eldest's office so you can find them." Monica started to turn to look at a sound from the other end of the bakery, where the cooling racks for freshly-baked bread stood. Before she could, though, her attention was caught by another small, adorable squeak from the kitten in front of her as they nestled closer into her hand.

"Oh?" Monica looked back down. Little Toreval was keen on being cuddled, it seemed. She supposed they might be cold, despite the warmth of City-on-the-River's pleasant jungle spring. Kittens did tend to get chilled easily. "Do you need more attention today, Toreval, is that it?"

The kitten nodded, apparently understanding enough of her words to agree with the assessment. Florivan kittens never ceased to amaze Monica with how quickly their intelligence developed, even though they were limited to squeaks and trills for communication until they reached the size and age where they began trading their soft silver fur for the smooth silver-striped blue skin that adults of their species bore.

Usually, though, Monica could get a general idea of which category of common kitten desires she was dealing with. Attention and warmth were the biggest ones, tied closely with hunger. Bearing in mind that they'd be almost human-sized when fully grown, it stood to reason that even little kittens like Toreval could seem like small fuzzy bottomless pits at times.

"Okay, then, sweetheart." Monica picked up the kitten and set aside her work in favor of gentle petting of their soft silver fluff. "I can take a cuddle break…"

✶

Toreval considered their Auntie Monica one of their favorite people in the whole galaxy.

She was certainly their favorite *human*. No matter that they'd only met three of those so far; Auntie Monica was clearly the best of the three.

The first human they'd encountered was the heavy-set, dark-haired man-Ambassador who tasted bad. It seemed he'd learned his lesson about asking Laryven if they wanted to be picked up and petted *before* he tried to do that, so Toreval could justify tolerating his continued presence in their life for the moment. They were grateful he hadn't given them cause to bite again—his hand tasted of bitter soap and icky metallic goo, and Toreval was still disgusted by the memory of it.

The second one was Miss Riley, the counterpart of the very shiny Europan Ambassador who worked with their nemesis. She was the shortest adult Toreval and their littermates had ever met, with warm brown skin and shoulder-length black hair that she wore close shaved on one side and finely braided with shiny beads and charms woven in on the other. Miss Riley was nice and always smelled like flowers, but for some odd reason, she seemed to be *afraid* of Toreval.

Toreval couldn't imagine why.

Auntie Monica, though, was always a good source of cuddles and snacks, and she was warm, too. Her apron even had nice pockets to sleep in! There was a lot for a kitten to like about her, really.

Today, though, it was her predictable response to being presented with the opportunity for cuddles that Toreval was interested in. All they had to do was keep Auntie Monica's eyes on *themself* for a few more minutes. Laryven and Liret would do the rest. They had lots of practice, after all—they'd been doing this sort of thing long before Toreval opened their eyes. They were far more successful now that Toreval was around to help them, though.

Toreval purred softly as their favorite human's warm hands stroked their head. Being the smallest and the best at being distracting was nice...

"Monica?" called Indigo Taivin from the other side of the beaded curtain separating the workroom of the bakery from the front cafe area, "Do you have any of those big towels folded yet? I have a basket here that needs one." Like all Florivans, their lightly-accented voice was underlaid with tones of softly ringing wind chimes.

"Yes," they heard their Navigator reply, "come get it. Busy hands!"

Taivin chuckled. Six words: that was more than usual for Monica. On an average day, she'd have left it at 'yes' and then waited for Taivin to ask for the towel to come to them before saying anything else. There had to be a kitten involved in her hands being busy. Their Navigator was *always* more talkative around the kittens.

Monica had always been a quiet sort of human. It confused Taivin at first, since the other humans they'd encountered before meeting her were so much the opposite. It took weeks of careful observation on their part to recognize that she was capable of saying more than ten words to anyone in a given day. When Taivin introduced her to their then-kitten youngest sibling, though, everything made more sense. Tivree brought out entire *paragraphs* of conversation from her, and all they had to do was squeak and wave their soft silver tail in response.

Monica saved her words for important things back then, even if she didn't mean to do it. Even now, having long since grown out of the shy streak she'd had when Taivin first met her, Monica still tended to keep her words to the point more often than not, unless the two of them were talking about something that truly interested her, like coffee or the collection of old Earth recipes she'd brought with her when they settled at Procyon. It was part of Monica's charm, really.

According to *her*, of course, Taivin themself usually supplied more than enough words for the two of them when other folks were around. Monica's first assessment of them had been a single, poignant word: chatterbox. Taivin couldn't deny it, really, then or now.

Still, they, too, had grown up over the years; they'd learned from their Navigator to appreciate the value of companionable silences.

Taivin couldn't remember now what it had really been like not to have their dear human counterpart in their life. Even if they and Monica weren't serving on a starship anymore or making use of their people's skills with the Strange, the veiled dimension most humans insisted on calling Quantum Space, they had a wonderful life all the same.

As Taivin came through the beaded curtain to retrieve the towel from the stack their Navigator was supposed to be folding, they saw the reason her hands were busy. They shook their head. True to form, Monica could never resist the call of a kitten.

"Well, now, hello, little Toreval." Taivin patted the little ball of kitten fluff on the head with one of their free lower hands while they deftly folded the thin towel with the upper pair. "Did you lose Laryven and Liret again?"

Little Toreval gave their reply in a series of bright, cheerful squeaks. It had been a very long time ago now that they were a kitten themself, but like all Florivans, Taivin had retained the ability to understand the simple form of the language they all knew from birth. Taivin understood well enough what the kitten meant: No, they hadn't lost their foster littermates today, but they were here all the same because they wanted their Auntie Monica's attention and warmth... and possibly a biscuit, if Taivin had come to offer one.

"Well, I wonder where those two little scamps are, then..." Taivin shook their head. "I wouldn't doubt they're up to their ears in some scheme or another."

Little Toreval gave them a perfectly innocent squeak and ear twitch in response: They didn't know what Taivin could possibly be talking about. *Their* littermates? Up to something? Impossible.

"Oh, of course you wouldn't know anything about it, whatever it is. No, no, you're *just* here to borrow my Navigator for a few minutes and convince her to give you a biscuit..." Taivin resisted the urge to roll their eyes. Foster child or not, this little fluffy thing was far too much like the Eldest. Little Toreval'd barely had their eyes open for three weeks, and they were already just as much of a troublemaker as their two foster littermates *combined*. They were simply cute enough to be able to get away with more.

"I don't know what they're saying," Monica said softly, giving the kitten a snuggle as she intoned the longest sentence she'd said all day within Taivin's hearing, "but they're adorable and they clearly wanted some attention. Probably just got cold and wanted to come in here where it's nice and warm and yeasty." She paused, standing and taking little Toreval over to the counter with her. "Here, sweetheart, *I'll* get you that biscuit... how does oatmeal raisin sound?"

Just as she handed little Toreval their treat, a chorus of excited squeaks from the door leading out into the main courtyard caught Taivin's ears. Little Toreval clearly heard it too. They gave Monica a sweet nuzzle of gratitude, hopped down from her shoulder, and bounced over to the door, still holding the biscuit in their upper pair of hands.

Just outside, Laryvyn and Liret were waiting for them—and holding between them a basket that seemed to be full of *something* they'd gathered from the bakery's display shelves. Within moments, little Toreval was perched approvingly on the handle of the basket and the two larger kittens were scampering away, carrying their prize between them.

Taivin laughed, dusting a bit of flour off their lower pair of hands. "Monica, dear... they did it to you again."

Monica laughed too. "Yep."

"I'd go after them if I didn't have things in the oven that need tending." Taivin shook their head. "Hopefully the Eldest will return the basket this evening so I can ask just *what* their three little scamps picked to take them for teatime."

Monica raises an eyebrow at them. She's a soft-spoken one, their Navigator—but they know exactly what she means.

"Well, now, it can't be *Navy* who put them up to it…"

Toreval and their littermates carefully carried the basket of teatime treats up the many, many stairs of the Council House leading to their parent's office. It was careful work. Not only was there the matter of stairs that were taller than Laryven and Liret, but also that of *stealth*. The three of them did their best not to be noticed by any of the adults who were going about their business.

After all, the special rolled nut bread their Nida liked was best when *warm*, and any delays could lead to cold bread. Toreval considered cold bread to be thoroughly unacceptable today. Laryven and Liret agreed with them. They usually did.

There was one obstacle left between the three kittens and their destination: Navy, their minder.

Hopefully, Navy still thought they were all snuggled into the nest of blankets and stuffed toys they'd made a point of building on the lowest shelf of the bookcase in Nida's outer office. Navy was very good at noticing when kittens had plans, most of the time. Moreover, they seemed to take great delight in *thwarting* those plans.

Luckily for Toreval and their littermates, though, today Navy was studying for some important thing or other. Toreval themself couldn't quite grasp what that meant. It involved staring at a holoscreen and making a lot of scribbles on a tablet, though—quite boring, in their opinion. Still, "studying" was clearly *important* to their big cousin, and Toreval had promised with Laryven and Liret to be very good and quiet kittens today so Navy could concentrate on it.

As the smallest, and therefore not able to help with carrying the basket, Toreval's job today was to sneak in first and see if Navy needed distracting. When they saw that their favorite minder-cousin was stretching out their arms in preparation to get up from the desk where they'd been all day, Toreval squeaked a soft direction to their littermates to wait for their signal. Distraction was needed.

They scampered up on top of Navy's desk swiftly. Once properly placed between Navy's eyes and the holoscreen where all of their scribbles were floating, Toreval squeaked a cheerful greeting.

"Ah, hello there, Little Toreval. How'd you sense I needed a break?" Navy obliged them with soft cuddles.

Toreval purred in response, swishing their long fluffy tail to signal their littermates. While Laryven and Liret quietly carried the basket over to their Nida's office door and stacked themselves up to open it, Toreval kept all three of their eyes locked with Navy's. They squeaked softly again, then turned to look at the screen for a moment. They tilted their head at an adorably curious angle for emphasis.

"What, this? You want to know what's keeping me from playing with the three of you today?"

Toreval nodded and squeaked a confirmation, both because they *were* curious about what Navy'd been up to all day and because Laryven was clearly having trouble getting the door handle to cooperate.

"Well," said Navy, patting Toreval's ears again as they gestured with their free upper hand to the screen, "like I told you this morning, I'm studying for my theoretical exams on human psychology and psychiatric medicine so I can start on my training to work with them the way Elder Hydrangea and Star Sapphire work with us… which means having to memorize a lot of terms and lists of symptoms. Humans are *complicated* in so many ways…"

While Navy rambled, Toreval's third eye switched focus to their littermates. Usually, Laryven and Liret could open any door they encountered quite swiftly. The one to Nida's office was being troublesome today. It was almost the wet season here in City-on-the-River, so the old wood was swelling—that's what Nida said when Liret complained about not being able to get out of the office when they wanted to this morning, at least.

Finally, with an extra acrobatic leap from Liret pulling down on Laryven at the exact angle to also shift the door's bulk, the latch cooperated and the door creaked open.

Loudly.

Navy turned toward the sound before Toreval could distract them again. "Kittens?"

Luckily, even with the basket held between them, Laryven and Liret could scamper faster than Navy could stand up and cross the same space.

Toreval rode in triumphantly on their cousin's shoulder into their Nida's inner office. They arrived just in time to see Laryven and Liret bounce up onto their Nida's big carved wooden desk and present them with the cloth-draped basket.

"Shiny!" said Laryven, speaking for all three of them, since they were the only one who'd mastered a grown-up word so far. They and Liret sat beside the basket and swished their tails at Nida happily.

"I'm so sorry, Eldest," Navy started to say while Toreval hopped down to join their littermates on the desk. "I don't know *how* they got away from me this time..."

"It's quite all right, dear." Nida laughed brightly, waving one white-silk-clad arm in a reassuring sort of gesture. "I did, after all, tell the three of them that teatime would happen when the meeting was over..." Nida looked to the humans sitting across the desk from them in the padded guest chairs, and to the shiny Europan gentleman in the bubble backpack on the corner of the desk closest to Miss Riley. "...And it seems my kittens have declared that it is now teatime, and thus our discussions *must* be over for the day. Care to join us?"

Toreval still didn't particularly like the human Ambassador, of course. After all, their first memory was of him upsetting Laryven—and that he tasted bad. But still, if Nida wanted to share tea with him, that's okay with them. At least Miss Riley and her shiny counterpart were here too. They both were nice enough to be worthy of sharing some rolled nut bread with Nida.

Navy let out a soft laugh of resignation. "I'll go get the teapot, then."

"Thank you, dear—that jasmine tea the Ambassador brought will be lovely with this." Nida turned their upper eye back to the humans, smiling broadly as they spread the basket-towel out on their desk and unpacked the collection of teatime treats Laryven and Liret had picked. "Of course, you're all welcome to stay a bit to share tea with us. We'll pick our talk back up tomorrow morning."

"Ah..." The human Ambassador seemed disappointed, but with a moment of consideration, he nodded. Toreval decided that must be because he respected the power of their own pointed stare and slowly swishing tail. "All right, then. Teatime is whenever your little fuzzy shark says it is, I suppose."

Miss Riley leaned over to whisper conspiratorially to Toreval and their littermates. The shiny charms on the braided side of her hair glinted in the light from the motion. "Thank you for the rescue, my little fuzzy shark friends. Eos here doesn't like these long-winded meetings any more than you do."

For his part, Ambassador Eos flashed a few brightly colored tendrils in Toreval's direction. Coming from him and Miss Riley, 'fuzzy shark' was more of a compliment than when the bad-tasting Ambassador said it.

"Have either of you tried our seed and nut rolls yet?" Nida asked their guests, clearly pretending not to hear what Miss Riley was saying. "My cousin Indigo makes the best ones in the city... ah! And the one my kittens brought for us is still warm."

Once their Nida served the treats and tea and Toreval had nibbled their share, they slipped back into the folds of the soft white silk layers that were their home. Safely tucked in their Nida's warm fur-lined brood pouch with Laryven and Liret, they settled down for a well-deserved nap.

They couldn't help being pleased with themself for having come up with such a good plan for bringing an end to the day's meetings.

Late that evening, as Monica and her counterpart were closing up the bakery for the day, the bells on the door tinkled softly. She stepped out through the workroom's beaded curtain to see the unmistakable figure of the Eldest of the Council waiting for her by the front counter. They had their lower hands resting on the head of their old, ornately-carved wooden cane, while their upper ones held a familiar basket. Their two youngest kittens and foster-kitten were nowhere to be seen.

"Good evening, Monica, dear!" the Eldest said softly, setting the basket on the countertop. "I came to return this."

Indi stepped through the curtain behind her, settling one of their upper arms around her waist as they looked up and grinned. "See? I told you they'd have been involved."

Monica patted her Florivan friend on the head as an acknowledgement of their correctness and then smiled at the Eldest. She tilted her head lightly, glancing down at the towel-draped basket.

"Ah, yes, I should probably return it *empty*, shouldn't I?" The Eldest let out a light giggle, lifting the edge of the towel. "They were just so cute sleeping among the crumbs..."

Peering in with Indi, Monica was delighted to see the two larger kittens curled up together in a tangle of limbs and tails, while the seemingly perfect fluffy sphere of little Toreval was nestled in the middle on top of them. She hadn't seen anything quite as cute since Woad's last litter grew out of their fur.

"All right," Indi said, echoing Monica's own thoughts, "that's worth letting them think they were getting away with something." They turned their third eye up to the Eldest. "How was the nut bread, by the way?"

"Delightful as always, dear." The Eldest reached their two upper hands into the basket and carefully picked up the whole bundle of sleeping kittens. They cradled all three of them close against their chest, lightly trilling something soft to settle the one who almost woke back to sleep. "Thank you for indulging my little couriers."

"Any time, Eldest." Indi took the towels out of the empty basket and added them to the laundry bin under the counter. "You know, if you ping me in advance I can have the basket *ready* for them so they don't have to climb all over the place to retrieve their snacks..."

"Now, really, Indigo." The Eldest flashed a conspiratorial grin. "Where would the fun be in that?"

Monica stifled a laugh. Aside from Indi and Woad, the Eldest had always been her favorite person on this planet— and this was exactly why. They were the sweet ideal of a grandparent, for sure, but they also had a sense of humor and a troublemaker's streak to match any kitten.

Indi shook their head. "Fair point... You know, Elder Lazurite's never going to believe half of what Little Toreval's gotten into by the time they wake up, at this rate."

The Eldest looked down at the three sleeping kittens in their upper arms and sighed softly. "As long as Lazi wakes up, in the end? I'll happily let them lecture me on anything they want."

As if knowing that they were once again the subject of conversation, the smallest of the kittens opened their eyes and looked around. They squeaked a charming greeting at Monica and Indi, then turned their eyes up to their foster parent.

"Yes, dear, we're about to go home and have dinner." The Eldest raised one hand off their cane to stroke Little Toreval's ears. "Now, say goodnight to your cousin Indigo and Auntie Monica?"

Little Toreval squeaked cheerfully again.

"Goodnight," said Indi.

"I'll see you tomorrow," Monica added, knowing all too well that the kitten would be back to pester her for treats and affection at their earliest opportunity. If she was lucky, all three of the kittens would spend some time with her while they waited for tomorrow's teatime snacks to come out of the oven.

That would suit her just fine.

Luck, after all, had always been on her side.

✴ **The End** ✴

CHARACTERS APPEARING IN *A CONSPIRACY OF FLUFF*

The following list of characters is divided by species and arranged in order of their appearance in the narrative. Only characters with significant "speaking roles" have been detailed here. All others present are listed as a group for the reader's reference; characters who are mentioned but do not appear are not included.

Florivans

TOREVAL
They/them. Kitten of **Elder Lazurite**, foster-kitten of **The Eldest**. Foster-littermate of **Liret** and **Laryven**.

INDIGO TAIVIN
They/them. Older sibling and member of the household of **Elder Woad**. Counterpart to **Monica Malarius**.

LIRET AND LARYVEN
They/them. Kittens of **The Eldest**. Foster-littermates of **Toreval**.

NAVY IRLEEIM
They/them. Adult kitten of **Elder Bughaw**. Student of psychology and apprentice-assistant to **The Eldest**.

Humans

MONICA MALARIUS
She/her. Counterpart to **Indigo Taivin**. Adoptive sister and member of the household of **Elder Woad**. A retired Astral Navigator turned baker.

AMBASSADOR WEXLER

He/him. A diplomat of the Sol Coalition, assigned to Procyon.

MISS RILEY

She/her. An Initiate of the Europan Mysteries and junior diplomat of the Sol Coalition, assigned to Procyon. Bonded companion of **Ambassador Eos**.

Others

AMBASSADOR EOS

He/him. A Europan Ambassadorial Observer. Bonded companion of **Miss Riley**.

THE NOVAN WAR ERA

Aliens at a Tiki Bar

★ A Strange Space™ Short Story ★

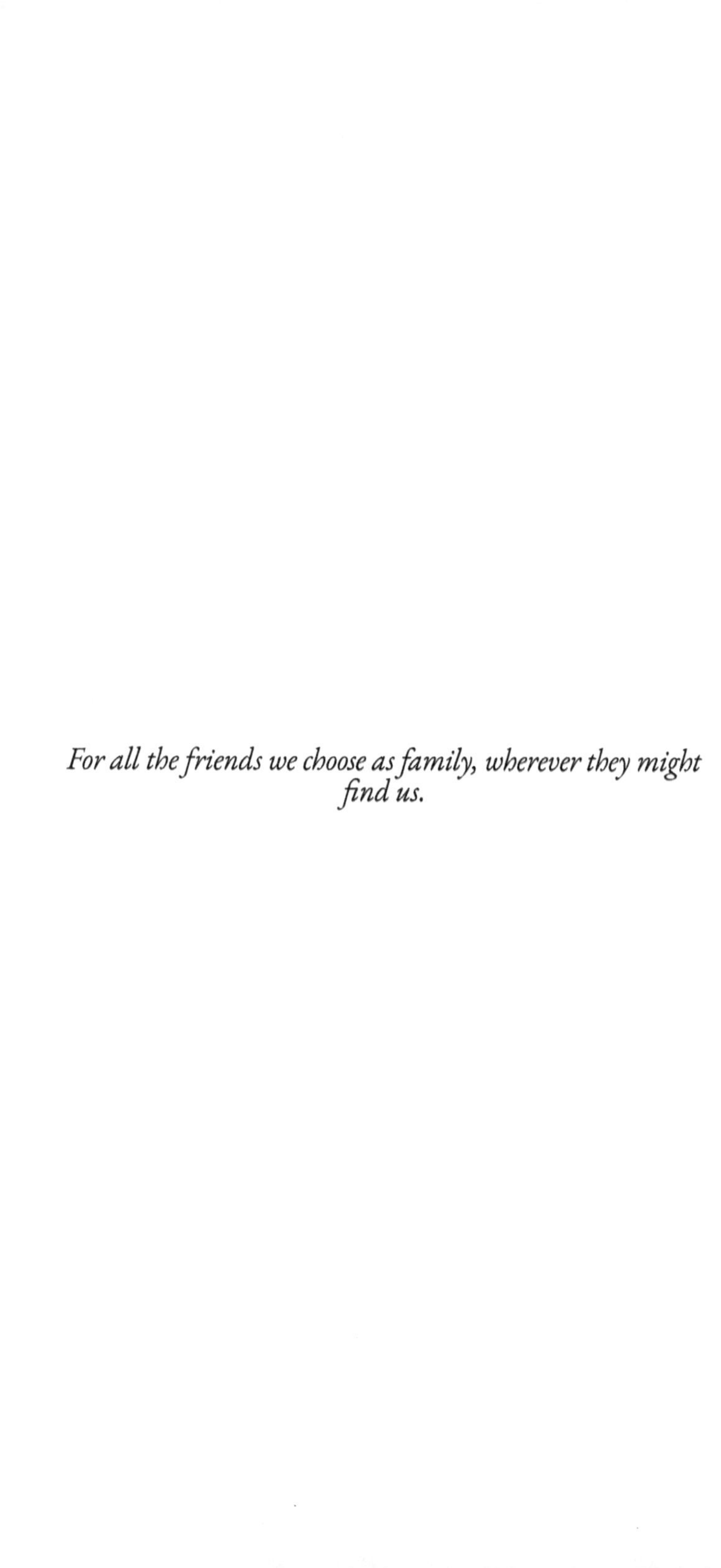

For all the friends we choose as family, wherever they might find us.

At the corner table nearest to the dance floor of one of Horizon Prime Space Station's more popular recreational facilities, two officers from the Defense Fleet starship SCV *Aegolius* sit together sharing a toast to celebrate the beginning of the first bit of leave time the two of them have had in more than six months. With the Novan War still ongoing, it's rare for Admiral Marvin's flagship to be in any port more than a few days at a time, let alone the full three weeks she'll be spending at Kapteyn b on this occasion.

The opportunity is not lost on *Aegolius'* Astral Navigator and his Florivan Quantum Space Drive Engineer counterpart. The two of them will not be needed back at their posts properly until the day their ship departs—and therefore, as is custom, get to spend the stay in port enjoying a well-deserved bit of rest and recreation.

The Florivan Elder Celadon Toreval and their human counterpart, Hsu Li, make quite the striking pair: one slim human man with a clean-shaven, tawny-pale complexion and long black hair; one shorter-than average Florivan with icy blue-green skin marked with silver stripes, four arms, a third golden eye in the center of their forehead, a long silver-tufted prehensile tail, and silver hair surrounding their large, tuft-tipped catlike ears which is longer even than the man's when it's not braided up into their current set of ribbon-woven braided buns. If anyone were to happen to glance towards the small table in the corner where the two of them are sitting, they'd be a hard sight to miss.

Toreval had chosen the table, of course. Their Navigator is used to their habit of sitting in a corner where they can see the whole of the room and keep their tail well out of the way of anyone walking past. He would no doubt have picked the same spot himself. Li doesn't mind having his back to the room, as long as Toreval remembers to warn him before anyone tries to set a hand on his shoulder to get his attention.

"So, Navigator..." Toreval raises all three of their eyebrows in a curious accusation. "Remind me why I let you keep talking me into visiting places like this?"

"Hey, now, *you're* the one who always says it's too quiet without Sparks around, Val." Li matches their expression as well as someone with only two eyes can. His tone is playful—and he's right, too. Toreval's youngest kitten left to apprentice on a civilian starship several years ago, but they still often find themself missing little Taldee's antics and enthusiastic chatter.

"I didn't realize 'quiet' was some sort of human code for 'say, why don't we go hang out in a busy nightclub,' Li." Toreval rolls their third eye, now, but with a hint of a smile. Their Navigator has known them long enough that he can usually tell when they're teasing.

"Well, I know you like coconut drinks best, so where else was I supposed to take you?" Li laughs brightly. "You *have* to admit the music is good, at least."

"Oh, it is. It's just a bit loud for my ears, that's all—and I *never* realized there would be so many people here tonight." Toreval takes another sip of their pleasingly coconut-tasting drink. They can't deny that it's their favorite flavor of Earth origin. The song playing over the speakers is pleasant, too, aside from the volume: all bell-like steel drums and some sort of guitar. The style reminds them of their home in the Procyon Sanctuary and the music played at City-on-the-River's various festivals.

Most of the more grating noise in the room is coming from the conversations at the tables around them. Humans seem to have an instinct to talk louder when they can't hear each other clearly; when a lot of them are in the same place trying to be heard over each other, it all adds up to shouting in the end. Toreval's not sure how any of them can understand a word of it. They don't have that problem with Li, though. Their Navigator's voice is smooth as silk and bright as sunlight and carries across a room just as clearly as it does over Toreval's earpiece when they're working in the Strange. Their highly tuned pair of catlike ears can pick Li out whispering from the other side of the most crowded room if they need to.

"We can go find another place if this is too much for you, Val." Li gently nudges their foot under the table. "I don't mind." He takes on a particular sort of lightly concerned expression as he says this. Toreval knows that look too well—it's the one that says he's started worrying about them again. He's been making that face a lot lately, although they can't entirely fathom why.

"No, it's fine, really." Toreval smiles reassuringly at him as they return the nudge. It's hardly Li's fault that their hearing is far more sensitive than the average human's, after all. "I have a nice corner here to sit in and watch the dancing from a safe distance—my ears are bound to adjust sooner or later."

"Okay, then. Tell me if you change your mind about that?"

"I will." Toreval turns their attention briefly to stirring the little purple paper umbrella around in a circle through the slush of crushed ice and fruit juices in their fat-bottomed glass, avoiding the short spikes of pineapple fronds that make up the rest of the garnish. They've yet to understand what those are for, but it's a very human thing to make drinks that look as nice as they taste.

"Do you want some of this to take the edge off?" Li holds out his own drink towards them. His tall, narrow stemmed glass is filled with brightly colored liquid, reddish at the bottom and gradually shifting to an electric green at the top. A twirl of lime zest perches on the edge of the rim to complete the decoration set of green umbrella and toothpick-speared cherries.

"Mm..." Toreval considers the offer for a few moments and then shakes their head. "No, thank you. I think I can manage without it. Besides, this isn't nearly as bad as the place you took me the *first* time we had shore leave together."

Li laughs brightly, then takes a sip from his drink. "You're never going to let me live that one down, are you?"

"Li, I was still finding glitter everywhere for *months*."

"Oh, I don't know, Val," Li quips, shooting them a brief, cheeky grin. "I rather think the glitter suited you."

"You would." Toreval can't help smiling, even though they roll their third eye at him again. Their Navigator has a way of being charming even when he's being a teasing young pest. That's probably part of why they keep letting him talk them into excursions like this every time *Aegolius* is able to stay in port long enough for its crew to be allowed shore leave.

As the ship's only Nav/Quan pair, Toreval and Li seldom get a night off at all unless *Aegolius* is in port. While starships are carried forward with solar sails during the day, the nightly jumps through the veiled dimension Toreval's people call the Strange are what truly moves them between planets and stars. The so-called 'Quantum Space Drive' is Toreval's responsibility; without them or another Florivan, the jumps are impossible. They keep the ship moving every night, and their Navigator keeps them anchored to the landmarks of Normal space and guided in the correct direction. It's exhausting work even on a calm night; any time Toreval has to maneuver *Aegolius* back and forth in a battle zone, it's even more so.

Early on in their service with the Sol Coalition Defense Fleet, Toreval learned that downtime of any sort is worth taking advantage of whenever one can find it. A chance to spend time with Li doing *anything* but making jumps through the Strange is something to treasure.

Assuming the repairs from *Aegolius'* last close encounter with the Novan Armada take the full three weeks the maintenance technicians said they would, Toreval knows they should have more than enough time even to take their Navigator down planetside for a few days to enjoy exploring one of Kapteyn b's many nature reserves before Jenny needs the two of them to get her flagship moving again. They haven't decided which one yet; possibly one of the deep winding canyons on the smaller desert continent, or the equatorial islands with their warm black-sand beaches. That will more than make up for the less pleasant parts of this traditional first-night-on-leave tour of the more *social* recreation options on the station.

To be fair to their Navigator, Li *does* enjoy the hikes and peaceful explorations of interesting landscapes just as much as Toreval does; he's just also the sort of human who needs to be close to members of his own species at least some of the time. It might be in their own nature to be able to be content having an alien for their sole companion, but Toreval has known from the beginning that it wouldn't be right to expect Li to be the same way. They're Florivan, after all: a member of a genderless, asexual species with no innate concept of relationships or intimacy beyond 'family' and 'friend.' Toreval may be one of the few individuals capable of bearing kittens, but that's a *private* matter between themself and the Strange. While they have a general understanding of how humans do things, it's still all a very alien set of concepts to have to keep in mind when dealing with Li and their other human colleagues.

In a lot of ways, this little tradition the two of them have grew out of Toreval's desire early on in their friendship to help Li understand that they wouldn't be preventing him from having the same sort of social life he had before he was their counterpart. Li hadn't intended to become their Navigator when they first met, after all. It was little more than a matter of impulsive convenience on their part. At the time, making their compact with him was the only option Toreval had to convince the rest of their people's Council of Elders to allow *them* to leave Procyon and volunteer their services to the Defense Fleet. As far as they know, Li has never regretted having gone along with it. Toreval certainly hasn't. They couldn't have asked for a better or more compatible human to share their life with, nor a more skilled Navigator.

It's out of a mix of affection and respect for their Navigator, then, that Toreval comes with him to these dancing-and-drinks sort of places whenever *Aegolius* first puts into port—even if they know they'll more than likely be returning to their ship alone and may not see much of him at all for a day or two afterwards. For his part, Li has always told Toreval that he likes them to be aware of his social connections. It's sweet, in a way, that he cares what they think about his choices of temporary human companions, even if Toreval has never quite understood why their opinion on the subject matters to him.

"So, Navigator," Toreval asks teasingly, pausing to take a sip through the cold metal straw that's sticking out of their drink beside the umbrella, "are you planning on asking someone to dance anytime soon, or are we *both* just watching tonight?"

"Oh…" Li glances out towards the dance floor briefly, then shrugs. "I might eventually."

"You should." Toreval gives him an encouraging smile. "It'd be good for you to do something other than sit around keeping me company for a change."

"I don't know about that, Val—you're better company than you think." Li chuckles and brushes some stray bits of his waist-length leaf-black hair back over his shoulder. He's got it down, tonight, held back from his tawny-pale face with four tiny intertwined braids on each side that Toreval had helped him put in. A flower is tucked neatly into the junction of the braids just above his right ear. The look suits him every bit as well as the high looped ponytail he wears when he's on duty.

"It's been months since we had time off at all, Li… besides, I thought you *liked* dancing with strangers?"

"Well, yes… among other things." Li smirks slightly over the rim of his glass. "But most of the people in here came off of *Aegolius*—they're hardly strangers."

Toreval glances around the room. "True."

"And I'm saving at least one dance for you, you know."

"Of course." Toreval takes a small sip from their drink, shaking their head. "But let me get used to tuning the noise out first, okay? Otherwise I'll just run into someone or get my tail stepped on again—and I'm not in the mood to accidentally start a brawl tonight."

"That doesn't happen *every* time you dance with me, Val."

"No, but it's happened enough times now that it's something I actively try to avoid."

"You know, Val, for someone with such good spatial awareness..." Li grins at them knowingly.

Toreval rolls all three of their golden eyes at him this time. "I have good spatial awareness when I'm not overwhelmed by loud music and multitudes of gyrating bodies under strobe lights, Li. I've been in parts of the *Strange* that are less chaotic than some of your haunts, you know?"

"I know, I know." Li laughs. "That's why I picked this place. No strobes, no glitter, just good music—you should see the cyber-rave den down on level 30, though. Now, *that*, my friend, is chaos."

Toreval flicks their ears in amusement. "No, I think I'll stick with whatever this is, thanks."

"It's supposed to be modern Kapteynic disco-tiki, I think."

"Right, that." Toreval has little understanding of the theming of these human social spaces—all they've been able to put together is that the room has been decorated heavily with bamboo and palm fronds and has a recording of a white-sand beach playing in a long loop on the holoscreen covering the far wall. A life-size sculpture of some sort of a shark hangs over the bar, while a similar one of a brightly colored jungle bird sits on a branch mounted to the wall just above their Navigator's head.

Most of the other people in the room are dressed to suit the theme with bright shirts and long floral cloths wrapped around bathing costumes. A little service robot at the door offers cut flowers and necklaces of greenery to everyone who enters, too; thus the large white orchid tucked into

Li's hair and the yellow-orange ones he'd *insisted* on adding at the top of the sheer green and ivory ribbons wound through Toreval's own braided silver buns and just behind each of their ears. Li's always pleased to see them wearing something resembling their proper color, even if it's only a few flowers. He's told them before that the amber of their Elder's silks suits their pale silver-striped blue-green complexion better than the Fleet's uniform colors ever will. Toreval trusts his eye for colors and aesthetics—it's one of the qualities they like about him, even. Still, they're the Fleet's Elder; wearing the emerald and ivory in their hair instead of their own household's amber is a symbol of that, and of their self-imposed exile.

Despite the casual atmosphere, Toreval and Li are both still in uniform tonight, if only for the sake of convenience. They'd come directly from their ship, after all, to see what Horizon Prime had to offer when Li settled on this as their hangout spot for the evening. Even so, the relative warmth of the room already has Li shrugging off his officer's green-and-ivory jacket and passing it over for Toreval to keep on the bench beside them, along with his signature matching scarf. He'd undone the top three buttons of his band-collared ivory shirt when they arrived, but Toreval knows that's more for aesthetic than comfort. Li likes to appear more casual and approachable when he's in places like this.

Toreval still has their own jacket on, although it's draped over their shoulders like a cape. It's warmer here than the rest of the station for sure, but even with the climate controls set to mimic a pleasant day on one of Earth's tropical islands, they haven't been sitting here long enough to start shedding layers like most of the humans have. Granted, Toreval has been wearing their jacket like this for the last few days anyway because both arms on their right side are currently imprisoned in casts and slings and they *can't* wear it normally.

While they're talking to Li about the merits of the decor and music, one of *Aegolius'* other young officers approaches their table. Toreval sees her before Li does and gestures to him with their third eye so he knows there's someone behind him.

Li catches the look and turns around, all easy smiles and charm when he sees her. "Why, Ensign Mazden! Good evening."

"Lieutenant Hsu; Commander Celadon." The young auburn-haired assistant to *Aegolius'* quartermaster smiles back and nods to them both. "I didn't realize the two of you came to places like this, but I thought I'd come say hello."

"Li likes dancing," Toreval tells her, winking briefly at their Navigator. "I just come along to drink coconut-based things and cause trouble."

Li laughs at that, raising his glass towards them. "Isn't half of my job keeping you *out* of trouble, Celadon?"

"Why, yes, Navigator, I do believe it is." Toreval clinks their glass against his with a chuckle at the oldest joke the two of them share.

"I don't suppose you'd be interested in dancing with me, then?" Mazden asks, twirling a lock of hair around her finger. "Since we're all out for the recreation part of 'R and R' and all?"

"I would be *delighted*." Li stands and offers Mazden his hand, and then turns back to Toreval once she's taken it, tilting his head slightly to one side.

They know what he's meaning to ask.

"Go on, you two, have fun." Toreval makes a shooing motion towards the dance floor under the tall potted palm trees. "I'll still be here guarding the table when you get back."

"Don't get into any trouble without me, will you?" Li teases, although in a lightly concerned tone that sounds *entirely* too much like Toreval's eldest kitten.

Toreval laughs. "I'll try, Li, but I won't make any promises."

The two humans scamper off to the dance floor, leaving Toreval alone at the corner table. They don't mind. It's nice to see Li spending time with a member of his own species for a change. Their Navigator is young and he's human— and the two of them are all too often in a situation where it's impossible for him to enjoy being those things. Toreval likes seeing this lively, less serious side of him, even if it means spending most of the evening watching over him from a distance.

They take a sip from their drink, still keeping their third eye on the dance floor. The inventive combinations of fruit juices are a nice addition to their evening, of course. The cold sweetness and tangy flavor almost compensate for the noise level.

Almost.

If it does get to be too much, Toreval knows they can always take Li up on his offer of a sip from whatever bright-colored spirits he's drinking and let *that* dull down the edges of all the information their highly tuned senses are pouring into them. They've done that before, once or twice, but they avoid it if they can. The sensation of not being able to feel the stars and the echoes of the Strange for hours if they misjudge the dosage is downright unsettling. The connected loss of the ability to perceive holoscreens isn't as bad, but it's still inconvenient.

Toreval surveys the room again. As usual, they're the only member of their own species around. Even on their ship, they're the only Florivan. That's a necessity, though; they've only been able to recruit so many of their people as volunteers for the Fleet, and they have to be spread to as many ships as possible. Having two Nav/Quan teams to a ship would be preferable, but the numbers just aren't there.

It's been almost five years since Toreval left their people's sanctuary at Procyon to become the first Florivan officially serving with the Sol Coalition's Defense Fleet. A hundred or so others have followed them, but they regularly struggle to keep the rest of the Council of Elders from forbidding further involvement. Without their people to jump the Fleet's ships through the Strange, though, Toreval is certain that the seven human star systems would already be conquered by the Novans—and their own home would be sure to follow.

Toreval had been the one to bring their people into this mess no one wanted—the ones who would come with them, at any rate—and although they *still* think they did the right thing, they do have to admit that it's lonely being the only one of their kind around. Before they took Li for their Navigator, they'd spent the majority of their life surrounded by family: first their siblings, and then later their kittens. Now, though, their youngest is off apprenticing on a cargo vessel and their other surviving kitten joins the majority of their own parent's household in refusing even to talk to them. Toreval has come to terms with the fact that their parent will never support their so-called defection to the human military, but losing their relationship with Ilmi hurts them more than any physical pain ever could.

Although Toreval does have a few dear friends and older siblings scattered through space and a relationship of mutual respect with the Admiral they've chosen to serve, the only person they're truly close to is Li. As their Navigator, their *anchor*, he occupies a special place in their life. If they were asked to define what that is, they'd say he's somewhere just a touch closer than even their siblings, on an equal level to the two almost-littermates this dreadful war has now taken from them. Toreval's affection for him certainly matches closely with what they feel for their kittens, too—and Li has already withstood more for their sake than any Florivan's counterpart before him.

There's only so much Toreval can offer him in return, though, which is why their Navigator is currently on the dance floor taking a well-deserved break from being at their side.

Toreval doesn't make a habit of dwelling on these things, of course, but it's difficult not to brood when one is set on spending the evening sitting alone in the back corner of a place meant for socialization. Once or twice, they've met other Nav/Quan pairs in places like this, but it rarely happens—usually, such meetings are in quieter surroundings with coffee or tea rather than cocktails. Of course, the coffee is for the Navigators, but it's a very nice-smelling poison.

Toreval takes another slow sip from their glass, watching the dance floor with two eyes and glancing around the rest of the room with the third. The song has changed again and Li's acquired an additional dance partner. He usually has several fluttering around him throughout the night when they go out like this—it'll be a surprise if Ensign Mazden keeps his attention for more than two or three songs by the end of it. She's a perfectly lovely person, from what Toreval knows, but Li never allows himself to become closely involved with people who serve on the same ship as him.

He's tried before to explain to Toreval just *why* that is, but it's all such an alien concept to begin with that they've simply accepted that it's how Li does things and left it at that. As long as no one is causing him pain, Toreval doesn't see any need to interfere with his personal matters.

As they continue their observations, Toreval notices someone walking toward them. They immediately shake off all of the brooding circling in their mind. *This* is unusual enough to require their full attention.

The human in question is tall and pinkish-pale with light golden-brown hair that's just long enough to be begging to be pulled back out of his clean-shaven face. A garland of flowers and greenery drapes around his neck. Underneath, instead of a uniform jacket, he has a green-trimmed ivory vest covered in pockets of different sizes hanging loose over his dark green shirt. Like Li, he's undone his shirt buttons—all of them, in fact, leaving the garment open and the details of his upper body free for anyone to observe.

Toreval is somewhat sure that if they asked his opinion, Li would say that the resulting effect is *quite* attractive. All they can tell for themself is that the young man appears healthy and well-groomed and seems to be around the same age as Li; perhaps a year or two younger, but it's difficult to tell with humans.

They assume at first that he must be going towards a different table, but he isn't. The human weaves his way through the crowd and comes to stand directly in front of Toreval.

"Mind if I sit with you for a bit?" The young human gestures vaguely towards the rest of the room with the drink he's carrying. "This seems to be the only free seat in the house."

Toreval tilts their head to one side, considering him carefully. It's unusual for anyone to approach them at all when they're in one of these places. Normally, unless Li's sitting there to draw attention from potential dance partners, Toreval is almost invisible in whatever corner they've claimed for the evening. The young human is right, though. Toreval can't see another free chair anywhere nearby—and Li's off twirling Ensign Mazden around the dance floor again, so he won't be back anytime soon unless the music turns slow.

"Go ahead," Toreval says, reaching over to move Li's half-full glass so it's next to theirs and out of the new human's way.

"Thanks." The young human sits down, still with his drink in one hand, turning sideways in the chair so his back is mostly towards the wall. From that position, he could easily look out over most of the room and still carry on a conversation with Toreval if he chose to. He stays quiet for a while, taking a sip or two from his tall, lime-wedge-garnished glass of ice chips and white liquid as he scans the crowd.

Toreval finds themself oddly hoping that he *will* strike up a conversation, even if it's just brief pleasantries and small talk. They're curious about him—and there was something compelling about his voice that they can't quite lay a finger on.

"Well," the young human says at last, looking back to Toreval with a wry smile, "It's the oldest line in the galaxy, but I just *have* to ask: What's a nice jumper like you doing in a place like this, anyway?"

Toreval chuckles and glances back over to the dance floor with their third eye, keeping the other two focused on the human at their table. "My Navigator likes dancing," they tell him, "and *I* like coconut drinks... so I come along keep him company until he finds someone interesting to dance with."

"Well, that explains it, then. They do a good lime-in-the-coconut here, by the way, if you haven't tried it." The young human takes another long swig from his glass. Toreval assumes that must be the name of whatever it is he's drinking.

"I haven't, but that does sound nice."

"I take it this Navigator of yours is over on the dance floor now?" The human turns his eyes that way, taking on a curious tone.

"He is."

"Don't tell me which one, then. I want to see if I can guess."

Toreval's long prehensile tail twitches curiously under the table. "I'd be interested to see if you could."

"Hmm..." The young human turns back to them, again with that same wry smile gracing his features. "Want to make a little friendly wager on it?"

"What *sort* of friendly wager?" Toreval would be lying if they said they weren't intrigued.

"Oh, let's say..." Toreval's new acquaintance pauses to take a sip from his glass and then gestures to them with it. "If I'm right, you let me take you and this Navigator of yours somewhere less crowded than this for dinner later."

"And if you're *wrong*?" Toreval picks up their drink again with their lower left hand and uses the upper one to rearrange the remaining slush of ice and juices with the straw before taking a pointedly long sip. "I can't say I can think of anything in particular I'd want from you."

"Well, then, let's say I'll owe you a favor sometime."

He's a cheeky one for sure, but Toreval finds they like that quality. They have a feeling their Navigator would be okay with the idea, too, regardless of the outcome of the bet. This young man seems to be the sort of human Li enjoys discovering, after all, and Toreval is certain he's not part of *Aegolius'* crew. If the insignia on the collar of his open shirt is any indication, though, he probably works in ship's operations on whatever vessel he does belong to.

"All right, then." Toreval smiles, flicking one of their ears lightly. "You have yourself a wager, mister—"

"The name's Elias," he says, holding out his right hand to them, "not that any of the folks I work with ever use it. And you are?"

"You can call me Celadon." Toreval nods briefly to their injured pair of arms and then offers their upper left hand instead. "But you'll have to switch hands if you want to shake on this properly, I'm afraid."

"Sorry about that, force of habit."

Elias leans over the table and gives them a brief but firm handshake, five pinkish-pale alien digits wrapped neatly around Toreval's own four light blue-green ones. His hand is warm, too—warmer than most humans they've met, even.

Warm.

That's what it is in his voice, too, Toreval realizes—deep, rich warmth with a compelling accent that marks him as coming from one of the inner worlds of the Teegarden system. If the coffee Li drinks had a *sound* instead of a smell, that would be this human's voice. Toreval doesn't know why, but they have an immediate impression that this is someone they'd become friends with easily if given the chance.

"Well, then, Elias!" Toreval says with a grin once he's released their hand, gesturing towards the dance floor, "go on, pick out my Navigator—if you *can*, that is."

"Oh, I think I can." Elias grins back and then turns his attention towards the dance floor. He watches the dancers carefully for several minutes.

Toreval wonders what he's thinking. For that matter, they wonder why he's suggested the bet at all. It's certainly an odd thing—although perhaps not nearly as odd as coming to sit with them was in the first place.

Soon, Elias looks back to Toreval, chuckling. "All right, Celadon. I think I've got him."

"Oh? Do you?" Toreval raises their eyebrows. They were expecting him to take longer to make a guess. After all, there *are* a lot of humans to choose from out there. They can still see Li clearly, of course. It seems yet another of the young officers from their ship has found him and taken the opportunity to find out just how good of a dancer he is.

"Yeah." Elias picks up his drink again and takes a swig, then gestures out towards the dance floor with his glass. "It's that one, I'd say: the dark-haired fellow."

"There's at least four humans with dark hair there, if you're pointing the way I think you are. Which one do you mean?"

"The shorter one in the group closer to us—You see him? Long hair, white flower, twirling the blonde girl around every chance he gets?"

"I see him." Toreval does their best not to betray their surprise. "That's your choice, then?"

"Yeah."

"Care to tell me your reasoning?"

"Sure." Elias is still watching the dancers. "Your Navigator has to be an officer of some sort, and there's only so many of those out there to pick from. I know everyone from *Surnia*, so that eliminates them—and anyway, *your* Navigator's bound to be someone particularly special." He gestures with his glass again. "That one's the most interesting man out there."

"You think he's interesting from this far away?"

"Yeah. Sort of... well, brightens up the room around him, if you know what I mean." Elias's voice takes on a soft, wistful tone as he says this. "If I win, *that's* the man I'd want to get to know better."

"Seems like you'd owe me a favor even if I lose, then."

"I just might at that." Elias turns back to them fully now, an overly confident glint in his pair of hazel eyes. "So? Am I right?"

Toreval chuckles. "You'll find out when my Navigator comes back to check on me."

"I can live with that." Elias raises his glass to them congenially before taking another swig. "You looked like you could use some company yourself, at any rate."

"Perhaps I did." Toreval swirls the last of their drink around with the end of their straw. "So, you're with *Surnia*, then?" They know the ship; it's the Fleet's newest carrier-class vessel that's just arrived from the shipyards at Teegarden. They have an informal appointment tomorrow to meet with *Surnia*'s Nav/Quan pair, too, since the ship will be joining the convoy *Aegolius* leads—and to catch up, naturally, since Indigo and Monica are two of Toreval's oldest friends and were among the first volunteers to follow them into the Fleet.

Elias nods. "Have been since we got her Drive bay set up last year. I was planetside at the Shell Island base before that—got called up to help put *Surnia*'s updated Nav-coms system in and it turned out Captain Brentwood liked the idea of having a darter mechanic who could double for a Nav-com tech if something went pear-shaped."

"And that's you, I take it?" Something about his tone of voice tells Toreval that there must be considerably more to the story than his summary lets on.

"It is." Elias takes another swig from his drink, crunching on a few bits of ice. "Nav's only really needed me twice since I transferred, though. As it is, I spend most of my time repairing darter radios and trying to keep it so my pilots have something resembling functional craft to fly." He chuckles, shaking his head. "You wouldn't believe some of the messes that bunch makes for me to fix, Celadon. I'm only responsible for the 2nd Squadron, of course, and with just one wing team you'd think it wouldn't be as much of a workload... but I'd *swear* the four of them are in an ongoing competition to see how many parts of a bloody darter they can break at the same time and still live to tell about it."

"Oh, I can imagine." Toreval nods softly and takes another sip from their drink. They've sat through enough of Jenny's command team meetings over the years to be well aware of the antics of *Aegolius'* own 1st Squadron pilots—particularly since Colonel Hannemann *himself* has to be subjected to one of her lectures about his seeming lack of an instinct for self-preservation and the need for him to set a better example for his pilots at least once a month. More than that, one of Toreval's dearest kittenhood friends is the psychologist who worked as a consultant with the Darter Development Project nearly from the beginning. Navy is still posted at the shipyards' Shell Island base, too, and keeps them regularly updated on all the odd stories that come out of the Fleet's darter pilot training program there. The stories are almost unbelievable, if one's never seen darters in action.

Toreval's seen them, though, both in demonstration flights and occasionally through the Drive bay's viewport while *Aegolius* was under attack and they were waiting for all of the darters to return and land so they could jump the ship to safety. It never ceases to amaze them that the human darter pilots are physically capable of doing what they do and living to tell the tale. It's a special sort of human that can handle flying through all the chaos of a deep space battlefront at all, really. Toreval's had more than a few of their Florivan volunteers take a former darter pilot for their counterpart, too. That special sort of human tends to be good at keeping track of star charts and three-dimensional reference points, both of which are important skills for a Navigator.

"Say, want me to grab you another one of those while we wait? Since it seems we're going to be waiting for a while and all?" Elias gestures towards the bar with his glass.

"That would be nice, thank you." This isn't the sort of place to have a robotic server flying around to deliver drinks—too much of a crowd and a chance of running into people. That, of course, is also Toreval's main reason for not wanting to leave their seat in the corner. The last thing they want this evening is to have someone tread on the tufted end of their long prehensile tail again.

"Piña colada, right?"

"Painkiller, actually. My Navigator thought the joke was too good to pass up given the circumstances with my arms." Toreval shakes their head. They'd refused to admit it to Li when he brought them the drink, but it *was* amusing. They're not sure if the 'cocktail' is worthy of the name, though, when all that's in their glass is the mix of fruit juices that go into the standard version. "I wouldn't mind going back to my usual now that you've mentioned it."

"All right, then. I'm pretty fond of the odd piña colada too, to tell you the truth. Might go ahead and grab one for myself while I'm at it and save a trip later." Elias grins at them, getting to his feet. "You strike me as the sort who likes extra cherries in their garnish. Am I right?"

Toreval stifles a surprised laugh. This young human is *far* more perceptive than they expected. "Yes, thank you—and without the spirits, please."

Elias raises an eyebrow curiously. "Can't have them or don't want them?"

"Mm... more the second one, but really a bit of both if I'm honest."

"All right, then. Good to know." With that, their new acquaintance disappears back into the crowd in the direction of the bar.

Toreval half wonders if he'll come back at all.

The whole encounter with Elias so far has been intriguing, but Toreval still doesn't know quite what to make of him. They do know they want to see how their Navigator will react. Turning all three eyes back towards Li, they can see that, conveniently, he's just now taking a break from the music.

"So, having fun?" Li asks when he reaches them. He leans on the corner of the table on one hand rather than sitting down. He's sweating mildly from all the dancing, but Toreval can tell he's been having a good time out there. They were right about him needing this sort of an evening—the youthful sparkle has finally come back into his dark brown eyes.

"I am, actually." Toreval passes his glass over to him.

"Well, now, Val, that's a surprise! A good one, don't get me wrong, but I know you're usually bored by this point." Li takes a long sip from the glass of bright-colored spirits. "What's going on?"

"I found someone interesting to talk to."

"Oh? Where?" Li's eyes scan the room.

"Somewhere off that way at the moment." Toreval makes a gesture in the general direction. "I'm not sure when he'll come back."

Amusingly, their Navigator's return has coincided with a group of humans in pilot's uniforms coming in and surrounding the place where they last saw Elias. Toreval has a suspicion those pilots are from *Surnia* as well—and if they are, then there's a strong possibility he'll be delayed in returning.

"Ah." Li takes another, smaller sip. "Well, I'm glad you're having a good time, anyway."

"I am." Toreval gestures for him to come closer. "Your braids are coming loose. Let me fix it?"

"Sure." Li smiles and slips into the seat beside them and positions himself so they can reach both sides of his head. "I thought it felt like they were falling..."

Toreval carefully takes the white orchid out and sets it on the table before they begin re-braiding their Navigator's hair. It's slower with just their two left hands, of course, but they can still manage. They're glad he doesn't mind letting them do things like this for him. Li's not particularly keen on being touched casually most of the time, especially when he's not expecting it, but he's comfortable enough with Toreval to indulge their tactile-affectionate instincts. He helps them with their own braids, too, most mornings, even when they're not injured and genuinely in need of the assistance. With their kittens far away and no other Florivans around to share their nest at night, Li's gentle gestures like that are the main thing keeping Toreval centered in the face of their species' gregarious, semi-eusocial nature.

"So," Toreval asks, passing one set of small intertwined braids to him to hold so they can fix the ones from the other side of his head, "how's the dance floor tonight?"

"Stellar!" They can't see the grin, but they can hear it in Li's voice. "You ready to come for a whirl yet?"

"I already *have* two broken arms, Li, do you really want to try for a leg too?" Toreval shakes their head, smiling. They do usually enjoy it when Li persuades them to join in, but there's far too many people out there for them to be comfortable with the idea tonight.

"All right, then. When it quiets down later, maybe?"

"If we're both still here when it gets quiet, then sure."

"I'm going to hold you to that, Celadon Toreval," Li teases, turning to look at them with a pointedly cheeky grin.

"I know you will, Navigator." Toreval matches his expression. "Now hold still so I can finish this—I swear, you're worse than Lapis ever was sometimes about trying to wiggle while I'm fixing your hair."

Li laughs and turns back around. "Hey, now, you and I *both* know Sparks has me beat there." He takes a sip from his drink, then makes an exaggerated effort to become perfectly still.

"...True. *You* at least only ever need to be told to settle down once. You're more like Jade, that way." Toreval holds back a sigh while they finish Li's side braids and begin connecting both sets together at the back of his head. It's been a long time since they had a chance to braid their youngest kitten's hair—even longer since they were able to sit like this with their surviving eldest kitten. The memories of home and the family they left to protect fill them with conflicting swirls of emotion.

As usual, Li seems to pick up on the direction their thoughts have taken. He doesn't say anything, since he's still making a point of being still and quiet, but when Toreval reaches over so they can retrieve the orchid, he settles a hand on their lower one and gives it a gentle squeeze. His eyes say the rest.

Toreval smiles and squeezes back. "There," they say, softly, as they tuck the white flower back into the smooth leaf-black silk of their Navigator's hair with their upper hand. "Now you're all set to go dance without your orchid escaping."

"Thanks, Val." Li holds their hand for a moment longer before the music shifts back to a more upbeat song. He stands and takes a final swig from his nearly empty glass and looks back to the dance floor, waving briefly at someone or other who's trying to catch his attention. He turns back to Toreval with that same cheerful teasing expression once more before he goes off to charm the other young humans some more. "Say hello to your invisible friend for me, will you?"

"Oh, I will, I promise." Toreval can't help chuckling at that, even after Li's blended back in with the rest of the dancers. They've decided it will be *very* entertaining to see how Li reacts if their new friend ever manages to appear in front of him.

Elias returns scarcely a minute later.

"One piña colada, hold the spirits." He places a new umbrella-garnished glass in front of Toreval and then pauses, raising an eyebrow. "All right, Celadon, what's so funny? Did I miss something?"

Toreval accepts the beverage, sliding it over closer with their working lower hand. The little paper umbrella is blue this time, in a shade that reminds them of their youngest kitten. They have an impulse to keep it, although they're not entirely sure why.

"Nothing much, *really*," Toreval replies with a light chuckle and a gesture of the umbrella before they close it and slip it into their pocket. "Just my Navigator."

The human's eyes widen as he lets out a disbelieving laugh.

"Seriously?" Elias glances back towards the dancers, shaking his head. "That's what I get for letting folks find me, I suppose."

Toreval looks over to the cluster of pilots at the bar they'd seen him talking with. A few of them are fully uniformed, while others have on the same sort of bright-colored thematic outfits as the majority of humans in this place—although most of them still have their signature short fitted ivory pilots' jackets on their person somewhere. The distinctive jackets each bear the pilot's surname and squadron markers on the back and are *highly* valued by those who earn them. In Toreval's experience, one seldom encounters a darter pilot without their jacket.

"Some of your colleagues from *Surnia*, I take it?"

"'Colleagues' isn't the word I'd use for Colonel Bell's rookies from the 18th, but yes." Elias shakes his head. "Even the Musketeers hardly believed me when I told them who I was sitting with, though."

Toreval raises their third eyebrow. "Because I'm not some charming young human who's caught your eye, I assume?"

"More because the rookies are all in awe of Florivans in general for one reason or another and didn't believe me that you were here in the first place." Elias chuckles and takes a sip from what little remains of his first beverage. "Or that *any* officer would accept my company, for that matter."

"I see." Toreval smiles. They're finding this human to be quite pleasant company, themself. They feel like there must be some context for his statement that they're missing—and that somehow, they'll likely be amused when they find out whatever it is.

"Granted," Elias adds, absently moving the garnish in his first glass out of the way so he can finish drinking it, "the Musketeers mainly didn't think I could possibly have found another person in the entire bloody *galaxy* who shares my love for coconut-based drinks without the strong stuff."

"Oh?" Toreval raises an eyebrow. "I was under the impression most humans came to places like this for the alcohol as much as for the socialization."

Elias gives them a bit of a cheeky smirk. "I socialize just fine *without* the lubrication. Makes it more interesting, really—especially the next day when folks have to ask what went on and I'm the only one who remembers."

"I can sympathize with that."

Li's responsible enough in his evenings out, usually, but Toreval can think of at least two occasions where they've had to explain to him just *how*, precisely, he'd ended up in one situation or another when he'd happened to overindulge. They count themself fortunate that's an infrequent occurrence.

Elias turns his attention back towards the dance floor.

Toreval knows who he's watching. They still haven't figured out why this human is sitting and talking with *them* instead of going out and joining the revelry himself. At the same time, it's oddly refreshing to have someone new to talk to without it being related entirely to their work.

A few moments later, Toreval catches a glimpse of people coming towards their corner. When they turn their full attention see who it is, they have to stifle a laugh. This is turning out to be quite the interesting evening indeed.

"Say, Elias?" They flick their ears towards the appropriate direction. "I think your friends have found us."

Toreval's new acquaintance turns his eyes away from the dance floor just in time to see the trio of pilots appear out of the crowd in front of them. He lets out a somewhat amused groan. "Of *course* they bloody did..."

"So, you really *did* find yourself a Florivan!" says the first pilot, plopping down into the free seat beside Elias. She's a tall, wiry woman with deeply tan skin and piercingly dark eyes, wearing a neat ivory headscarf which conceals all of her hair.

"Will wonders never cease? Our Rudy, out here making friends with *officers*?" The second pilot pulls over an extra chair and turns it around before sitting down and resting her arms on the chair back that's now in front of her. With her tawny-pale complexion and shoulder-length leaf-black hair, to Toreval's eyes she looks like she could easily have ancestors in common with Li.

"Mind if we sit with you?" asks the third, gesturing to the remaining empty seat beside Toreval. She's a highly muscular sort of human with incredibly curly white hair pulled into two poofy ponytails at the base of her neck and the palest skin and eyes Toreval's ever seen. The true color of her eyes is somewhat obscured by the lightly tinted lenses of the wraparound sunglasses she's wearing. They suspect she's one of the members of her species with some degree of albinism, although they don't feel inclined to ask about it at the moment.

"Go ahead, please." Toreval takes a sip of the sweet frozen coconut-and-pineapple concoction Elias retrieved for them. Something about the three women is familiar, although Toreval can't quite place it at the moment. That in itself piques their curiosity. It's going to be interesting to see how Li reacts when he returns and sees that their quiet corner table is filled with people, that's for sure.

"So, Celadon," says Elias, gesturing to each of the pilots in turn, "here we have the three lady Musketeers of the 2nd Squadron: Pilot-Majors Toussaint, Ioane, and Albright."

"We have a d'Artagnan, too," says Albright, the pale woman sitting beside Toreval, "but the silly man has gone and misplaced himself and we're *still* waiting for the Prelvee to return him."

"But that's our Sarge for you—ever the galant darter in distress." The dark-haired pilot in the backwards chair, Ioane, giggles softly.

"Hopefully we'll teach him not to need rescuing all the time one of these days." The third pilot, Toussaint, laughs and reaches up to readjust the folds of her neatly placed ivory headscarf.

If Toreval's guess is right, all three pilots are closer to their own age than to Elias' or Li's. For humans, that puts them somewhere around "not quite middle aged"—but it's hard to tell for sure without asking directly.

"Your misplaced young friend sounds like quite the character," Toreval comments, looking between the three pilots.

"Oh, he is!" Toussaint declares, "That's why we picked him for our fourth. Good pilot, our Sarge, too—just a bit green, you know?"

"I know the type." Toreval takes another sip from their drink. They've seen a lot of young, inexperienced humans since they first joined the Fleet—some of them will become fine officers one day, but thanks to the Novans, many others will never have the chance.

"What's our Rudy up to that has him lurking in a corner with the highest-ranking officer here, anyway?" Ioane leans over the chair back, looking to Toreval curiously.

"Oh, I wouldn't say either of us is particularly 'up to' anything." Toreval can't help chuckling. "We do have a bit of a wager going on, though."

"Oh?" Toussaint looks between them and Elias.

"It's nothing, really," he says, glancing absently at the dance floor. "Just a friendly sort of thing to pass the time."

The three pilots share a knowing look.

"So there's a cute guy involved, then?" Albright pulls her sunglasses down a bit and turns her pale eyes pointedly over the rim of them towards Elias.

"Now, Penny, let's not tease him *too* much." Ioane reaches over and nudges Albright's arm playfully. "It could be something else entirely, you know."

"So what's the bet, sir?" Toussaint asks again, looking back to Toreval. "And how do we get in on it?"

Elias' expression in response to all this is a combination of affectionate annoyance and stifled embarrassment. He does his best to hide most of it behind a long sip from his drink. Toreval can't help but picture these three pilots as his older sisters—the dynamic between them, at least, reminds them of a trio of littermates teasing a beloved younger sibling.

"Well," Toreval says, gesturing with their lower-left hand since their upper one is occupied with holding their drink, "do you see all of those young humans enjoying themselves on the dance floor?"

The three pilots turn to look that way in almost perfect unison.

"Yeah," says Ioane. "They're pretty hard to miss. What about them?"

"One of them is my Navigator." Toreval pauses to take a sip from their drink. They absently stir the slush of frozen fruit juices around for a moment. "The bet is whether my new friend here has managed to spot him."

"*Interesting...*" There's a definite grin in Toussaint's voice, although she doesn't turn around to show it. "All right, sir, I'm in. What's the stakes?"

Elias looks to Toreval with a brief, meaningful glint of pleading in his hazel eyes.

Toreval takes this to mean he'd prefer the pilots *not* know the part about him asking to take them and Li out to dinner when he wins. From what they understand of the way humans do things, the good-natured teasing would be merciless if that came to light.

"Oh, nothing too terribly important... Just a favor to be determined at a later date." Toreval raises their glass to him slightly, knowing the pilots all have their eyes on the dance floor.

Elias nods in gratitude and returns the gesture.

"You're *learning*, Rudy," Albright comments with a chuckle. "Okay, then, I'm in too. How about you, Abigail?"

"I'm in. Haven't won a favor from an officer in a while— this should be fun!"

Toreval is starting to think they're going to be owed favors by half of *Surnia*'s crew if this keeps up. They're amused by the prospect.

The three pilots turn back to them.

"So," asks Ioane, "are we shaking on this or...?"

"Forgive me," Toreval says with a chuckle, nodding towards the casts on their right side, "I'm somewhat short on hands at the moment. Would a toast be official enough instead?" They raise their glass towards the four humans.

"*Stars*, sir!" Toussaint exclaims. "I hadn't even noticed you were injured."

"It's nothing, really—I had a disagreement with the ship's artificial gravity fields at the end of a tactical jump the other day."

"Ah, yes, our old foe: *Gravity.*" Albright raises her glass dramatically and clinks it against Toreval's.

"Gravity indeed!" Ioane laughs and does the same.

"Come on, Rudy," adds Toussaint after her turn at the toast, "you too, yes?"

"Fine, fine." Elias gives them an amused head shake as their matching glasses touch. Toreval winks their third eye at him. They've decided they like this human—they're looking forward to seeing what their Navigator thinks of him.

The ritual complete, the pilots turn their attention back to the dance floor to make their choices.

"I'm going to say..." Albright folds her hands together, leaning her elbows on the table. After a long pause, she gestures vaguely towards the dance floor with her pressed-together index fingers. "Ah, the ginger fellow with the goatee."

"Aw, Penny! I was going to pick him." Ioane looks back to Albright with a mock pout.

Albright just grins and takes a sip from her lime-and-mint garnished glass of crushed ice and pale amber liquid.

"Who do you want instead, then, Abigail? I'll pick last." Toussaint is intently watching the dancers, her head moving slightly from side to side as she follows someone or other with her eyes.

"Hmm... how about the tall one with all the twists in his hair who's *dancing* with the ginger? His aura is the more Nav-ish of the two anyway."

Albright giggles softly. "You and your auras..."

Toreval focuses their eyes to get a better look at the two humans the pilots are talking about. The tall young man with the rich copper-brown complexion Ioane has chosen is familiar to them—he's one of the prospective Navigators they and Li have helped train who currently serves as an assistant to SCV *Strix*'s Captain Setiaiwan. They make a mental note to ask Ioane at some point what she means about him having a "Navigator aura"—particularly after she's had the chance to meet Li for a comparison.

"Good choices," says Toussaint, "but you're both wrong."

"Who are you picking, then, Anna?" Albright asks.

"That one: Blonde, bright yellow floral shirt."

"Ah. He's a good pick too." Albright takes another swig from her glass. "Which did you pick, then, Rudy?"

"Not any of the ones you did," he says. Following the line of his gaze, Toreval can tell he's still watching the cluster of dancers around Li.

Toussaint nudges him with her elbow. "But which one?"

"You'll find out when he comes over here and Celadon admits I've won." Elias laughs and turns back to the table. He nonchalantly plucks one of the cherries off the end of the garnish spear in his drink.

"Oh, *stars*, girls!" Toussaint lets out an exaggerated chuckle. "I think we missed spotting a real catch out there."

"I was picking for Nav-ish-ness," protests Ioane, "not attractiveness. You *know* I can't tell what that's supposed to be."

"Don't worry, Abigail, yours is cute too," Toussaint tells her. "Younger than I care for, of course, but definitely on the high end of the sexy scale in general. I mean, seriously, *those cheekbones...*"

"It's like you're speaking a completely different language—and not one I care to have translated, at that." Ioane turns back to the table with a groan and shakes her head, looking to Toreval with a small eye roll.

Toreval indulges her with a matching movement of their third eye. They always find it somewhat pleasant when they encounter a human who shares their lack of personal interest in the subjects of attraction and romance. They wonder where on the various orientation spectrums Ioane would place herself, but they find it best to let humans volunteer that sort of information rather than ask for it or try to guess.

That's one of the things Toreval finds fascinating about living among humans, though: there are an almost *infinite* variety of characteristics, identities, preferences that the species exhibits, both biologically and mentally. They never tire of seeing how all those different qualities can manifest into an individual.

"I still can't believe you found someone who likes those things without the rum too," Albright tells Elias, changing the subject with a disgusted gesture at his glass. "I mean, if you're going to drink something that tastes like *sunblock*, it might as well be high-octane sunblock."

"I take it you're not a fan?" Toreval asks, taking a pointedly long sip from their own drink.

"I spent my entire childhood back on Mars smelling like the stuff because it was either that or stay *indoors* all the time, even though the city dome shielded out enough UV to protect everyone else." She lets out a light huff of mock annoyance. "Coconut is preferable to sunburns, but it's *not* something I want in a drink."

"I just don't see how any of you stand the sweetness," says Toussaint. "It just gets in the way of the other flavors."

"*Most* people don't like being pickled in bitter herbs and rocket fuel, Major Toussaint," Elias looks askance at her glass of swirling pale green liquid. "How you can drink that stuff and live is one of the great medical mysteries of our time."

"Oh, he's got you there, Anna!" Albright chortles and reaches across the table to clink glasses with him.

"It's an acquired taste." Toussaint rolls her eyes.

Toreval can't help but be amused listening to the exchange. "You sound like my Navigator when he starts talking about coffee."

"Coffee is another thing altogether," Toussaint declares. "It *needs* sugar to be drinkable."

"You're wrong and you know it." Elias shakes his head. "All coffee needs is a splash of milk. Nothing fancy."

Toussaint nudges him with her elbow, holding up three fingers on the other hand. "Three words, Rudy: Hazelnut caramel mocha."

"There's barely even any bloody coffee in that!"

"Oh, no," says Ioane with a dramatic groan, "here we go again."

"Subject change!" Albright holds up a hand before the other humans can say anything else. She turns to Toreval, shifting to a bright easy-going smile. "So, which ship are you with, anyway, Celadon? If you don't mind my asking?"

"I don't mind at all," Toreval replies. They're unaccustomed to such enthusiastic company, but it's a nice change from their usual routine. "SCV *Aegolius*."

All four pairs of human eyes widen at once.

Toussaint chokes on the sip she'd been taking from her drink. "Seriously?" she sputters between soft coughs.

"The flagship?" Albright shakes her head. "You're *that* Celadon? I knew you were an officer, but—*stars*!"

Ioane looks over to Elias, still shocked. "You're after the *Admiral's* Navigator—and sitting here drinking rum-less piña coladas with a Florivan Elder like it's just an average Tuesday night for you?"

"To be fair..." Elias says, recomposing his expression back into the easy-going confidence he's had since he first sat down, "Celadon didn't mention whose ship they served on until just now."

Toreval takes a long sip from their drink before saying anything. The reaction is amusing. They always forget how concerned humans can get regarding hierarchical matters in the Fleet. They're the Youngest of their people's Council of Elders, yes, and serve closely with Jenny as the 'exiled' Fleet's Elder—but they hardly consider themself to be *important* in the way humans so often seem to think they should be.

"I didn't realize it mattered," Toreval says at last, smiling over the rim of their glass.

"It's... more just a surprise that the person all the *other* Fleet jumpers report to would be hanging out in a tiki bar," Albright replies. After a moment, her composure apparently recovered, she smirks at them. "Not to mention that we've heard a lot about *you*."

Toreval arches their lower eyebrows curiously. "Dare I ask?"

"Well," says Ioane, "we were test pilots back at Teegarden before the war even started…" She giggles softly. "Navy might have mentioned your name once or twice when they were lecturing us on getting into too much mischief for our own good."

"Ah." Toreval holds back a sigh. "Of course they would have." Navy might be the psychologist working with the Fleet's pilots at the Teegarden Shipyards *now*, but they'd been tasked with minding Toreval and their equally mischief-prone almost-littermates long before that. Toreval's not sure they want to ask just yet what these pilots have heard about them from their old kitten-sitter.

"Not to mention," adds Ioane, with a subtle note of sadness coloring the edges of her tone, "that Sky back on the *Athene* was a good friend of ours—they had a lot of stories about you, you know?"

"I promise, I'm *terribly* boring compared to whatever Sky might have told you." Toreval chuckles, despite the pang of regret and loss that name sparks in their soul. *Athene*'s Florivan QSD officer was one of the two kittens Toreval had been raised with—the ones their heart always said were their littermates, even though the two of them were several years older and belonged to Toreval's foster parent. Sky Laryven and Stream Liret had been among the first who followed them into the Fleet, too. Now, both are yet another name on the list of loved ones Toreval has lost to the Novans and their quest to conquer this part of the galaxy. It's been more than a year since their deaths, but Toreval feels the loss just as keenly as ever.

"So, you *aren't* the same Celadon that jumped off a balcony and told your Elders' Council where to shove it when you joined the Fleet, then?" Albright raises an eyebrow, still wide-eyed under her tinted lenses.

"Well... I didn't use those words exactly." Toreval had *wanted* to say something of the sort at the time, to a certain extent—not that they would ever admit that to anyone besides Li.

"And you never *really* cussed out one of the T'irsh-fel observers for trying to interfere with you during a jump-tactic demonstration either?" Toussaint asks, stifling a laugh. "We heard that story from Indigo a while back— they join our standby-duty card games sometimes."

"No, actually." Toreval's ears twitch with amusement. They're not surprised their old friend is well acquainted with these pilots, somehow. "I'm not sure how they've come to misremember the details... but *that* was my Navigator."

"Really?" Elias raises his eyebrows, clearly intrigued.

Toreval nods solemnly, taking another sip of their drink. "He's normally quite mild-mannered, but he takes our safety protocols for working in the Strange *very* seriously... and the observer had attempted to open one of the viewports near our Drive bay twice already before he tried to break the door seals to come in and pester me."

"Oof," says Albright, "no wonder your Navigator ripped him a new one. That'd what, have killed every human on the ship? Worse?"

"Worse, most likely; we were running battle tandem exercises with *Glaucidium* and *Otus* at the time. I wouldn't have been able to control the shockwave hitting them if I'd had to jump us out mid-transit." Toreval calmly slides one of the cherries off the end of their drink's garnish spear and takes a nibble from it. "Probably would have taken out all three ships."

"I'm surprised you *didn't* cuss him out yourself," says Albright. "I mean, I'd've decked the guy if it was me."

"Well, I would have had to get in line, really, between my Navigator and the Admiral. Besides," Toreval says, finishing off the cherry and winking briefly at the humans, "it was far more effective to shame dear Captain Zox *politely* in front of the entire T'irsh-fel admiralty when the observers made their reports after the exercises were over, since I *did* need to formally apologize to him for how rude my Navigator had been and all... I haven't had any problems with a one of them since."

All three pilots burst out laughing. Toussaint chokes on her drink again.

Elias shakes his head and chuckles quietly, passing her a napkin.

"Now that's more like it," Albright says once they've all quieted down. "No wonder the scuttlebutt goes around that if we ever get to the end of this mess, none of the galactic powers will survive being in negotiation talks with you."

"I hadn't heard that rumor," Toreval admits, laughing lightly. They hadn't been aware that they had any such reputation to begin with. "In any case, I sincerely doubt I'll be the one doing any negotiating—my people are *officially* a neutral party in this war, you know. I'm nothing more than the Admiral's volunteer jumper and advisor on things involving the Strange, that's all."

"*Sure*... but still, Celadon, remind me never to get on your bad side." Albright reaches over and clinks her glass lightly against theirs once again. "And hey, since Florivans are pacifists and all—if you ever need someone to kick a few butts on your behalf, let me know? I get bored just sparring with *Surnia*'s security team."

"She means it," Ioane adds with an amused fondness. "Penny's something of a judo champion, among other things. Captain Brentwood hasn't found *anyone* yet who can match her, and trust me, she's tried."

"Thank you, then, Major Albright." Toreval nods softly. "I seldom need to have anyone fight on my behalf, but I will keep that in mind." They take it as an offer of friendship more than actual martial loyalty, but that's a touching gesture all the same.

"Never figured a Fleet legend like *you* would be a tiki bar type, you know," Toussaint comments, taking a more cautious sip from her drink now that she's finally caught her breath.

"I'm not, usually, but my Navigator is—and where he goes, so do I." Toreval looks between the humans sitting around their table and finds themself smiling. "Although I will admit this place is starting to grow on me."

"That's good to hear," says Ioane. "Maybe we'll see more of you while our ships are in port, then."

"I wouldn't mind that." Toreval smiles, then glances over to the dance floor. The music's changed to one of those slow sorts of songs that Li usually saves for later in the evening when he's settled on one particular dance partner. He doesn't seem to have done that yet tonight. In fact, he seems to be taking his leave of the dancers for the moment. They watch him go towards the bar—probably to refresh his drink, since the glass he's left with them is empty. Toreval chuckles and looks back to the pilots and Elias. "So, about that wager! You're all confident in your choices?"

The humans give them a chorus of affirmative replies and nods.

"Good, then!" Toreval grins at the four of them. "Well, if one of you would be so kind as to pull over another chair... he should be coming back any moment now."

Toreval gives Elias an encouraging wink with their third eye, although they don't know for sure if he sees it. He's too busy watching the young man walking over from the bar, tall glass of brightly colored cocktail in one hand and shorter glass of cream-colored juices and pineapple fronds in the other.

"Well, now, Celadon!" Li slips gracefully into the chair Ioane has just pulled over, sliding the shorter glass across the table to them. "I leave you for twenty minutes and you're forming your own squadron already?"

"Oh, no, just making friends and gathering favors..." Toreval does their best to sound as innocent as they possibly can. "You know me, ever the troublemaker."

"As always," Li laughs. "Are you going to introduce me to your new friends, then?"

"Why, of course." Toreval gestures to him with their piña colada glass as formally and dramatically as suits the occasion. "Elias; Pilot-Majors Toussaint, Ioane, Albright... may I present my Navigator: Lieutenant Hsu Li of *Aegolius*."

"Nice to meet you all." Li gives Toreval a look that says he knows they're up to something, but he hasn't figured out quite *what*.

Toreval pulls their glass back to drain the last of the frozen slush of coconut and pineapple before adding, "I believe that settles the bet?"

"It does indeed," says Toussaint, lifting the last of her drink in toast. "And you have certainly bested us, sir." The other pilots follow suit, and then all three cast amused glances in Elias' direction.

The young man in question is sitting there half entranced, his eyes tracing over Li's face as if he's trying to memorize every detail of a mirage. Toreval has seen the look before—their Navigator has that effect on a lot of humans. A glance to the other end of the table tells them that for his part, Li is *equally* intrigued by Elias. Somehow, Toreval isn't surprised.

"Dare I ask what the bet was, Celadon," Li asks, "or just *what* you've won from them?"

"Oh, just a silly little game, really, Li..." Toreval smiles at him. "My new friends were challenged to pick a Navigator for me from the crowd."

"Oh, were they?" Li chuckles and takes a somewhat distracted sip from his bright-colored beverage. "And did anyone manage to win?"

Toreval nods over towards Elias. "Behold, the winner! He has *excellent* taste in Navigators, if I do say so myself."

"Really now?" Li raises his glass to the other young man. "Congratulations are in order, then... it's Elias, yes?"

Toussaint takes the opportunity to give Elias a teasing nudge. That seems to jolt the younger human out of his daze.

"Petty Officer third class Elias Rudolph, at your service, sir—darter maintenance and Nav comms, SCV *Surnia*." Elias somehow manages not to knock any of the glasses on the table over in his rush to give an exaggerated sort of salute.

"No need to be so formal." Li chuckles brightly, his eyes never leaving those of the other young man. "You were fortunate, Elias. Celadon practically *never* loses wagers."

"Thank you, sir." The traces of a blush color Elias' cheekbones.

"Please, no more of the officer nonsense." Li is smiling now in that way he has that seems to light up any room. "I use my name when I'm off-duty, you know?"

"Of course, sir—"

"—Li."

"Li." As it turns out, Elias has a smile of his own that's equally brilliant.

"So, Celadon," asks Li, turning back to Toreval with a curious tilt of his head, "what has Elias here won from you, anyway?"

"Oh, nothing much, really." Toreval shrugs. "I owe him dinner and a to-be-determined favor and... I *believe* we said a dance was included in that, yes?" Toreval is sure Elias catches their wink this time. He's finally turned his eyes back to them, at least.

"Um... yes, I think it was." Elias pointedly does *not* make eye contact with any of the pilots who are watching the exchange.

Toreval smiles innocently as they look back to Li. "Although considering that I'm not in the best shape for dancing tonight... would *you* mind covering that part of my debt, Navigator?"

Li looks at them for a moment, almost confused, then takes a long swig from his drink and laughs. "You arranged all of this to get out of going on the dance floor, didn't you? Celadon, really, I thought we agreed you wouldn't be the *manipulative* sort of cryptic with me anymore."

"Who's being manipulative?" Toreval smirks teasingly at him. "It just happens to be convenient for all concerned, Li, that's all—assuming Elias doesn't mind the substitution?"

"Oh, I don't—not at all—but I might call that favor in for a song or two once you're healed up." Elias seems to have recovered his composure and caught on quickly enough.

"Naturally," Toreval says, smiling. "Piña coladas and dancing, just as soon as these casts come off."

Even if Li hasn't caught on precisely, at least he seems content to go along with all of this. He takes one more sip and then passes Toreval his glass and stands up again. "Well, then! It seems I have a debt to pay off. Shall we?"

"I would be *honored*." Elias stands as well, maneuvering himself around the seated pilots to take Li's offered hand.

Toreval watches, amused, as the two young humans disappear in the direction of the dance floor. They didn't set out to find Li a dance partner, but they're quite pleased with the one they've acquired for him.

The pilots seem equally amused.

"Well, now," says Albright with a giggle, "if that's not the most adorable thing I've ever seen, I don't know *what* is."

"Want one of us to walk you back to your ship later, sir?" asks Toussaint. "I don't think you'll be getting your Navigator back tonight."

"Oh, I wouldn't want to intrude on your evening." Toreval smiles and takes a sip from their drink. "But I do appreciate the offer."

"You won't be intruding on *my* evening, at least," Ioane tells them cheerfully. "It'll save me having to go home entirely alone once these two get distracted by whoever manages to catch their eye in the end and wander off."

"We don't always wander off, Abi," Toussaint teases, "do we?"

"Well," Ioane admits, "not *always*—and I don't take offense that you do, mind, that's my signal that it's time to go home and enjoy the relative peace and quiet while it lasts—but we've been cooped up on Surnia long enough this time that I'll be surprised if you don't tonight."

Toussaint shakes her head, letting out another good natured chuckle. "Point taken. I thought I was the one who was supposed to know the odds on everything..."

"And yet, here you are, defeated in a wager by Rudy, of all people." Ioane grins. "If that doesn't make for an interesting turn of fate, I don't know what does."

"Rudy may not give that Navigator of yours back at all, you know," Albright tells Toreval, taking another sip from her drink. "I've never seen him smitten that thoroughly before."

Toreval shakes their head lightly. Humans are so odd sometimes. "I rather like your young friend, you know," they say. "He's a sweet sort of a scoundrel, from what I've seen of him. If my Navigator enjoys his company, why should I want to interfere?"

Ioane nods. "Either way, you get a new friend to hang out and drink piña coladas with?"

"Exactly." Toreval stifles a giggle. Somehow, they're not surprised that she's the one who understands their position. "Several new friends, even."

They watch with the pilots for several songs, absently making small talk about their mutual acquaintances in the meantime. For his part, Li seems to be having a grand time—and no intent of changing to another dance partner at all. In all the time they've known him and been coming to these sorts of recreational spaces with him, Toreval has never seen Li taken with someone so quickly.

"New bet." Toussaint turns around from watching the dancing as another song ends, setting her empty glass down on the table with a sharp clink.

"What now?" asks Albright.

Toussaint grins. "Those two. I'm calling it right now, that's six months to a proposal at the most."

"Seriously, Anna?" Ioane shakes her head in disbelief. "How in the *stars* could you tell anything from that exchange just now? They just met."

"No," Albright says, catching the grin, "she's right, there's something nice and sparky there. I'd say a year, though—being on different ships is going to interfere something fierce."

"To be fair," Toreval comments, "that might work in Elias' favor. Li never allows himself any interest in crewmates."

"Ooh, that's good to know." Albright sets her now-drained glass down as well.

Ioane groans and swirls the remaining blue liquid around in her glass. "There's no way I could guess on this one. You're *sure* they're going to be a long-term thing at all?"

"Just pick a number, then, Abigail—or do you really want to bet against them getting together? I mean... just look at that." Toussaint gestures out to the dance floor. "That's just *begging* to be a thing."

"I'll take your word for it," Ioane replies, "but I think I'll sit this one out."

"All right, then!" Toussaint says triumphantly, "It's you and me, Penny. Stakes?"

"Nothing too big," Albright tells her. "We'll have to wait *ages* to find out who wins regardless. How about first round of drinks at the wedding reception? Abigail, you can be sure to remind us then."

The other two pilots nod, then all three look over to Toreval.

"You want in on this, sir?" Toussaint asks, still grinning broadly.

"Oh, no." Toreval lets out a small laugh. "I'll stand as a second amused witness to your wager, nothing more. As I said, I don't interfere with my Navigator's social life."

"If you don't call what you just did interfering, I'm afraid to know what would be," Albright teases. "Although you can interfere *me* up a cute officer anytime you like."

"Me too," Toussaint adds, stifling a laugh. "Do you think you can interfere me someone who's athletic *and* can hold her own at competition-level sudoku?"

"Well..." Toreval smirks over the rim of their glass. They look forward to contacting Navy and asking what they think of these pilots, that's for sure. "None of this was really my doing at all, you know. It took Elias all of two minutes to decide that Li was my Navigator and suggest the bet—I'm sure they'd have found their way to each other sooner or later."

Toussaint giggles affectionately. "That's our Rudy for you. Once he's made up his mind, there's no changing his course."

"To tell you the truth, Li's much the same about a lot of things..." Toreval absently swirls the last of the liquid around in their glass. "I'd be grateful if the two of them do get along in the long run. It'd be nice to see him have a friend of the same species, at any rate."

Ioane looks over to them, tilting her head to one side. "You worry about him?"

"Mm..." Toreval turns their third eye back to the dance floor. They don't know how to even begin to explain the fullness of the concern they have for the young man who shares their life. "Li is my Navigator," they say at last, "I worry about his wellbeing almost as much as I do my kittens."

"Well," Toussaint says, standing and gesturing in the direction of the bar, "I'm getting us another round. Same as always, girls?" After the other pilots have nodded their agreement, she turns back to Toreval, that same wry smile coloring her features. "For what it's worth, sir, I don't think you need to worry about him being lonely anymore."

Toreval watches the dancers for a few moments longer as everyone rearranges themselves for one of those long slow sorts of songs Li normally avoids.

In the middle of the dance floor, their Navigator is still right there with Elias, close as any pair out there. There's a graceful ease between the two of them like nothing Toreval's ever seen in all the time they've come to these places and watched Li charm everyone who comes near him. Li looks happy, too, in a way that seems to make him shine brighter even than he normally does to Toreval's eyes. They've never seen a dance partner whose introduction made him smile quite like that.

"You know, what, Major Toussaint?" Toreval says softly, more to themself than anyone. "I think you might be right."

✶ **The End** ✶

Characters Appearing in *Aliens at a Tiki Bar*

The following list of characters is divided by species and arranged in order of their appearance in the narrative. Only characters with significant "speaking roles" have been detailed here. All others present are listed as a group for the reader's reference; characters who are mentioned but do not appear are not included.

Florivans

Elder Celadon Toreval

They/them. Also known as "Val." Primary Quantum Space Drive Engineer, SCV *Aegolius*. Youngest of the Florivan Council of Elders; Defense Fleet Elder. Counterpart to **Lt. Hsu Li.**

Humans

Lt. Hsu Li

He/him. Lead Astral Navigator, SCV *Aegolius*. Former personal assistant to **Admiral Marvin**. Counterpart to **Elder Celadon**.

Petty Officer 3rd Class Elias Rudolph

He/him. Also known as "Rudy." Darter Maintenance Technician, Second Darter Squadron, assigned to SCV *Surnia*.

Pilot-Major Abigail Ioane

She/her. Second Darter Squadron pilot, assigned to SCV *Surnia* (previously SCV *Athene*). Former Project Snail Darter test pilot.

PILOT-MAJOR ANNA TOUSSAINT

She/her. Second Darter Squadron pilot, assigned to SCV *Surnia* (previously SCV *Athene*). Former Project Snail Darter test pilot.

PILOT-MAJOR PENNY ALBRIGHT

She/her. Second Darter Squadron pilot, assigned to SCV *Surnia* (previously SCV *Athene*). Former Project Snail Darter test pilot.

An Interlude of Colors

★ A Strange Space™ Short Story ★

For Sharon T. Hinton, my wonderfully supportive Astral Navigator from the Strange Space™ Fan Club who requested this story.

The kittens and I had far too much fun fulfilling your request!

It's a good day, as far as the Florivan kitten known as Mirawynd reckons things. They've spent most of it exploring the starship SCV *Aegolius*, which is always fun as far as Mirawynd is concerned. They're used to living on a different Defense Fleet ship called *Surnia*, but their most recent adventure involved changing ships for reasons little Mirawynd doesn't quite understand. Conveniently, though, their temporary home also happens to be where half of their family lives, so they've had all sorts of people to visit today.

At the moment, Mirawynd is hanging out in the ship's "Nav Closet" with three of their most favorite humans. They're currently nestled under the warm ivory scarf their Entile Celadon's Navigator always wears with his uniform.

He's wearing it now, even—just with Mirawynd tucked inside it and resting mostly on his shoulder. Li is a very nice human all around, with long black hair, dark eyes, and a tawny-pale complexion. He also has the warmest, brightest voice of any human Mirawynd has ever met. They've liked Li ever since they met him, especially because he always has a donut hole or two for them at the end of the night if they're a polite kitten and sit quietly while he's working. It's no wonder he's one of their two second-favorite humans.

Mirawynd's own human, a more pinkish-pale fellow with short, scruffy sandy-brown hair and a matching beard, is sitting on one of the rolling stools on either side of Li's Navigator-in-charge chair. *This* is their favorite person in the whole galaxy.

They've been his companion ever since they were a much smaller kitten and their parent tasked them with keeping him safe. The other humans they live with call him "Sarge" most of the time, but his proper name seems to be "Julian." Mirawynd simply thinks of the young man as *their* human, although his nickname is one of the best words they've learned how to say.

Their human is a darter pilot, properly, but Li borrows him from *Surnia* regularly to make him practice Navigator things. This suits Mirawynd just fine, since it means they get to spend time with their Entile Celadon's family and sleep in Li's scarf.

On Li's other side sits another Navigator-in-training who looks similar to Mirawynd's human, but far younger and somehow less scruffy. This is their Cousin Ocean's human, George, who is also a pilot. Mirawynd likes him, naturally, especially because he knows lots of songs and doesn't mind them squeaking along when he's singing. They have to agree with their big cousin that George has a wonderful singing voice.

Ever since *Aegolius* picked them up from their latest big adventure, Mirawynd has spent a lot of time napping in Li's scarf while he teaches their human and George to be good Navigators like he is. It's a cozy way to spend an evening, for sure, and there are always interesting things to watch on Li's collection of information screens too—not to mention the possibility of tasty snacks at the mid-shift break. Mirawynd is a growing kitten, after all, and always open to sharing snacks with their favorite humans.

Mirawynd isn't sure how long they've been napping in the folds of Li's scarf when they awaken to the sound of the door to his little screen-filled room opening.

"Hey, there, handsome. You need a refill on that hummingbird nectar?"

Mirawynd's tufted catlike ears prick up. That warm, richly accented voice is unmistakably that of their other second-favorite human, Rudy.

Mirawynd slips their head out of the scarf-nest so all three of their golden eyes can see the source of the voice and squeak a sleepy hello in his direction. The ruddy-pale man in question is standing in the doorway holding a tray with two covered mugs and a tall lidded cup with a straw. His shoulder-length hair is golden-brown, and has once again escaped the hair-tie it's supposed to be in and fallen into his face.

"You have the best timing, Elias." Li brightens and spins his chair towards the door. "I was just thinking about sending someone down to the mess..."

"Well, it's as good an excuse as any to come up and say hi to my husband while I'm on my break without his boss getting onto me for distracting her Navigator." Rudy grins at him, holding out the cup with the lidded straw.

"She's your boss too, you know." Li smiles and accepts the drink. "But thank you."

Mirawynd's human finally lets out the chuckle he's been stifling. "I will *never* get used to seeing your soft side, Rudy," he teases.

"Don't push it, Sarge." Rudy rolls his eyes, although with a soft blush coloring his cheeks. "Or is that your way of saying I should take *your* cup down to the medbay for Dr. Kiely instead?"

"No, no, I'll be good. You brought coffee for me too?" Mirawynd's human still has that teasing sparkle on the edge of his voice.

Rudy hands him a mug, rolling his eyes. "I brought one for the kid here, so I bloody well couldn't leave you out." He turns to George and offers him the final, smaller mug. "Breezy said you were a cortado man?"

"Yes, sir. Thank you." George accepts it, slightly awkwardly.

"Kid, I don't outrank you, remember? No need for the bloody honorifics." Rudy laughs. "Besides, you're family now."

"Right." George nods, slightly hesitant. "Still getting used to that."

Mirawynd takes this as an appropriate moment to emerge fully from Li's scarf, revealing all four of their slim, silver-furred arms as well as their legs and long fluffy prehensile tail. They hop to George's shoulder to give him a reassuring nuzzle. "Mine."

"See? Even Wyndi agrees." Rudy grins, turning his attention back to Li. "Try to keep this little brother of yours out of trouble tonight, will you? Sid and I have too much work to do on his darter to have time to come rescue him." He pauses, looking to Mirawynd's human with a firmer tone. "That goes *double* for you, Sarge."

"Hey, now!" Mirawynd's human laughs. "You don't outrank *me* either, you know."

"No, but if you want that bird of yours to keep flying..."

"*Li?*" Mirawynd hears their Entile Celadon's voice call over the intercom headsets the Navigator and his two students are wearing, "*We're ready for those points now.*"

"Ah, right on it, Celadon." Li gives Rudy a little wave and turns back to his displays. "Sergeant, I believe you have the list this time?"

While their human and George are busy helping Li, Mirawynd leaps over to Rudy's shoulder and gives his cheek a brief nuzzle. "Wyndi help?"

"Oh, I'm sure you've been a very helpful kitten today." Rudy obliges with a light scratching of the itchy bald spot between Mirawynd's shoulder blades where their soft coat of fur has shed off and revealed the silver-striped bright blue skin underneath, just like their ears, face, and hands have. "Do you want to come help me now, is that it?"

Mirawynd swishes their tail cheerfully. Working with Rudy is one of their favorite things in the whole world. "Wyndi help!"

"I'll take that as a yes, then. Sarge? I'm taking your counterpart," Rudy calls behind him as he leaves. "Don't forget to come pick them up when you're done for the night."

Mirawynd's human waves an acknowledgement.

Mirawynd settles into a contented perching position on Rudy's shoulder and sets about fixing his hair into braids so it will stay out of his face better. He doesn't even try to protest this time.

"All right, Wyndi," says Rudy, reaching up to pat their head. "We just need to make a stop at the quartermaster's office to pick up some parts from the ship's stores, and then we'll be set for work."

"Shiny!" Mirawynd claps their upper pair of hands and swishes their tail excitedly. They like *Aegolius'* quartermaster almost as much as they do Lieutenant Young on their home ship, *Surnia*.

"I had a feeling you'd say that..."

When they arrive in the Quartermaster's office, Mirawynd is overjoyed to see that one of their favorite not-human people on the ship is there too. Her name is Isolde, and she is a magnificently sleek cat with white fur and golden-brown patches on her nose, ears, paws, and tail. Mirawynd hops off of Rudy's shoulder and scampers up to Isolde's nest basket on the end of the long desk to say hello.

Isolde returns their greeting trill with a yawn and a chirrup of a mew. She accepts Mirawynd's gentle petting of her head, and gives the fluff on top of their own head a small lick in return. Mirawynd is glad she's decided they're big enough now not to need to be held down and cleaned. When they first met Isolde, she had a litter of little cats who were just about the same size as their small, then-fully-silver-furred self, and she insisted on treating them the same way and giving them a bath every time she encountered them. Granted, they'd also met because Mirawynd was dusty, cold, and lost in one of the ship's cargo bays. Isolde had found them and brought them back to the nest where she was keeping the rest of her own kittens.

"So, Mister Rudolph," says Lieutenant Smithfield from behind the desk, "are you here to pick up your box, or do we need to go down to the parts stores with my minions to scrounge something up for you that wasn't on the list you sent over?" The Lieutenant is Isolde's human and the ship's quartermaster. She's the deep, cool-toned brown sort of a human, with long black hair that she keeps in a multitude of tiny braids with sets of sparkly beads on the ends.

Rudy tilts his head curiously. "Well, it was just the list—what's this about a bloody box?"

"You didn't get my message? I did ask Lt. Hsu to forward it to you."

"Huh. Must have slipped his mind... or gotten buried in my inbox." Rudy chuckles. "What's the box, then?"

"I don't rightly know." The quartermaster shrugs. "All I know is the manifest from our last supply transfer out of Teegarden had a crate marked explicitly for you, to be delivered the next time you were on the ship. Do you want to go down and collect it while my minions are sorting out your list?"

"Why not?" Rudy lets out a chuckle. "You've got my curiosity up. Did the manifest at least say who it's from?"

Lieutenant Smithfield pulls up a holoscreen and taps at it for a few moments. "Ah, here it is. One box of 'miscellaneous technical supplies,' marked for Petty Officer First Class Elias Rudolph of SCV *Surnia*, care of Lt. Hsu and Commander Celadon... blah blah blah... ah, sent by Dr. Navy Irleeim, Lt. Commander, Psychologist, Teegarden Shipyards."

"Oh, now I know this is going to be something interesting..." Rudy gives her a curious, questioning expression. "Dr. Navy hasn't sent me any messages about a box, but I'm sure whatever it is, it'll be worth my time to open it."

"All right, then." The Quartermaster closes her holoscreen after a bit more tapping at it, then pops up the countertop door on the side of the desk and directs her floating chair around it. As long as Mirawynd has known her, she's always floated around in her special chair instead of walking. "Isolde, honey? You coming with us?"

Isolde perks up at the mention of her name, then languidly stretches and slips down into her human's lap, curling up into a neat kitty ball much like Mirawynd does when they take a nap.

Mirawynd hops back over to Rudy's shoulder. They swish their tail with eager curiosity. "Box?" This is one of their favorite words. Boxes tend to have interesting things inside, after all, and are good for playing and napping in once they've been emptied.

"Yeah, Wyndi," Rudy says as he follows Lieutenant Smithfield and Isolde out of their office. "Looks like your Entile Navy sent us a box..."

When Elias Rudolph first joined the Defense Fleet's ranks, it had been as an assistant to the head mechanic of the development project for the small, swift spacecraft his small squadron of pilots now fly. He'd enjoyed working with Zoë, and gotten to be on pretty good terms with her Florivan counterpart, the Shell Island facility's psychologist.

Dr. Navy is in charge of mental healthcare for all of the pilots training at the Teegarden base and has been tasked with assessing and maintaining pilot sanity ever since the early years of the project's development—long before humanity was brought into the Novan War. Like the rest of the mechanics now responsible for a squadron of darter pilots, Elias is both amused and proud to count himself as one of Dr. Navy's "agents" looking after the wellbeing of the pilots he works with.

Every so often, Elias receives a message from Dr. Navy asking him to run some test or other for their research. He sends them memos on what the 2nd Darter Squadron has gotten up to every month, too, if only so he has someone to complain to about his pilots and the amount of trouble they get into.

His latest such memo was *particularly* lengthy, considering all of the nonsense his pilots dragged him into over the last fortnight. Elias counts himself lucky that there are only four pilots in his squadron. He's not sure how someone like his friend Sidney survives working with the 6th Squadron and its sixteen fools with no sense of self-preservation. Numbers aside, though, Sid has assured him that the Mustangs are the easier lot to handle more than once—particularly now that Pilot-Corporal Barker's Florivan counterpart is on hand to help control the squadron's chaos.

As he follows Aegolius's quartermaster through the ship's main cargo bay, Elias can't help but wonder just what his psychologist friend is up to this time. They've never sent him a box before. The Florivan kitten perched on his shoulder is just as curious, if the interested swishing motions of their tail are any indication.

"All right, let me see…" Lieutenant Smithfield guides her hover-chair through the stacks of neatly arranged crates and boxes. "Cargo taken on four weeks ago… non-perishables… ah, forty-two stroke nineteen J." She stops in front of one of the stacks of boxes. "Your package is the top crate here, Mister Rudolph." She reaches up and pats the side of the box in question. "Think you can get it down onto that artigrav sled by yourself?"

Elias looks the box over, then gives it an experimental lift. It's heavier than he expected for its size, but it's still manageable. He nods to the Quartermaster, then sets the box onto the artigrav sled with the one holding all of the parts and tools he came down to get in the first place that they just collected from her assistants. "It's just this one, right?"

"Yes, as far as my records show." Smithfield taps a few things on her hover-chair's holoscreen interface before turning it towards him. "And if you'll just sign here that you've received it, you can be on your way."

Elias takes his stylus pen out of his pocket and signs, then looks to the kitten on his shoulder. "Well, Wyndi!

Let's get this stuff down to the hangar before Sid starts wondering what's taking us so long, shall we?"

Wyndi squeaks excitedly and hops down onto the box to inspect it. "Shiny!"

The Quartermaster giggles, then yawns. "I'll leave you to it, then. It's about time Isolde and I turned in and left the ship to you nocturnal types." She guides her chair towards the cargo bay's doors, waving for Elias to follow her with the artigrav sled. "Krista's my minion-on-duty tonight if you wind up needing anything."

"Thanks." Elias nods. "Here's hoping we don't. If we do, it means there's something broken we don't know about yet."

"Heh." Smithfield shakes her head. "Good luck with that, then. How many darters did you say you had to overhaul tonight?"

"Three, really, but we're focusing on the kid's tonight since he and Sid have to go back to *Gymnasio* in the morning..."

"Hey, Sid!" Rudy waves to the short, bald human with the exquisitely curled blonde mustache who's waiting for the two of them in the hangar where the 2nd Squadron's darters are now residing, along with the darter belonging to Cousin Ocean's Navigator, George.

Mirawynd waves too. They only met Mister Sidney a few days ago, but they already like him. He's a mechanic like Rudy is, and he keeps one of the pockets of his uniform vest filled with small round lemon sweets that he's proven happy to share with polite kittens like Mirawynd.

"Evening, Rudy; Wyndi." Mister Sidney yawns, covering his face with one hand. "What's with the box? I didn't think our list was that extensive tonight."

Rudy chuckles, parking the artigrav sled on which Mirawynd and the box are riding directly in the open area between the darters. "Turns out Dr. Navy had sent me something or other. Haven't opened it yet, but as long as I was pestering the Quartermaster anyway..."

Mister Sidney's eyes light up. "Oh, our good friend the Doctor, is it? Well, come on, then, man. Let's see what that's about before we get started—if we're lucky, Zoë's gone and snuck something useful into it for us."

Mirawynd watches from their perch on top of the box, swishing their tail with curiosity while Rudy starts undoing all of the latches around the edges of the box's lid.

"You know, Sid," Rudy says, looking up before he finishes with the last latch, "that reminds me. I need to get a note passed to Zoë about what we're up to—if anyone has an idea of how we can pull this off without breaking the bird, it's her."

Mr. Sidney chuckles. "Pass a hello along for me, then. You can send the notes on what we're up to when you write to the good Doctor and thank them for the box."

"Okay, Wyndi, off." Rudy offers his hand to Mirawynd to help them climb up to his shoulder. "I can't open the bloody thing if you're sitting on top of it."

Mirawynd obliges with a cheerful squeak. They're more curious than ever about what might be inside the box that Entile Navy—whom they've only met in vid calls—has apparently sent.

"Huh." Rudy tilts his head curiously at the contents of the box before pulling out a paper envelope. "Well, looks like Dr. Navy hasn't given up passing notes the old fashioned way yet." He opens it and skims over the text before laughing and passing it to Mr. Sidney. "Oh, now, this is going to be interesting." He pulls out his pocket-com and sends a message off to someone or other before putting it back into his vest.

Mirawynd hops down to inspect all of the jars and big sheets of paper that are neatly arranged in the box. Each jar looks like it's filled with something brightly colored. There's a jar for every color of the rainbow, too. They can't smell through the jars to know what the bright stuff *is*, unfortunately.

"Huh." Mr. Sidney says, squinting at the paper. "What is this, Florivan script? Last time I checked, our friend the Doctor wasn't into sending coded messages... at least, they never send any to me."

"No," says Rudy, laughing. "That's what happens when someone tries to write standard with six kittens hanging off their arms. Navy still has the same brilliant penmanship they've always had."

"And you can *read* this chicken-scratch?"

Rudy shrugs, stifling a chuckle. "Li's handwriting is worse, believe it or not. I think Dons and I are the only people who can decipher that." He takes the letter back and holds it up to read aloud. "Let's see... ah, here's the part I wanted you to see: 'You'll find here the contents of an experiment my niece did with my kittens that I'd like you to attempt recreating with little Mirawynd and your squadron. Instructions are on the data chip, but Zoë assures me that it should be reasonably self-explanatory for you. I'm curious how such artistic activities can be used to reduce stress.'" Rudy pauses, sharing a meaningful look with his friend, who's now examining the jars and things in the box with Mirawynd's help. "If this crew doesn't need a bloody stress-relief activity, I don't know who *does* after what we've been through lately."

"Agreed." Mister Sidney shakes his head. "Yours more than mine, but if whatever this is works out, I'd be happy to try it on the Mustangs too. The boys go *looking* for trouble when they get bored and stressed like this... You wouldn't believe the number of times Breezy and I have had to intervene before they all wound up in the brig for some juvenile prank or other."

"Oh, I've *met* your boys, Sid. I believe it. And you still think my lot are worse?"

"They're the *Musketeers*."

"Point taken."

Both men get a good laugh about that, although Mirawynd doesn't quite understand the joke.

"So," Mister Sidney asks, once he's contained his amusement again, "is that all our friend the Doctor said?"

"Mostly. There's some family business and such in there too... as far as all this? Only other thing is that they made a point of saying that the contents of the jars are fully non-toxic and washable, but may leave a stain on light-colored fabrics if they're not washed off within a few hours."

"Well, then!" Mister Sidney grins ear-to-ear under his mustache now. "This is going to be interesting for sure." He's looking closely at the label on one of the jar lids. "I suppose we can set this up for the Musketeers when they inevitably come to try to pester us while we're working tonight."

"I sent Ioane and Nyx a ping to come down and bring Dons' kittens," Rudy says with a smile, tucking the folded-up letter into one of his vest's inner pockets. "But for the moment, let's just get to work on what we're actually up to, shall we?"

"Sounds like a plan to me."

"Wyndi help?" Mirawynd asks, stretching up out of the box and holding their upper pair of arms towards Rudy.

"Of course you can help, Wyndi." He lifts them up and reaches into one of his other pockets to pull out the special collar and belt he keeps there for them. "Here's your anti-statics, let's get you suited up and then we'll start taking those relay systems apart."

Mirawynd squeaks happily. The anti-statics were one of his first gifts to them, and keep their fur from getting all sparky around the sensitive electronics he works with. Helping Rudy has always been one of their favorite things.

"I swear, Mirawynd, m'dear," says Mister Sidney, getting his toolkit out and set up, "you're a better assistant than anyone I have over on *Gymnasio*—Except maybe Breezy, but they're too much of a pilot to be able to focus half the time..."

Some time after Rudy and Mister Sidney start their work taking parts off of one of the darters and laying them neatly on the floor underneath the wing, several more members of Mirawynd's family appear in the hangar.

The two adults who enter are one of Mirawynd's other pilots, Abi, and their recently found cousin, Nyx. Mirawynd's two littlest cousins, Teryin and Tesnee, are with them. Since Mirawynd's keen catlike ears only pick up the muffled sound of their little cousins purring, they must be snuggled somewhere in the pockets of Abi's jacket.

Abi is a relatively short, tawny-pale human with straight black hair cut just below her chin. As usual, she's wearing her darter pilot's ivory jacket with the 2nd Squadron's crossed swords and fleur-de-lis design on the back. She also has on the special breathing mask she's been wearing ever since she was hurt while out flying at the end of their most recent adventure.

Mirawynd and their little cousins had to help take care of her, too, then. They still take turns watching over Abi and soaking up the shiny energy that's stubbornly clinging to her lungs. Today is Teryin and Tesnee's turn, which is why their two tiny silver-furred selves are somewhere inside Abi's jacket.

Cousin Nyx, meanwhile, is a Florivan like Mirawynd— only all grown up and without fur to speak of, except if the asymmetrically cut silver hair on their head and the tuft at the end of their long prehensile tail is counted. Instead, they have inky blue skin with silver stripes and wear a soft ruby-colored tunic and trousers to keep them warm. Unlike most Florivans, Cousin Nyx only has two arms, both on their left side. From what Mirawynd understands, their cousin *used* to have right arms, but lost them in an accident a long time ago.

Mirawynd bounces over to greet their cousins and Abi, starting with Cousin Nyx. They hop up to their big cousin's right shoulder so that it's easier for their left hands to reach. "Hello!"

"Hello, Wyndi." Cousin Nyx happily accepts Mirawynd's greeting snuggles and pats them gently on the head. They look over to Rudy and Mister Sidney. "So, what was that cryptic ping about, Cousin Elias?"

"We were on our way down to the pilot's den to beat the gals and Colonel Hannemann at cards, you know," says Abi, using the voice of the little wrist-com she's wearing since her own still doesn't work well. The special respirator mask she has to wear around other humans to protect them muffles what little voice she has left of her own anyway.

"Ah, nothing serious… just a little gift Dr. Navy sent for the kittens." He slides his top half out of the access port on the wing of George's darter that he's had himself wedged into and gestures to the box of bright-colored treasure. "Thought since you two have the cuties, you might be willing to try your hand at it."

At the sound of Rudy's voice, Mirawynd's smallest cousins squeak excitedly and emerge from within Abi's zipped-up darter pilot's jacket. Before Abi or Nyx can catch them, they've both leapt up to the darters wing and are happily snuggling with Rudy, squeaking with joy to have found him. He is, after all, *their* favorite human.

"Ah. Hello, Teryin, Hello, Tesnee… no, sweethearts, you can't get in my pockets right now." Rudy laughs, trying to sound stern even though he's giving both of the tiny, fully silver-furred kittens a thorough petting behind their ears all the same. "I'm *working*, and you're not trained to help yet like Wyndi is."

Abi giggles from inside her respirator mask. *"Aww... you don't want to take a break to cuddle with your step-kittens?"*

Rudy rolls his eyes. "I'll get to hold them later, when I'm not in the middle of all of this. And don't you go calling them that too. It's bad enough that the Admiral does."

Mirawynd takes the opportunity to hop down from Cousin Nyx's shoulder and into the box of treasures. "Shiny!" they call, and then add in squeaks and a cheerful beckoning trill to encourage their little cousins to come see what they've found.

Teryin and Tesnee are soon in the box with them, excitedly peering at all of the jars of color and sniffing at the crisp white paper. They squeak appreciatively and swish their tails as all three of them turn their expectant faces up to Abi and Cousin Nyx. The two of them are too small and young to be able to use grown-up words like Mirawynd can.

"Play?" Mirawynd asks, cheerfully swishing their tail too.

"That's right, Wyndi." Rudy calls from the wing of George's darter, already wriggling back into his access port. "Put your static bands in my tool roll so they won't get dirty, and then you and the cuties can finger-paint with the Major all you like until the rest of the family gets off their shift—ah, hand me that micro-circuit probe, will you, Sid?" With that, both mechanics have essentially turned their attention fully away from the kittens, the box, and Cousin Nyx and Abi.

Mirawynd does as they've been told and puts their special collar and belt away, and then scampers back over to the box Abi is helping their cousins unpack.

"Shiny," says Mirawynd, hopping up to Abi's shoulder and giving her neck a nuzzle.

Abi nods, then taps the interface on her wrist-com again so it will talk for her. *"I assume that tarp under my bird is laid out for us to make a mess on?"*

"It is, Major!" Mister Sidney calls down.

"Try not to get the bloody paint anywhere else," Rudy adds, his voice echoing from within the access port. "It's washable, apparently, but neither of us has time to mop this place tonight if you make a mess."

Abi chuckles inside her mask, then pushes the artigrav sled holding the box over and turns it off so it's resting on the floor on the corner of the big tarp.

Cousin Nyx rummages through the box with their upper hand, then sets three pieces of paper down on the floor in the middle of the tarp while Abi and Mirawynd carry all of the jars of bright colors over. "Well, Abigail, I'll admit this is something I'm unfamiliar with."

"What? You and Thalassa never finger-painted when you were little?" Abi gives them a teasing nudge. *"We did a bit when I was in nursery school. Sort of standard sensory development activity for human kids, really."*

"No, we didn't, as far as I remember—Nida likes bright colors as much as the rest of us, but they aren't exactly keen on messes. If Joseph ever let us get into his watercolors, I don't remember it." Nyx smiles softly. "I'd assume this is precisely what it says on the tin?"

"Pretty much! Allow me to demonstrate..." Abi takes off her jacket and tosses it up onto the wing of her darter so it's out of the way of the paint, then sits down crosslegged in front of the three sheets of paper. She picks up a jar of

paint. Once she's got it open, she sets the jar next to her piece of paper and dips her fingers into it, getting paint all over them. The bright blue goo is almost the same color as Mirawynd's bald patches. Then, Abi carefully draws a few lines on the paper with her fingers to make something that loosely resembles a flower.

Mirawynd claps appreciatively. "Shiny!" They look up to Cousin Nyx with a swish of their tail and a happy squeak, then add the new word their cousin has taught them: "Flower! Shiny *flower*!"

"Yes, Wyndi!" Cousin Nyx reaches over and pats them on the head with their lone lower hand. "It *is* a flower." They're smiling more brightly than Mirawynd has ever seen them in the short time they've known each other. "Okay, Abigail, I can see how this is going to be fun." They sit down beside her. Wyndi hops into their lap, since Teryin and Tesnee are occupying Abi's for the moment.

"Hmm... let's go with green, shall we?" Nyx holds the jar in their lower hand and uses their upper one to unscrew the lid. They experimentally dip two of the long inky-blue and silver-striped digits from their upper hand into the paint, then make marks on the paper to add a stem and some leaf shapes to Abi's flower. "What do you think?"

Abi giggles. "*I think we're going to have as much fun with this as the kittens.*"

"Wyndi help?" Mirawynd asks, peering into the jar of green.

"Yes, Wyndi." Cousin Nyx holds the jar steady for them. "Go on, it's okay to get a little messy tonight."

Teryin and Tesnee watch curiously as Mirawynd dips both of their upper hands into the paint and makes marks and handprints of their own on the paper to add a "ground" for Nyx and Abi's flower to grow in. The paint is a bit cold, but it has a pleasingly goopy and smooth texture. They're not sure what they think of the smell, which is somewhere between flowers and soap. It's definitely not a food-type smell. Mirawynd decides they like making paint messes, regardless of the smell. Their tail swishes with excitement as they look up to their big cousin. "Shiny! More, please?"

"Of course." Cousin Nyx wipes their painted hand on one of the rags from the neat pile Rudy and Mister Sidney had laid out for them, then starts helping Abi open the rest of the jars of color. "Let's get a few more options out, shall we?"

Teryin squeaks with interest from Abi's lap, then cautiously plunges their whole upper-left arm into the blue paint. They don't seem to like the feeling of it all over their fur, though, so they shake their arm and send splats of paint flying all over the place.

Abi wipes a splat of paint off of her mask, then gently presses Teryin's paint-covered hand onto the paper. *"Here, sweetheart, see? It's okay."*

Teryin seems more excited about the paint after that, although they still seem to have to shake their arm off every time they dip it in the jar. Tesnee, in contrast, enthusiastically has all four hands in the paint before anyone can try to help them. They paint swishes and spots all over the new piece of paper sitting between Abi and Nyx.

Mirawynd contentedly stays in their big cousin's lap for a while to help them paint. They're not sure what the point of finger-paints is yet, but it's a fun game.

A while later, Mirawynd is sitting with their two little cousins in between Cousin Nyx and Abi and working on a picture to take to their Entile Celadon. Suddenly, they feel a sensation of damp coldness on the end of their tail. They look over to see that Tesnee has *dipped* said tail into one of the jars of paint.

Mirawynd squeaks at them in protest, flicking their tail away. As they do, its paint-covered tip streaks across the paper, making a rather large and swishy line of paint. Tesnee giggles and chitters at them excitedly, then dips their own tail into the paint too so they can use it as a brush. Tesnee looks back up at Mirawynd with more excited squeaks, thrilled to have found a new way to make paint marks. Out of the three of them, it's clear that Tesnee is the one who likes paint the best.

Mirawynd looks at their now-paint-covered little cousin, then to their own paint-dipped tail, then back again. They swish their tail and paint a long streaky line on the paper beside all of Tesnee's marks. They have to admit, tails make excellent paintbrushes. They giggle and wave to Teryin with the paint on their tail to show them too.

Soon, all three of them are sneaking over together to dip Cousin Nyx's tail tuft in some purple paint so that *they* can learn how to make tail marks too.

After all, why should painting be limited to *fingers*?

Elias is busy sorting all of the small, delicate components that go into a darter's communications array when he hears the distinctive chattery commotion of the rest of the Musketeers entering the hangar. He looks over just in time to see Major Albright, Major Toussaint, and the First Squadron's Colonel Hannemann each be pounced by a paint-covered and rather excited Florivan kitten.

"There you are, Abigail!" Major Albright laughs, carrying one of the two smaller kittens over to where Major Ioane and Nyx are sitting on the tarp. She reaches an ice-pale hand up to wipe the paint off of her cheek and the special pink-tinted wraparound lenses she wears to protect her highly sensitive eyes. As usual, she has her curly white hair pulled back into a pair of short poofy ponytails. "We were wondering where you and Nyx were!"

"So *this* is why you didn't show up to play cards with us?" Major Toussaint asks, deftly preventing the other of the two smaller kittens from getting under the folds of her ivory headscarf. Her deeply tan cheek now has a bright blue kitten print across it, but she doesn't seem to have noticed. "What's going on here?"

"A delightful mess," Nyx tells her. "Won't you join us?"

Major Toussaint tosses her jacket up onto the wing of Major Ioane's darter so it won't get any more paint on it and then plops down beside them. "Don't mind if I do. This is better than trying to play cards with Gunther, that's for sure."

"He and Penny are ganging up on you with the martian rules Poker again?" Major Ioane asks.

"And then some—I swear they're making up half of them just to frustrate me."

"The whole point of the game is to make up the rules as you go," Major Albright teases. She finishes wiping the kitten handprints off of her jacket with one of the few remaining clean rags, then sets it up on the wing of

Major Ioane's darter with the others and joins them all in the middle of the tarp. "Stars, I don't think I've done this since I was *six*."

Major Ioane teasingly flicks a bit of paint at her. "*How long ago was that, again?*"

"Oh, now," Major Albright teases back, "don't you start on me, young lady. I know where you sleep, and Bell isn't here to enforce her ban on juvenile pranks…"

"*No, but you'd have to get through my team of elite Florivan bodyguards first!*" Major Ioane's face is covered, and the voice of her wrist-com is a bit monotone, but Elias knows for sure that she's got that Cheshire Cat grin of hers on as she says this.

"So I'll stop by the mess and get a waffle or two to bribe them… you do like waffles, don't you, Nyx?"

Nyx laughs. "Oh, sure—my Nida's Navigator is martian too, you know—but not enough to abandon my post as Abigail's guardian…"

Elias rolls his eyes. He can't help hoping that his pilots will get distracted before they start another ship-wide prank contest—if only because there's a certain cranky Admiral aboard who will doubtless hold *him* responsible for it. He has enough problems with staying out of trouble with her on his own without the Musketeers making it worse.

"What is all this, Rudy?" Colonel Hannemann asks, passing by the tarp and coming over to loom near Elias instead. Wyndi's swishing tail is already putting paint all over the man's shirt and up into his short-cropped brown hair. His darter pilot's jacket is slung casually over the other shoulder, almost miraculously free of paint. "I thought you two were just doing maintenance in here tonight."

"We are," Elias replies, looking up at the freckle-and-stubble-covered face of the ship's head pilot. He makes a vague gesture towards the tarp. "That over there is an activity Dr. Navy sent for the kittens."

"Oh, so this is *Navy's* doing." Colonel Hannemann chuckles and looks back to the tarp under Major Ioane's darter. As the former head of the darter development project, he's known the enigmatic Florivan psychologist longer than any of them. "That explains it. And the activity is...?"

"Pai..." Wyndi begins, clearly struggling with the pronunciation of the newest word in their vocabulary. They pause, looking up to Elias with that same adorable look they always get when they're concentrating. "Pai-ih-neen?"

"'Pain-ting,'" Elias corrects, saying the syllables as clearly as his accent will allow. "But you were close that time, magpie. Keep practicing."

Wyndi squeaks happily and looks up to the Colonel with a swish of their tail. "Pai-nin'!"

"I see, Wyndi, yes." Colonel Hannemann gives the kitten's head a pat. "Well, that explains all the colors."

"It does." Elias shrugs and goes back to sorting his component parts. "Anything else I can help you with?"

"No, but I was headed up to the mess to get snacks for the card game I think we just canceled. You want coffee or anything?"

"Sure. Splash of milk, nothing fancy. Sid!" Elias calls up to the darter access port. "Colonel's getting us coffee."

Sid laughs. "Wish I could train Colonel Vasquez to do that!" He slides out of the access port just long enough to wave at the man. "Black with a shot of hazelnut syrup, sir, thanks!"

"Got it." Colonel Hannemann looks between the two Musketeers who have now joined their wing-sister on the floor with Nyx and the kitten on his shoulder. "You coming with me, Wyndi? You can help me pick snacks."

"Snack?" Wyndi's eyes light up. "Wyndi help!"

"Just don't go letting them track paint all over the ship," Elias calls as the man and the kitten leave. "I'll never hear the end of it if you do..."

Mirawynd and their friend Colonel Hannemann are almost done collecting a tray full of snacks and securely lidded cups full of various nice-smelling liquids when they encounter two more of their friends who live on this ship.

"Ted! Glimmer!" Mirawynd waves excitedly from the Colonel's shoulder, still doing their best to be a good kitten and not get paint on anything other than him.

"Evening Ruttiger; Glimmer." The Colonel nods a greeting too.

"Ah," says the young man with the fancy bubble backpack who's just walked in and is now approaching the two of them, "hello, Mirawynd. Good evening, Colonel."

Ted is the same sort of pale and freckly human that the Colonel is, but thin-framed rather than muscular, and with short-cropped red hair and a perfectly clean-shaven face. His left eye is brilliantly green, while an ivory eyepatch that matches the rest of his uniform covers the place where his right one used to be. Ted is pretty high up on Mirawynd's list of favorite people—he even helped them save their human from a monster once.

"Pleasant evening to both of you!" says the pleasingly accented deep male voice that Ted's backpack generates for the person who rides in it. *"Wyndi, I see you are brightly colored! Is this usual for your species?"*

Glimmer is the only Europan Mirawynd has ever met, but they like him a lot. He's made of a squishy round-ish body that's a bit smaller than Mirawynd themself and has two big, dark eyes, along with a lot of shiny tendril arms that shimmer and change colors all the time. Glimmer "talks" with his colors and gestures, but Ted is the only person who can completely understand what he's saying. Mirawynd and their little cousins are getting better at reading him, though, since he makes a point of telling the three of them stories whenever he gets the chance. Mirawynd's human can sort of read Glimmer's way of speaking, too, but Glimmer still has to talk *very* slowly for him to catch everything.

Wyndi answers his question with a squeak and a swish of their tail. "Wyndi pai-nin'!"

"What is 'painin'?"

"They mean finger-painting," Colonel Hannemann explains. "They and Celadon's cuties were given some paints to play with—we're just up here getting picnic supplies since the Musketeers and I are on stand-by duty tonight and it's better fun than our card game was."

One of Glimmer's tendrils slips out of the backpack through the special hole at the top with the shimmery field that keeps his cold water inside and taps Ted on the shoulder. *"Please explain?"*

"It's sort of an art thing that kids do to build their hand-eye coordination." Ted's tone has more amusement in it than his usual shyness. "You're all painting *with* them, Colonel?"

"Yep!" Colonel Hannemann grins. "Say, you're off-duty now, aren't you?"

"Um... yes... I was just going to get some dinner and turn in..."

"Well, then! You two should bring your food and come down and paint with us. Don't you think so, Wyndi?"

Wyndi swishes their tail with excited approval. "Shiny!"

"I don't know..." Ted starts to say.

"Will Major Albright be there?" Glimmer asks, his tendrils flashing lavender interest and excitement. Penny is one of his favorite humans. *"I wish to ask her if she will take us flying again."*

"Glimmer, we talked about that..." Ted lets out an awkward laugh. "If you want to fly, you have to teach Sergeant Potts to read you better so I don't have to go too."

"I take it you two enjoyed your little adventure with Penny the other day?" the Colonel asks, on the edge of a chuckle.

"Well... *Glimmer* enjoyed it." Ted seems to be making a point of not giving his opinion.

"It was a fascinating experience," Glimmer says. *"I found it most enjoyable, even if my dear Initiate here was unsettled by the sensations."*

"He's really just a thrill-seeker." Ted shakes his head. "Any new experience opportunity shows up, and he's going to talk me into coming along for the ride. You'd think I'd get used to it."

"Oh, new experiences is it, Glimmer?" Colonel Hannemann grins, sharing a glance with Mirawynd. "Well, then! You two *should* spare a few minutes and come down to the hangar with us..."

When they all arrive at the hangar, Mirawynd's two little cousins immediately scamper over from the painting area and bounce up to Ted's shoulders to greet him and Glimmer. They're both so colorful now that the only silver bits still showing are their faces.

"Hello Teryin and Tesnee!" Glimmer waves his tendrils to the two smaller kittens. *"You are amazingly colorful tonight. I approve!"*

"Ack!" Ted fruitlessly tries to brush the colors off of himself. "You two are positively *covered* in paint, aren't you?"

"It's washable paint, kid," Anna calls, giggling. "Don't worry, it'll come out—but you might want to take your jacket off."

"I'm already painted," Ted replies with a sigh, coming over to stand next to the pilots and look down at all of the paint-covered paper strewn about the tarp. "I'd rather keep my shirt clean."

"Fair enough," says Colonel Hannemann. He sets the tray of snacks and drinks down on the lid of the now-empty box, then picks up the two coffee cups he'd marked for Rudy and Mister Sidney.

While he goes to deliver those, Mirawynd hops down from his shoulder and picks up one of the pieces of paper they'd decorated earlier. They bring it over to Ted and hold it up high so he can see. "Pai-nin'!" Mirawynd tells him, "Shiny fun!" The excited swishing of their tail makes streaks of blue and green spread on the tarp behind them. The tarp is starting to turn into a wonderfully colorful painting in itself.

"*It does look like fun,*" Glimmer intones from within the backpack bubble. One of his tendrils snakes out of the little shielded hole near Ted's neck and curiously touches Tesnee's paint-covered head. It immediately recoils and flails around for a bit before wiping the paint off on one of the handful of clean spots on left Ted's back and retreating into the bubble of the backpack. "*Paint tastes bad. Ted, you will do the painting on my behalf, please?*"

Ted shakes his head, lightly concealing a trace of a laugh. He sets Glimmer's backpack down next to Penny and then takes a seat himself on the other side of it. "Fine, I suppose a few minutes of finger-painting before I turn in for the night wouldn't hurt..."

"Well, Mister Rudolph, I be here and I brought me kit, so why—" Dr. Kiely breaks off mid-sentence when she sees the scene before her. She sets her hands on her hips and stands there stunned for a moment. As usual when she's on duty, she has all of her wavy red hair pulled up into a bun. Her sharp green eyes flash up to meet Elias' with a look he knows all too well.

"Your patient's the lanky one, Kiely," Elias calls from his perch on one of the wings of the darter he and Sidney are working on. He pauses to take a sip from his coffee. "Kid went and stood up under the bloody wing and bonked his head—and try to settle his friend there down while you're at it, will you?"

The trio of paint-covered kittens are busy sitting on top of the young man who's laid out on his back under the wing of Major Ioane's darter next to a backpack with a rather concerned Europan flashing all sorts of unintelligible things with his tendrils. Elias is pretty sure that Ruttiger's not hurt badly, of course, but considering how upset the kid's best friend is, it stood to reason to call his squadron's favorite doctor down to have a look at him. If nothing else, he knows that the Europan is fond of the doctor too—if anyone can get Glimmer to calm down and stop doing his impression of a sapient strobe light, it's her.

Dr. Kiely sighs and goes over, shooing the kittens away so she can get a better look. "So, how bad do ye feel, Mister Ruttiger?"

"I'm fine, really," the kid says, awkwardly waving a hand toward the backpack while the other one is resting over his eyes. "I just... wounded my pride a bit. Again."

"Aye, of course ye did." Dr. Kiely shakes her head. "Ye be just like me Julian, always finding new and inventive ways to get yeself hurt. So ye hit your head?"

"Well, I slipped on the paint and twisted my ankle first... and then when I caught myself so I wouldn't fall, I hit the wing and fell anyway."

Dr. Kiely waves her portable roboscanner over the kid's head for a minute or two and then lifts the hand over his eye. She seems pleased enough by whatever it is she sees.

"Hurt?" Wyndi asks, still at Ruttiger's side and holding their tail with concern just like the two smaller kittens are. Kittens tend to take injuries to people they like *very* seriously, in Elias' experience.

"He be fine, Wyndi. He just needs to learn to watch where he's walking in here, that's all." Dr. Kiely scans Ruttiger's ankle, then helps him sit up. After a moment, she takes out a handkerchief to wipe all of the kitten-prints off of his face. "Ye ankle ain't anything worse than a minor sprain, so I'll put a cold wrap on it and give ye something for the headache... but perhaps ye should stay *away* from the darters for a while?"

"I wouldn't mind that, ma'am."

"Good." Dr. Kiely looks at the bright colors on her handkerchief now. "Why *do* there be paint all over the place, anyway?"

"*We're finger-painting with the kittens,*" Major Ioane tells her.

"Finger-painting?" Dr. Kiely echoes in disbelief.

Wyndi squeaks something to the other two kittens, then scampers off and retrieves a piece of paper covered in kitten-prints and streaks of color. "Shiny!" They say, holding it up for Dr. Kiely to see. "Reba play?"

Dr. Kiely sighs, holding back a laugh. "That explains why ye be so many colors, at least. Well..." She pulls out her pocket-com and checks the time, then smiles. "Aye, fine, let me see to Mister Ruttiger here first, and then I'll paint with ye. I go off-duty in ten minutes anyway..."

Elias finishes the last of his coffee and chuckles. He makes a mental note that he'll have to include the fact that no one on this ship seems to be able to turn down an opportunity to finger-paint with the kittens on his report for Dr. Navy.

Jenny Marvin has always been the sort of person who gets restless in the middle of the night. Ever since she took command of "her" Defense Fleet and its flagship, *Aegolius*, she'd given up on trying to force herself into maintaining a single continuous sleep cycle. The midnight break between Quantum Space Transit cycles has always woken her up, no matter what ship she's on; she chooses to take advantage of that rather than be annoyed by it.

So it is that her habit on each of the ship's nights is to rise from her bunk and, in her best Fleet-issue loungewear with her light brown curls loosely contained by a headband instead of in her usual smartly arranged bun and hairpins, wander through her ship to make sure that all is well and her night watch crew doesn't need attention. It's rare that anything more than a minor issue arises, too, and she can sleep soundly after her "midnight stroll."

The members of her crew who are typically on night watch are accustomed to this, and seldom comment on it. More than once, she's startled a newer midshipman or two by appearing so unexpectedly and casually. Jenny finds that more amusing than anything, when it happens.

Tonight, as Jenny steps into the port-side secondary darter hangar to look for her pilots who are on standby duty since they weren't in their "den" playing cards like she expected, a streak of bright-colored motion comes out of nowhere and leaps up onto her shoulder.

"Aunt Jenny!"

It takes a moment for the admiral to realize that the brightly colored squirrel-sized critter hugging her neck is, in fact, the Second Squadron's little Florivan "mascot"—and with her friend Celadon's two more chipmunk-sized youngest kittens clinging to their back, no less. All three kittens are covered head to tail in bright-colored goo, not that they seem to care. They're clearly more interested in excitedly squeaking and distributing themselves around Jenny's shoulders to give her the usual enthusiastic greeting nuzzles she's come to understand kittens give anyone they consider family.

Jenny lightly pats Wyndi on the head to settle them down. Her russet-brown hand is covered in splotches of color when she lifts it. "Land sakes, kittens," she says, tired enough that she's not bothering to hold back her Smoky Mountains accent, "What *are* you covered in?"

"Pai-nin'!" Wyndi replies, pointing excitedly towards the cluster of darters on the other end of the hangar. "Aunt Jenny play?"

Aware that this is the most information the kitten is likely to give her—and knowing a certain surly mechanic is *doubtless* responsible—Jenny sighs and pulls her composure together, then strides purposefully over to the darters. "Dare I ask what's going on here?"

The sight before her is odd. There's a color-spattered tarp on the floor under one of the darters. Paint is tracked on seemingly every available surface, too. Even the darters have been painted, mainly with kitten prints in scampered lines up and down their sides, but also with bright-colored renditions of the squadrons' insignias. Sitting in the middle of it all is the majority of the Second Squadron, along with Colonel Hannemann, Dr. Kiely and her Florivan botanist friend, and even Jenny's own personal assistant and his ever-present Europan sidekick. All of *them* are covered head to toe in colorful splotches too.

"Ah! Admiral Marvin, Ma'am!" Ensign Ruttiger, as usual, is flustered by her sudden appearance and tries to stand to attention. He's immediately tugged back to the ground by the doctor, just before he can strike his head on the underside of the darter's wing.

"Sit, boy," Dr. Kiely admonishes. "I'll not have ye hurting yeself again slipping on the paint because ye stood up too fast without looking."

"My dear Lady," calls Glimmer's ever-cheerful and chivalrous computer-generated voice from Ted's backpack, *"please, do come join us! The kittens have assisted me in painting a tribute gift for you!"*

Jenny crosses her arms, even as said kittens scamper down from her shoulders and into the lap of Major Ioane. "What is all this mess, then? I seem to recall the majority of you are on standby duty tonight."

"We are, ma'am," says Hannemann with his usual cheeky grin. "The kittens invited us to finger-paint with them instead of playing cards. Best stress-relief activity anyone's come up with since the last time you let us put on a talent show..."

"Is that so?" Jenny takes out her handkerchief and does her best to wipe the paint off of her neck. There are at least six different reasons she no longer allows this man to put on talent shows, and two of them involve *far* bigger messes than this. "And I take it that you were invited too, Ensign Ruttiger?"

"We were..." Her assistant hesitates, then shrugs. " It's... well, you know how it is when Glimmer wants to try something new, and the kittens *insisted*..."

"I see." Jenny walks around the group to the darter where the two mechanics she hadn't seen initially are working. Both of them are suspiciously clean. "Why do I have the impression this was *your* doing, Mister Rudolph?"

As usual, Rudolph doesn't even bother looking up from what he's doing. "Your intuition's good as ever, I'd expect—but if there's a problem with it, you can take it up with the person who *sent* the paints to me."

Jenny is about to say something scathingly witty in return, but a rather insistent tug on her trouser leg stops her. "Aunt Jenny!" says Wyndi, holding up a piece of paint-covered paper in their upper hands and waving their equally paint-covered tail in excited swishes. "See! Pai-nin'!"

She bends down and pats the kitten on the head, taking the paper. "It's very pretty, Wyndi. You've been busy."

The kitten purrs and then takes hold of her wrist and looks up to her with wide, hopeful eyes. "Aunt Jenny stay? Play pai-nin'?"

"Well, sweetheart..."

"*Oh, please do!*" Glimmer waves a shimmering tendril from Ruttiger's backpack. "*I would be most pleased to hear your opinions on this activity—perhaps my dear Lady the Admiral will honor us by participating?*"

With a look between the now three expectant pleading kitten faces in front of her and the beckoning tendril from her Europan friend, Jenny sighs. "Not a word of this to *anyone...* but fine, I'll stay for a bit." She locks eyes with Hannemann and Albright in turn. "And you two had better have all of this cleaned up before the morning watch comes in here so I won't have pilots tracking paint all over my ship. Understood?"

Both pilots grin and salute her, speaking in unison. "Yes, ma'am!"

"Good." Jenny takes a seat next to her assistant and accepts the piece of mostly clean paper the kittens enthusiastically carry over to her. "Okay, then! What shall we paint?"

She wasn't ready to go back to sleep yet, anyway.

Mirawynd is quite happy to be sitting in their favorite auntie's lap, helping her paint pictures of something she calls "chickens." Aunt Jenny claims they're some kind of bird, but Mirawynd has never met one themself. In fact, they've only ever met one bird in their entire life: their cousin River's pet quail, Captain Coturnix. From what they understand, he is considerably smaller than whatever a chicken is.

"So, Glimmer?" Aunt Jenny asks over the top of their head, "You're actually getting something out of this?"

"*Of course, my dear Lady!*" Glimmer waves several of his tendrils with shining colors for emphasis. "*It is a most delightful activity—ah, please use the red again, there, Ted?*" He pauses to tap his human on the shoulder and point at the spot on his paper before turning his attention back to Aunt Jenny. *"I do not care for the taste of the paint, of course, but it is pleasing to see all of the humans relaxing and creating pictures with it. Particularly you, my dear Lady—I had been concerned for your well-being of late."*

Mirawynd hops up out of Aunt Jenny's lap and scoots the jar of red paint over where Ted can reach it. They dip their tail in the paint, too, so they can use some for their own chicken picture. He gives them a small pat on the head in thanks. They're not entirely sure *what* he's painting for Glimmer, but it's very pretty with all of the different colors.

"I see what you mean, Glimmer, but you really don't have to worry about me."

"I have pledged my undying loyalty to you, my dear Lady." Glimmer swishes a particularly bright green gesture with several of his tendrils in the water. *"It is my honor to swim alongside you; so too, it is my duty to be concerned with your well-being. I have been informed that prolonged stress of the type you experience is ultimately toxic to humans, and it is pleasing to see that this antidote activity is effective."*

Aunt Jenny looks to Reba. "Why do I sense a conspiracy here?"

"It ain't my conspiracy, Admiral, I be nothing more than a civilian what's volunteered to take these accident-prone pilots off Dr. Inman's hands so he can focus on the rest of ye crew." Reba laughs. "But ye have to admit the Ambassador here has a point."

"Glimmer *may* have overheard us discussing your meeting schedules, ma'am," says Ted, sheepishly focusing his eyes on the paper he's painting for Glimmer. "And Europans are nothing if not perceptive..."

Aunt Jenny shakes her head. "Oh, now, don't you start on me too."

"You are enjoying the activity, though, my dear Lady? It is reducing your accumulated stress toxins?"

"I am, I suppose," says Aunt Jenny. "it's not exactly protocol, but if it keeps these pilots out of trouble for a few hours... I'd say that would reduce my general stress levels, yes."

"Does that mean you'll help us clean up, Admiral?" asks Penny, grinning as she looks over her shoulder from the wing of her darter. She's standing underneath it holding Teryin and Tesnee up so they can paint pictures on the underside of it for her.

"No, Major," Aunt Jenny replies dryly, "Although I'll admit I look forward to seeing how you get all of the paint off the ceiling..."

"Oh, we'll just turn the gravity controls off in here." Anna shrugs. "Easy enough."

"How *did* the lot of ye manage to get so much paint up there?" Reba asks, looking up at the collection of paint splatters above them.

"Trust me, Reba," sys Nyx solemnly, while all of the pilots share a giggle, "you don't want to know."

Mirawynd's ears perk up at the sound of the hangar doors opening. They immediately scamper over to Penny's darter to collect their cousins so the three of them can greet whoever it is that's come to play with them now. The best part of painting, they've decided, is that all of their favorite people keep coming in to paint *with* them.

Teryin and Tesnee squeak excitedly as they take their usual places clinging to Mirawynd's back. Mirawynd arrives at the hangar door with their little cousins in tow as soon as it opens.

"Sarge!" Mirawynd calls when they see who it is. Their human has finally come down from the Nav closet, along with George and Cousin Ocean. They couldn't be happier to see his scruffy face. Mirawynd immediately clambers up onto their human's shoulder to inspect him for injuries and give him a hug. Their cousins squeak greetings at him too.

"Ack, Wyndi, what in the *stars* have you gotten into this time?"

"Pai-nin'!" Mirawynd explains, swishing their tail with excitement. They tug on his collar and gesture towards the tarp and the empty space beside Reba. "Sarge play?"

Cousin Ocean giggles, their deep greenish-blue ears and tail twitching to match. "It does look like fun! Come on, George!" They take their Navigator's arm and lead him over to the tarp before he can even think to protest. They plop down beside the Admiral and tug the young human down beside them. "Mind if we join, ma'am?"

Aunt Jenny holds back a laugh, tilting her head at them with a raised eyebrow. "Don't you two have a shift to pick up in twenty minutes?"

Mirawynd's human follows, setting Wyndi and their cousins down before he takes the seat next to Reba. She leans over and nuzzles his cheek briefly, the way the two of them always seem to greet each other lately.

"No, Ma'am," says George, hesitating. As the youngest human in their little family, he still seems to be a bit intimidated by Aunt Jenny. Mirawynd doesn't quite understand that, considering how nice their favorite auntie is. "Commander Celadon decided to give us the rest of the night off, since we're ahead of schedule for arriving at the convoy's morning rendezvous point."

"Ah, is that so?" Aunt Jenny looks to Mirawynd's human now.

"Yes, ma'am," he replies, setting his somewhat paint-marked jacket aside. "They said we were a jump and a half out."

"All right, then. Carry on." She shrugs and goes back to the chicken painting she was working on. Teryin and Tesnee bounce over to help her.

Mirawynd tugs on their human's pant leg to catch his attention, holding up the painting they made for him. "Sarge! See? Shiny pai-nin'!"

"Very shiny, Wyndi." He chuckles and gives their ears a ruffle. "You've really gotten into this, haven't you?"

"In the sense that they look like a wee fuzzy rainbow, yes." Reba giggles.

"So do you, you know," Mirawynd's human reaches over and wipes a bit of paint off her forehead. "Having fun?"

"Aye." Reba gets a sneaky sparkle in her eyes. "And *ye* be awfully clean still, Julian..." She looks over to the rest of Mirawynd's pilots. "We should fix that, ladies, don't ye think?"

Penny grins, dipping her fingers in a jar of blue. "Why, Dr. Kiely, I couldn't agree more!"

"Oh, no." Their human's eyes widen as the realization dawns on him. "You wouldn't dare..."

Aunt Jenny looks thoughtfully down into the jar of red she's been using. "You have a good point, Dr. Kiely.

I'd even go so far as to say your young man here is out of uniform for this mission..."

Elias dusts his hands off on the rag he keeps tucked into his belt. "Well, Sid, that should about do it for tonight."

Sid nods, tucking the last of his personal tools into their places in his kit. "Yeah. I'll let you know how testing all of it out goes over the weekend." He looks over towards their collection of paint-covered pilots and officers. "I'm not about to let Breezy and Barker into this bird until they're clean, though."

"Fair enough." Elias chuckles. "Think we should have them wash the birds off too before they clean themselves?"

"Nah, I doubt it'll make our lot any more of a target than they already make themselves. Dangerous creatures are supposed to be brightly colored and all that." Sid pauses. "Besides, I'm sure Dr. Navy would want to know how long the paint lasts in flight scenarios."

"Point taken." The sound of the kittens excitedly greeting someone at the hangar doors catches Elias' attention. He can't help smiling when he recognizes the voices of their latest painting conscripts.

"Oh, stars, little ones..." he hears Dons giggling, "I hardly *recognize* you with all of the colors."

"Are we sure these are your kittens, Val?" Li asks in that delightful teasingly serious way he has. "I was sure Teryin and Tesnee were still silver—although I think there *might* be a Wyndi underneath this rainbow here..." Elias turns to look just in time to see Li wiping paint off of Wyndi's face with the free end of his scarf.

Wyndi giggles and gestures towards the tarp protecting the one part of the hangar that isn't covered in paint. "Wyndi pai-nin'! See?"

"Ah, a trio of painted kittens, is it." Li carries them over to where Elias is standing. "And it seems everyone here but you and Mister Sidney have been painted as well?"

Elias shrugs, trying not to laugh. "We've been working."

Meanwhile, Dons has gone over to the tarp to let their kittens show them all of the paintings. "Yes, dears, I see." They make a show of holding up each painting and making approving trilling sounds. "And you've decorated the darters too?"

"Well, of course!" says Major Toussaint, "We all have a bit of kitten luck to fly with now."

"Oh, is *that* what we're calling the mess now?" Admiral Marvin crosses her arms. "Luck or not, you lot are still cleaning it up."

"Why, Jenny!" Dons laughs. "I hardly noticed you under all those colors, you blend in so well. It seems the kittens have blessed you with their luck too!"

"Thankfully, Celadon," the Admiral quips, "'luck' is washable."

"Oh, you're all adorable." Dons takes out their pocket-com and gestures for everyone to gather in front of the painted darters. "Come on, I need a picture of all of you to send to the Eldest."

"And to keep for yourself, Dons?" Elias asks, sharing a knowing look with his husband.

"Of course! It's not often I get to have cute pictures of my Fleet family all at once... and so colorful!" They come over and hand Li the other two kittens so they can set up their pocket-com for remote control and be in the picture with everyone.

"Come on, then, Elias, Mr. Sidney!" calls Ocean. "It wouldn't be a family photo without you!" The young Florivan laughs knowingly. "Besides, Nida will want to know who gave us the paint."

"Fine, fine." Elias shakes his head and goes over with Li to join the rest. He's more amused by all of this than he's willing to show. One does have to keep up appearances around one's pilots, after all.

"How in the stars *are* you still clean, anyway?" Li asks, passing Wyndi over to Sarge and Dr. Kiely.

"The kittens listen to me sometimes too, you know," Elias replies.

Dons' kittens giggle and squeak from Li's now paint-covered shoulders, but thankfully don't make any attempts to jump to Elias' own or try to get down into his shirt. That's unusual; usually he can't get them to leave him alone.

"Ah, now, that just won't do." Li smirks and reaches up to pet each of the kittens, getting some paint on his hands. "As it is, *you're* going to have to be the one to get all of the paint off of these two..."

"Navy said the stuff's washable." Elias shrugs. "Shouldn't be a problem."

"In any case." Li reaches over and dabs a spot of paint right on the end of Elias' nose. "There. *Now* you're properly dressed."

The kittens seem to take this as a sign that they are, in fact, allowed to hug him now. Before Elias can react, one of them is on each side of his neck, with all four of their small arms and even their tails wrapped around him. Wyndi, naturally, leaps over from Sarge's shoulder to join the fun. They land on Elias' head and hug him from up there.

"So much for staying clean." Elias sighs. How else can he react to three affectionate little purring paint-covered critters? He reaches up to give each of the smaller kittens a pat on the head. "Thanks for waiting until I was done with the electronics, at least."

"Aww." Sarge leans over and gives him a nudge in the ribs. "Now if *that's* not the cutest thing I've seen today…"

"Don't start on me, Sarge." Elias growls, holding back a laugh.

"No, Mister Rudolph," says Admiral Marvin, "he's right. Quite adorable, I'd say."

"Oh, no," Elias groans, "not you too—"

"All right, everyone, hold still!" Dons bounds over and takes their place between Elias and Li, hugging both men close to their now-paint-covered self. "Photo time!"

After Dons has taken far too many pictures of all of them, they and Li leave to finish their last QSD jump cycle of the night. Elias wipes his hands off on his now-colorful belt rag and gets the last of his tools put away. The kittens stay clinging to him the whole time, for reasons he can't fathom.

"So, Rudy," says Sarge, wandering over with Dr. Kiely on his arm and a stupidly broad grin on his face. "Since you're already laundering two kittens tonight…"

"Yeah, yeah, Wyndi can have a bloody sleepover with us." Elias rolls his eyes. "As long as you two help clean up this place."

"Deal!"

"Wyndi *splash*?" the kitten perched on his head asks, eagerly swishing their paint-covered tail.

Elias chuckles, although softly enough that hopefully no one else will hear it. "Yeah. Let's go have a splash and get the three of you clean before the Admiral changes her mind about not blaming me for this mess."

✶ The End ✶

CHARACTERS APPEARING IN *AN INTERLUDE OF COLORS*

The following list of characters is divided by species and arranged in order of their appearance in the narrative. Only characters with significant "speaking roles" have been detailed here. All others present are listed as a group for the reader's reference; characters who are mentioned but do not appear are not included.

Florivans

MIRAWYND

They/them. Also known as "Wyndi." An orphaned survivor-smallest kitten. Second Darter Squadron mascot. Counterpart and ward of **Julian Potts**. Great-grandkitten of **Elder Marine**.

TERYIN AND TESNEE

They/them. The youngest kittens of **Elder Celadon**.

NYX YRITAL

They/them. A botanist, formerly of the staff at the Mayview Outpost. Kitten of **Elder Caeruleus**. Heart's-sibling of **Reba Kiely**. Counterpart to **Abigail Ioane**.

OCEAN MARBREE

They/them. Also known as "Breezy." Secondary Quantum Space Drive Engineer, SCV *Gymnasio*. Adjunct officer to **Colonel Esteban Vasquez** of the 6th Darter Squadron. Counterpart to **Pilot-Corporal George Barker**. Heart's-sibling to and member of the household of **Elder Celadon**.

Elder Celadon Toreval

They/them. Also known as "Dons," "Val," or "Donnie." Primary Quantum Space Drive Engineer, SCV *Aegolius*. Youngest of the Florivan Council of Elders; Defense Fleet Elder. Counterpart to **Lt. Hsu Li.** Adoptive entile of **Mirawynd** and heart's-sibling to **Elias Rudolph**. Parent of **Teryin** and **Tesnee**.

Humans

Lt. Hsu Li

He/him. Lead Astral Navigator, SCV *Aegolius*. Former personal assistant to **Admiral Marvin**. Called "Beacon" by Florivans generally and "Sunshine" by **Elder Azul**. Husband of **Elias Rudolph** and counterpart to **Elder Celadon**.

Pilot-Sergeant Julian Potts

He/him. Also known as "Sarge." Second Darter Squadron pilot, assigned to SCV *Surnia*. Counterpart and guardian to **Mirawynd**. Childhood best friend and sweetheart of **Reba Kiely**.

Petty Officer 3rd Class Elias Rudolph

He/him. Also known as "Rudy." Darter Maintenance Technician, 2nd Darter Squadron, assigned to SCV *Surnia*. Husband of **Hsu Li** and heart's-brother of **Celadon Toreval**.

Lt. Smithfield

She/her. Quartermaster, SCV *Aegolius*. Keeper of the ship's cat, **Isolde**.

Chief Petty Officer Thomas Sidney

He/him. Also known as "Sid." Chief Darter Maintenance Technician, 6th Darter Squadron, assigned to SCV *Gymnasio.*

Pilot-Major Abigail Ioane

She/her. 2nd Darter Squadron pilot, assigned to SCV *Surnia.* Former Project Snail Darter test pilot. Counterpart to **Nyx Yrital.**

Pilot-Major Anna Toussaint

She/her. 2nd Darter Squadron pilot, assigned to SCV *Surnia.* Former Project Snail Darter test pilot.

Pilot-Major Penny Albright

She/her. 2nd Darter Squadron pilot, assigned to SCV *Surnia.* Former Project Snail Darter test pilot.

Pilot-Colonel Gunther Hannemann

He/him. Commanding officer of the First Darter Squadron, assigned to SCV *Aegolius.* Former head test pilot of Project Snail Darter.

Ensign Theodore Ruttiger

He/him. Also known as "Ted." An Initiate of the Europan Mysteries. Personal assistant to **Admiral Marvin.** Bonded Companion of **Ambassador Glimmer.**

Dr. Reba Kiely

She/her. A civilian physician who did her residency at the Teegarden Shipyards medical facility. Childhood best friend and sweetheart of **Julian Potts.** Heart's-sister of **Nyx Yrital**

ADMIRAL JENNIFER MARVIN

She/her. Also known as "Jenny" or "She-the-Defender-of-Stars". Head of the Sol Coalition Defense Fleet. Commanding officer of SCV *Aegolius*.

Others

ISOLDE

She/her. Quartermaster's Cat, SCV *Aegolius*.

AMBASSADOR GLIMMER

He/him. A Europan Ambassadorial Observer. Attendant to **Admiral Marvin**. Bonded Companion of **Ted Ruttiger**.

THE POST-WAR ERA

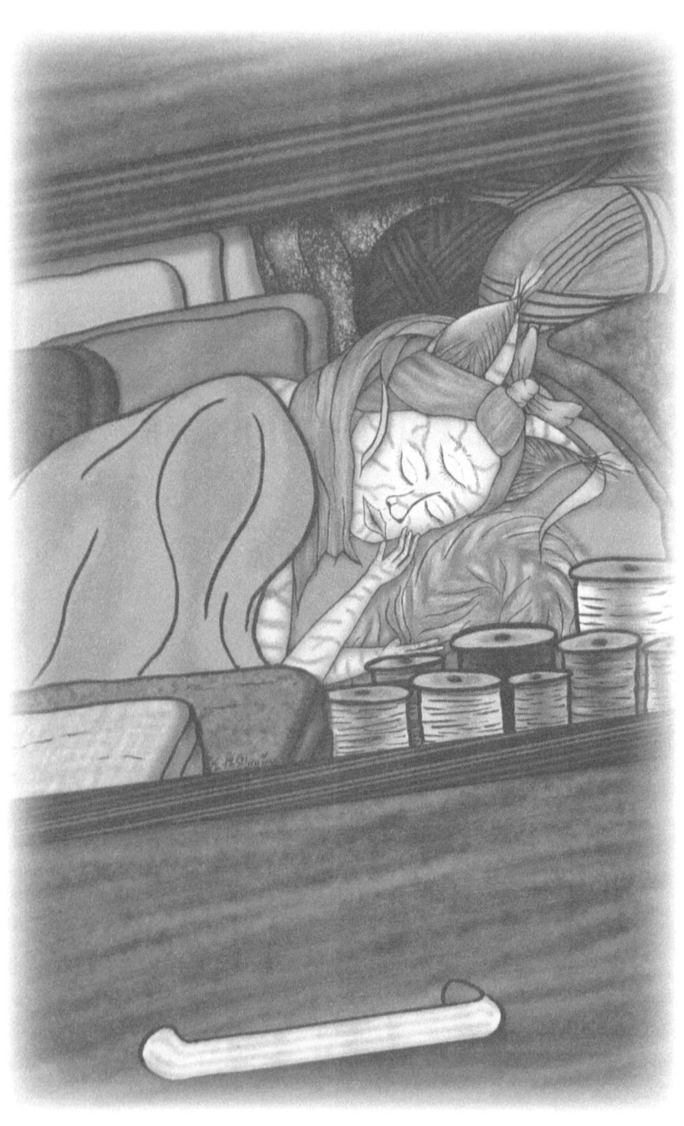

A Mystery, Unsolved

★ A Strange Space™ Short Story ★

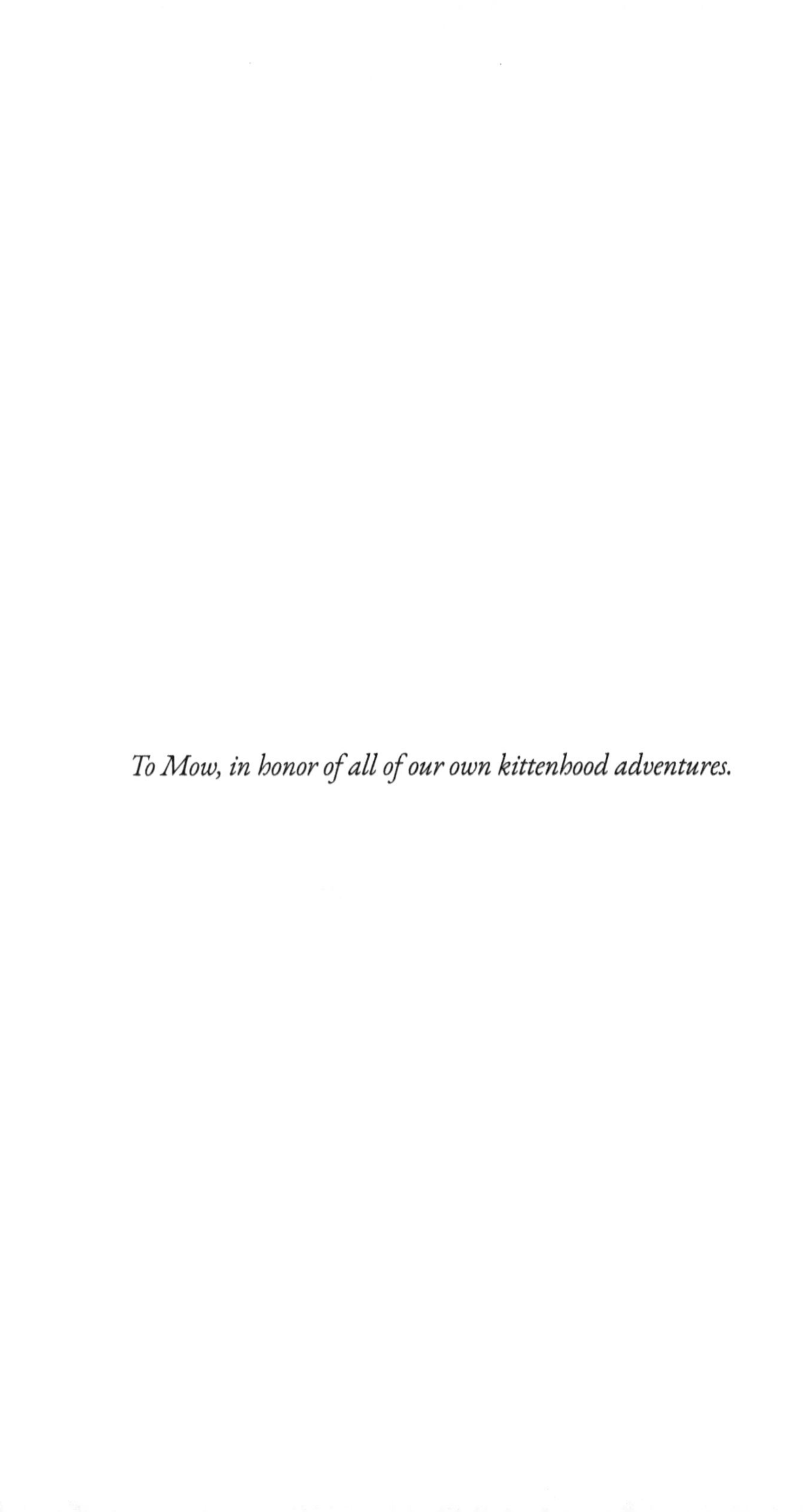

To Mow, in honor of all of our own kittenhood adventures.

“Hello!”

“Ah... hello, there, little one. Wandered off from your Dad’s watchful eyes again, have you?”

“Dad busy!”

“Heh. Is that right?”

“Yes!”

“Well, then. I suppose it wouldn’t hurt if you sit with me for a while...”

“What is?”

“This? Oh. Just a little something to pass the time. It’s a bit of a hobby I picked up as a boy—my granddad was an Artisan who specialized as a tailor—and I’d thank you *not* to go telling the whole station about it, mind.”

“Is shiny!”

"You like the color, I take it?"

"Yes! Pink is Sky's favorite!"

"Is it now? I would *never* have guessed. You always wear a bow like that, don't you? My granddad was friends with one of your Elders when I was a kid, but I don't think any of the kittens they brought with them when they visited ever wore one."

"Is *shiny*!"

"Heh. So it is. Well, then. Let's see... Here we go! I don't usually have people who can appreciate these little things around to give them to—want to try this on?"

"For Sky? Shiny bow for *Sky*?"

"Yes, Sky, this is for you. I don't have any hairpins for you to put it on with, but it should fit just fine."

"Is shiny! Help fix?"

"Of course."

"Thank you!"

There comes a time in every parent's life, regardless of how it was that they came to be the one in charge of a young creature's upbringing, where they have to stop and wonder just *why* and *how* their child has done something.

In the case of one Lt. Commander George Barker of the Alpha Centauri-New West Space Service Academy, moments like that happen no less than twice a week.

The frequency of perplexing moments in Barker's life may, of course, have more to do with the fact that his children aren't the sort of semi-helpless toddlers that humans their age would be. Instead, they're a trio of small, still-somewhat-fuzzy Florivan kittens whose general intelligence and dexterity far outpace their grasp of spoken language and whose curiosity can seldom be contained. The kittens' parent had been Barker's Florivan Quantum Drive Engineer counterpart back when he was a starship's Astral Navigator. Upon their death, he'd retired from the Defense Fleet and taken a position as an instructor at AC-NW to raise the little ones they'd left behind. Like their parent, the kittens seem to take an instinctive delight in confusing him; Barker still can't decide if that's a *family* trait or a Florivan one, but most of the time he finds it endearing all the same.

The larger two of Barker's kittens have lost the majority of their soft coats of silver fur now and are beginning to look very much the miniature of the adults of their genderless, asexual species. Adult Florivans are roughly humanoid and slightly smaller than human-sized, with an extra pair of arms, silver-tufted prehensile tail, large catlike ears, and a third golden eye in the center of the forehead to match the lower pair, all wrapped up in smooth blue skin bearing tiger-like silver stripes to match the silver hair they retain at the top of their heads.

In the cases of Sky Miradyn and Storm Melbryl, respectively, the former has ended up a lighter, brighter blue and the latter a more grey-toned one. Both are roughly the size of a rather large squirrel. As their silver kitten-fur now remains only on their bellies and tails, Barker has taken to tying his old Fleet-issue handkerchiefs around their small bodies as sarongs to keep them warm in the cool air of the AC-NW Space Station and help them adjust to the concept of wearing clothing in general.

The third kitten in Barker's care is still more chipmunk-sized and has only just begun to shed patches of fur off of their tufted ears. The deep blue-green skin peeking out from those patches reminds Barker more than a bit of his former counterpart, too. Enough of the kitten's eventual skin color has not yet been revealed for them to have been presented to their people's Council of Elders and receive a proper public name, though. For now, they're known simply as Merlani.

When the kittens were all Merlani's size and smaller, they would spend much of their day sleeping nestled in the inner pockets of their adoptive father's uniform jacket. As Sky and Storm are now too big for that, the kittens have taken to borrowing said jacket at their usual nap-time and making a nest with it in the lower drawer of Barker's desk so the three of them can curl up comfortably together. This suits Barker just fine, since it means the kittens are keeping each other warm and he knows where they are while he's busy with his never-ending pile of instructor's paperwork.

At the moment, the kittens are snuggled in the drawer taking such a nap. Barker himself is focused on marking all of the potentially disastrous errors one of his first-year Tactical Pilot cadets has made on their latest flight plan submission. He's in the middle of making a note on the assignment reminding his student why one cannot ignore a moon's gravity well when setting out to dock with an orbiting ship when he's interrupted by a small but insistent tug on his shirt-sleeve.

Barker turns to see Sky perched on the armrest of his chair, looking up at him with the same excited sparkle in all three of their eyes that their parent used to get just before the two of them went out flying. It's just as cute an expression in miniature, even if the memories it calls up are bittersweet.

"Now," says Barker, "what's this about, Miradyn? I thought you were sleeping still."

Sky's upper pair of hands holds out a piece of dusty-pink ribbon with a large, long-tailed bow sewn neatly to the middle. Their lower pair of hands fold together in an adorable pleading pose. "Please, Dad? Mir's bow fell off."

"Ah, yes, so I can see." Barker chuckles and takes the ribbon, setting aside the datapad containing the assignments he was in the middle of grading. He pats the desk in front of him. "Hop on up, then. I'll fix it."

Sky happily bounces up onto his desk and turns around so he can better reach their head and the shoulder-length silver hair the bow is supposed to be holding back from their face.

Barker never expected back when he first set all three of the then-tiny silver fluffs he'd just inherited from his Florivan counterpart into a basket with bright-colored bows tied behind their ears to distinguish them for a set of family photos that one of the kittens would become so fond of the accessory they'd never want to be without it. Sky had, though, and Storm and Merlani were all too happy to donate the ribbons *they'd* worn for the photos to their littermate's cause. Barker has gotten rather good at tying ribbons ever since.

"Thank you!" Sky waves their long, still-fluffy silver tail happily. The tip of it tickles Barker's nose. "Is *new* bow!"

"So I noticed—just where did you find this, anyway, Mir?" Barker asks, lightly combing out the static tangles in Sky's hair in search of the small bobby pins he usually uses to keep their bows in place. He had, after all, tied and pinned the ribbon they were wearing earlier that day himself.

After a glance down into the drawer where Storm and Merlani are still curled up asleep together, Barker is not so much surprised that once again one of the kittens has managed to slip away and have some sort of an adventure while he was working as he is that it's *only* one of the kittens who's done so. Usually, Sky and Storm disappear in tandem if they're going to escape, and then Barker learns they've gone because little Merlani wakes up cold from their absence and comes to him seeking snuggles and his help in finding their littermates.

"Is secret!" Sky replies, lightly purring and leaning into his hand in the way the kittens always do in response to having their ears petted. "Friend makes for Mir! Is shiny!"

"A new friend?" Barker asks, raising an eyebrow. He's grown somewhat accustomed, over the last three years, to the oddly quick way the kittens seem to latch onto some people—but at the same time, he's well aware that none of them are out of their 'if it is shiny and interesting I should bring it home and add it to my nest, regardless of who's possibly looking for the unattended shiny thing' stage. Barker has become well acquainted with the heads of several different Academy and Station Operations departments just from having to return some of the odd things the kittens have borrowed.

"Old friend!" Sky giggles with a happy bell-like undertone that's all too like the one their parent once had whenever they were in the midst of causing benevolent mischief.

"I see. Someone I know, then?—ah, hold still so I can pin this on straight, will you?"

Sky does their best to stay still. It's not an easy task for them. Kittens are wiggly by nature. "Secret friend with shiny ribbons!"

Try as he might, this is about all Barker can get them to say on the subject.

✸

"Hello!"

"Why, hello there, Sky! I was wondering if you'd come by to visit me again. Which of your siblings is this?"

"This Storm!" Sky tugs on one of the other kitten's hands excitedly. "See? Storm!" They turn to their sibling and gesture to the human with their tail. "See? Shiny-maker!"

Storm hops up onto the back of the chair behind the human and curiously peers over his shoulder at the shimmering yellow fabric in his hands. "Is making shiny things?"

The human laughs again and holds up the small garment he's been constructing out of bits of cloth and ribbons so the kittens can see it better. "My grandchildren haven't grown out of playing with dolls yet, and I like having something to keep my hands occupied while I'm on duty. Night shift guarding the station is usually just a lot of lonely sitting around keeping an eye on the monitors, you know? I'll be sending this down to Titania Colony for them once it's done."

Sky nods appreciatively and leans up over his arm from the other side, setting their lower pair of arms on top of his for stability. "Is *very* shiny," they say, tail waving happily.

"I had a feeling you'd like it, if you appeared again while I had a chance to show you. So, who's responsible for the two of you tonight?"

"We stay out of trouble!" Storm says proudly. "Dad said."

The human raises one eyebrow. "And where is your Dad, then?"

"Dad meeting with Entile Lari and Auntie Mandy!" Sky answers.

"Ah. That'll be Commanders Larimar and Hodgkins from Nav/Quan, I'd imagine? Stands to reason—it's the right time of year for everyone to be having extra staff meetings."

"Is too many meetings," Storm tells him solemnly.

"Heh. It always is." The human nods, reaching over with one hand to tap out a message on a nearby computer interface. "Well, you can sit with me until he's done with his meeting, then. I'll send him a ping so he knows where to come find you."

"What is?" asks Sky, still fascinated by the tiny piece of clothing in the human's hands.

"Oh, this?" He holds it closer so they can inspect the details. "It's a doll-sized version of a Martian-style ballgown."

"Needs more ribbons!" Sky reaches out with their upper hands to touch the dress and see how all of its decorations are attached. They make an appreciative little bell-like trilling sound as they examine the under-layers of the skirt.

"Sky likes ribbons," Storm comments in a matter-of-fact tone.

"So I noticed," the human chuckles. "I see you're still wearing the one I made for you. You like it?"

"Is *shiny*!" Sky says. "Thank you!" They reach up for effect and fluff the trailing ends of the hair ribbon perched behind their ears.

Storm looks more closely at the tiny dress, then giggles. "Is Mer-sized!"

"Is!" Sky agrees with another excited wave of their tail. "Could make a shiny Mer!"

"Mer?" the human asks.

"*Merlani*," Sky corrects, turning all three of their large golden eyes up to him. "Is littermate!"

"Ah. Yes, I remember the little darling now. That's their family nickname, then?" After a moment, he looks down at the dress in his hands and then at the two handkerchief-clad kittens perched on either side of him. "Say, now. You two are old enough to be trading fur for clothes..."

Some weeks after the incident with the "secret hair ribbon," a new addition is made to the list of things the kittens have brought back from their explorations of the station that utterly baffle George Barker. This one tops even the time Sky had somehow managed to stash an entire set of engineer's circuit-probes and micro-wire tools into the cubby-hole under his desk which the kittens had been using as a place to hide their collection of treasures at the time.

On this particular day, Sky comes back from *supposedly* spending the day in the company of one of Barker's senior Tactical Flight students without the handkerchief sarong he'd helped them tie around themself that morning. Instead, they're dressed in a white kitten-sized blouse with four long ruffle-cuffed sleeves underneath a pastel pink jumper dress with lace and embroidered flowers at the edge of each of the three tiers of the skirt and a particularly fluffy petticoat underneath. Sky's outfit also includes a large bow secured to the center of a wide lace-edged hair ribbon made with holes for their ears to comfortably slip through and long ruffle-cuffed socks to match their blouse.

"So, care to explain this?" Barker looks to the cadet standing in front of his desk with a raised eyebrow.

The two kittens the cadet had been tasked with watching excitedly scamper over to greet their smaller sibling who'd stayed with Barker while he was off the station running Quantum Space Transit drills with the senior Nav/Quan students. The three of them start up a cheerful conversation of their own on the corner of Barker's desk that's mostly in kitten-squeaks, seemingly oblivious to the adult conversation going on above them.

"I don't really have an explanation, sir," the cadet says sheepishly. "They were both very well-behaved all morning, really, but Sky disappeared while I was in my applied physics class... and when they showed back up at the end of the lecture, they were dressed like *this*."

"So this *isn't* your doing. Is that what you're saying, Mendoza?" Barker absently rubs at his beard, giving the cadet a disbelieving look.

"Yes, sir." The cadet smiles lightly in spite of the serious tone she's trying so obviously to keep in her voice. "If I may say so, sir, I think it's quite a cute outfit on them."

"It is," Barker agrees, shaking his head. "But forgive me, cadet, I'd be happier with the cuteness if I knew where it came from. Thank you for watching Sky and Storm today, though."

"Any time, sir."

After dismissing the cadet, Barker turns to his kittens. "Miradyn, sweetheart? Come here, will you?"

Sky bounces over excitedly and does a twirl for him, their tail waving happily under the ruffles of the little layered skirt. "Dad! See? Is shiny and *swishy*!"

"You're cute as can be, Mir," he says, "but where in the stars did you find something like this?"

"Secret friend!" Sky raises their two left hands to their lips and makes a dramatic shushing sound. "Secret-making shiny things for Mir!"

Barker raises both eyebrows now. "Secret?"

"*Secret*!" Sky replies, giggling and doing another twirl. "Dad likes?"

Barker sighs and ruffles the kitten's ears, careful not to disturb the perfectly-matching headdress tied into their hair. "It isn't anything I'd have thought to put you in, especially since you're in for a growth spurt soon if Larimar and your Entile River are to be believed... but it's sweet and ruffly and cute and it suits you. So yes, I like it.

Do I get to know who your friend who made this for you is so I can thank them?"

"Is secret!" Sky says again, already purring and clambering up into his arms for additional cuddles.

"You are so much like your Nida sometimes..." Barker chuckles and then pulls out his pocket-com. "Come on, let me at least take a few pictures of how cute you are so I can pester your mother and River with this adorable little mystery too."

A few weeks later, Barker's adorable little mystery deepens.

"*So, George,*" says Commander Fenton, head of the AC-NW Nursing Program on the interdepartmental video intercom from her office, stifling a laugh. "*I know you Navigators are known for taking on odd senses of humor, but this is something I never expected—even from you.*"

"Trust me, Mariah, I keep my sense of humor to myself more often than not these days..." Barker runs a hand sheepishly over his sandy-brown beard. "What's this about, then? One of my students gotten into trouble again? I'd hardly expect a social call from you in the middle of the day."

"*Oh, now, George, don't pretend you don't know! Your little stepping up of our running joke is adorable, don't get me wrong, but I have to say it's distracting my cadets a bit more even than Storm's visits usually do.*"

"Storm's with you? Great *Scott*. All three of the kittens are supposed to be with *Indigo* right now for one of their Florivan culture lessons..."

"Oh, are they? Well, then, maybe it's Lieutenant Indigo I should have called about this..." She chuckles again and waves off to the side of her office the camera isn't covering. *"Storm, dear, come over and say hello to your Dad."*

Storm bounces into the frame on Commander Fenton's desk. *"Dad! Hello!"*

Barker can't help but let out a startled, yet appreciative laugh when he sees them.

Storm is dressed in a perfect miniature of the Commander's own cream-colored uniform, complete with a tiny nurse's cap pinned into the small silver bun that's been arranged just behind their ears and a long lab coat with a slit down the back so their tail can move freely. They even seem to have the same multitude of pockets on the little scrub-pants they're wearing under the coat.

"I take it from your reaction that you didn't have a hand in this?"

"Well, now, Mariah, I can't say that I did..." Barker raises an eyebrow. "You expect me to believe it's not *your* doing?"

"It isn't—although I wish I had thought of it, considering that Storm here seems determined to make themself our mascot."

"They *are* a bit young to be signing up for the Nursing program, Mariah." Barker laughs again, shaking his head. "You're adorable, though, Storm. Where in the world did you get a getup like that?"

"Secret-friend!" Storm replies, happily waving their tail and making a grand gesture with all four of their arms.

"Oh, is *that* how it is?" Barker asks. "So this was a gift from the same person who made the dress and things for Sky, then?"

"Is secret!" Storm excitedly unzips the front of the miniature uniform jacket they're wearing to show him the shirt underneath over the video intercom. *"See? Is extra warm!"*

"It looks very warm, sweetheart." Barker turns his attention back to Commander Fenton. "I have no idea who's making these outfits for the kittens, but they do good work. I'll be down to get Storm out of your hair in a few minutes, Mariah."

"Thank you—I'll send you the photos we've taken with my students, too. I'm sure the rest of your family will want to see this."

"River's going to want copies of those for their picture-album, that's for sure." Barker finds himself grinning as he ends the call. He fishes his pocket-com out of his jacket and sends a message to the Nav/Quan department's Lieutenant Indigo to ask if he needs to be looking for more than one escaped kitten. "Breezy," he says to the air as he heads for the door, "these kittens of yours are something else..."

"Hello!"

"Ah! Good evening Sky, Storm. You've escaped from another of your Dad's meetings tonight, I see?"

"Yes!" Sky and Storm happily hop up onto the human's desk and then reach down to help their smallest littermate scamper up to join them. Both of them are wearing the outfits he's made for them, although Sky has the simpler of their two ribbons in their hair and Storm is without their little nurse's cap.

"Ah, and hello to you too, Merlani!" The human smiles and waves to the smallest kitten. "I don't think I've ever seen you where you weren't with your Dad before."

"Is 'Cin now," Storm tells him.

"'Cin-cin like our Nida!" Sky adds.

"Oh, is that so?" The human takes a closer look at the kitten, who is sporting a large patch along their shoulders where all of the silver fur has come off and revealed the deep blue-green color they'd inherited from their parent, although the rest of their small body is still covered in a coat of soft silver fluff. His eyes soften for a moment. "Yes, I can see the resemblance—you're going to be a perfect miniature of Breezy someday, aren't you? Well, then, little Ocean, it's good to meet you again."

"Hello," says little Ocean, waving shyly with one of their upper hands. Their lower pair are occupied with holding tightly to the folds of Sky's skirt for security.

"See, 'Cin?" Sky gestures excitedly to the human. "Is *shiny-maker!*"

"I am at that!" The human chuckles, then takes a swig from the glass of iced tea on the desk beside him. "So, little Ocean... I've made it a bit of a hobby lately to sew things for people who can actually enjoy wearing them instead of dolls. Now that you've got your public name, would you like me to make something for you too?"

Little Ocean nods their fuzzy head and then looks to their littermates with a questioning squeak. They're small enough still that words are harder for them to form than for the other two kittens, even though they're all the same age.

"'Cin gets *cold*," says Storm, climbing up and taking their usual cross-legged position on the back of the chair above the man's shoulder.

"Even with all that fur? Well, now, we'll see what we can do about that..." The human pulls up some files on the holoscreen of his pocket-com and flicks through them until he comes to the folder of images he's looking for. "Here, little Ocean, come have a look. You'd like something with a bit of room for you to grow so you can still wear it after you get to the same size as Sky and Storm, I'd imagine. Which of these do you like?"

It takes a few minutes, but soon little Ocean is sharing bell-like squeaks with their littermates and gesturing excitedly at one of the images.

"Shiny!" they say, looking up at the human with wide eyes, all their earlier shyness forgotten. Their tail swishes with interest. "Warm?"

The human pulls the photo up bigger to inspect it. A wide grin spreads across his face. "Yes, I think that'll do the trick."

A few weeks after the family's official celebration of their smallest kitten's finally having grown enough to receive their public name, George Barker finds himself making the long trek up to AC-NW's main station security office.

It's hardly the first time. With cadets under his watch across two different departments and three rather curious little Florivan kittens who tend to go off exploring *precisely* when he isn't expecting them to, Barker has gotten to be of a rather good acquaintance with the station's security staff.

In addition to that, AC-NW's chief of security is a man who served on the Defense Fleet's SCV *Gymnasio* with Barker and his counterpart during the Novan War. Back then, Barker found Q. Lawrence Pettigrew to be something of an imposing figure—an impression he still has, not that he'd admit it openly. The then-already-middle-aged Pettigrew had been assistant chief of *Gymnasio's* security staff when Barker first joined the crew as an exceedingly young junior-ranked darter pilot. Even after Barker found himself with the post of the ship's secondary Astral Navigator, thanks to a just as young Ocean Marbree's abrupt decision that he was going to be their counterpart, he'd still been a bit intimidated by Pettigrew whenever they'd run into each other.

The fact that the two of them are of old acquaintance does nothing to make the old soldier any less impressive now.

"Ah, I was wondering if you'd gotten my message yet, Barker," says Pettigrew as Barker walks into the office. He leans down and opens one of the lower drawers of his desk. "I believe you're here to collect someone from my lost-and-found box?"

"Better than retrieving someone from the brig," Barker quips.

"Better than back in the day when it was Breezy coming to retrieve *you*." Pettigrew replies, raising an eyebrow with a smirk in a way that makes the deep scar down one side of his face contort his whole expression into something which, as a teenager, Barker had initially found *terrifying*—although he now knows it as a sign of fond amusement.

"Yes, that too," says Barker, nodding with just a touch of sadness coloring his tone before he changes the subject. "Although I *will* say, I think this is the first time it's just been this one that's ended up being bought to you. Usually when little Ocean's feeling brave enough to go adventuring alone, they'll end up in the Geology department's display cases—and Lakshmi knows how to reach me."

At the sound of their adoptive father's voice, little Ocean bounces up out of the desk drawer they've been napping in and excitedly scampers across Pettigrew's desk. They're dressed in a long, loose-fitting little poncho made from bright green fleece that's secured under their lower set of arms with a simple black ribbon for a belt.

"Dad! See! *Shiny*!"

"There you are, Cinna-bun!" Barker picks the kitten up with a chuckle. "And I see you've met Sky and Storm's 'secret tailor' too, have you?"

"*Warm* shiny!" says little Ocean, happily cuddling against Barker's hands for a few moments before climbing up his arm to take their usual post on his shoulder.

"It does look like a warm jacket," Barker agrees, still doing his best to not laugh too much. "And it has a hood?"

"See!" Little Ocean pulls the over-large hood of the green poncho up over their ears. "Warm *frog*!"

Barker can't help laughing aloud now. The hood of the poncho has a pair of large embroidered spheres attached to the top, made to look like a pair of frog's eyes to go with the bright green of the rest of the little garment. This is simultaneously the funniest and the cutest thing one of the kittens has brought him yet.

"Great *Scott*," Barker says, once he's recovered his composure, "if you aren't the most adorable little four-armed frog in the galaxy, I don't know who is."

"Frog say 'ribbit!'" little Ocean informs him, quite pleased with themself. This is the closest thing to a full sentence they've ever said.

"They do at that, Cinna-bun." Barker turns back to Pettigrew, who's been watching the whole exchange with a stoic sort of amusement. "I don't suppose *you* have any idea who this mystery tailor is that keeps putting my kittens into cute little outfits like this?" He shakes his head. "I don't know whether to be worried or just grateful they're apparently friendly, anymore."

"Well, Barker," says Pettigrew, raising an eyebrow again, "I don't think these little mischief-makers of yours would hold *still* long enough for anyone who wasn't acting out of good faith to even take their measurements. Do you?"

"...No, you're probably right about that."

"If it's any consolation, Barker, I've had a good look at the seams on that poncho little Ocean has on—the construction's just as good as anything my granddad would have made back on Mars." Pettigrew pauses to answer an intercom message from one of the station's other security officers, then turns back to Barker and little Ocean. "Well, at any rate, it'll be interesting to see what else turns up, if this 'mad tailor' of yours is still at large."

"I'll send you pictures of the other things the kittens have shown up wearing," says Barker, chuckling. "Best I can figure is that one of my students is playing pranks on me... but none of them have admitted to having this sort of skills. I've asked."

"Please don't say you want me to launch an investigation into a few harmless acts of garment-making."

"What, you're not curious?"

"Oh... there's little goes on around this station I don't hear about sooner or later, Barker. If there's someone going about sewing outfits for the kittens in their spare time?" Pettigrew makes a vague gesture at the wall of security monitor screens behind him. "Well, let's just say I'd know if they meant any harm."

"I'd suppose you would." Barker strokes his beard thoughtfully. "Well, at any rate, I can always ask Taimri to find them for me the next time she and River stop by, and save you the work. She's pretty curious about all of this too, you know."

"Knowing that Ranger wife of yours and Breezy's sib and how they are with mysteries..." Pettigrew pauses to chuckle lightly under his breath. "I'd end up involved anyway, one way or another."

"Well, I'd almost think—"

"—Dad!" Little Ocean taps on Barker's cheek to get his attention. "Look! Mer frog! Ribbit-ribbit!"

"Heh. Yes, you're the cutest little frog around." Barker laughs again and shakes his head. "I'd better get you back home before Storm and Sky manage to escape too. Thanks for keeping an eye out for my kittens, Pettigrew. I appreciate it—and I'm sorry they keep getting in your hair."

"I don't mind them so much—they behave well enough when they show up here. Better than you ever did, at that! Goodnight, Barker, little Ocean. Say hello to Sky and Storm for me."

"Bye-bye!" little Ocean waves happily from Barker's shoulder as he heads out the door. "Thank you!"

"Now, Cinna-bun," asks Barker, patting the frog-jacketed kitten on the head, "what's that about?"

Little Ocean giggles brightly and snuggles up against his neck, purring. "*Secret*!"

✶ The End ✶

Characters Appearing in *A Mystery, Unsolved*

The following list of characters is divided by species and arranged in order of their appearance in the narrative. Only characters with significant "speaking roles" have been detailed here. All others present are listed as a group for the reader's reference; characters who are mentioned but do not appear are not included.

Humans

Q. Lawrence Pettigrew

He/him. Chief of Security, Alpha Centauri-New West Space Service Academy.

George Barker

He/Him. Lead Tactical Piloting Instructor, Alpha Centauri-New West Space Service Academy. Adoptive father of **Ocean Merlani, Sky Miradyn,** and **Storm Melbryl.**

Mariah Fenton

She/her. Head of Nursing Program, Alpha Centauri-New West Space Service Academy.

Florivans

Ocean Merlani Barker-Hämäläinen

They/them. Also known as "Mer," "'Cin-cin," and "Cinna-bun." Adopted kitten of **George Barker.** Littermate of **Sky Miradyn** and **Storm Melbryl.**

Storm Melbryl Barker-Hämäläinen

They/them. Also known as "Mel." Adopted kitten of **George Barker.** Littermate of **Sky Miradyn** and **Ocean Merlani.**

Sky Miradyn Barker-Hämäläinen

They/them. Also known as "Mir." Adopted kitten of **George Barker.** Littermate of **Ocean Merlani** and **Storm Melbryl.**

The Ones Who Wear White Hats

✦ **A Strange Space™ Short Story** ✦

For my mother, whose love of my "kitten stories" keeps me motivated to write more, and for all the other nurses in my life.

WHEN GEORGE BARKER WAS A MUCH YOUNGER man, he'd been a darter pilot in the Sol Coalition Defense Fleet—lied about his age to join and everything.

Then, through a small twist of fate involving one of the old songs about sailing ships that sticks in the back of his mind from time to time, he found himself suddenly with an alien best friend and a career as one of the Fleet's handful of Astral Navigators.

Somehow, in all the time that passed in between those two points, Barker never really considered the thought that one day he would retire from the Fleet at all—much less become an Academy instructor and adoptive father of three.

It's been almost two years now, but in some ways he's still adjusting to this latest redirection of his life.

"All right, that's all the errands done," Barker says to no one in particular as the door to his office slides shut behind him.

On the opposite side of the small room, a viewport stands open with a clear view of the stars and just a fraction of one of the nearby moons. Throughout the day, as the Alpha Centauri-New West Space Station rotates in its orbit of the system's largest gas giant, the view changes to show more or less of the planet itself. It's not the *best* view from the station, by any means, but for a man who's spent most of his adult life out guiding a starship through the void, having a view of any kind is a nice, homey sort of touch.

"Now, let's see..." Barker goes through his regular routine, lightly patting the head of each of his charges in turn as he counts them to make sure they haven't misplaced themselves again. "One kitten on the shoulder, one sleeping in the pocket..."

Usually, the third Florivan kitten is either on his other shoulder or curled up in one of his uniform jacket's large inner pockets with their smallest sibling. Barker sighs when he realizes that they're nowhere to be found.

He looks to the kitten sitting on his shoulder, who had only minutes ago awakened from their nap and emerged from his pocket themself.

"Sky, where's Storm gone? I could have *sworn* all three of you were here the last time I checked."

The small Florivan tilts their head to one side and gives him a a questioning look with all three of their golden eyes. Most of Sky's body is covered in soft silver fur. The places around their upper shoulders and catlike ears where they've shed the fur are a smooth cheery light blue accented by silver tiger stripes. Their four arms and long, tufted prehensile tail are still fully furry. In general shape, Florivans are remarkably similar to humans—at least when compared with most of the other sapient species in the galaxy—but for whatever reason, their kittens start off looking like something small and cute that would be kept for a pet. Little Sky and their missing sibling are both just about the same size as a small Earth squirrel, now, but their smallest sibling sleeping in Barker's pocket is still closer to chipmunk-sized.

Barker sighs. The two kittens who've shed enough fur to receive their public names still don't always recognize that the words are attached to them.

"Miradyn, sweetheart," he says to the kitten, briefly tickling them behind one of their ears, "we've been over this. 'Storm' is Melbryl. Where's *Mel* gone?" He helps Sky re-tie the bright pink ribbon they insist on wearing as a sash around their fuzzy little waist into a proper bow at their back.

"Mel!" says Sky, in a happy little bell-like voice. "Mel ix... ex?" They pause, squeaking softly to themself for a moment or two as they usually do when trying to remember how to say one of the words they've picked up recently. Their tail swishes proudly when it comes to them. "Mel *explore*!"

Barker runs a hand over his short-cropped dark beard and rolls his eyes. "Great Scott, of *course* Mel's off exploring... I should probably have asked why *you* hadn't disappeared along with them instead. Do you remember where they hopped off?"

Sky mimics his gesture with one of their upper hands and then waves their tail excitedly. The fluff of it tickles Barker's ear. "Riki!"

"Really? But we left Cadet Rodricks in the infirmary *hours* ago..." Barker shakes his head and turns back out into the corridor. He's glad that the kittens are at least old enough now to be able to answer questions when he needs them to.

Florivan kittens, Barker has learned, are remarkably intelligent from the moment they open their eyes. It takes a few years, though, for them to be able to communicate in anything other than adorable little squeaking and bell-like trilling sounds. He has plenty of practice by now, though, in understanding what his little silver-furred children are trying to say with their body language and limited vocabulary.

"Where, Dad?" Sky asks, lightly tapping his ear.

"To get Mel before they cause too much trouble—and you stay put for now, Mir, you got me? I don't want to have to chase you down today too."

"Yes, Dad!" Sky briefly nuzzles against his cheek before taking up a more comfortable position to observe their surroundings from the safety of his shoulder. "Mir stay."

"Thank you. I'd appreciate it if you did." Barker reaches up and affectionately rubs the kitten's ears and head as he walks. Down in the breast pocket of his jacket, the smallest of the three is still contentedly curled up asleep and purring softly. "Really, though," he says, more to himself than to the kittens, "If your Nida could have seen how much trouble I have keeping track of the three of you, they'd *never* have let me hear the end of it..."

Almost as soon as Barker arrives at the Academy's Medical Education Center and Hospital, a young nurse-cadet stops him.

"Excuse me, sir?" They gesture at Sky, who's still sitting on Barker's shoulder. "Are you supposed to have another of those?"

"Yes, as a matter of fact I am." Barker pats Sky on the head again—more as a reminder to the kitten not to scamper off than anything else. "This one has a littermate who's a bit more of a teal-grey color on the parts where they've lost the fuzz. Have you seen them?"

"I have! Actually, the little darling's been bouncing around here all afternoon. Commander Fenton has them right now, I think." The cadet stifles a giggle. "They sort of disrupted her lecture earlier."

Barker rubs at his beard again. "Of *course* they did... Mind showing me to her office so I can collect them?"

"It's this way." The cadet gestures for him to follow. "They're very cute little creatures, sir. We've had a bit of a debate going on about where they'd come from, actually."

"I'm sure you did."

A short walk later, and Barker finds himself standing in the doorway of an office marked "Commander M. Fenton: Head Instructor, Nursing".

A woman with greying dark brown curls is sitting in a high-backed chair at the desk, although turned towards a second desk and set of holoscreens at the moment so the hair and the cream-colored folds and single black stripe of a nurse's uniform cap are the only parts of her that can clearly be seen from the door.

"Commander?" The nurse-cadet taps on the doorframe. "This gentleman's come to collect our little visitor."

"Oh, has he? Thank you, Cadet Moonsamy. I'll deal with him; you can return to your duties." The Commander turns around and fixes Barker with an assessing sort of gaze while the Nurse-cadet departs.

Storm, for their part, is contently sitting on one of Commander Fenton's shoulders holding some kind of biscuit that they seem to be halfway through nibbling down. They give Barker and their littermate an excited little wave with one of their lower hands.

"Sorry to bother you, ma'am." Barker dips his head politely. "Heard you had a bit of a pest problem in your lecture earlier?"

"Yes, I did," Commander Fenton says dryly. "You wouldn't *believe* how hard it is to get first-year cadets to stay focused on a wound care seminar when someone as cute as this is scampering around the room trying to 'borrow' the rolls of bandages from them."

"Ah..." Barker awkwardly rubs at the back of his neck. "That would be a bit difficult, I'm sure. Apologies, ma'am. Florivan kittens have something of a 'make a nest out of shiny things' phase they go through—"

"—Mel!" the kitten on his shoulder interrupts, unable to be still any longer. They jump down and scamper across the desk to meet their littermate.

"Mir!" echoes Storm, hopping down to meet them on the desk. They offer Sky the other half of the biscuit and point at Commander Fenton with their tail. "See? *Friend*!"

"Shiny!"

"—And these two are still learning not to go around pestering people. I *am* sorry for the disruption." Barker shakes his head, trying to ignore the half-squeaked conversation the two kittens are having in the middle of the desk. "I brought them by to visit one of my students— he's in with a broken leg—and it seems whatever Storm saw going on as I was leaving was too tempting for their fuzzy little brain to ignore."

"They're cute enough that I'll let it slide this time, mister...?"

"Barker," he says, "Lt. Commander George Barker; I'm over in Tactical Flight and Nav/Quan. Have been for a couple of years now, but I don't think we've officially met before."

"Mariah Fenton," she says. "Nice to meet you—try not to make a habit of letting your charges disrupt my students, George."

"I'll do my best." Barker chuckles. "The three of them are a bit of a handful, but usually they're more obedient than this."

"*Three*? There's another one of them somewhere around here?"

"Oh, the other one is a bit smaller—and better behaved, thankfully—they're still in the middle of a nap at the moment." Barker offers his hand to the two kittens on the desk. "Sky, Storm, come on now, we don't want to bother the nurses any more today."

"Yes, Dad," the two kittens say in unison, reluctantly hopping onto his arm and climbing up so one of them is perched on each of his shoulders.

"Dad?" The Commander raises an eyebrow.

"*Legally*, yes—I was their parent's Navigator." Barker's eyes grow sad for a moment, but then he brushes it off. "Thanks again for watching Storm for me—I'll try to keep them from exploring in this part of the station from now on."

"Thank you."

"Is this Lt. Commander Barker?"

"*Yes, it is,*" says the voice on the other end of the relay call. "*What can I help you with?*"

"Well, sir, I'm Midshipman Gregory, one of Commander Fenton's graduate students..."

"*Ah. Let me guess. You have a small Florivan causing mischief again?*"

"Yes, sir. Two of them sat in on our basic first aid workshop today with the second-year folks from Nav/Quan, but then one didn't leave when the rest did—the Commander said to call you?"

"*Ah. That'll be Storm, then?*"

"That's the name the Commander called them, sir, yes."

"*Naturally. Well, I'm out on a deep-space exercise with some of my Flight students at the moment... Storm's not causing any trouble for you, are they?*"

"Oh, no, not at the moment. I've got them helping me tidy up the classroom, actually—Storm? Come here and say hello, sweetheart."

Melbryl scampers over from where they're being a very helpful kitten and rolling up the practice bandages into nice neat bundles with the metallic side facing out just like their new friend Gigi showed them. They like playing with the nurses and all of their shiny soft things. "Tidy up the bandage pile" isn't nearly as fun of a game as "gather all the bandages into a pile," but Gigi has promised them biscuits later as a reward, so making a *tidy* pile of shiny soft things isn't too bad in itself.

"Dad! Hi!" Melbryl squeaks, hopping up onto the nurse-cadet's shoulder, still holding a long gold-backed cloth bandage in their lower pair of hands. They wave to their father's image on Gigi's holoscreen. "Look! Shiny!"

"Ah, yes, Storm, I see the shiny thing." Dad laughs and turns his attention back to Gigi. *"Well, if you can't get ahold of Nav Cadet Tomlinson or QDE Cadet Cerise—that's the pair who's supposed to be watching Storm and Sky for me this weekend—there's a Ranger ship that should be docking at AC-NW in an hour or two. You can turn Storm over to the Rangers when they get there."*

"Sir?"

"Don't worry—" A series of bright beeps cut off whatever he was about to say. *"—Ah! Sorry to leave you hanging, Miss Gregory, but I need to get back to work. Storm! Be good for the nurses!"*

"Yes, Dad!" Melbryl waves happily to him again as his face blinks off of the holoscreen transmission.

Gigi stands there acting stunned for a few moments, then sighs and taps a few of the translucent buttons hovering in front of her.

A bright cheery flash of colors and squiggles appears on the holoscreen. Melbryl taps their new friend's cheek to catch her attention and makes a questioning squeak. They understand most talking, of course, and they're starting to be able to use some words themself, but they haven't even begun to learn to read yet.

"Oh! It says that Cadets Tomlinson and Cerise are unavailable for direct pings until this evening." Gigi shakes her head and taps out a message before making the holoscreen disappear and fully turning her attention back to Melbryl. "Looks like you'll get to stay with me for a bit longer, Storm."

"Shiny!" Melbryl excitedly swishes their tail and holds the bandage in their lower hands up to her.

Gigi laughs. "Yes, the outer barrier coating is shiny. Let's see about tidying the rest of those up, shall we?"

Once all of the shiny soft things have been organized to Gigi's liking, she carries Melbryl down to the station's lower docking ring.

"Really, though, Storm," she says, settling down onto a bench in the waiting area near the set of airlocks the docking officer told her to go to. "I wish I knew why he wanted you given to these Rangers, whoever they are."

Melbryl isn't sure what the fuss is about, themself. They'd have been perfectly happy to continue helping the nurses with their shiny things instead of coming down to a colder place like this that isn't *nearly* as interesting.

At the same time, "Ranger" is a word that Melbryl *knows* has an important meaning—although they don't remember what that is. They give the nice nurse-cadet a reassuring nuzzle and then hop up on top of her head behind her neat little black-striped cream cap to keep a better watch on everything going on around them while they try to remember.

Melbryl has a distinct impression that Mir would know what "Ranger" means. Mir is generally better at understanding all the things that Dad and the other adults talk about than they are. Mir, however, isn't here. Dad told them to help Cerise keep their Navigator, Tomi, out of trouble while he's gone, so Mir is wherever *Tomi* is. Melbryl likes their nurses better than Tomi and the rest of Dad's human students, though, so they're more than happy to have left that task to Mir and Cerise.

A ding from the waiting area's intercom speaker sounds before a computerized voice begins talking. *"Docking completed at Airlock J-18: LSRV Atascosa."* A second ding signals the end of the message.

"Ah! That's the one we're waiting for, Storm! Hopefully the Rangers will be in a good mood when I pass you on—not that I mind your company, of course, but I *do* have a lot of studying to do tonight and you're too distractingly cute for your own good."

"Friends, Gigi?" Melbryl asks, leaning down to look into the nurse-cadet's eyes. Her tan human face is awfully odd-looking upside-down, of course, but Melbryl has decided they like her. She does, after all, have both tasty biscuits and lots of shiny soft things to share.

"Yes, Storm, of course we're friends. I just don't have time to play anymore today, that's all. " She chuckles and plucks Melbryl down from her hair, setting them back on her shoulder instead. "And I'll thank you to not mess with my cap any more—re-pinning it twice since you introduced yourself is more than enough."

A few minutes later, one of the airlock doors makes a bright chiming sound and then slides open. A tall, rosy-pale woman with a white cowboy hat steps out. Beneath the hat, her ash-blonde hair is tied neatly into a braided bun at the base of her neck. She's dressed in an old western style outfit, complete with a dark brown vest over her crisp cream shirt and matching boots and silver-buckled belt. All three of Melbryl's eyes, though, are immediately drawn to the shimmery turquoise swirls of the woman's tie and the brilliantly shiny silver star-in-a-circle badge pinned to her vest.

This person, Melbryl remembers, is *family.*

She's why "Ranger" is an important word!

"Äiti!" Melbryl calls to her. They excitedly swish their tail and wave to the woman with three of their hands. With the fourth, they tug on the collar of the nurse-cadet's jacket to try to get her to walk that direction. "Gigi! Äiti! Äiti *home!*"

"Settle down, Storm, will you?" Gigi pats their head before getting up from her chair. "Ms. Ranger, Ma'am? Excuse me... I'm sorry to bother you if you're on official business, but I was told to deliver Storm here to you when you arrived."

"Not a bother at all, Cadet." Äiti laughs brightly and holds out her arm for Melbryl to jump to. "Hello, my little Melppu! Did you miss me?"

"Äiti *missed!*" Melbryl excitedly makes the leap and scampers up to hug her neck.

"You've grown a lot since I saw you, yes?" Äiti gives Melbryl an affectionate scratch behind their ears as she looks back to Gigi with a smile. "I'm surprised. Usually George brings all three of the kittens to meet us when we dock. Did he send you for an advance party?"

"...Sort of, ma'am?"

"You're one of his students, yes?"

"Ah, no. I just transferred in as a graduate student in the *Nursing* program—Storm keeps haunting our training areas, and when I tried to get in contact with Lt. Commander Barker to return them today, he said to give them to you? He didn't have time to explain, exactly, but I can see Storm knows you..."

"That's George for you." Still occupied with giving Melbryl a much-overdue snuggle, Äiti shakes her head and makes a small clucking sound with her tongue. "You'll have to forgive my husband, cadet, he still thinks like a Navigator—forgets other folks don't know all the details, yes?"

"Ah..."

"Don't worry, I'll remind him he needs to explain things better." Äiti stops petting Melbryl's ears and gestures towards the nurse-cadet. "Storm? Say goodbye to your friend, I'm sure she has other things to do today."

Melbryl waves to the nurse-cadet, who still looks a bit perplexed for some reason. "Bye-bye Gigi!"

"Ah. Right. Thank you, ma'am. I'm sure I'll see you soon, Storm." Gigi nods, then turns and disappears down the corridor.

"Something happening out here, Tam?"

An adult Florivan emerges from the door behind them, followed closely by a young human. Both of them are dressed like Äiti, although the Florivan is wearing a filigreed bolo tie and the human has a bandana tied around his neck instead. The Florivan is a grey-toned version of Mir's color, only *bigger*—about the height of Äiti's shoulder—and not furry. The silver hair on their head is pulled into a pair of braided buns at the base of their neck just like Äiti's. Melbryl immediately recognizes that *this* person is family too.

"Oh, nothing serious, Jokeni. That nice nurse cadet was kind enough to deliver one of your fuzzy little niblings to us, that's all."

"Only one?" The Florivan tilts their head and fixes all three golden eyes on Melbryl.

"Entile River!" Melbryl leaps to their shoulder and gives them an excited hug.

"Hello, Storm." Their entile happily accepts the offered cuddles. "Now why in the *stars* are you alone?"

Äiti answers for them. "From what I understand, there's a pair of Nav/Quan cadets somewhere who have Sky... George probably has Merlani with him, wherever he is."

"And this cute little creature is...?" The young human's voice is warm and bright and lightly accented and catches Melbryl's attention immediately. He is probably the tallest human Melbryl has ever seen—even taller than *Äiti*—and that alone is mesmerizing. He's a medium sort of tan, with just a hint of short darker brown locks showing around the parts of his head his hat doesn't cover.

"One of my adopted children I mentioned you'd be meeting, Merek," Äiti replies, chuckling. "My husband was the Navigator of River's littermate. The kittens know him as their dad, and they've settled on calling me their äiti—it's my ancestral language's word for 'mother.' Now, don't be shy, it looks like we have custody of this one for the moment—and you might as well get used to the rest of the family, since you're going to be with us for a while, yes?"

Melbryl considers the young human closely. They reach up and tug on their entile's hat with one hand to get their attention. "Friend?"

"Storm, really!" says Entile River, chuckling. "You're every *bit* the little pest now, aren't you?" They let Melbryl step off their shoulder onto one of their upper hands and hold them up to the young human. "Here, you want an introduction? Say hello to Merek. He's our new trainee Ranger—fresh from Waco, even! I wouldn't be surprised if there's still a bit of Texas dust on his boots somewhere."

Melbryl squeaks curiously, tilting their head to one side as they gauge the distance, and then makes a perfect leap off of their entile's hand and onto the young man's shoulder to inspect him more closely.

"Hello!" Melbryl lifts up the edge of his hat so they can poke at the tufts of brown hair underneath. They do their best to imitate the sounds Entile River used to make his name. "Mi... Mee-reek?"

"I..." He smiles, although a bit awkwardly for some reason. "Well, it's actually 'Meh-rehk.'" He pronounces the sounds very slowly and crisply, so they're easier to hear.

"Meh-rehk?" Melbryl asks. They taste the sounds for a moment, then pause in their investigation of his hat and tap on his cheek. "Merek!"

"That's it," he says. "Good job."

Melbryl is quite pleased with themself. Usually it takes a few more tries to get words right, but names are *important* so they and Mir have been trying hard to learn how to say them. "Merek *friend*?"

Merek lets out a small chuckle. "Sure, we can be friends... um..."

Their new friend seems to be looking for their name, since Entile River didn't tell him. "Mehl-brihl," they say, waving their tail happily. They make sure to say the sounds carefully so he can learn them fast too. "Melbryl!"

"Melbryl, yes. Hello." Merek looks between Entile River and Äiti. "Are they always like this?"

"Friend!" Melbryl says, looking back to their mother happily. "Shiny!"

"Only with people they find interesting," Äiti laughs. "This one's properly called Storm, but they're still learning to *tell* people that."

"Hello, *Storm*, then," Merek says. He sets one hand up on top of his hat to hold it down, now that Melbryl is trying to investigate it again. "Nice to meet you, but—"

Melbryl is nonetheless successful in their quest to slip up into the space inside the hat and on top of his short fluffs of soft brown hair. It's dark and warm and smells like hat—a good sort of place to hide, in their opinion. Melbryl looks forward to playing the hide-under-the-hats game with their littermates later, now that there's a new hat-cave to add to the playing field. They like this new human already.

"—Captain River? A little help here?" Melbryl hears him ask, although they don't see why he'd need help.

"Taimri?" says Entile River, "Remind me when we see that husband of yours to talk to him about the sort of *manners* he's teaching the kittens?"

A muffled laugh from Äiti. "Will do, Jokeni."

"Good. Now bend down so I can reach, Merek, will you? I doubt you want *me* to have to climb up there too..." After a few moments, Entile River raises the brim of the hat and fixes Melbryl with a firm look of their third eye. "Come out from there, kitten. Merek is a friend, but you shouldn't pester him like this."

"They're very... cute, Captain Hämäläinen, these children of yours," Merek says haltingly as he lifts the hat all the way up off his head before Melbryl can pull it back down to hide again. "And you said there were *three* of them?"

"There are! Here, let me help," says Äiti, gently reaching up to give Melbryl a brief scratch behind the ears. "They'll calm down a bit once they get used to you, yes? And once we reunite them with their littermates so they're not so excited about being the center of attention."

Melbryl gives their mother's hand a nuzzle, but doesn't make a move to come down from Merek's head. They like the higher vantage point and warmth such a tall human's head offers, even when there isn't a hat covering it.

"Come now, Storm, leave him be." Entile River reaches up again and tries to catch them.

"Friend!" says Melbryl, dodging their entile's hand.

"Storm Melbryl Barker-Hämäläinen. That's *quite* enough." Entile River reaches for Melbryl with both their upper hands now.

Melbryl likes the new human. They want to stay with him for a while and soak up his warmth and listen to the bright compelling tone in his voice some more. They can't quite find the right words to say all of that, though, so they settle on something simpler to say as they push all of the hands away: "*Mine!*"

"Oh, is *that* how it is?" Entile River's voice shifts to the gentler but still firm tone that says that Melbryl is amusing them and in trouble all at once. "Well, yours or not, you can't go around pestering people like this. Manners, Storm, remember? At least come down from his head."

Melbryl makes a reluctant sighing sort of squeak and slips down to their new friend's shoulder, ears and tail drooping. They look up to his two very green human eyes with the widest and saddest expression that they can muster. They don't know how to explain that they would promise to be good and not pester him too much if they could stay on his shoulder, but they *very much want to stay there* for reasons they don't even understand, so they settle for the look and tilting their head to one side.

"You never told me Florivans could *weaponize* cuteness," Merek laughs awkwardly as he puts his hat back on and looks away from Melbryl to their entile. "If they'll stay out of my hat, I guess I don't mind letting Storm ride on my shoulder for a little while."

Melbryl's eager set of eyes turns to their entile as well. They set all four of their small hands together and use their most polite and pleading voice. "*Please*, Entile River?"

Entile River sighs and rolls their third eye dramatically. "Oh, fine—but if Merek says to give him space later, you'd *better* respect that."

"Yes, Entile River!" Melbryl waves their tail happily. They're incredibly pleased to have a taller person to ride with. They briefly hug their new friend's neck and then settle happily onto his shoulder.

Merek reaches up a hand cautiously to pat Melbryl's head like Äiti always does.

Melbryl is more than happy to let him. Their new friend's hand is nice and warm, after all, and this part of the station is *cold*. Their purr starts up softly.

Entile River shakes their head now, half-chuckling. "And as for *you*, Mister Fiala: if Storm ends up imprinting on you and making a fuss when we have to leave, well... just remember that I've warned you."

"Warning noted, Captain River." From the tone of his voice, Melbryl assumes he's making a show of being formal.

"Well, now that *that's* settled," Äiti says brightly, making a wide sweeping gesture towards the corridor in front of them, "We're a bit overdue for a proper lunch while we wait for the rest of the family to find us. This way, Merek—I did promise to show you around AC-NW, yes?"

"I believe you did, ma'am."

Some years later, Melbryl is nearly fully grown and only a few years away from being considered an independent adult. They've just finished their evening Quantum Space Drive jump simulation training, and now they're in one of AC-NW's washrooms changing out of their charcoal-colored Nav/Quan Cadet's uniform and into the crisp cream scrubs they wear for their secondary specialism classwork.

Melbryl is the only cadet they know who has to regularly change clothes between classes. Then again, Medical is the only section of the Academy that has a different uniform to begin with.

Melbryl slips all four arms into their large-pocketed lab coat. Their long silver-tufted prehensile tail finds its way out of the long slit down the back of the coat so it can move freely. They double-check that their crisply folded student's cap is pinned in the correct place in front of their braided bun and between their ears. It hasn't been long since the school term started, but they're still proud of the single grey stripe on the side of the cap and the cuffs of their sleeves marks them as a second-year student nurse.

With all of their clothes correct and their other uniform neatly folded and tucked into their bag, Melbryl heads down to the Academy Medical Center to check in with the Nurse-Instructor in charge of the night shift.

Granted, "night" is a terribly arbitrary thing on a starship or a space station like AC-NW. There's usually a designated day and night period set up for the sake of the humans aboard, though, and the activity patterns of the place fall into step with that. For their part, Melbryl likes their turns on the night shift best—and not just because it fits better with the rest of their somewhat overbooked class schedule.

Check-in complete, Melbryl makes their way down the low-risk recovery hallway, quietly stepping into each room to either check and record the patient's vital signs or simply confirm that they're stable, comfortable, and already sleeping as needed. As a second-year student, of course, there's not much more they're actually *allowed* to do yet. If there was something wrong, they'd have to ping the Nurse-Instructor.

Melbryl's favorite part of making rounds like this is visiting with the patients who happen to be awake. There always seem to be interesting people to meet when they get to take the night shift.

Tonight is no exception. When they check the information screen outside the last room at the end of the hall, Melbryl learns that the room's occupant is apparently a Ranger—and one who's just today been moved from the Intensive Care Unit, at that. They've always liked meeting Rangers, and not just because of the family connection. The people who sign up to be part of humanity's neutral peacekeeping and emergency assistance service do tend to be interesting folks. The fact that some of them also captain small, swift-moving ships as Nav/Quan pairs like Melbryl's mother and entile do only makes them more fascinating. The mythic connection to their ancient Earth-bound predecessors doesn't hurt, either; Melbryl has many fond memories of reading "Old West Ranger adventures" with their father and littermates when they were younger.

As the door to the room slides open, they see that the man inside is sitting up in his bed reading something or other on a holoscreen. "Good evening, Ranger!" Melbryl says, stepping into the room. "How are you today?"

The Ranger looks up from whatever he's been reading on his holoscreen and smiles at them. He's young-looking, as far as humans go, with brown hair and skin that's a medium tan shade. "Hello, there. You're one of the Nursing Cadets?"

"I am," Melbryl replies. "I'm assisting the night shift this week. I'm here to check your numbers and make sure you're comfortable."

"Check away, then." The Ranger shoots them a cheeky smirk. "I have to say, you're a bit of a surprise. The charge nurse earlier mentioned it was supposed to be a Cadet Barker—"

"—That's me!" Melbryl holds back a laugh while they let the medical computer system scan their eyes and tiger-like silver facial stripe pattern to confirm their identity so they can access the patient's records and add the new notes on his condition. "Let me guess, you thought I'd be human?"

"I suppose I did, yes. Barker's not exactly a typical Florivan public name, is it?"

"Oh, it isn't. My Nida's Navigator raised me," Melbryl explains simply, just as they have so many times before. "My sibs and I have his surname. My public name is Storm—you can use that, if you like."

"Ah—say, wait—Storm?" A flicker of startled recognition flashes across the Ranger's face. "Your Dad's married to a Ranger, isn't he? Works as an instructor around here somewhere?"

"That's him! Why? Are you a friend of Entile River's, then?"

"You could say that—" The Ranger laughs, then sounds as if he's remembered why laughter isn't recommended for patients with broken ribs. Once he can get words out again, he shakes his head.

"Something funny, Ranger?" Melbryl can't see why the coincidence is so amusing. There's not that many Rangers in the galaxy—they'd always assumed most of them knew each other.

"Oh, *definitely.*" The Ranger grins at them. "We've met before, Storm Barker!"

"Have we?" Melbryl looks up from the auto-reading blood pressure cuff they've just slipped over his arm and tilts their head curiously.

"I did my rookie training under Captains Hämäläinen and River about oh... ten years ago now? Just got transferred back to Centauri Company last month—I'm assigned with *Atascosa* for the time being."

"Ah! That explains things!" Melbryl chuckles and then takes a few moments to check that all the information has gone into the computer correctly before they remove the cuff from the Ranger's arm. "I remember Entile River saying the two of them had been assigned an 'accident-prone junior partner' that they'd had to bring to the Medical Center in a stasis pod, but they weren't here long enough last week to say much about it."

"Heh. That *would* be how River described me... Went and put myself on the wrong side of an avalanche, I'm afraid."

"That's not a very healthy thing to do, Ranger."

"I figured that out, yes." The Ranger chuckles, wincing lightly, and then holds out a hand to them. "And you can call me Merek."

"Ranger Merek, then." Melbryl shakes his hand gently. It's warm, in that healthy human way. They pause, considering his face carefully. "You *do* seem familiar, but if I was still a kitten when we met..."

The Ranger shoots them a teasing grin. "I take it you don't remember making a nest in one of my boots or trying to add my badge to your little collection of borrowed medical tools, then?"

"Ah... no, but I'll apologize for that anyway." This whole interaction is reminding Melbryl a lot of when they turned up for their first day of classes as a Nurse-Cadet and most of their instructors made a fuss about some bet that had been made when they were a kitten—and gave the whole incoming class a good-natured teasing lecture about not falling asleep in the practice bandage storage closet and getting trapped.

"I could have sworn your Dad took pictures..."

"He probably has *several*, knowing him. Now, are you going to continue trying to embarrass me, or can I finish putting your vitals in the system?" Melbryl keeps their tone playful. They do have an old memory of a tall warm person with a distinctively pleasant voice who had been around sometimes when they were little, after all—and this man's voice fits that memory perfectly.

"No, no, go ahead—although forgive me if I can't quite believe that the little silver pest I met back then is all grown up now." The Ranger relaxes, although he still sounds amused. "So your secondary is medicine, then?"

"Yes." Melbryl nods and gets back to work. "Specifically field medicine and nursing—I'm double-specialized, actually—aiming for Advanced Practice Nurse and Emergency Medical Response qualifications."

"Neat. Don't think I've run into a ship with a Florivan medical officer yet."

"There's a few out there, actually... not many, but I'm certainly not the first." Melbryl pauses to finish making their notes and then flashes a smile at him. "You seem to be recovering well, Ranger Merek. I've got to go do the rest of my rounds now, but if you're still awake when I come by to check on you later, we can talk some more."

"Ah, now, there's a delightful prospect to fight the boredom—say, I don't suppose you still play mancala?"

"Oh, I do!" The game of counting and capturing bright-colored glass pebbles had been a kittenhood favorite of Melbryl's. "When I'm on a shift break sometime, I wouldn't mind a game."

"I'll hold you to that, Storm Barker."

A few days later, during their free time between classes, Melbryl is sitting in a chair pulled over by the Ranger's bed with the old wooden mancala board they've borrowed from Dad set up on a small table between them. They've lost count of who's in the lead as far as matches go already. The two of them have been chatting more than actually paying attention to things like scores.

"So, have you taught this training partner of yours to play yet, Storm?"

"Wila?" Melbryl shakes their head. Their lower pair of hands continues sowing the little glass stones into the carved spaces on the board. "No, she's more the 'can't sit still long enough to play a silly board game' sort. Your turn."

"Ah. Pity." The Ranger scoops up the pieces that have collected in one of the spaces on his side of the board and begins distributing them. "I'd have thought a Navigator would have more patience than that."

"I think some of them have to grow into that?" Melbryl shrugs and mentally maps out a few options for moves they could make while they wait for him to finish. "The rotation's almost over, though—I'm hoping I'll click better with whoever they pair with me next."

"Not planning on keeping her?"

"We get along fine, but Lavender—they're one of the un-partnered third-year cadets—well, they're really close friends with her. I'm almost *certain* they're going to offer her their compact at the end of the year..." Melbryl pauses to count as they place the next set of stones into place. "... And I don't want to get in the way of that."

"Makes sense enough. Someone else you've got your eyes on, then?"

Melbryl's tail swishes softly as they shake their head. "Not particularly. The Nav Cadets are all nice sorts, don't get me wrong, but none of them have made all that much of an impression on me yet—does that make sense?"

"Considering that y'all choose your counterparts for life? Yeah, it does—your move, Storm."

Melbryl focuses for a few moments on the satisfying clinking sound of the game pieces falling into their new positions. The Ranger's right, of course. The whole purpose of the Nav/Quan program at any of the Academies, aside from training folks in how Astral Navigation and Quantum Space jumping work in the real world, is to help young Florivans like themself find the human who best suits them as a counterpart.

It's one of the most important choices any Florivan makes, considering how limited the population of their genderless, asexual species still is after their sanctuary planet was destroyed during the Novan War. Not only that, but every starship that uses the veiled dimension their people know as the Strange as a shortcut around the vast distances of interstellar space has to have a Florivan Quantum Space Drive Engineer aboard to make that means of travel possible. A Florivan's human counterpart, too, becomes a member of their *family*: chosen sibling, dearest friend, anchor. That relationship makes the separation from their blood kin bearable and the work that they do safer—and, in some ways, makes it possible for them to do the work that they do at all.

"It's actually unusual how quickly Sky found Joy, I think?" Melbryl says at last, at the beginning of their next turn. "The Commanders warned us when we first signed that it usually takes at least a full rotation cycle if not two or three to find someone who really clicks."

"How long did it take the two of them?"

"They were partnered in the first round at the beginning of our first year." Melbryl can't help giggling. "It was amusing to watch, for sure—Sky'd only been training with her for a *week* when they told me they were set on asking her to be their Navigator."

The Ranger catches a giggle himself. "How'd your Dad react to that?"

"He wasn't surprised, for some reason—said Sky takes after our Nida for being quick to hear and latch onto someone, whatever that means." Melbryl stifles another giggle. "And considering Joy has the same taste in outfits with too many layers of frills and lace that Sky does, it stands to reason the two of them were meant to be each other's counterparts."

"Ah. And your other sib's signed somewhere else?"

"No, not yet. Elder Celadon wanted to keep Ocean in their apprenticeship a bit longer—we're hoping they'll end up coming home to AC-NW too, though. Maybe give us a chance to all be together as a family again for a while, you know?"

"That'd be nice, I'm sure."

"What about you?" Melbryl asks on a curious whim, "Did you ever go through the trial rotations they do for Rangers?"

"A few times," he admits with a shrug, "but none of the folks who were there to see if they could pair with one of us could even hear me over the Nav comlinks—and I'm sure I don't have to tell *you* how much of a dealbreaker that is."

"They really couldn't hear you? That's surprising." Personally, Melbryl can't understand how anyone *wouldn't* be able to anchor on to a warm, smooth voice like his— they can't help but think it would come through clear and bright even through the heaviest fog. The special intercom channels used on starships can only reach partway, after all; the rest of the work of keeping a Navigator in contact with their counterpart relies heavily on the Florivan's instinctive ability to anchor themself to the voices of family members so they won't get lost in the Strange.

"Not a one—your entile can, though, oddly enough, and so can Captain Lapis, which is why the two of them keep recommending me for trials any time someone asks them…" The Ranger runs a hand awkwardly through the back of his hair while he watches Melbryl drop their latest group of stones into place. "I don't know, maybe that's just wishful thinking on my part. It's not so bad being a lone Ranger, you know—more of us out there that don't have counterparts than do, really."

"Well, *I* think your voice is nice. If Entile River says you're a good candidate for someone's counterpart, I'm sure they're right."

"Thanks, Storm. I appreciate that." The Ranger smiles at them and makes his next move. Somehow, it's enough to win him the match.

"Good game," Melbryl tells him.

"Want one more round before you scamper off to class?"

"Yes, if you're up to it."

The Ranger is already re-arranging the stones for the new match. His smile turns into a grin. "I'd be delighted, Storm."

A week passes, and then three.

Melbryl finds themself spending more and more of their free time keeping the Ranger company. Whatever opinion Merek may have had of them when they were a kitten, there's something undeniably *pleasing* about the friendship they've been forming with him.

Soon, Melbryl's mother and entile return from finishing up their latest assignment to visit the family while they wait to hear where they're headed next—and to retrieve Merek from the Medical Center, since he's finally been cleared to return to duty.

Towards the middle of the visit, Melbryl finds a chance to talk to their entile alone about some of the things that are starting to swirl around in the back of their mind. Aside from their littermates, River is their only living direct relative. The rest of their entiles are all members of their adoptive grandparent's extended household. Melbryl can't help being relieved that they're here in person—otherwise, they'd have had to have this conversation over the relays, and it's just not the same asking for advice that way.

"Entile River? Can I talk to you?" Melbryl taps lightly on the deck plating above the access compartment their entile is currently half-laying, half-floating in to re-tune *Atascosa*'s recently damaged artificial gravity system.

Although neither Ranger has been eager to explain *why* and *how* the gravity plating ended up damaged, the fact that Entile River's had to disengage it completely and set the whole of *Atascosa* into its natural microgravity state while they make repairs is a sign the damage must have been considerably worse before they reached the station. Fortunately for Melbryl, their species is halfway native to the Strange and almost equally at home weightless as in an earth-level gravity environment.

Their entile reorients themself enough that they can pop their head up out of the access port. "I can take a break, yes. What is it, Melbryl?"

"Well..." Melbryl takes a breath and then asks an easier question first. "How'd you end up with Äiti?"

"What?" Entile River gives them a look that says they suspect that's not the real question. "I thought you knew that story, Mel."

"I know you two always joke about it and that it had something to do with pirates and the War... but that's it."

"*Smugglers*, Melbryl. Not pirates, thankfully. Ones Tam and the Ranger who was supervising her training were trying to catch—there's not much to tell, really. Elder Caeruleus was an old friend of her mentor's, and after your Nida left us to join the Defense Fleet... well, the smugglers they'd been tailing were infiltrating civilian relief ships like our *Dinochirus*, and Caeruleus pulled a couple favors to get this pair of undercover Rangers on board."

"But what does that have to do with you and Äiti?"

"Caeruleus kept me back as an apprentice the same way Elder Celadon's kept Merlani. Taimri came into my life around then. We were friends; I wasn't interested in any of the Navigator prospects I'd been introduced to, and since Tam was a *Ranger*... it all worked out in the end. Attempted kidnappings and matters of who rescued whom from the smugglers notwithstanding." Entile River makes a little shrug and shakes their head. "But I'm rambling. Why do you want to know all of a sudden, Mel?"

Melbryl hesitates. "Is it *that* different, making your compact with a Ranger instead of a Navigator?"

Entile River raises all three of their eyebrows just enough to indicate that they're suspecting the reason for the questions. "It's *different*, but a lot of things are the same. Smaller ship, faster jumping through the Strange. Less of a crew around you, though—usually it's just me and Taimri and whoever's been assigned to some mission or other in the neighborhood of wherever we're going, or the occasional dignitary or specialists we carry along. And then there's the work itself." They make a vague gesture with one of their lower hands, keeping the upper pair crossed over their chest. "I don't do all the same things your mother does, of course, but I'm still a Ranger too, mind you. There are some assignments where I have to step in to be the voice of reason when the humans we're dealing with can't hear each other anymore. It's an added layer of responsibility—not everyone's cut out for that."

"Ah." Melbryl nods, running the silver tuft at the end of their long tail through their lower set of fingers to straighten it out.

Entile River's eyes soften. "Something troubling you, kitten?"

"You said you were friends with her… but how'd you know *Äiti* was the one you wanted to make your compact with, in the end?"

"To tell you the truth, Mel… when I was your age, I didn't intend to take a counterpart at all."

"You *didn't*? But why not?" Melbryl has only ever heard of one Florivan who doesn't have a human counterpart, but that's their entile who is the agent of the Elders' Council and does things differently to begin with. From what they know, even Entile Jade has a collection of human friends they visit as they travel.

"Back then, not all of us had one. Or *needed* to have one… I'd always planned on going back to Procyon once our apprenticeship was over. I was going to go full into agriscience and be the one who stayed planet-side at the Sanctuary to help our Nida with our new litters of younger siblings… Needless to say, that never happened. " Entile River sighs, ears drooping lightly to mark the sense of loss the way they always do on the rare occasions they talk about the world the Novan War took from them. "When Marbree chose your Dad for their Navigator and volunteered for the Fleet, I was more alone than I'd ever been in my entire life... and by the time Caeruleus finally cleared me to move on from my apprenticeship, I didn't have a home to return *to*."

For a moment, Melbryl wonders what all of that must have been like—and then at the same time, in the back of their mind, makes a distinct mental note that they *have* to talk to the littermate *they've* had to leave essentially alone when they're done here. It's been too long since they've had a chance to visit with Mer properly as it is.

Entile River's ears resume their normal posture and their eyes turn back to meet Melbryl's. "All of that was going on while Tam and I were getting to know each other. I don't know quite how to explain *why*... but being around her made everything I was going through easier to bear. Your mother may have her odd streaks, but even then, she was this warm, optimistic person who was aiming her whole life towards helping out folks who'd get overlooked otherwise. I may never have intended to take a Navigator's compact, but I liked the idea of having her for a *friend*... and I found myself wanting to help people the same way she did. Is that enough to answer your question?"

"Yeah... it does." Melbryl doesn't know what else to say. Their entile's never told them so much about any of that at one time before.

"Good." Entile River reaches out and pulls Melbryl into a hug for a few moments before ruffling their hair with one hand and gesturing at the scattered tools and parts floating around the two of them. "Now, Mel, give me a hand with these, will you? I know you're not aiming to be a mechanic, but you never know when it'll be a good time to know how to mend gravity platings..."

Early in the station's morning some weeks later, Melbryl sprints down the corridors towards the lower docking ring. They've not even bothered to change out of their sleep clothes or braid up their hair yet—getting to the ship in time to say the things they need to say is too important.

Luckily for Melbryl, *Atascosa* is still right where they'd hoped to find her. Not only that, but their mother and entile are right outside the ship's cargo bay where the airlocks are connected, sorting out some sort of checklist.

"Äiti! Entile River! You're still here!" Melbryl scampers up to the two of them, almost breathless from their run. "I was afraid I'd missed you."

"Of course we're still here—we don't launch for another hour—but I thought we all said our see-you-laters after dinner last night?" Äiti laughs and reaches out to ruffle Melbryl's ears and long mess of unbraided hair.

Entile River raises an eyebrow at them. "I was under the impression you and Miradyn had training exercises to attend this morning?"

"We do." Melbryl folds all four hands behind their back and swishes their tail nervously. "I'm... going to be a bit late, that's all."

"*Goodness*, Melppu." Äiti laughs again. She clucks her tongue at them and shifts effortlessly into her native language. "I haven't seen you this reluctant to let us leave the station since you were a kitten and all three of you were trying to stow away."

Melbryl's third eye flashes to the man who's awkwardly stepped past the three of them—likely wanting to avoid intruding on the little family moment—and is now busying himself with shuffling some small boxes around.

"It's not just that, Äiti..." they reply, switching languages to match. "I—I needed to say something before you left."

"To us?"

"No..." Melbryl shakes their head softly. "To Merek."

Äiti and River share a look, and then a matching pair of knowing smirks.

"Oh, is *this* what you said they were being vague asking you about, Jokeni?"

"I *do* believe it is, Tam." Entile River nudges Melbryl forwards with two of their hands. "Go on, kitten, we'll give you some space."

Melbryl hesitates for a moment, and then bounces up all the way into the ship's cargo hold and taps Merek on the shoulder.

"Come to say goodbye to me too, Storm?" He sets the box he was holding down on top of some others of a similar size before fully turning his attention to Melbryl.

"No."

"No?"

"I..." Melbryl takes a breath to center their nerves. They don't even know why they're nervous asking something they're so certain about themself. "I came to ask if you would consider staying?"

Merek being Merek, he doesn't seem to catch what they're asking at all. "I'm a *Ranger*, Storm. I've got to leave to help with this new assignment headquarters sent us—we told you that, didn't we?"

"Right... you do..." Melbryl's ears twitch as they rearrange which of the four hands behind their back is holding which.

"I do."

"Then... you have to come back when it's over! Alive and uninjured, I mean. Please."

"I'll do my best?" Merek chuckles again, the same way he does when he tries to tell his stories about what they were like as a kitten. "That's usually the goal with these things."

"Good." Melbryl smiles, gaining a bit of confidence. "*When* you come back, then—do you think you could get assigned to AC-NW for... oh, let's say three years?"

"I don't think the station's had a Ranger posted on-site before, but nothing's impossible... why?"

"That's how long it'll take me to finish my ANP training."

"I'm not sure headquarters would reassign me just so I could keep a good friend company." Merek laughs again and readjusts his hat. "But I promise I'll come back to visit whenever *Atascosa*'s heading this way—"

"—No, I mean..." Melbryl looks back to their mother and entile, both of whom are doing their best to pretend not to be listening even though it's obvious they are.

Äiti gives them an encouraging 'go on' sort of gesture.

Melbryl takes a deep breath and then looks back up into the tall Ranger's eyes with determination. "When you come back, Merek, I want you to *stay* so I can claim you for my counterpart."

"Really?" A flash of elated shock crosses his face.

"If you'll have me," Melbryl continues, trying their best not to sound too pushy. "I've always liked the idea of being a Ranger, you know—and *you* need a qualified nurse by your side so you don't keep winding up delivered to the ICU in a stasis pod."

For a few moments, everything is silent.

Melbryl looks down, suddenly nervous for some reason and unable to meet Merek's eyes while they give him a chance to process the request. It's a *lot* to ask of a human, after all—even one who's familiar with their people and how the world works for them.

The silence ends with the sensation of a familiar wide-brimmed felt hat being set behind Melbryl's ears and then tilted back so it can sit on their head without falling off. When they look up, they see Merek smiling at them.

"I would be *honored* to accept your compact, Storm Barker—If you're certain that's what you want?"

"I am." Melbryl doesn't know how they could be *more* certain about anything. They remember liking this man when they were a kitten. They *know* they enjoy being around him now. They've talked to their mother and entile about him enough, too, to know that he really *is* the wonderful person they've gotten to know since he appeared as one of their patients.

They can't imagine wanting anyone else to be by their side.

Merek nods. "When we get back from this assignment, then, I'll make it official."

"You don't *really* think I'd change my mind, do you?"

Merek chuckles again and shakes his head. "No, probably not—and I can't say I'd want you to."

Äiti and River seem to take the ensuing hug as a sign they can safely approach without interrupting.

"So!" Äiti teases, "I'll be telling the Major we need a badge made for a new recruit, yes?"

"Merek's going to be my counterpart," Melbryl tells her, releasing the hug but still standing beside their Ranger.

"Is that so?" asks Entile River, looking to Merek with a grin.

"I am," he replies, chuckling. "You were the one saying I'm too accident-prone to be a loner, weren't you?"

"I suppose I was at that. Well, *this* was a long time coming, at any rate. Storm was trying to put a claim on you before they could even talk in sentences, after all! Now, as much as I hate to break up such a sweet scene, since as far as custom goes that little bit of declaration to a family member and a superior officer is enough to mark a compact and I'd *love* to properly celebrate this... and go tell George he owes me scones from a certain wager I just won..." Entile River laughs brightly, grinning at both of them. "But we have a ship to get ready to launch. Storm? You can have your Ranger back when we come home to roost."

"Yes, Entile River." Melbryl says, still all smiles. "You'll all be careful, then? I'll come after you if you aren't."

"I promise we will." Äiti pats them on the shoulder. "You have our relay frequencies, you can keep in touch. Now shoo, yes? Or do you want *me* to tell your father why you're going to be late to the class he's teaching?"

"No, Äiti, don't worry—I'll tell him." That's a conversation Melbryl definitely wants to have a chance to prepare for and have themself. They look up to their Ranger with a smile. "I'll ping you later, okay?"

"Okay." Merek shoots them a teasing grin. "Now go get yourself sorted out so you're not having to run to class late and out of uniform, all right?"

One more round of farewell hugs later, Melbryl scampers off.

It's only when they get all the way back to their quarters to change into their uniform that they realize they're still wearing their Ranger's hat. By then, there's no chance of returning it to him, since *Atascosa* has already launched for parts unknown.

Melbryl decides they'll keep it safe for him instead.

If they do say so themself, Merek's wide-brimmed white felt hat is *precisely* the accessory their Nav/Quan uniform was always missing.

✶ The End ✶

Characters Appearing in *The Ones who Wear White Hats*

The following list of characters is divided by species and arranged in order of their appearance in the narrative. Only characters with significant "speaking roles" have been detailed here. All others present are listed as a group for the reader's reference; characters who are mentioned but do not appear are not included.

Humans

George Barker

He/Him. Lead Tactical Piloting Instructor, Alpha Centauri-New West Space Service Academy. Husband of **Taimri Hämäläinen** and adoptive father of **Ocean Merlani, Sky Miradyn,** and **Storm Melbryl.**

Mariah Fenton

She/her. Head of Nursing Program, Alpha Centauri-New West Space Service Academy.

Virginia Gregory

She/her. Graduate-level Nursing student, Alpha Centauri-New West Space Service Academy.

Taimri Hämäläinen

She/her. Also known as "Tam." Ranger co-captain of LSRV *Atascosa*. Counterpart of **River Myrval.** Wife of **George Barker** and adoptive mother of **Sky Miradyn, Ocean Merlani,** and **Storm Melbryl.**

Merek Fiala

He/Him. Trainee Ranger, assigned to LSRV *Atascosa* under Captains **Taimri Hämälainen** and **River Myrval**.

Florivans

Sky Miradyn Barker-Hämälainen

They/them. Also known as "Mir." Adopted kitten of **George Barker** and **Taimri Hämälainen**. Nibling of **River Myrval** and littermate of **Ocean Merlani** and **Storm Melbryl**.

Storm Melbryl Barker-Hämälainen

They/them. Also known as "Mel" or "Melppu." Adopted kitten of **George Barker** and **Taimri Hämälainen**. Nibling of **River Myrval** and littermate of **Sky Miradyn** and **Storm Melbryl**.

River Myrval

They/them. Also called "Jokeni" by their counterpart. Ranger co-captain of LSRV *Atascosa*. Counterpart of **Taimri Hämälainen**. Entile of **Sky Miradyn, Ocean Merlani,** and **Storm Melbryl**.

Ocean Merlani Barker-Hämälainen

They/them. Also known as "Mer." Adopted kitten of **George Barker** and **Taimri Hämälainen**. Nibling of **River Myrval** and littermate of **Sky Miradyn** and **Storm Melbryl**.

The View from a Distance

★ **A Strange Space™ Short Story** ★

To the tiger who sits and eats tea cookies with me.

"This seat taken, cadet?"

The young man in the pale grey uniform of a first-year student startles at the sound of a voice behind him. When he turns and sees the owner of the voice, he immediately scrambles to his feet from the barstool where he's been sitting, knocking his pocket-com to the floor in the process. He bends down to get it, striking his head on the edge of the bar counter on the way back up.

He recovers quickly and rushes to salute the Academy Instructor who's just walked up beside him. The Alpha Centauri-New West Space Service Academy isn't a military institution, but enough of the instructors are veterans of the Defense Fleet that the old-fashioned respectful protocols are in common use, just as they would be on most starships. The Fleet insignia pin on the right lapel of this particular instructor's charcoal grey uniform jacket marks him as one of those veterans, just as the gold winged star pin over his breast pocket announces his status as a qualified pilot.

"No, sir. It's free. If you need me to move—"

"—Great *Scott*, but you're a twitchy one." The instructor makes a vague gesture at the barstools. "Sit down, will you?"

The cadet halfway trips himself climbing back onto his stool. He nearly knocks over his glass in the process.

"You can calm down, cadet, I'm off-duty—and you're not in my department to begin with, as far as I remember." A twinkle of gruff amusement forms in the corners of the instructor's dark blue eyes. "I always remember the twitchy ones. They make good pilots in the end, usually, but *stars* does it take a long time to get them there."

"Ah—Yes, sir; apologies, sir." The cadet is still sitting stiffly, rubbing the sore spot beneath his short blonde hair with one hand.

"Nothing to apologize for, cadet. Now, relax before you hurt yourself again." The instructor takes his seat on the tall, black-upholstered bronze stool beside the cadet with all the grace of a cat alighting on a windowsill. He takes his uniform jacket off and drapes the ivory-collared garment over the free stool on his other side. The regulation short sleeve shirt he has on underneath is the same colors: loose charcoal jersey with wide ivory bands around the cuffs of the sleeves. The colors match well with the instructor's beard and close-cropped hair, which is dark, but beginning to take on a salt-and-pepper tone around his temples.

Leaning on his elbows on the smooth, sparkling black counter top, the instructor raises a ruddy-pale hand to catch the attention of the bartender. In moments, the multi-limbed hovering robot in question has made its way over. It tilts the black and silver assortment of visual displays and sensor inputs that serves as its head to one side in acknowledgment of the instructor.

"Query: What will it be for you this evening, Lieutenant Commander Barker?"

"Coffee: cortado, dash of vanilla." The instructor glances over to the cadet and then adds, gesturing vaguely at the stasis case on the far end of the room, "and two of those pastries with the red stuff, Buzzy, if you don't mind."

The bartender-bot pauses to process the more informal portion of his order and associate the request with items in its known inventory and recipe book. After a moment, it turns a small orange light with a question mark on above its center-most camera. "Please specify flavor of pastry: Cherry or raspberry?"

"Is that what it is? Hmm. Let's go with cherry, then."

The robot beeps musically in acknowledgment and buzzes off.

The cadet shifts awkwardly in his seat, glancing over at the instructor. He checks his pocket-com for damage. Finding none, he flips out its holoscreen in compact mode. He sets the device down on the bar so the screen is in front of him and easy to tap through with one hand. With the other hand, the cadet reaches forward and picks up his drink. It's something dark and foamy in a tall glass, already well towards being emptied. He takes a sip. His hand tremors lightly as he sets the glass back down.

The instructor is still leaning on his elbows, only now with his hands together, the fingers interlaced. His eyes turn across the bar to the wide viewport on the far wall.

Outside, the green and orange marbled sphere of the gas giant below floats serenely against the star-punctuated darkness of open space and the luminous expanse of the galactic center, attended upon by thirty-four moons of various sizes. The station's orbit and slow daily rotation are bringing the system's two suns and the planet's horizon into perfect alignment with the middle of the viewport behind the bar.

The robot bartender returns. Like some incredibly dexterous clockwork jellyfish, it balances a small yellow plate with two cherry danishes on one of its many appendages and a matching saucer holding a small glass cup filled with steaming brown liquid on another. It deftly sets both the plate and saucer down in front of the instructor.

"Query: Will there be anything else, Lieutenant Commander Barker?"

"No, not just now. Thank you, Buzzy."

The robot gives him another series of acknowledging beeps and then spins around and buzzes off to assist another patron.

There aren't many people around at this hour. It's the lull of the station's designated late nighttime, after all, and a Wednesday. Aside from a handful of maintenance technicians on break at the back table and the trio of visitors from a newly docked ship whom the robot is now busy serving, the room is practically empty. The cadet and the instructor are the only ones sitting at the bar, with six empty stools to the left of the cadet and three to the right of the instructor.

Perhaps this proximity is why the cadet keeps glancing up from his holoscreen so furtively.

The instructor quietly unclasps his hands and picks up the little glass cup between his thumb and two fingers to take a long, slow sip of his coffee. His eyes never leave the viewport.

The cadet taps to refresh his list of messages. He grimaces and shakes his head a little and then reaches for his drink again, barely looking up.

"Nice one out there tonight, isn't it?" The instructor's question isn't so much a question as it is a statement of fact.

"Hmm? What did you say, sir?"

"The *view*, cadet. You should try looking at it sometime."

The cadet glances up to the viewport briefly before setting his glass back down. "Oh, yes, sir, very nice." Almost immediately, he returns his attention to his holoscreen.

"Sit here long enough, this time of night, and you can see whole storm systems form down there."

"I... wouldn't know, sir."

The instructor takes another long, slow sip and then sets the cup back on the saucer. He turns his attention to the plate, methodically tearing off part of one pastry. "You didn't strike me as a stargazer, no."

The cadet looks over towards the instructor without making eye contact. He shrugs. "I'm on the Astrophysics track. I like stars well enough, sir..."

"Got other things on your mind, then?"

The cadet glances down, refreshes, and then lets out the briefest of sighs. "...I suppose I do, sir."

"Figured as much." The instructor still has his focus on his pastry and the viewport. He falls silent, never turning his gaze in the cadet's direction.

Outside the viewport, the smallest starship that's been docked with the station leaves for parts unknown. She's the fast moving sort of craft originally designed for small crews doing cargo runs between planets, and is shaped a bit like a fat blue and white goldfish—although her golden solar sail 'fins' are currently folded in and stowed in their protective housings. A five-pointed star set into the middle of a wide ring is emblazoned in silver on each side in front of the main sails, with 'LSRV *Atascosa*' painted across the center of the star.

The ship passes slowly across the viewport in front of the planet as she departs, firing small jets of blue flame from her tail end to push her forward. After clearing the station's flight zone, the ship shimmers for a few moments as if hit with glittering strobe lights from all directions and disappears. *Atascosa* has jumped into the veiled dimension of Quantum Space for the first leg of her journey. Only her Astral Navigator and their Florivan Quantum Drive Engineer counterpart know for sure where she will reappear to sail on the solar winds.

"Fair breeze follow with you, Taimri," mutters the instructor as he watches *Atascosa* disappear. He briefly raises his cup towards the viewport as if making a toast.

Several minutes later, the cadet finally looks up from his holoscreen and speaks again. "It's... it's just that I'm worried, sir."

The instructor finishes the last of his coffee. The second danish sits alone and untouched on the plate in front of him.

"Worried, cadet?" The instructor waves absently to the robot bartender, still looking out to the stars and the planet below. "What does a bright young spark like you have to worry about this late at night?"

The cadet hesitates, taking a nervous gulp from the dregs of his glass. He refreshes his messages again, then looks back to the instructor. "It's... well, it's my girlfriend, sir."

"Oh, is it? Young love, *drama*, all that mess?" The instructor turns his eyes to the cadet briefly with the edge of a wry smile. "I have been there, young man—and I do not envy you."

The robot bartender buzzes over and picks up the saucer with the empty glass cup in one of its mechanical tentacles.

"Say, Buzzy, can I get another of those? And a refill of whatever the cadet here is drinking, too."

`"Order confirmed, Lieutenant Commander Barker."`

"One of these days, Buzzy," the instructor quips, "I'm going to convince you to call me George when I'm off duty."

The robot tilts its mechanical head at the instructor for a moment again before beeping and hovering away.

"...Thank you, sir."

"Looked like you needed one. Saves the bot a trip, at any rate."

The cadet glances down at his holoscreen again and sighs.

The instructor looks over to him now, raising an eyebrow. "She not answering your pings, then?"

"Oh, no, she's... Well. She has this thing going on this week. Some sort of 'survival training' out on Moon Eight. Her whole cohort's down there for it."

"Ah—she'll be in Nav/Quan, then?"

"Yes, sir. You know about it?"

"I get the odd memo from them, now and again."

The robot returns, setting new beverages down in front of each of them. "Cortado with vanilla; Beta Centaurian oat stout over ice. Query: May I assist with anything else?"

"Oh, is *that* what it is? Can't account for taste, I suppose—No, Buzzy, that's all for the moment. But say, before I forget, have the usual ready for me at 01:45, will you?"

"Order confirmed, Lieutenant Commander Barker."

"Thanks." The instructor picks up his refreshed cup of layered espresso and steamed milk. He makes the same brief toasting gesture towards first the cadet and then the window before taking his first sip.

The cadet awkwardly mirrors the gesture before he gulps some of his own drink. He glances down at the screen once more, then flicks it off and nudges the whole pocket-com away with a groan.

"You were saying, cadet?"

The cadet takes another gulp and then sighs, now joining the instructor in staring out the window. "It's just... Well. I mean, I *know* she's busy, you know? I'm just waiting for her to have time to ping me back. That's all."

"Naturally."

The instructor slides the plate with the untouched second danish over in front of the cadet.

The cadet doesn't notice it initially. When he does, he looks to the instructor with confusion.

The instructor just shrugs and goes back to watching the stars and the planet's swirling clouds of gas.

After a hesitant nibble at the edge of the pastry, the cadet speaks again. "I guess... Well. I'm still getting used to her having such a different schedule. We've been together since secondary school, you know?"

"Oh, have you?"

"Yeah, pretty much *forever*, really. I don't think we were ever apart before she came to the Academy—I'm a year below her, see—and she used to send me messages all the time while we were long-distance and she was studying Astral *Cartography*... but she switched tracks last term when Nav offered her a place, so we're not in the same department like I always thought we'd be—and she's just... Well. *Busy*."

The instructor takes another slow, silent sip of his coffee.

"I mean, I'm *happy* for her and all—who wouldn't be?" The cadet gestures vaguely in the direction of the viewport. "Nav's practically impossible to get into and she's *brilliant* and deserves it—but..."

"But?"

The cadet absently picks up his glass and swirls the dark brown liquid and chips of ice around for a while before taking another gulp. "...I signed to the Academy here at New West because *she* was here, you know, sir? And now... Well. I hardly ever even get to see her."

"Is that so?"

"She's always in *simulations* or *training* or working on extra assignments... I wait outside the lecture hall for her most days just so I can say hello before she goes to lunch and *I* have to go to class. Then she's too tired after all of her extra classes to meet up and do anything in the evenings—when she's actually *free* in the evenings—so we only really get to spend time together maybe twice a week. And all of her *new* friends get to see her all the time, and..." The cadet hesitates, then sighs. "Well. She has this Florivan 'training partner' she's gotten close to, and *they're* always around now unless she specifically sets aside time for us to be alone."

"Things change, I suppose."

"Not with *us*."

The instructor looks over at him again with the same raised eyebrow. "So what's your problem, then, cadet, if change isn't it?"

The cadet breaks the eye contact and looks down into his glass instead. "She's my *world*, sir. And I know it's old-fashioned, but when she gets back... Well. I'm going to ask her to marry me."

"That's a problem?"

The cadet reaches over and flicks the holoscreen back out on his pocket-com and refreshes his messages. He grimaces.

"No... We love each other, sir. I know she'll say yes—we've talked about it being something we might want to do after we graduate before, even—but... Well. She's in *Nav*."

The instructor nods and takes another slow sip of his coffee. "You don't get along with her current training partner, then?"

"I... They... They're just so..." The cadet lets out a frustrated breath. "Well. I don't think they like me, sir."

"Why not?" The instructor raises both eyebrows this time.

"I don't know, sir. I've *tried* to be nice to them, but we just... Well. We don't have *anything* in common at all."

The instructor sets down his cup, absently stroking his beard with one hand. "Oh, I can think of at least one thing you'd have in common."

The cadet shrugs. "It's like oil and water, sir. And if she ends up sticking with them *officially...*" He trails off, shaking his head and taking a long drink from his glass.

The instructor gives him a knowing look.

"You don't like the idea of sharing her, do you, cadet?"

There's a long, tense pause before the cadet answers. "... Not especially, sir. At least, not with *Lazuli*. I've met some of the other Florivans she could have paired with. They're perfectly lovely and I get along just fine with all of them— it's just *this* one who drives me up the wall, you know?"

"Ah."

"I just... Well. I don't know what to do, sir."

The instructor turns his gaze back out towards the planet. He's silent for a few minutes, stroking his beard absently and watching the swirls of a large storm matrix on the planet outside shift and reform. When he does speak again, his tone is even and clear, as if he's chosen his words with extreme care. "Cadet, I've known a *lot* of Navigators over the years... And there's very few of them I've met who haven't been in the middle of a situation like yours—at least, not if they go in for romance and the like in the first place. Some of them work it out, some of them don't."

The cadet briefly glances down to refresh his messages again.

"The problem," says the instructor, "the real core of it, is that a lot of humans get *possessive* of people they love. Worst case, it makes them forget that the other person has the right to have friendships and a life outside the relationship—sometimes makes them forget that *they* should have those things themselves, too. Breaks things sooner or later all the time, that does—and that's just with humans by ourselves. You put a person with that sort of possessive streak in love with a Navigator? It's just *asking* for trouble."

"I'm not—that's not..." The cadet hesitates, abandoning whatever he'd begun to say. "I don't understand, sir."

The instructor laces his fingers together again and rests his chin on them as he leans on his elbows and looks out towards one of the larger moons that has just begun to rise past the horizon of the planet.

"Let me put it this way, cadet: One of those Nav folks I knew back in the day? She's been married to the same man for over thirty years now; childhood sweethearts, too, even. He's the best of friends with her counterpart—never saw them as a threat to his relationship with her, just accepted from the get-go that they'd become part of her life and worked to make sure they were a welcome part of his too." The instructor pauses for a moment, his tone growing darker. "But I *also* knew a Navigator back in my Fleet days who got himself married oh... five times?

Seriously involved a few more than that. Loved every one of the people he was with, too, but sooner or later... well, things didn't work out."

"...Why not, sir?"

The instructor picks his coffee up again before answering. "It was a lot of things that made those relationships fall apart, of course; different career priorities, too much distance—more than one of his spouses had *affairs*, even."

"Oh... that's... Well. Unfortunate."

"It was." The instructor gestures lightly with the little glass cup. "But he *also* kept falling in love with people who had that possessive streak. There was always this point of contention where the person he'd given his heart to would end up being jealous of the close friendship he had with his counterpart. Eventually, all of the other problems would add up and he'd be forced to choose between being with that person and being a Navigator—and no matter how much he'd loved them, there's only one choice a Navigator can really make in a situation like that."

"I don't see why, sir." The cadet's expression is halfway between confused and offended. "If he *really* loved them—"

"—Cadet, do you have any siblings?"

"Sir?"

"Just answer the question."

"Um... Well. Yes, sir. I have an older brother."

"You close?"

"Pretty close, sir."

"What would you do if your girlfriend told you that if you *really* loved her, you'd give up your career and your entire relationship with that brother of yours? Never speak to him again, even."

"She'd never—"

"—If you *had* to make that choice, Cadet. Think about it. What would you choose?"

The cadet goes silent for a long time. He stares down into his glass and then takes a swig. "I... I don't know, sir."

The instructor gestures vaguely towards the viewport with his cup. "*That* is as close as I can get you to what this Navigator's spouses asked of him, in the end."

"Really, sir? I don't see how..."

The instructor takes on a curiously meaningful tone now, as if he's presenting a lecture to one of his students. "How much do you know about the way Nav/Quan works, cadet?"

The cadet hesitates, clearly confused. "A starship's Astral Navigator has a Florivan QSD Engineer counterpart assigned to them who runs the Quantum Space Drive to move the ship between points in space? The Navigator says where to go, and the Florivan puts it into the Drive system to jump the ship back and forth out of Quantum Space. Everyone knows that."

"Correct," says the instructor, "Except for one thing: Florivans aren't *assigned* to their Navigators. They *choose* the human they make their compact with, and in most cases they stay beside that person for the rest of their life."

"That's not the same thing?"

"It's not." The instructor shakes his head. "The bond a Florivan builds with their Navigator goes just as deep as the closest of siblings or the best of friends—deeper, in some ways, because out there, jumping a ship through Quantum Space, *lives* depend on the two of them having that kind of trust. More than that, Florivans don't have the luxury of spending their lives surrounded by their own people like we do, either, anymore, and they're a semi-eusocial species by nature—they take such care in choosing their counterparts because *we* can't run the Drive without them and *they* can't bear being entirely alone. They need someone whose voice can anchor them when they're working just as securely as their parent or siblings could. The two aren't just coworkers, cadet. They become *family*." The instructor drains the last of his coffee as punctuation. "I don't think any person who's really meant for Nav could abandon that for *anything*."

The cadet continues silently staring down into his glass.

"What I'm saying, cadet," the instructor says, glancing over as he sets the little glass cup down onto the saucer with a bright clink, "is that if *you* do love this girlfriend of yours, you might want to think long and hard about whether you're prepared to follow the course she's charting—knowing full well that if she *does* graduate from the Nav program in the end, she *will* have a Florivan counterpart in her life, regardless of who they are or whether you get along with them. That's what Nav *is*. If you can't learn to live with that, you're both better off finding someone else to fall in love with."

The cadet is silent for a long time. He and the instructor sit there at the bar, staring out at the clouds of green and orange gas swirling across the planet's surface in an endless cycle of currents and spirals.

"...Sir?"

"Yes, cadet?"

"What happened to your friend, in the end?"

"Him?"

"Yes, sir—Well. If you don't mind me asking, I mean."

"I don't." The instructor gives a little shrug and takes up that same posture again with his chin resting on his interlaced fingers and his elbows on the bar counter. "Well, after his last wife left him—after almost four years, too, longest he'd ever been able to stay with *anyone*, married or not—he sort of just gave up. It just wasn't worth it to him to have to go through the inevitable breakup. Put him in a pretty dark place for a while, too, like he barely existed at all when he wasn't working."

The cadet swirls the ice chips through his glass again, leaving a trail of tiny bubbles behind them. He looks like he wants to say something, but can't settle on what an appropriate response would be.

"His counterpart did their best to bring him out of it, though." The instructor shakes his head with a light wistful amusement. "They never *did* think he should give up on romance, actually, even though they couldn't relate to the desire for it. They just... always wanted him to be happy, and they knew he was the sort of human who *needed* another human in his life. Even conspired to play matchmaker and set him up with their littermate's counterpart, believe it or not."

"Really, sir?"

"Yeah. If I remember right, their reasoning was that if the problem was that all of his previous partners couldn't cope with him being a Navigator, then maybe someone who was in the same situation *could*." The instructor chuckles for a moment, idly spinning his wedding band around on his finger with his thumb. "They'd have been pleased as punch if they'd gotten to see how well that worked out."

"They didn't?"

"No." The instructor's eyes go to some distant spot between the stars. "Accident, during a rescue mission."

The cadet awkwardly runs his finger over the rim of his glass. "That's... Well. Unfortunate, sir."

"It was. He retired, after that—didn't really have the heart to even try to find a new counterpart—and he had other responsibilities to take care of after they were gone. They'd left him some very *important* ones, too."

The robot bartender buzzes back over, carrying a pair of steaming mugs and a small plate piled with mound-shaped cookies covered in powdered sugar. It sets both mugs and the plate between the instructor and the empty stool beside him.

"It is 01:45, Lieutenant Commander Barker. Two green teas, hot, one with honey; one plate of tea cakes. Query: Do you require anything else?"

"No. Thank you, Buzzy."

The robot beeps in acknowledgment and zooms away.

The cadet's pocket-com lights up with a series of bright sounds. He scrambles to pick it up and read through whatever messages are now waiting for him.

"Your girlfriend?"

"No." The cadet shakes his head, looking at the screen in utter puzzlement. "Her *training partner*."

"Oh?"

The cadet reads through the messages that are still pinging in, the puzzled expression shifting to one of apprehensive surprise. "They're wanting to know how I'd feel if they ask her to be their Navigator after finals are over."

"You didn't expect to be asked?"

"Not really. I... Well. I didn't think they *cared* what I thought at all."

"I suspect they care more than you realize, cadet."

"Maybe, sir."

The cadet is too busy with the back and forth of his pings to notice when a small Florivan child scurries into the room and clambers up onto the stool on the other side of the instructor. They're wearing a soft cotton martial arts outfit sized for a human six-year-old, modified to accommodate their second pair of arms and long tufted tail. The white cloth of their top and belt stands out against their silver-striped dark teal skin.

Once they're comfortably perched on the tall barstool, the Florivan child pulls the instructor's oversized uniform jacket on over their upper pair of arms. They have to push the too-long sleeves back considerably for their slender four-fingered hands to show. That done, they tap the instructor lightly on the shoulder.

The instructor turns to them with a smile, setting a hand between their large catlike ears and briefly ruffling their chin-length locks of silver hair.

The child looks up at him with three wide golden eyes and smiles back, leaning into his touch with a momentary hint of a cat-like purr.

"So, Cinna-bun, how were lessons?"

"Okay." The Florivan child's voice bears the signature bell-like after-tones of their species, light and clear like a small set of wind chimes in a mild breeze.

"Just okay?"

"Yeah..." The Florivan child's tail waves slowly under the too-long jacket, although only the silver tuft on the tip of it shows. "Cousin Indigo said to tell you they want to talk about stuff when they're done with the rest of Sky and Storm's lessons tonight."

"Ah. Okay, then." The instructor nudges the plate over closer to the Florivan child and then sets one of the still-steaming mugs where they can reach it without having to stand up on the stool.

The Florivan child brightens and takes one of the tea cakes, leaving a little pile of powdered sugar behind.

The instructor does the same, washing it down with a sip of his tea.

The Florivan child turns their lower two eyes to the viewport, the third one still focused on the instructor. "Did I miss seeing the ship?"

"Yeah."

The Florivan child nibbles on their cookie some more. "Oh. I was hoping I'd get to wave at them."

"I watched them for you."

"Thanks. Do you think Äiti and Entile River will get to stay longer next time?"

"I hope so." The instructor makes a vague gesture at the viewport. "Maybe *next* time your mother will be able to persuade Ranger headquarters to schedule things better so they're not leaving in the middle of the night unexpectedly like this."

The Florivan child nods and reaches for the tea mug. Taking a sip, they look around the instructor at the cadet. After a moment, they tilt their head curiously to one side. "Who's your new friend, Dad?"

On the other side of the instructor, the cadet is still engrossed in his messages and has yet to look up.

"Astrophysics cadet..." The officer pauses, stifling a chuckle. "You know, Cinna-bun, I don't think I ever caught his name? We just happened to meet while I was waiting for you."

"Oh. Does *he* like tea cookies?"

"I'm not sure, kitten, but I suppose you could ask."

The Florivan child nods with a very intentional seriousness.

The instructor watches with amusement as they climb down off of their stool, still wearing his jacket, and then back up on top of the empty one beside the cadet.

Once perched there, the Florivan child looks expectantly at the cadet.

The cadet is in the middle of tapping some sort of message out on his holoscreen.

The Florivan child waits impatiently.

After a minute or so, the cadet finishes with whatever he was typing and looks up. He turns to the instructor. "I'm sorry, sir... did you say something?"

The instructor shakes his head, chuckling. "Not to *you*, cadet, no."

The Florivan child reaches up now and taps the cadet on the shoulder. The cadet startles and nearly falls off of his barstool. Catching himself, he whirls around and finds himself face to face with a set of three adorably eager golden eyes.

"Hi! I'm Ocean! Do you like tea cakes?"

"I... um... Well. Hello, yes, why?"

The Florivan child waves excitedly towards the instructor, who stifles a laugh and slides the plate down to them. They pluck two tea cakes off the plate, one in each of their upper hands, and hold one out to the cadet.

The cadet hesitates for a moment and then accepts it. "... Thank you."

The Florivan child gives him an incredibly pleased grin and sets about munching on the cookie remaining in their hand. "Do you have a name?"

"Um... Well. Yes, of course. It's Tim."

"Okay!" With that, the Florivan child picks up the plate with the last cookie. Holding it carefully in their upper pair of hands, they scramble down from the stool.

The cadet turns around to watch as the Florivan child scurries around him and then climbs back up to sit on the stool next to the instructor, where they set the plate down triumphantly.

"I found out what his name is, Dad!" The Florivan child picks their cup of tea back up and takes a sip.

"Oh, *did* you?" The instructor, for his part, is doing a good job of not bursting out laughing. He does stroke his beard in mock contemplation, though—and in doing so, covers most of the wide grin he's wearing with his hand.

The Florivan child nods solemnly over their tea, although their large catlike ears are still perked up and their tail is swishing excitedly beneath the borrowed jacket. "I did! He's a *Tim*!"

"Great *Scott*, I never would have guessed! Good job." The instructor ruffles the Florivan child's hair again and nudges the plate towards them. "Last one's yours, Cinna-bun."

"No, Dad, I *counted*. That one's yours."

"Is it?"

The Florivan child rolls their third eye with a smile and holds up five fingers between their two lower hands so they can fold each one down as they explain. "There were *five*. That's two for me and two for you—and one to share with Tim! And *you* only took *one*. So this is yours." They push the plate back in front of the instructor.

"So it is, then." The instructor picks up the last tea cake, then looks back to the Florivan child with a smirk. "Want half of it?"

"Yes, please!"

The instructor breaks the tea cake in two pieces, sending a poof of powdered sugar up into the air. He hands the larger piece to the Florivan child before popping the rest into his mouth and washing it down with the last of his tea.

The Florivan child giggles and does the same with their portion.

The cadet has been staring at the two of them the whole time. He's about to ask a question when his pocket com begins pinging again. He scrambles to tap back through the holoscreen menu to see the new messages. His eyes widen considerably when he reads them. He blinks rapidly and then looks to the instructor again. "I don't know how they knew, sir... but they just asked if I wanted any help with arranging things for when I ask her."

The instructor halfway grins at him. "Well, then. There's hope for you yet, I'd say."

"Sir?"

"Or do you consider that offer of theirs bad news?"

"Oh, no, sir, it's..." the cadet pauses, a soft hint of a smile showing for the first time since he sat down. "Well. It's good, I think."

The instructor dusts the remaining powdered sugar off of his hands and stands up. "Glad to hear it, cadet. Think about what I said, though, will you?"

"I will, sir."

"Good." The instructor gives the cadet a reassuring pat on the shoulder and then turns to the Florivan child and offers a hand to help them down from the stool. "Come on, kitten, we'd best get a move on."

The Florivan child's ears perk up excitedly. "Judo time?"

"Yep. We have ukemi to practice."

"Fall breaks *again*?"

"Forward rolls and sides for sure."

"I *do* get to learn how to throw people like you and Äiti do eventually, right?"

The instructor chuckles. "Only after you learn the basics, Cinna-bun. If you're going to join Major Norton's beginner's class next month, you need to be ready to take falls without breaking an arm or three. Your Entile River would *never* let me hear the end of it if you got hurt."

The Florivan child seems satisfied with this answer. They take hold of the instructor's hand and follow him for a few steps before pausing to turn and wave at the cadet. "Goodnight, Tim!"

The cadet turns and waves back. He still looks perplexed, but the Florivan child's sheer precociousness seems to have won him over.

Soon, the cadet is the only patron left in the bar at all. He taps a few more messages back and forth on his holoscreen while he finishes the last of his drink. Before he leaves to seek his bed, he spends a long time sitting there alone, looking out at the view.

The planet continues to swirl with clouds of green and amber gas. Another moon rises over the horizon, a pale blue and grey orb set like a perfect sea glass marble against the star-studded black velvet of the expanse of space.

Somewhere on that moon, another pair of cadets is sitting on top of a large boulder near their classmates' campfire and looking up at the planet and the stars. The point of lights that is the Alpha Centauri-New West Space Station seems to sparkle in the desert twilight as it crosses the sky.

One of them, a Florivan, twitches an ear at a soft melodic ping and slips a bright blue hand into their jacket to withdraw a small silver device. They flip open the holoscreen just long enough to read the message that's just appeared and tap back a speedy response.

"What's that all about, then?" The human beside them asks, brushing some of her stray curls out of her face, "You've had pings flying around on delay for an *hour* now."

"Oh, just someone I needed to clear the air with, that's all."

"You're *scheming* something, Lazuli, aren't you?"

"Oh, no. Not me... at the moment... technically... but if someone else was, I might be involved."

"Well?" The human nudges her friend playfully. "Are you going to tell me about it?"

"Oh... You'll find out soon enough." The Florivan grins and sets one of their upper arms around her shoulders, taking on a pointedly conspiratorial tone. "So, Julietta... remind me again what your opinions about *flowers* are?"

✶ The End ✶

CHARACTERS APPEARING IN *THE VIEW FROM A DISTANCE*

The following list of characters is divided by species and arranged in order of their appearance in the narrative. Only characters with significant "speaking roles" have been detailed here. All others present are listed as a group for the reader's reference; characters who are mentioned but do not appear are not included.

Humans

TIM DALTON
He/him. First-year Astrophysics Cadet, Alpha Centauri-New West Space Service Academy.

GEORGE BARKER
He/Him. Lead Tactical Piloting Instructor, Alpha Centauri-New West Space Service Academy. Adoptive father of **Ocean Merlani.**

JULIETTA PETERSON
She/her. First-year Astral Navigation Cadet, Alpha Centauri-New West Space Service Academy.

Florivans

OCEAN MERLANI BARKER-HÄMÄLAINEN

They/them. Also known as "Cinnabun." Adopted kitten of **George Barker.**

LAZULI TERYL

They/them. Third-year Quantum Space Drive Engineering Cadet, Alpha Centauri-New West Space Service Academy.

Fox in the Cave

★ A Strange Space™ Short Story ★

To the friends I've found along the way.

"*WHY, YES, FOXY, the intercom is working! Will you look at that? How unusual. We've only been using it ever since we left Central.*"

David rolled his eyes and switched over to the inter-ship radio. Intercom static only made the annoying tone of his training partner's voice more grating. "Shuttle twelve calling in, Central—all shuttle main systems ready to go; waiting for Quantum Space Drive checks to verify."

"*Status confirmed, Cadet Foxbury; standing by for final verification.*"

David switched back to intercom, not bothering to hide his irritation anymore. "Could you just for *once* in your life be serious about your systems check?"

"What's there to say? Everything's golden down here! Let's get this over with."

David groaned. It was going to be one of *those* days, apparently.

"The checklist is there for a *reason*, Cobalt Mereday. Use it, would you?"

"Fine, fine, Foxy, whatever you say. Proceed with your checklist."

"Finally. Drive bay door seals?"

"Engaged; inner layer's showing green. Door latch was a little sticky, nothing major. I'm all locked in down here."

David made a note on his secondary checklist for maintenance to review later. "Drive controls?"

"Heh. All set and ready to dip into the Strange!"

"Internal artificial gravity system?"

"Floaty!"

"Cobalt."

"Fine. Disengaged. Turned it off as soon as I got the door to cooperate."

"Quantum Space analysis computer?"

"Can't you tell that's working from your end? I mean, you have an interface to it and everything—"

"—It's on your checklist, Cobalt."

"Can't see why, but fine—green lights all across. Happy now?"

"Marginally." David was sure from his talks with the other Nav cadets that they couldn't *possibly* have this much trouble with their Florivan counterparts.

"You're really no fun today, Foxy, you know that?"

"I thought I told you to stop calling me that."

"Did you? I thought you <u>liked</u> your nickname and being treated like a Navigator."

"I am a Navigator, Cobalt."

"Not yet! And you're certainly not <u>mine</u>, so I have to call you something else, now, don't I?"

David absently rubbed at the bridge of his nose. A four-armed walking migraine, that's what he'd been assigned—not a training partner.

"Let's just finish the checklist, all right?" He readjusted his headset and switched to the Quantum Space adjusted channel he'd be using during the transit cycle. "Primary Nav-com?"

"I'm getting a bit of static, did you—"

A cacophony of ringing and feedback filled the shuttle until David found the short he'd somehow missed when he checked the system the first time and managed to shut it off. Silence re-established, he flipped back to the main intercom channel.

"Sorry about that. Try testing it from your end, will you?"

"My ear is going to be ringing for hours! If I find out you did that on purpose, Foxy..."

"Tech issue, Cobalt, unintentional."

"That's a really loud unintentional you've got there!"

An alert popped up on the holoscreen in front of David. "All right, we've got ten minutes before this thing starts. Give me your viewport confirmation over the earpiece so I can finish the checklist."

David couldn't make out the grumbling from among the static as everything switched over, but he had a feeling he didn't want to know what was being said. His shifts assisting the Commanders with the jumps out from Earth had been so much easier. Cobalt had been almost *cooperative* then.

"*Okay, Foxy, I've got you in my other ear now—try not to deafen me before we even get started.*" Their voice came through clear over his headset now.

The Nav-com channel was always clearer, though, as long as the tech held. If the two of them were on a proper starship doing this, David wouldn't have to bother with the shuttle's glitchy mains to begin with. That'd be someone *else's* checklist.

"I'll do my best, Cobalt. Hopefully the tech doesn't have any more surprises for us today. Viewport?"

"*Shutter's open, no glitches. You got the Nav port open still?*"

David looked up at the main viewport. Shuttering it was the last thing on his checklist. "Yeah, I was just about to close it."

"*Take a good look first, Foxy—they've set us down in a great spot. You can probably see both galaxies from your end, not just black and Central's nest hiding most of the stars.*"

"You'll get the better view soon enough." David tapped back into the radio channel. "Central, this is shuttle twelve: Drive checks verified, we're ready to go on your mark."

"*Status confirmed, Cadet. Stand by for orders.*"

"Standing by, Central." David switched out of radio mode and turned his attention back to the annoying voice on his headset, glancing up through the viewport at the expanse of deep space.

"*Well? How's the view?*"

"...It's a nice one, you're right. Pretty collection of stars."

"You really need to learn to describe things better than that, Foxy."

"I'll leave the describing to you."

It *was* a nice view, though. Compelling, even.

Annoying as they were, Cobalt was usually right when it came to opinions on stellar vistas—and the Academy's Sub-Solar training ground had nothing but choice ones, placed as it was directly 'below' the rest of the system's orbits. From his current position, David could see the stars of both the greater Milky Way and Andromeda cutting through the void.

He didn't have words for it the way his training partner did, though.

When they'd first arrived at Central two days ago, David had been sick of hearing the Florivan's voice over the headset and exhausted enough from drawing the last duty shift of the journey to want nothing more than to get to his bunk to catch some sleep. He didn't know how anyone could run Nav/Quan for full shifts—just the four hours at a time assisting his instructors had been exhausting.

Sleep had been forced to wait, though, because an equally exhausted Cobalt had insisted on dragging him up through the station before he ever found out where his bunk *was*. Cobalt hated him, but for some reason they'd been *determined* to be the one to show David his first view from Central. It couldn't have been from any one of the viewports they'd passed on the way, either—No! It *had* to be from the polyglass observation dome at the top of the whole place.

David had resented his training partner more with every additional ladder he had to climb.

Just when he'd had *enough* and was in the middle of telling them how pointless the whole endeavor had been, two pairs of four-fingered blue hands had reached down and pulled him into the dome from the last ladder tube and he was weightless and all the stars of the cosmos were stretching out around him.

He hadn't known the right words for it then, either.

Cobalt had filled the silence for him. Somehow, in their odd, nonsensical way, the troublesome alien knew *just* how to say what space made you feel when you were truly aware of being surrounded by it for the first time. It was the only conversation he'd ever had with them that didn't end in an argument of one kind or another.

A short-lived truce, granted, but it had been almost *nice* while it lasted.

David didn't have time to get caught up in the wonders of space today, though. He closed the viewport shutters.

"You have enough stars to get your bearings down there?"

"Yeah—better than last time I was out here, even. Once you have landmarks for me I'll be golden."

Last time, right, David thought.

This exercise was his first time running Nav on his own in interstellar space, but Cobalt had done all of this before. Childish, difficult, and given to flights of fancy even more than the average Florivan: Cobalt had been at the Academy longer than anyone in the Nav/Quan program. No partner they'd been offered could come close to handling Cobalt for two *months*, let alone the full two years that were required for a pair to graduate.

The going theory among the Astral Navigation cadets was that being assigned to David with no option to switch was Cobalt's punishment for driving so many other prospective Navigators crazy—at least one of them literally, if the rumors were true. The thing no one could figure out was what *David* had done to deserve the pairing.

He was a T12 primary, after all, and high classed across all his other assessment letters. The only thing marring David's transcript was that he'd missed most of his freshman year in the NavTech track and had to submit all of his assignments over the relays because his flight in from Mars had been re-routed through *Europa* to avoid a solar storm—which was hardly *his* fault. The Nav/Quan instructors had been willing to overlook that whole fiasco based on the potential they saw in him. They'd told him as much.

Cobalt must have been thinking about similar things, sitting in the silence of the shuttle on standby.

"Hey, Foxy, who knows? Maybe we'll get some new jumpers next year so we can be rid of each other."

"Wouldn't that be a breath of fresh air?"

"Agreed! You'd think they'd have noticed we have an established hatred going on here by now."

"The Commanders are trying to prove some sort of a point to you, I'm sure of it."

"Oh, probably <u>several</u> points, Foxy—and I don't agree with any of them."

"I'm sure you don't."

Over his headset, David could hear echoes of Cobalt drumming their fingers on something—probably the viewport's polyglass. *"All I'm saying... is that they're never going to let me have a new Nav cadet to work with until either you wash out or we have new folks to rotate with."*

They had a point. Since no new Florivan Quantum Space Drive Engineer cadets had signed to the Academy and Cobalt was the only one who hadn't already chosen their Astral Navigator, there hadn't been a need for any other new Nav cadets. A Nav/Quan pair stayed together for *life* once they graduated, meaning any human who failed to become someone's counterpart after a year left as 'Nav certified' only. The instructors had promised that David would be allowed to stay an extra year, given the circumstances—but only if he didn't wash out like so many of Cobalt's other training partners had.

David was determined not to be the next to give up, though, even if he *was* stuck training with the most annoying person in the history of star travel for the moment.

"So?"

"So... we might as well try to win this capture the flag nonsense so they'll get off our case in the meantime. Deal?"

"Deal." David chuckled. It was an unexpected olive branch, but he'd take it. "Why does the idea of *you* calling something nonsense send chills down my spine?"

Any response Cobalt might have made was cut off by an announcement from Central coming in and overriding the shuttle's intercom. The uniformed visages of the Nav/Quan instructors filled the holoscreen: one human man—tall, pale, and bald, with a salt-and-pepper beard; one Florivan—four-armed, three-eyed, and silver-striped blue, with a long, complicated braid of silver hair coiled around their catlike ears.

"Cadets! Commander Cerulean and I have placed six marker buoys for each of you! Find the best path available to

reach and tag each marker before returning to Central. Try not to get lost—I've got a bet going with Sec/Tac that I won't have to hunt anyone down this time." Commander Potts had been a darter pilot in the Sol Coalition Defense Fleet before he became an Astral Navigator. David assumed *that* was where he'd picked up the eccentric streak.

"*Remember, Navigators, the boundaries of your fields are marked on your charts based on the starting point we've placed you in. Keep in your fields so you don't interfere with each other's paths.*" Commander Cerulean blinked their golden eyes in sequence and grinned. "*I'm awarding points for style, too, since most of you have done this before.*"

"*Good luck, Cadets! Make us proud!*"

The holoscreen flipped back to his usual readouts. David pulled up the last of the star charts he'd need once they started making jumps.

"*Well, now, that's every bit the encouraging speech I was expecting! You ready to go, Foxy?*"

"All set for Quantum Space jump; engage Drive in ten."

"*Ha! Ten it is then. Which marker do you want first? Ten... nine...*"

David looked over the list of coordinates. "Looks like we've got one close by; once you take us in it should be at 4 by 4E and 9, in line with the Andromeda edge."

"*Six—gotcha on that one, Foxy! Big rock by the river—one, zero...*"

The whole shuttle seemed to vibrate around David for the few seconds it took to transition into the veiled dimension of Quantum Space—what Cobalt's people simply called 'the Strange.' Other than the dimmed-down blue lighting, nothing really changed from his perspective.

Only the computer readouts indicated that the shift had occurred.

Five full minutes of silence ticked over on his display while he made conversions from his list of coordinates to have hexadecimal points ready to call down when Cobalt asked. All the two of them had to do now was work together so they could jump back out at the right place to tag the marker.

David wondered how long they were going to take this time. He couldn't ask, though. He had to wait for Cobalt to call up to him. That was the first thing all Nav cadets learned: Don't interrupt at the beginning of a jump, or at the end, because your counterpart has to concentrate to get the Drive stable so you won't drop out in the wrong place.

Another two minutes passed.

Time didn't always flow right in Quantum Space. David sometimes felt like the waiting was twice as long as his display showed. *No wonder this place drives people insane*, he thought—and not for the first time.

Finally, Cobalt's voice rang out through his headset again.

"All right, Foxy! I've got us up a tree at the edge of the valley, ready for your landmarks. What do you have for me for North?"

"8 by 12D and 5F max forward."

"All right, northern mountain plotted in. Give me the rest in sequence?"

David obliged, reading off the other three coordinates he'd selected from the list of points designating the confines of their training space. Quantum Space either didn't have dimension at all, or it had too many varieties of it—possibly both. Either way, it didn't cooperate with the usual ways of figuring out where you were in the universe. Somehow, Cobalt would plug all of the coordinates into the Drive in a way that could get the shuttle to wherever they wanted to go without crossing the space between the points.

No amount of technical papers David had ever read could even explain how the Drive worked. Some of them *tried*, but those tended to end without accomplishing more than coining new words to describe what little was already known. David was *sure* the best Navigators got told more of the reality of it, eventually. Like a lot of things where Florivans were involved, it seemed that this was information that had to be *earned*. David had no idea what one had to do to earn it—he'd asked, but even Commander Potts had just chuckled and told him to be patient.

What David *did* know was that the combination of flux and physical impossibility involved in reconciling the two dimensions was the main reason Quantum Space Drive Engineers had to be Florivan. No human mind could handle it, and Quantum Space destroyed AI systems. A human couldn't even stand in an active Drive bay to observe—at least, not if they wanted to be alive and sane at the end of the day.

Florivans, though, were halfway native to Quantum Space. What few of them remained in the galaxy had gladly given the Drive to humanity, but they still had to be the ones running it.

"Okay, cardinals in. Can I get a sky and a sea floor?"

Cobalt always gave him planetside terms when they were calibrating. David himself thought it was a bit of unnecessary fancy. Commander Cerulean had used the proper Nav terms during the training shifts on the way to Central, so he was starting to think it was just more of Cobalt's nonsense.

"Let's go with C by 58 and 2D for max up and 6 by 20 and 0 for max down."

"Going for those style points, Foxy?"

"You wanted to win, didn't you?"

Cobalt's laugh was like wind chimes ringing in the breeze. *"Style it is! All right, Foxy, where's my tree?"*

"Starting point is 0 by EE and 4."

"You said the first boulder goes at… 4 by 4E and 9?"

"Right. And Sol is your primal like always. That should be everything now."

"It's a nice bit of the Strange to wander in, that's for sure. The river looks swifter than I remember it. A bit deep, too—if we weren't trying to win I'd look for a pond for a swim instead."

"Cobalt, don't start with the nonsense again."

"You wanted style points, didn't you? I'll tell you when I reach the boulder."

The routine was simple once they'd tagged the first marker.

Jump to Quantum Space.

Recalibrate with Cobalt where they were; wait for them to move the shuttle to the next marker.

Jump out.

Tag the marker.

Confirm location; start again.

David was surprised to see that the two of them were actually making decent time with the first five markers. Usually in simulations, something would throw the process off and he'd be stuck waiting what felt like *hours* for Cobalt to respond to his calls.

Cobalt was being efficient today. That in itself was almost unsettling. David decided it must be because they were familiar with the training ground.

"*—All right, that's enough!*" Static over his headset almost drowned out Cobalt's voice.

What's gone wrong now? David wondered as he swiftly double-checked the readings on the interface with Cobalt's earpiece. *I thought I fixed that thing!*

"Repeat that, Cobalt? I'm getting interference."

"*Do you have numbers for—storm clouds I keep having to outrun? This latest one is really—on my nerves.*"

"Storm clouds? Clarify that, I didn't have any zones marked that I haven't already given you."

"*Big dark broody clouds—lightning—condensing. I may have—take us back to Normal—catches me. Where—about—15 by EF—?*"

The static only got worse, no matter what David did from his end to clear up the channel. This had *never* happened in any of the simulations. Unexpected phenomena in Quantum Space happened sometimes, but there was no way of knowing whether this would be the sort that destroyed ships.

Better to play it safe, David thought.

"You cut out there, but I think I get you. Whatever's going on, we don't need to be in it."

"*You and—understatements—*"

David double-checked his charts. *Oh, that's not good either.*

"Don't disengage the Drive yet! Cobalt, can you hear me?"

"*—Clear—kind of busy—running away from—can I jump?*" The static warped their voice. It almost sounded like they were having trouble breathing.

"Listen, Cobalt, your 'storm' has us drifting on the computer readouts. If we come out at 15 by EF and anything between 1 and *F8*, we're not just out of bounds, we're in the middle of a debris field."

"*—Try best—not much choice—jump—*"

The shuttle started shaking violently. *That* had never happened in simulations before either.

"Cobalt? What in the *stars* is going on down there?" David was frantically running checks. Whatever was causing the shaking was now affecting other systems. "Answer me, Cobalt Mereday! I need to know where we are—"

Alarms blared from the quantum analysis computer and the proximity alert system all at once.

The shaking stopped with one last sharp jerk, sending David flying across the Nav compartment and into the bulkhead on the other side.

"*—Twelve, please respond!*"

David opened his eyes at the sound of shouting from the inter-ship radio. He didn't know how long he'd been unconscious. Everything was dark save for the red glow from the emergency lights and the flashing communications panel.

He pulled himself up to the chair at the console. It wasn't easy. His head was pounding and his right ankle disagreed with all forms of locomotion. He hoped it was only sprained.

"Foxbury here, Central, this is shuttle twelve."

"We've been trying to reach you for an hour now. You're not in your assigned field and we can't find you on the scanners. What's your status?"

"I'm not sure where we jumped out. Probably around... hmm... 15 by EF and something? That's the last mark I remember. My main systems are dark, but life support and gravity seem to be fine for the moment."

"What happened? Your field wasn't anywhere near those coordinates."

"Something went wrong in the last jump—Cobalt called it a storm?—I couldn't understand them through the interference."

Right, David thought, *Cobalt*.

"Just a minute, Central, I need to try getting through to them. They may have a better idea where we are." He switched over to the main intercom. "Hey, Cobalt? What's your status down there?"

No response—just static and alarm echoes.

It took David a lot longer than he'd have liked to find where his headset had landed and link back into the Nav-com system.

"Respond, Cobalt Mereday, will you? Central's trying to find us."

The main channel was out. The secondary didn't give him static, just an odd electronic hum.

Something was definitely wrong.

He'd have to go check on them.

David tapped back into the radio. "Central, I can't get a response from them at all."

"You're breaking up, Cadet Foxbury, please repeat."

Just what he needed: more interference.

"Central, I can hear you. I'm putting you on my headset—I can't raise Cobalt from here so I'm going down to them."

"Standing by."

David got up and limped over to the ladder that led down from the Nav compartment. Their training shuttle was modified from the sort used to ferry cargo and people between ships and surface—he'd thought it cramped before, but now it felt enormous.

He slipped halfway down the ladder and ended up sprawled on the floor for a few moments while he caught his breath.

"Can you hear me, Cadet Foxbury?" A different, but familiar wind-chime toned voice replaced that of the Central dispatcher.

"Loud and clear, Commander Cerulean."

"Good. We've got a fix on your position now, but I can't get close with a tow 'til you shut down your Drive. You're flickering in the thickest part of the debris field."

"What do you mean?" David asked through a wince.

"You're drifting in and out of the Strange. Cobalt probably lost consciousness before they could complete the jump."

"So this is what happens when the Drive shuts down incorrectly, then? Or are we going through something new?" David didn't really expect an answer, but the Commander's voice was a welcome distraction from the pain he felt limping through the empty compartment where passengers would usually be. *Maybe it's not just the ankle?* he wondered, *cracked ribs would make sense...*

"Not unheard of, but quite rare—and dangerous. We're bringing a tow shuttle down to get you, but I might have problems pulling you all the way one side or the other because of the debris around you."

"Nothing's going to be easy today, is it?"

"I'm afraid not, Cadet."

David made it to the other end of the compartment and looked over the system check lights around the heavily reinforced Drive bay door—which in any other shuttle of this kind would only have led to a cargo bay. Everything looked to be running correctly still, except for the engagement indicator light, which kept blinking on and off at random. He thought it looked like some of the blinks were getting further apart—something like thirty seconds for the longest ones.

Maybe the Drive's stabilizing on its own?

He pounded loudly on the steel door. "Cobalt! Answer if you can hear me!"

No response.

David tried getting through to them over the headset again, only to be answered by the same electronic hum.

"Commander, I'm outside the Drive bay now and they're still not answering me. Indicator lights match up with what you're saying. I'll have to go in and get them."

"I caught most of that, Cadet. Better you wait for me. You know the risks if you're exposed to the Strange or any miasmas that are still in there."

"I was out for an hour, right? Longer, maybe, if this 'flickering' effect is distorting time for the shuttle?"

"That's correct..."

David dug through the maintenance equipment box beside the door. He found a set of analysis specs at the bottom and put them on. The lenses wouldn't be the *best* shielding, but if he remembered correctly from his studies, they might buy him a few extra seconds to get in and drag his training partner out.

"Cobalt's probably had it worse than me getting thrown around in there. If they're hurt badly enough that they're not responding, by the time you get here it might be too late. The way I see it, I don't have much choice *but* to go in, Commander."

The two of them might have had a well-established mutual hatred, but that didn't mean David could let the irritating Florivan *die* if there was something he could do about it.

There was a silence, then David heard a deep sigh over the radio.

"I'm not going to be able to get you to wait, am I?"

"No, you're not." David started disengaging the overrides on the door's electronic seals. There was a triple-redundancy system he had to get through to be able to open it from the outside, all designed to keep any

Quantum Space miasmas from leaking into the rest of the craft. "Besides, if we have to shut the Drive down so you can get us out of this mess, Cobalt has to be the one to do that—unless you want to try talking *me* through it before I go blind and crazy in there?"

"*You're partially correct about that...*" David heard a distinctively resigned sigh over the radio before Commander Cerulean spoke again. "*Very well, Cadet, I can see you have considered the situation and its risks. We've switched you over to a Strange-filtered channel; you're coming in much clearer now. I'll stay on the com with you as long as I can. I don't doubt you'll need my guidance once you breach the door.*"

"Thanks, Commander. I'm ready to open it now."

David had been watching the indicator light carefully. If he went in just as it switched to show Normal, he'd hopefully have a full thirty seconds to get to Cobalt before the full effects of Quantum Space hit him. Assuming, of course, that he could get there quickly while putting as little weight as possible on his injured ankle, that *might* be just enough time.

It took him three painful attempts to get the last physical latching mechanism disengaged. Somewhere in the back of his mind, David remembered Cobalt saying it was sticking. That felt like an age ago.

"All right, I'm going in."

"*Good luck, Cadet.*"

On.

Off.

Wait for it... now!

David flung the door open as quickly as he could.

It was only after he'd taken his lunge in that he remembered that the artificial gravity field in the Drive bay had been turned *off* at the beginning of the jump cycle. He realized what was happening just in time to catch on to one of the bits of tech attached to the ceiling before he could impact with it and go flying back in a different direction.

Fortunately, microgravity training was required for Nav cadets. Equally fortunate was the fact that all of his weight was no longer on his injured ankle and he could move more freely. Weightlessness was unexpected, but it was something he could work with.

Five seconds gone. David took stock of the situation.

The Drive bay was lit only by the red warning screens of the various bits of computer tech scattered along its walls and ceiling and the dim glow of stars outside the viewport. Cobalt was floating as a crumpled ball near the far corner of the room: all four arms curled inward, knees protectively up to their chest, long silver-tufted tail wrapped around catlike. Their hair had escaped from its usual bun and was floating all around them as a long shimmering silver mess obscuring their face. The three small gold hoop earrings they always wore along the edge of their left ear glinted in the scattered light.

Cobalt wasn't moving, and clearly hadn't in some time, since they were floating in place with no signs of lingering motion to carry them around. David realized now that he would have slammed right into them at full speed if he hadn't caught on to the ceiling when he did.

Fifteen seconds.

David pushed off against the ceiling at an angle that would carry him over to his unconscious training partner. He caught Cobalt's shoulder as gently as he could while his momentum drove them both to the corner, where he grabbed hold of a raised place on the wall with his free hand.

"Commander, I have them!" David shifted positions so he could get a better look at Cobalt's condition. He brushed their hair out of the way and checked for a pulse. It was weak and irregular, even for a Florivan, but still there. That was a relief.

"How are they, Cadet?"

"They're alive, thank the stars, but barely breathing. Looks like there's bleeding from their ears and nose, probably more but the light's weird and it's hard to tell." David remembered well enough from his required first aid workshops that neither of those was a good place to see the inky blue spots of blood pooling against someone's skin. In microgravity, too, with the strange ways liquids pooled together and stuck to surfaces instead of falling away, it was a miracle that Cobalt *was* still breathing at all.

"Do you see any other injuries?"

"Not yet." David tried to wake his training partner as gently as he could. "Cobalt, can you hear me?"

Twenty-five seconds.

The unconscious Florivan shifted positions slightly, curling up just a bit tighter. Something was off about the way the light was hitting them, but David was too distracted to think of why that might be.

"Are they responding to you at all, Cadet?"

"Maybe? I don't know, I'll try—"

Flash!

Light burst behind David's eyes.

Deafening colors swirled all around him.

He squeezed his eyes shut. *Even with the specs,* he thought, *better not to look unless it's absolutely necessary.* He tried to focus on counting the time that passed.

Ten seconds. Twenty. Thirty. Thirty-five.

Flash!

He was still in the shuttlecraft's converted Drive bay, holding Cobalt's unconscious tangle of limbs close with one hand and the wall with the other. A few stray locks of their hair had floated in front of his face.

David did his best to shake off the afterimages. The whole of his vision was doubled with bright tracings of the wrong colors. The light was playing tricks on him now. It looked so much like there was a strobe somewhere playing just over Cobalt's body, but he couldn't identify the light source.

"Great... just what I need: hallucinations."

"Focus on my voice, Cadet Foxbury." Commander Cerulean sounded concerned now, in a way David had never heard before. *"Where are you? What are you seeing?"*

"Looks like Cobalt's—hang on a moment, Commander." David shifted positions so that when he pushed off from the corner, he would be able to catch onto the hand rail by the door frame without causing them further injury. "It kind of looks like they're flashing? Like we're under strobes? The lights in here are still—shouldn't be shadows like that—I'm sure it's just my eyes."

David pushed against the corner, sending the two of them floating across the Drive compartment.

Flash!

Swirls of green and orange swept over him just before he managed to close his eyes again. It didn't cut it all out, but he was glad for the specs. He could hear Commander Cerulean echoing in his headset. The characteristic bell-like after tones of the Florivan voice cut through the colors with surprising clarity.

"That's not a hallucination, Cadet."

There was a smell now. *Citrus?* No—it was a darker sort of vegetal than that.

David felt as if he was still floating under the same momentum, although with a *thickness* to the air around him that shouldn't have been there. He reached out, hoping the hand bar would be in the right place if the next shift ever came.

Flash!

Somehow, David's hand caught hold of the rail beside the door frame even before he realized it was there to grab. He clung onto it and took a deep breath in hopes he could clear some of the miasma out of his lungs. The air helped a little.

David opened his eyes. All he had to do now was pull himself around to the other side of the door, Cobalt in tow, and try not to drop them when the artificial gravity field took hold.

He forgot all about his injured ankle until the moment the full weight of both himself and his unconscious training partner was placed upon it. The ankle quite rightly buckled under all that, sending David to the floor with a sharp jolt of pain. Cobalt landed on top of him.

Yeah, he thought, *definitely a cracked rib in there somewhere.*

Flash!

Too many colors. Eyes closed.

Salt water. *An ocean?*

"Cadet Foxbury? Can you hear me?" Commander Cerulean's voice was faraway now, garbled by the salt in his ears.

David tried counting seconds again, but the pain in his ankle and ribs was too distracting to keep track. Something was making his skin prickle, too—all static electricity and lemon juice.

Flash!

When he had caught his breath, David gently rolled Cobalt over onto the floor beside him. He checked their pulse and breathing again. Both were the same as before: thready, but still there. David couldn't ignore that the same impossible strobe effect was *still* playing over their body even in the brighter lights of the outer compartment.

"Commander?" He reached up to readjust his headset so he could hear them again.

"Yes, Cadet, I can hear you. What's happening?"

"I just got Cobalt out of the Drive bay and the light still looks all strobe-y when it hits them. I... I really don't trust my eyes right now. How *isn't* this a hallucination?"

"They're flickering. I was afraid of this."

"I have no idea what that means." David struggled to his feet, leaning heavily on his uninjured leg. He tapped through the controls for the door until it started to slide shut. "I'm sealing off the Drive bay now before we get pulled in again—"

"—*Cadet, listen to me. There's no point wasting time trying to seal the door. Once you breached the seals, the whole shuttle was drawn in and flooded with lingering miasmas. You'll have to get through to Cobalt somehow while you wait for me.*"

"I don't understand, Commander."

"*It's the only way they'll be able to shut down the Drive. Even though you've got them out, you're still going to be shifting in and out of the Strange with them—eventually the bit of Normal space left inside the shuttle is going to collapse entirely.*"

"I *really* don't understand."

Nonetheless, David went back over to where he'd left his training partner and knelt beside them. Cobalt looked incredibly fragile, even with the weird play of lights distorting everything. He could see bruises starting to form through the multitude of rips in their uniform. There was a large, charred-looking spot on the left side of their abdomen between their two sets of arms that he hadn't noticed before. He gently moved their tangle of limbs out of the way before he inspected under the torn fabric. There were scorch marks on their skin, but no blood.

David did his best to gently maneuver Cobalt into a position where they could at least have an easier time breathing. He didn't like that shallow, raspy sound, assuming it was real. He ended up sitting against the nearest bulkhead with their head and shoulders propped up against half his lap over his folded uninjured leg. Leaving his other one stretched out hurt less.

"*You'll need to call them back out.*"

"Commander, I'm not sure if you've noticed, but Cobalt doesn't listen to me when they're *awake*, half the time!"

Flash!

Brilliant yellow fireworks.

David couldn't tell if his eyes were closed or not anymore.

The lights and colors shifting around him as he kept hold of Cobalt's unconscious form were the same either way.

"You have to <u>try</u>. You're the only anchor Cobalt has right now."

"This makes no sense, you realize that?"

"You're halfway in the Strange. Sense is different here."

David couldn't tell if the flashes were growing longer or shorter apart. *What's the record for human exposure survival?* he wondered, *six minutes continuous? Eight? How long are these adding up to?*

"How would I even—"

"—You're my Mereday's Navigator, even if it's just for training. They're tuned to your voice."

"If by 'tuned' you mean *hates me*—"

Flash!

Normal?

David's eyes felt like they'd been rubbed with sand when he opened them.

"Listen to me, David. You don't have time to question this. They're caught halfway in the Strange—<u>you</u> have to get them to come out of it before we lose both of you. That's all you need to know. Let Mereday know that you're there. Talk to them. Call them back."

"How is that supposed to—"

"—Just do what you can!" He'd never heard that tone of desperation in Commander Cerulean's voice before. *"I'll be in position to jump to you soon. When you get pulled along,*

focus on this: You're in my caves facing the sunrise—I'll find you there, David, I promise."

"Caves?"

No response.

Okay, then, David thought, trying to process the conversation despite his growing headache from the lights and the pain in his ankle. *Call Cobalt out of the Strange. Somehow. None of this makes sense. Tuned to my voice? Caves and sunrises? Either I'm losing my mind or Commander Cerulean already lost theirs.*

Flash!

Clouds.

Lightning.

The taste of roses and blood.

Flash!

Silence punctuated by raspy breathing.

"You know, Cobalt," David said, squinting down at them, "I think we've blown our chances of winning. They'll probably wash us both out after this... assuming we survive. Not the way I wanted to get out of being stuck with you, really."

David thought he saw Cobalt's central eye twitch for a moment without opening. *That's something, at least! Talk to them, huh?*

"Cobalt, can you hear me? Commander Cerulean is coming to find us. They said I have to call you back so you can shut down the Drive—not that *that* makes *any* sense to me at all." He paused to brush a stray lock of hair back out of Cobalt's face. "They said we're in a cave, if that means anything to you? I may have hallucinated that, though—it sounds like some of your landmarking nonsense. What does a cave and sunrise have to do with finding us, anyway?"

Flash!

Dripping water.

Darkness.

Each slow drip echoed around David.

He tried to count the drips.

One. Two... Five... Twelve...

Each drip felt as if it fell further and further apart.

Twenty... Thirty-eight... Eighty...

Flash!

David squeezed his eyes open and shut a few times to try and even out the double-vision. There were colors moving in his peripherals that shouldn't have been there.

I can't believe I'm doing this. It makes no sense. He let out a frustrated groan that turned into a cough as a stray bit of sharp color found its escape from his lungs. *What was I even <u>thinking</u> going in after them?*

"Come on, Cobalt, respond. I have a feeling we're both done for if you can't wake up."

Flash!

Cold.

Damp.

Stretched-out melting pinks and purples turning golden in the distance.

This is insane, David thought, trying to focus on anything other than the sensations of a sunset sky filtering into his skin. *This whole thing is insane to the point of almost making sense.*

There was no way the Drive could do any of this. Not if it existed the way it'd been explained in NavTechs, at last.

It was so frustratingly nonsensical—just like Cobalt. David hated it.

Flash!

"Why don't they *train* us for this? I have no idea what's happening, Cobalt, but I'm sure you would—and you wouldn't tell me, would you? Another bit of Nav info I have to earn?" David paused for a moment and reached up to try to rub a bit of stray sunset out of his aching eyes. He couldn't, though; the specs were in the way and he didn't dare take them off. "What are you all so afraid of? That I'd not be able to handle it all at once and quit? Or break and stare into Quantum Space on *purpose*, like Johnson says happened to your first Navigator?"

Flash!

Impossible colors filled the air around him.

It hurt to breathe them in.

Somewhere far away David thought he heard the colors singing. Or screaming. Or both?

Flash!

"Well, *apparently*—" David coughed, his throat raw from that last lungful of color. "—I'm bouncing back and forth in Quantum Space with you now anyway." His head was pounding with a migraine the likes of which he'd never imagined could exist. The mounting frustration with the whole situation didn't help. "And if by some *miracle* I don't go insane... I'm done with waiting to be told! If we get out of this, Cobalt Mereday, I want *answers*."

Cobalt took a sudden deeper, gasping breath.

The 'flickering' slowed down.

By all the stars, thought David, blinking a few times to try to make sure he was seeing things correctly. *How is this working?*

Flash!

Commander Cerulean said to call to them—but how? David's thoughts circled endlessly around the puzzle of it all.

Flash!

The Commander called me Cobalt's anchor—but what does that even mean?

Flash!

Cobalt <u>hates</u> me—don't they?

Flash!

Dark, cold, damp, dripping water.

Warmth at his back, growing lightness.

The hallucinations were getting more vivid—or they were back in Quantum Space. David had lost track. He couldn't tell whether his eyes were open or closed at all anymore.

Enough of this!

"Cobalt Mereday, I swear!" David half-shouted, still hoarse from the colors he'd been breathing. "If we both survive this, you are going to find a *sensible* way to explain just what's going on even if I don't end up believing you. Now *come back to me!*"

Flash!

The flickering stopped.

A minute passed.

Two minutes. Five.

David realized his eyes were closed. They still *hurt*, but there was only a single steady source of light when he cracked them open briefly to check. He could feel the cold steel of the bulkhead at his back. This had to be the shuttle.

It's over? That <u>worked</u>?

No more flashes, no more flickering.

David opened his eyes fully. It *looked* like the shuttle he remembered. After a few moments of squinting in the glow of the overhead lighting, he cautiously took off the specs. The lenses were nearly opaque now, as if they'd been etched with fine sand. He rubbed at his eyes, but found no grit there to hold responsible for the lingering sensation of dryness. To his surprise, they weren't dry at all to his touch, but filled with unfelt tears which were now free to stream down his cheeks.

A familiar groan.

David looked down.

Cobalt's third eye cracked open just long enough to meet his gaze before closing tightly again.

"If your headache is *half* as bad as mine after all this..." David trailed off, leaning back against the wall and letting his eyes slip closed again. His eyelids were still filled with afterimages, but at least those didn't feel as real and painful anymore.

Everything *else* hurt, though. David was exhausted, too, even more than he'd been after their arrival at Central— more than he'd ever been in his life.

He felt one of the injured Florivan's hands haltingly moving around until it found his own. Four long slender fingers, cold to the touch, interlaced weakly with his.

David squeezed the hand lightly. "Yeah, Cobalt. Don't worry. I'm here."

He could feel himself starting to drift off. The light echoes in his eyes were giving way to darkness at the edges.

Cobalt's hand squeezed back.

Darkness and murky dreams of caves and flashes of light and snippets of Commander Cerulean's voice echoing around him.

"Made it—*yes*, Sarge, I *know* jumping through was risky, but we *both* know there was no way you could have gotten any closer between the debris and the miasma clouds."

Footsteps and cool alien hands on his shoulder and cheeks.

"Cadet Foxbury? *David*? Can you hear me?"

He could, all faraway and echoing and soft like windchimes, but he couldn't answer—it was just a dream. Hadn't he been back in the cave? Wasn't he still there?

"—Ah, yes, Sarge, I've got them both now. Mereday's stable, thank the stars—no condition to handle much more of this if I separate them—I'll fly us out where you can dock on, but it'll take a while to clear out all of the miasmas—"

More darkness.

David opened his eyes, then closed them again.
There was too much white. Too bright.
Everything hurt. He couldn't remember why.
I'm alone?
That wasn't right.

Where's—
Something sharp touched his arm.
He drifted back to the darkness.
To unknown dreams.
Alone.

✷

Wandering endless systems of caverns, he was carried on water dripping slowly through the stones.

Alone.

Without being or form.

Without name or memory.

Lost.

He was the water dripping down from above.

He was the water filtering through centuries of mineral formations.

He was the flow of the stream carving the caves ever deeper, down and down into the deep places where light had never touched.

The water flowed through the caves. The water dripped down from above. The water pooled on the edges of the stones and built them into cathedrals no eyes would ever see.

The water was time, and the water was timeless.

The cave was dark, and the cave was endless.

An eternity of water dripping, water flowing, had carved through stone and built stone again.

The labyrinth the water wove brought him ever deeper, ever further from whatever, *whoever*, he'd been before—if ever there had been a before, or another place at all.

Alone beyond being alone.

Lost beyond being lost.

Then, after ages of floating, a faraway voice.

"Foxy? Where are you?"

He knew that voice.

It called to him, echoing on the walls of the caves with an after-tone like clear bells ringing.

"Come on, Foxy, I know you're in here <u>somewhere</u>!"

He flowed toward the voice.

It was a long way to flow. He'd been so far in the depths, so deep in the darkness.

"Foxy? Come on, now, don't make this difficult."

He followed the path of the water that had carried him down. He flowed upwards along the stones after the echoes of the voice's call.

Hadn't the water come from somewhere?

The voice was waiting for him there. He needed to find the voice.

Finally, he was on the surface of a deep pool in a wide, high-ceilinged chamber of the caves, flowing in a shimmering reflection where before there had been none.

"Ah! There you are, Foxy! It took you long enough."

The voice had a form, shining in deep blue and silver light. It sat on a stone above his reflection, not reflecting itself but reaching out to touch the surface that contained him.

"You know, Foxy? I've decided I may not hate you all that much after all."

An alien hand twined with his.

Gently squeezing, it gave him substance again.

It pulled him up from the reflection, up from the water, up into *himself.*

"*Come back to me, David Foxbury.*"

The darkness gave way.

David's eyes fluttered open, then closed again.

Reality coalesced around him.

He was laying on a bed in some sort of medical observation room. He could smell faint traces of sanitizer spray and hear the steady beep and hum of some sort of monitoring equipment. He was *warm*, tucked up under a soft blanket. His head was aching with a migraine the likes of which he'd never felt before.

He wasn't alone. Someone was beside him, holding his hand.

David couldn't remember how he'd gotten there, or why. *The shuttle... something happened, and Cobalt had to jump us out... and then?* David tried to remember, but found nothing more than a strangely garbled collection of images and sounds that made no sense no matter what order he tried to put them into. *We crashed in a cave? No, that's not right.*

Thinking about it only made his headache worse.

Strangest of all, though, was the sight that met his eyes as they finally opened again found focus on the three weary, concerned golden ones just in front of him.

"... Cobalt?" David asked, barely able to manage a whisper.

The familiar Florivan lying curled on top of the blankets beside him let out a sigh of relief and squeezed the hand they were still holding fast between two of theirs.

"Don't worry, Navigator. I'm here."

David squeezed back with a weary smile.

✦ **The End** ✦

CHARACTERS APPEARING IN *FOX IN THE CAVE*

The following list of characters is divided by species and arranged in order of their appearance in the narrative. Only characters with significant "speaking roles" have been detailed here. All others present are listed as a group for the reader's reference; characters who are mentioned but do not appear are not included.

Humans

DAVID FOXBURY

He/him. Also known as "Foxy." First-year Astral Navigation Cadet, Earth Central Space Service Academy. Training partner of **Cobalt Mereday.**

JULIAN POTTS

He/Him. Also known as "Sarge." Lead Astral Navigation Instructor, Earth Central Space Service Academy. Counterpart to **Cerulean Mirawynd.**

Florivans

COBALT MEREDAY

They/them. Also known as "Coby." Quantum Space Drive Engineering and Biosciences Cadet, Earth Central Space Service Academy. Training partner of **David Foxbury.** Adopted kitten of **Cerulean Mirawynd.**

CERULEAN MIRAWYND

They/them. Also known as "Wyndi." Lead Quantum Space Drive Engineering Instructor, Earth Central Space Service Academy. Counterpart to **Julian Potts.** Adoptive parent of **Cobalt Mereday.**

Rooftops and Space Whales

✦ A Strange Space™ Short Story ✦

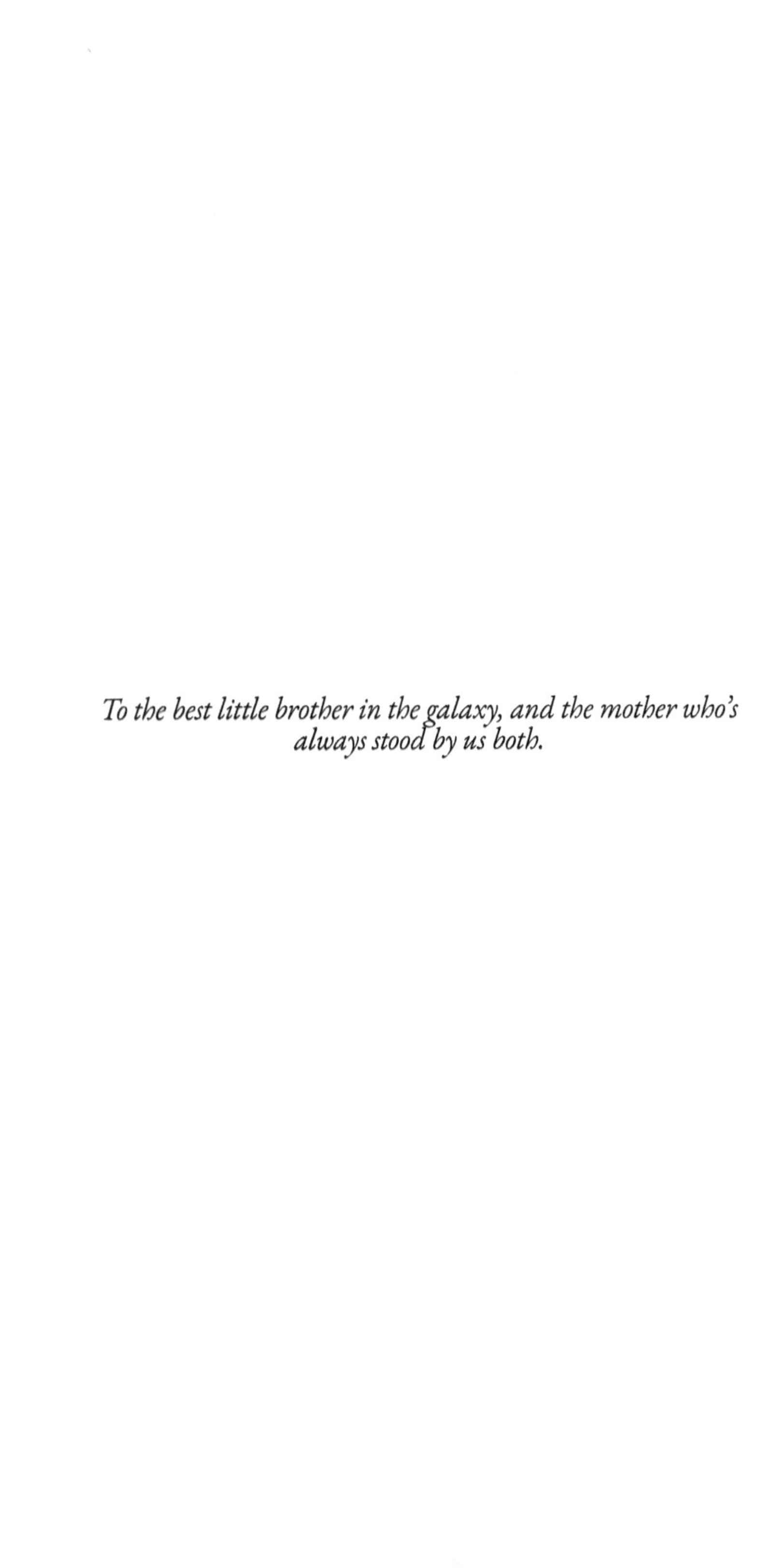

To the best little brother in the galaxy, and the mother who's always stood by us both.

S tars were hard to see at Isidis Dome City on Mars, even from the rooftop garden of Habitower 68-F. The light of the city below was too strong as it bounced off the inner force field of the atmosphere dome. Only the brightest of stars could compete with that.

Still, it was the best view available. More than that, it was better by far to be squinting up through three layers of auroras and shielding to see distant pinpoints of ancient light than to be stuck inside listening to the twins' bragging.

Newly nine-year-old Avis Foxbury flopped herself down onto the smooth white pebbles of the roof garden path and stared up at where the stars should have been. She was either fuming or trying to hold back tears, but even she couldn't have said which.

"Provisional class S8 with leadership potential—bleh! S for *stuck-up* and... and..." And Avis didn't know any other insults, now that she thought about it. She settled for blowing a rather wet raspberry up at the dome.

Tonight was *not* supposed to be about her cousins and their latest assessments. They weren't even supposed to be over for dinner.

No one was, just her and the parentals. They were never both home at the same time like this, but they'd arranged everything so she could spend her birthday at home with them instead of at Auntie Jee's or the minder's.

She'd been wishing her favorite great-aunt was there too tonight, but Auntie was getting to be important at Mars' Capital Dome this week for the Settler's Festival. She had promised Avis they'd celebrate again when she got home. That was okay, though, Avis had assured her; she was going to have *both* parentals home, wanting to spend time with *her*, and that was extra-special in itself. She couldn't remember the last time they'd done something like that.

Avis had come home from nursery school in the best mood, full of plans for what she'd do with her parentals after dinner and cake—and then the rest of the clan started arriving.

She'd thought it was for her at first, a special surprise or something. The first few family members to show up even remembered that it was her birthday. Six of her parentals' siblings, three grandies, and twelve cousins later, the house was nothing but chaos and loud voices talking over each other. After that, Avis had stopped counting the family members and trying to remember how they were related to which one of her parentals.

There were too many people, and it was too loud, and they were all talking about the twins and their provisional assessments. She'd barely been able to shut out the noise enough to nibble at her dinner enough to say she'd eaten if Mother got around to asking her and slip away. Now she was on the roof with the ferns where it was quiet, staring at stars that might not even be there.

She was quite sure that no one was going to notice that she was gone at all.

A mild breeze rustled the ferns on either side of her. Avis squinted up at the stars again. She finally found one and stretched a hand up towards it.

She'd show her cousins—and all the rest of the family, too, someday.

She was going to be an *explorer*. She'd go to the stars herself, and then when she came home they'd have to notice her because she'd be *important* and *useful*. No, she'd never be like her cousins, because *they'd* all be stuck under some boring colony dome where there were never any adventures and no one could see the stars—

"There you are, squirt!"

Avis bolted up, scattering gravel everywhere. *That* voice wasn't supposed to be here.

She turned around towards the door up from inside and blinked her star-squinty eyes back clear. A tall young man in a charcoal gray starship uniform was standing there grinning at her, the longer loose brown curls at the top of his otherwise short-cropped haircut almost glowing in the light behind him.

That person, she knew, shouldn't be standing there.

It couldn't *possibly* be him.

But it *was*—he was home!

"David!" She ran to the best older brother in the whole galaxy and hugged tightly around his legs, since that was all she could really reach.

David ruffled her own chin-length mess of mousey brown curls and laughed. "I missed you too, Squirt," he said, hoisting her up into a proper hug. "Looked all over the party for you—figured you'd skedaddled up here again."

Avis buried her face in the soft crinkly fabric of her brother's uniform. He still smelled like himself, too, mostly: like sandalwood and mint and electronics, but now with a bit of something like lavender thrown in. She hadn't seen him in person since he left for the Academy four years ago. If it weren't for the hug and the familiar smell, she wouldn't have believed he was really there.

Her brother had left for the Sol Central Space Service Academy when she was five. Him going away to school wouldn't have been a problem, except that the Academy was on *Earth*, which was too far away for anyone to take her to visit him. She'd started to think she'd never get to see him again at all, except on the other side of a Relay vid-call. Those just weren't the same. Holoscreens couldn't hug you.

"You're *home*."

"That I am, Squirt! *Spirit* put into the spaceport this morning. We're here for a week to stock up before we go out jumping through Quantum Space to the Centauri Triad, and then Sirius. Since I'm not needed until the day before we leave orbit and it'll be a long while before I get to visit again…" She couldn't see his face to be sure, but the tone of his voice said he was grinning as he said this. "…Well, anyway, Prime Navigator Kumar sorted it out so I could stay with you and the parentals while we're in the neighborhood."

Avis nodded, understanding now. Her brother was a T12 primary, after all—just as high-classed as a person could *get* in their finals—and almost done training to be a real Astral Navigator. David was the one who'd told her all about stars and exploring, back when she was little. She'd known he had to do his final year of training as part of the crew of a proper starship, and that MSS *Spirit* was the first ship being sent out to see a new star system in person in a very long time. No one had bothered to tell Avis that her brother's ship was visiting Mars on the way there.

"Besides," David asked, ruffling her hair again, "how could I miss my favorite little sister's birthday?"

Avis giggled, looking up at the cheeky grin she hadn't seen in ages. "I'm your *only* little sister."

"Same thing, Squirt." David carried her over to their favorite star-looking bench by the passionfruit vines. "Want to mark stars for a bit? I'm not too keen on being crushed by the mob Pops spilled the beans to about me dropping by."

"*You're* why they're all here!" Avis didn't know whether to be annoyed with her brother for being the source of the chaos or with their parentals for not telling her he was visiting in the first place.

"Yeah, sorry about that… wanted it to be a surprise. Didn't work out like I hoped."

Avis decided it didn't matter that the rest of the family had showed up. *David* was on the roof with her, and that was the best birthday surprise she could have asked for.

A good half an hour passed.

David sat on the bench beside Avis, pointing out the brighter stars and naming them and telling her all about his ship and the upcoming expedition he'd been chosen for as Junior Assistant Astral Navigator. She listened intently, wrapped up in his uniform jacket now and snuggled against him because the breeze had turned chilly and she'd left her jumper downstairs. Her brother was warm enough for both of them.

"So, Squirt," David asked after a while, stretching out his long legs from where he'd had them crossed since they sat down, "what got you up on the roof this time, anyway?"

Avis pulled her knees up to her chest and wrapped her arms around her own legs, hiding her face in the little space between the gathering of limbs. She didn't really want to think about it again, but now she was. It took her a few minutes to find an appropriate answer.

David gave her all the time she needed to find it.

"Cousins," Avis said at last, softly.

"Nico and Tony pestering you about your basics again?"

Avis didn't bother looking up, letting out a muffled groan of frustration.

"Ah. That'll be a yes." David was silent for a bit, then ruffled her hair reassuringly. "Don't let those two get to you, Squirt. Just because they're accelerated and Aunt Cathy treats them like they hung the moons doesn't mean they're better than you."

Avis let out a muffled groan. The twins were only a year older than her and they already had their provisionals—and they'd been *six* when they got their basics. Every other kid she knew had one set of assessment letters or the other by now.

Letters were *important*.

"Come on, now. After next week you'll have a base letter too, and I'll just bet it'll be something great."

"Nico said if I end up un-classed again I'd have to stay in the nursery school for *forever...* "

"That's not true for one red minute and you know it, Squirt."

"Maybe... but Tony..." Avis hesitated. Tony was the *worst* of her cousins, because he liked sneaking and eavesdropping on the grown-ups. She could never tell if he was telling the truth about the things Aunt Cathy and Mother said about her.

David waited patiently. He gave her hair another soft ruffle. David had never been the sort to rush her into speaking before she was ready.

Avis finally let the words out, her voice dropping to a whisper. "Tony... he said Mother and Pops could get a nice smart puppy to be their daughter instead after I fail my next assessment and prove I'm really broken so they can give me back, like they always wanted to anyway, and—"

Before Avis could finish or choke on the tears she hadn't realized were blurring her eyes, her brother had her caught up into a tight, comforting hug. "Avis. I *promise* you. No matter what Tony or Nico or *anyone* says, you're wonderful just like you are. No puppy in the galaxy could hold a candle to you." He tilted her chin up gently so she was looking right in his eyes. "And the only person Mother and Pops would ever let take you away from them is *me*."

There was something in her brother's expression that made Avis believe him. She nodded slowly.

"And," David added, tucking his uniform jacket back around her now that he was done hugging her cousin's cruel words away, "no matter what letters you get when you do pass your assessment, you're *still* going to be my favorite little sister. Nothing's going to stop us exploring the stars together someday—we'll work it all out. Okay?"

"Okay." She nodded again. She wished her brother was home all the time to reassure her like this. Even with his warmth to steady her and calm her worries, it still felt like she'd failed at being a person somehow. Being around her cousins always made her feel like that—Tony at least seemed to delight in making sure she remembered where she stood in the family.

Avis did her best to shoo those thoughts away. Her brother was here, and David was usually right about things. She still couldn't get one specific thought out of her mind, though. "But David," she said, turning her eyes down towards the gravel, "I tested wrong *seven* times already. What if I fail again, and they give up on testing me..."

"The assessors won't give up on you. Some people just take longer." David sat a hand on her shoulder. "One of my buddies up at the Academy was ten before he got his basics, and y'know what? Del only graduated a year ago and he's *already* a junior officer on a starship."

"Really?" Avis looked back up to her brother and unfolded herself a little. No one ever told her about people who hadn't tested well doing anything important. Lately, it felt like everyone but David and Auntie Jee was set on pointing out to her how bad it was to not know one's letters—and how disappointed they'd be if those letters weren't good ones.

"Yep." A pause, and then another of her brother's signature cheeky grins spread across his face. "Hey, want to meet him?"

"Um... inside?"

"Nah, he's with *Curiosity's* crew. I did bring a friend down with me from *Spirit*, though! They're running interference with the family so I can catch up with you. I'll introduce you when they get up here."

Avis wondered which of David's new Academy friends he'd brought, if it wasn't the one he wanted her to meet, but didn't have a chance to ask.

David reached around her to pull his pocket-com out of his jacket and started fiddling with the holographic touchscreen that popped out of the little silver device. "Come on," he said, "I'll call in over the Relays and see if we can pester Del for a bit. I've got access through *Spirit's* systems now—we might as well get some use out of it! Let's see, last he said, *Curiosity* was in port at Earth and he had a few days of leave... Which means wherever Del is, Chirps should be around too! You'll like her."

"...Okay."

Avis had heard the names before, on the rare occasions her brother could find time to call home. They had been cadets at the Academy too, so they had to be high-classed like David and destined for important space service careers. If she remembered right, Del and Chirps were the ones he'd lived with. That was pretty much all Avis knew. None of his friends had ever been around whenever Mother or Pops had called David and let Avis talk to him when they were done.

The call connected over the relays with a high-pitched series of beeps. They were almost immediately greeted by a deep, highly annoyed voice booming out of the pocket-com's tiny silver speaker.

"Tarnation, Davey-boy, don't you know it's past midnight on this side of the planet? Let a guy sleep, why don't you? Not all of us are nocturnal like you Nav types, you know!"

"Now, Del, if I know you as well as I think I do..." Her brother paused to stifle a laugh. "It may be midnight in London, but you're up watching ancient cinema with Chirps anyway, aren't you?"

"`He is, David, and you are interrupting the gunslinger's third-act monologue.`" The second voice was odd. It sounded a bit like one of the nursery school robo-minders, but feminine and less formal.

"Hey, Chirps! I was going to call you next if Del wasn't being predictable." David laughed again. "Switch to vid, already, will you? I've got my kid sister here to meet you."

"`All right, let me put Del's pocket-com where you can see more than just his silly face fur when we switch.`"

"My mustache is exquisite, Chirps, what are you talking about?"

The holoscreen expanded and flickered with static for a few moments before being filled with color and movement.

Avis hid her face back under the security of her brother's uniform jacket. She wasn't sure she wanted attention after all.

"No need to be shy, Squirt," David said, "I've told them all about you."

Avis reluctantly looked up at the floating image. In it, a man with a dark mustache sat on a red couch with a window somewhere behind it showing a view of a city at night. The man, she assumed, had to be Del, but she had no idea where the other friend was.

"...Hi."

"*Nice to meet you, little lady,*" said mustache-man, "*bet you're awful glad to have your brother home?*"

Avis nodded.

"*Well, now, I'm Randal, and this is... Chirps! Get your tail feathers over here and say hi to the cute little girl. The 'com's secure enough without you fussing over holding it.*"

A flash of white and blue fluttered across the image and landed on mustache-man's shoulder as a small bird.

"`I was just making sure it wouldn't fall.`" Surprisingly, the not-quite-a-robo-minder voice seemed to have come from the bird. The bird bobbed its head and spread its wings widely as it continued to speak. "`Hello, little sister of David! I am Salzar-Newman's Bernadette of Venture! You may also call me Chirps, if you like, it's shorter to say.`"

Avis looked up at her brother and whispered, "Your friend is a *bird*?"

David chuckled. "I may have left a few things out while the parentals were listening. You know how they get. Bernadette is a very *special* bird."

"Oh."

"*So, little lady,*" asked Del, "*what can we do for you?*"

Avis wasn't sure what to say. She looked up to her brother.

David seemed to know she was still feeling too shy to ask. "It's her birthday and we were on the subject of classification basics."

"*Oh, well, now, that makes sense.*" Del nodded, his tone shifting a little more serious. "*A bit nervous about your first assessment, then?*"

"Eighth..." was all Avis could manage to say.

"*Eh, next time's the charm, then, little lady. Took me a while, myself, but I'm sure Davy-boy's already told you that. Once it clicks how the tests work you never think twice about them.*"

"...Really?"

"*Yeah. I was a shy little rascal around the assessors. Sure enough, though, once I got the hang of the system and practiced the interview portion with my Uncle Nimbus a few times, it wasn't too hard to get classed up proper.*"

Avis nodded, comforted but not entirely convinced. "But if I don't get rated high enough..."

"*No use worrying 'bout what's not happened yet, little lady.*"

"Besides," said the bird, gesturing with one of her wings, "you have opposable thumbs! Those mean you can do whatever you want to do as long as you put in the time to learn how to do it."

Avis giggled. Her brother's friends were a good kind of silly.

"See, Squirt?" David asked, "Nothing to worry about."

Avis nodded. She believed him.

"And hey, little lady, once you get your assessments back, call us up again and we'll celebrate with you. David can give you our Relay codes and help you set the party line up."

"We'll be sure to do that, Del. Thanks. I'll let you get back to your film now."

"Right-o, Davey-boy. Say hi to Coby for us once you get back up to the ship?"

"Heh, I'll do you one better. Coby's downstairs distracting the family for me."

"You left them alone with your family?" The bird's voice sounded almost alarmed. "Your whole family? David! You know how they get overwhelmed… and with what you've said about just your parentals—"

"They *volunteered* for it, Chirps."

"I did," said a voice from behind Avis and David in the garden, strangely accented and with an after-tone like the breeze through the wind chimes. "Worry not, my sweet feathered sister, I have managed to escape—even though my Navigator here *distinctly* failed to mention that there would be three fascinated xenobiology dabblers to escape from in addition to his father."

"I told you already, Coby," David said, half turning to look over the back of the bench, "It wasn't *supposed* to be the whole clan tonight, or I'd have given you fair warning on what to expect from all of them."

Avis curled into her brother's side under the jacket, wishing she was invisible. Meeting David's friends through a screen was one thing, but in person? She wasn't sure she was ready for that. She didn't have much choice in the matter, though. Within a moment or two, Avis felt the creaking of the wooden slats of the bench as someone leaned over the back of it, but didn't look out of her jacket of invisibility. She wasn't ready for this.

"*Coby!*" said the bird's voice, "*You are missed! Del is being all sorts of boring without you and David to argue with! How'd you escape the rabid xeno-sci folks?*"

"I politely asked if there was a place I could meditate and realign myself with the stars while I waited for my Navigator to return from the very important communication he had *obviously* disappeared to take."

"*And that worked?*"

"Well, I *may* have also started a heated discussion about the merits of certain Martian sports teams and then stepped aside once they were no longer paying attention to me."

"*Starting arguments again to cover an escape from human awkwardness?*"

"Arguments might as well be part of the Strange to me, you know that."

"*Good on you, Coby!*" said Del's voice, laughing. "*We'll leave you to chastise your Navigator. Safe travels to both of you. And happy birthday to you again, little lady!*"

The call ended.

Avis stayed under the jacket and close against her brother's side, still paralyzed by the stupid shyness that had ruined every assessment she'd ever taken. She wanted to disappear.

"You can come out, Squirt. Coby's nice." David reached under the jacket to ruffle her curls. "A bit of a pest, sometimes, but they're friendly. I promise."

"You didn't tell me your sister was *invisible*, Foxy," said the wind-chime voice from the back of the bench. "Has Del's facial hair frightened her?"

Invisible? Well, she wanted to be.

"Nah, Coby, Avis is just a little shy with new people, that's all."

"She seems very good at being invisible. Is there a code word that makes her manifest?"

"Now, don't you start getting nonsensical again."

"How about... butterscotch? Like the sweets I have in my pocket to give her if she reappears."

"*Cobalt...*" Her brother was using his version of Pops' stop-being-silly-child-I'm-trying-to-work voice, for some reason.

"What? It's a *nice* word and one is supposed to bring gifts for the birthday child. Besides, Heather used to play this game with me all the time when I was a kitten! Let me try again. Butterscotch? Bu-tter-sco-tch."

Avis giggled. It *was* an objectively funny word, she had to admit, especially when stretched out long and strange like her brother's friend was saying it.

"Aha! It's working! I can almost see her."

"Cobalt!"

"Butterscotch!"

Avis, still giggling, popped her head out from the protective invisibility field of jacket and older brother and immediately found herself looking up into a very strange face leaning over the back of the bench.

There was a proper alien looking down at her, of the sort that were almost human-like except for the parts that *weren't*: deep blue skin traced with silver tiger stripes; three eyes, golden, one in the center of the forehead above the other two; silver hair pulled back in a braided bun; kitty ears with silver fur tufts at the tips and three small gold hoops pierced through the left one; extra pair of arms underneath their first set. They were dressed in the same sort of soft grey cadet's uniform as David, but with a jacket that had the correct number of sleeves.

Avis couldn't decide whether to be shy or fascinated. She'd never met a Florivan in person before. She knew Auntie Jee worked with one, sometimes, though, and she'd always said good things about them—and *this* one was David's friend, so they had to be nice like he said.

"And there she is!" the Florivan exclaimed, nudging her brother with one of their lower elbows, "See, Foxy? I knew it would work."

"Cobalt Mereday, you are something else *entirely*, you know that?" It was only mock annoyance in her brother's voice now. Avis was sure of it.

"I *am*, and you find it refreshing, and that is why we are friends. And here is her reward for becoming visible!" One slim four-fingered hand from their upper pair extracted a small cloth bag from one of their jacket pockets and offered it to Avis. "Happy birthday, young human! I've been looking forward to meeting you."

"Thank you." Avis accepted the gift and found that there were in fact a good number of paper-wrapped brown candies in the bag. She took one out for herself and pressed another into her brother's hand.

"Coby's the Junior Assistant Quantum Drive Engineer for *Spirit*," David told her, unwrapping the sweet and popping it into his mouth. "They're my counterpart."

"I am at that," agreed the alien, adding almost affectionately, "And your brother is my Navigator."

"You enjoy saying that too much."

"I enjoy being able to say it *officially*, Foxy."

Avis knew abstractly that it was a Navigator's job to help their Florivan partner fly a ship between planets and stars, but she'd somehow never heard anything about her brother having been paired with a specific Florivan yet.

"So you work together?"

"We've been working together for a few years now, actually. We got stuck together when I first transferred to Nav training and then it turned out they were friends with my crazy housemates..." David chuckled and absently ran a hand over the back of his hair. "Well, things just sort of worked out from there, eventually."

"Yes, yes, your *wonderfully* eccentric housemates." Coby slid themself catlike over the back of the bench to sit beside her, the fluffy silver tuft at the tip of their long blue tail waving in her brother's face briefly as they did. "You can see it, Miss Avis, can't you?" Coby asked, gesturing widely with two of their four arms as if presenting a particularly interesting scenic view, "There I am complaining to my little feathered sister—"

"They mean Chirps, Avis—"

"Yes, of course I do. Complaining to *Bernadette*," said Coby, pointedly pronouncing each syllable of the bird's name, "that I'd *finally* been given a new training partner, only to find out it was this hardheaded first-year who was too intelligent to know how to listen to anyone who wasn't a textbook—"

"Hey, now..."

"You're better now, Foxy, but you *have* to admit it was the case at the time."

Avis looked back and forth between the two of them, not entirely sure what to make of the banter, except that David hadn't had friends like *this* before he left for the Academy. All she remembered of his study partners from secondary school was that they didn't like being interrupted by her—or her in general, really—but they'd all put up with having her around because *David* wanted her around.

"Point taken," her brother said at last, leaning back and staring up at the stars beyond the atmospheric domes. "You may proceed with the embarrassing story."

"Thank you. Anyway, Miss Avis, there I am telling my dear little sister all about the trouble this *particularly* grating cadet has been giving me in simulations... and who should walk in with her much more interesting housemate—"

"They mean Del, Squirt—"

"Yes, of course I mean Del." Coby's voice turned very formal. "You should know better than to interrupt me, Navigator." The equally serious expression only stayed in their eyes for a few moments, though.

"Fine, fine." David laughed. "We're not working now, though, there's no real danger in it."

"Hmm. Maybe not, but it's still *rude*, and you did leave me with your overly scientifically curious relations earlier." Coby's tone was teasing now, accented by a dramatic wave of their long tufted tail.

"All right, all right, you win. Sorry again about that. Finish the story for her."

"I will," said Coby, turning back to Avis, "if I can remember where I'd gotten to."

"You were talking to the nice bird and mustache-man came home?"

David snorted at the description, but seemed to be making a point now of not interrupting.

"Aha! Exactly. Anyway, Del comes back in with this new housemate I'm supposed to *finally* be meeting, since we'd all given up on him existing at all at that point... and who happens to be loudly complaining about *his* training partner being full of nonsense and impossible to work with."

"Really?" Avis asked.

"Really, Miss Avis! And who should it turn out to be but this brother of yours, the very same troublesome cadet I had been telling Bernadette all about! Took the two of us a good hour to recover from our mutual friends trying to introduce us. Hated each other for about six months after that, too, I think."

"It was eight."

"Was it?"

"Central, remember?"

"I do... Yes, you're right. Most of a year, then."

"There has *got* to be a simpler way to tell that story, Coby."

"Well, now, where would the fun be in that?"

"...But you're friends now?" Avis asked, still confused. She had very little experience with the sort of friendship Academy cadets apparently took on. Or friendship in general, for that matter.

"Oh, yes, Squirt," David replied, "we're friends now. Wouldn't have brought Coby down to meet you otherwise."

"I have a feeling it will be *much* easier to become friends with you, Miss Avis. Assuming you would like to be such?"

Avis looked to her brother, who nodded encouragingly, and then back to the Florivan. "Okay!" She had now decided she liked her brother's new friends a lot more than his old ones. The new ones were a good kind of odd.

"Excellent! New human friend acquired!" The Florivan had now somehow transitioned to sitting upside-down with their feet slung up over the back of the bench, one set of spindly blue-fingered arms folded neatly behind their head and the other over their chest. "Feel free to ask any questions you're trying to hold in, Miss Avis, I'm much more inclined to answer *you* than your prying relations downstairs."

"Were they *really* that bad, Coby?" David chuckled.

"The identical pair of boys wouldn't stop pestering me about quantum physics and what my comparative classification would be if I were human."

"Those two are *always* pests, Coby—and they're at that stage where they're letter-obsessed. I was the same when I was that age."

Avis couldn't picture her brother ever being *anything* like the twins, herself.

"I'm sure you were. It would explain a lot from when we were enemies."

"It... probably does, yes," David admitted, although Avis couldn't see why.

"And!" Coby continued, "Your..." they looked over to Avis curiously. "Who *is* the pompous gentleman with the bushy white eyebrows, anyway?"

"Grandfather Maxwell." Avis sighed softly. He was one of the ones who was openly disappointed in her for not having her letters yet, and had said as much to everyone no less than twice tonight.

"Ah, that's right. Him. Foxy, that grandfather of yours had the gall to start asking me about biology."

"How's that a problem? That *is* what your degrees—"

"My *personal* biology, Foxy."

"Ah." David grimaced. "Okay, I owe you big for that one. Sorry, Grandfather did his doctoral thesis in comparative anatomy. I *really* should have warned you."

"You *should* have."

Both of them grew silent.

"What's space like?" Avis asked, finally, now that there was a lull in her brother's conversation with his friend.

"Space?" repeated Coby, reaching the two hands that had been crossed over their chest up towards the sky and interlacing the long fingers around whichever star they were looking at. "Normal or Strange, Miss Avis?"

She looked up to David.

"Ah, right. Florivans call Quantum Space 'Strange'. That's what they mean." He gestured at the dome and the night sky beyond it. "All of that up there is 'Normal.'"

"Oh! Um... either? Both?"

"Okay, then." Coby paused for a moment as if gathering their words and then smiled softly. "Normal is *big*... and cold, for the most part. Mostly empty, but beautiful. You feel small in a big vast blackness, but there are stars and nebulas and galaxies and the light of them keeps you from being entirely alone. And then there are *planets* and each one is its own little thing in the big darkness with something interesting going on..."

Avis could almost see the scene the Florivan was describing, like pictures in one of the galactic science for kids videos she'd watched in nursery school. She couldn't quite grasp the science parts yet the way the other children did, but she loved the images of space and its faraway wonders.

"When you see it all through the viewports for the first time it's like being part of the whole universe—even if you *are* very, very small. Kind of like the feeling you get in a forest, or out in that big desert here, or somewhere where the lights of the city don't touch you. You'd agree, Foxy?"

"Yeah. It's really... something." David shifted to look upwards too, resting his arms behind his head in almost the same way his friend had. Avis wondered if either of them knew they did that the same way. "I never have the words for it, Squirt, not like Coby does, but it's amazing."

Avis was silent for a while, staring up at the stars beyond the dome with the two cadets. She wanted to see the things *they* were going to see. She wished she could just go out into space with her brother and his friend instead of staying here to keep failing the assessment tests over and over again and disappointing her parentals.

Finally, after a long silence between all three of them staring up past the dome, she got up the courage to ask the rest of the question again.

"What about the other kind of space?"

"You want to take that one, Foxy?" She could actually *hear* the grin in Coby's tone without having to look.

"Do you *ever* get tired of teasing me?"

"No, Navigator, and you don't get tired of teasing *me* either. That's why we're friends."

Avis didn't quite get what the teasing even was this time. She tugged on her brother's sleeve and gave him her best please-explain look when their eyes met. This was a big part of why she missed him all the time. No one else could understand her without words so well except Auntie Jee.

"Humans can't safely come in contact with Quantum Space like Florivans can," her brother said, finally, "not without shielding and lenses, and even then it's... well, *dangerous* to try to do it. That's what Coby's poking at, mostly. When we're jumping *Spirit* through there, most of the ship is closed off and all of the viewports are shut so no miasmas can leak in. I have to navigate off of starcharts and quantum computer data and calculate landmarks for them, but Coby's the one on the other side of the ship's safety seals running the Drive."

"Oh." That made sense, Avis supposed. No wonder navigators had to be so high-classed and worked with alien partners. She looked back over to Coby. "But what's it like, then?"

"We don't normally try to explain that... well, for a lot of reasons, but especially because what we experience is so different from how the Strange shows itself to humans. But for *you*, Miss Avis? I'll make an attempt."

In the silence while Coby was gathering their words, Avis couldn't help but feel like it was something very special that she was being told: a secret, even, from the tone they'd used.

"It's everything normal space is, but smaller and very different," the Florivan beside her began, gesturing as they spoke with the two upraised hands. "You can hold a lot of it in your mind all at once, but there's never really enough room to see anything more than a tiny bit in focus. It's beautiful and odd and *warm*, and it moves around you like ripples in a calm lake. It smells like green tea sometimes–the nice parts do, at least–and other things depending on how the different stars and planets are arranged. You close your eyes..."

Avis couldn't help closing her own, transfixed by the strangely accented tones of Coby's voice. She wondered for a moment if her brother did the same, or if he'd heard all of this before and was just waiting for his friend to finish talking.

"...You can close your eyes, and it's there inside you waiting like a place you've been a thousand times before that's different every single time. When you open them, you can see it all, and you know the landmarks because they're *your* stars, your mountains, your streams. You define them and they define you. They're yours and they're real—as real as this bench, as real as the voice of your anchor, your Navigator in your ear telling you where you need to go, how far you need to carry the ship, where the things around you need to be. You walk along the edges of the stellar wind currents, swim in them, even, sometimes... It's a different kind of smallness from what you feel in the Normal, but at the same time it's all part of that too..."

Their voice sounded somehow very far away.

"It sounds like the most wonderful thing," Avis said quietly, still with her eyes closed, hoping she wasn't interrupting. She could almost picture the things they were saying, the same way she could see her memories of planet videos and nature hikes.

"It is, Miss Avis. Not without its dangers, of course, even for us, but the Normal isn't all safety either..." Coby lowered and folded in their hands over their chest again. "I wish I could show it to the both of you—safely, I mean. The way it looks to me."

"So it's like exploring a dream when you remember you're dreaming?"

"I'd say that's about as close as a human could come to grasping it, what with the way your brains are made to work. That's why it's so hard to find a decent Navigator, you know? I went through *dozens* of them before Sarge and Nida stuck me with your brother."

"Which is why all the other Nav cadets had a betting pool going on for how long I'd last with you." David interjected.

"Yes... did you ever hear who won?"

"Well, I haven't washed out *yet*... and you've declared our compact in front of my sister now... so I think we do?" David laughed. "Johnson still seems to think I'm going to snap during our first solo jump shift trying to wrangle you out of the clouds, though."

"Heh. We'll show him, then, won't we?"

"We will." David rested his hand on Avis' shoulder and she opened her eyes to look up at him. "Just like *you're* going to show those assessors what you're made of, Squirt."

"...Right." Avis really didn't want to think about that anymore, but she was starting to feel just a little bit better about it.

"*That's* why you were on the call with Del and Chirps, then?" Coby asked, seeming to have missed the theme of Avis' anxieties somewhere along the way.

"Yeah, can you think of anyone better to talk to about it? My family's nuts over classifications—-you may have noticed."

"Point taken, David, but you were going to introduce her to *me* anyway." The tone wasn't quite pouting, but for a moment it came close.

"You were older before you got your base letters too?" Avis asked, encouraged by the thought that people like her weren't as unusual as her cousins kept saying. She liked her brother's Florivan friend—the idea of being like them was nice, somehow.

Coby laughed quite a bit at that. "Oh, no, Miss Avis, I'm sorry... we don't get letters, you see. Minds that can fathom the Strange don't work with your human classing assessments. We tend to break them."

Avis had never heard of a person without letters before, and didn't know at all how to respond.

"What's so important about getting letters at one point in time or another, anyway?" Coby asked, looking to David. "She'll have some given to her eventually, she's human. I don't remember anyone *ever* putting so much pressure about it on Heather when we were growing up."

"Your family isn't exactly standard-issue, Coby," David replied. "Especially around here. Mars as it is now was *built* by the people who developed the assessment matrix... and our family's been here since the beginning."

"Right... so it's important here like it is to the Academy administration. Got it."

"It's not just getting the letters," Avis said softly, leaning back against her brother again and staring upwards at the stars. "If you want to be somebody *useful*, you have to have the *right* letters. Like David."

"Ah... I'm not sure I'd agree, but that's how your world works, I suppose. Who do you want to be, then, that it's already worrying you so much how to get there?"

Avis looked up to her brother again, confused.

"Coby's *trying* to ask what you want to do when you grow up."

"Oh!" She stood up on the bench, pointing as dramatically as she could up at the dome and the stars beyond. "I'm gonna be an explorer like you! And visit new *planets*, and see *stars*, and talk to aliens... um, *other* aliens! ...and... and ride space whales! ...um..." Avis trailed off, suddenly feeling shy again.

She wasn't supposed to say things like the part about space whales. The minders at nursery school said they weren't logical and it would throw off her assessments.

All three of Coby's golden-yellow eyes blinked in sequence as they scooted into a different position that had a better view of her. For a moment, Avis was afraid they were going to laugh at her like her cousins had all the times she slipped and said something that was nonsense like that.

"What sort of space whales, Miss Avis?" The tone wasn't mocking at all. Unlike anyone else she'd ever accidentally told something like that, Coby sounded *fascinated*.

"What kind?" Avis had never tried to describe one before, since she always assumed she'd also be the one to discover things like space whales in the first place. "Um... big grey ones, maybe?" she answered at last, finding the memory of the Earth whale documentaries she'd been watching when the idea first appeared. "The kind that filter feed, because they'd probably eat space dust?"

"Oh, of course! I worked with some baleen whales back on Earth for a while. Feeding on galactic detritus makes far more sense than there being interstellar krill out there..." Coby looked thoughtful for a moment, then smiled at her. "Your space whales do sound amazing! I'd be pleased to meet one."

"They would be! And they'd be *friendly*, and I'd learn how to ride one! You could come with me too, and we could ride them together..." This was too exciting. No one *ever* let her talk about things like space whales that might not be real. She could almost see herself riding one now through one of the nebulas in the posters on her bedroom walls.

"Coby..."

"Don't worry, Foxy, I *promise* I won't throw off her assessments. I just want to hear the future explorer talk about her space whales. What else would you do with them, Miss Avis?"

"Oh, I..." she hesitated for a moment, but the sparkle of sincerity in their three golden eyes reassured her. "I would teach them to dance!" Avis hopped off the bench to the garden path and twirled like she always did in the nursery school physical activity section at music time. "I'd teach them to dance," she said again, "and whales can already sing, kind of, and once they were ready I'd bring them home and we'd show everyone how wonderful dancing space whales are."

"Coby, I don't think…"

"Hush now, Navigator, you know better than to interrupt."

Avis only barely heard the exchange between her brother and his friend, she was too busy trying to work out what else to tell them about her future exploring.

Then, somehow, she found herself dancing with Coby, holding on to the lower pair of their hands while she led them in circles around the rooftop garden to the rhythm of the whale songs she remembered from her documentaries and the formal dancing music from nursery school.

Her brother was left speechless on the star-watching bench, and if he continued to protest Avis didn't hear him.

"What else would you see, bold explorer that you are?"

"I'd… I'd see where stars are born! And I'd find the glowing fish that swim between them to keep them company when they're babies so they don't feel lonely."

"Oh, glowing fish too, Miss Avis? Stellar!" The Florivan laughed, picking her up in a momentary gliding twirl. The movement was thrilling, and perfectly in time with the crescendo of the whale's song. She almost thought they could hear the music she was remembering too, but that couldn't be.

Avis giggled as she landed and asked, almost too earnestly, "Baby stars wouldn't need blankets, would they, Coby? I could ask Auntie Jee to weave one for us..."

"You know, I've never thought before to ask a star if it was cold? They always feel rather warm to me. I suppose we'd have to ask, but we'd need an *awfully* big blanket to wrap one up snug."

"Maybe just socks, then?"

"Socks would be perfect, Miss Avis, and so many things you would meet might have cold feet, too."

"Like alien caterpillars? They would have lots and lots of feet..."

"Precisely, Miss Avis, precisely! Oh, you *are* so clever at this. Tell me more." They spun her around again, and Avis felt for all the world like she was actually dancing among the marvels she was describing with Coby.

She could almost see the stars beyond the dome as descending as tiny points of light sitting in the flowers growing in the rooftop garden, where she could pick them up and hold them in her hands if she weren't holding tight to the long blue fingers of her new friend.

"Those caterpillars, they... they might turn into butterflies with galaxies in their wings, couldn't they? And they'd be *big*, so if you don't know they're there you can't see them at all!"

"Why, Miss Avis, that would be wonderful!" Another twirl, and the silver tuft on Coby's long blue tail brushed through the ferns around them and sent the tiny stars flying upward all around Avis. "And you and I would suspect they're there now, so I'm sure we could find one if we wanted to..."

"Can we?" Avis asked, staring up into the shining trio of eyes that she was sure now could see anything they wanted to. "Could we ask it to tell us what it's like to fly in space like a butterfly, and if they ever wonder what it's like to be on a planet like we are?"

Avis could almost see it, the butterfly's wings flapping ever so gently so it wouldn't blow her space whale away while they talked. The butterfly would teach them butterfly songs, and show them the sort of flowers it liked best that only galaxy butterflies could see—

"Oh, I'm sure we could, miss Avis—"

"*Cobalt Mereday*! Enough, please!" David's voice rang out clear as a bell tolling in a silent room.

Avis was in the garden.

On the rooftop.

Her brother was there.

There wasn't any music to dance to.

Space whales *weren't* real.

Avis didn't know what to say. Her mind was spinning and it had all felt so—so *real*—and she was tired, she realized, and it was late, and somehow Coby had brought her back to the bench and she was next to her brother again. She curled up next to him and rested her head on his leg.

David draped his jacket back over her. She hadn't realized how cold she was until she felt his warmth again. "We'll take you downstairs to sleep in a bit, okay? I just need to talk to Cobalt for a little while before we do."

"... okay." She closed her eyes. "David?"

"Yeah?"

"Can I go to space with you and Coby?"

"Of course you can, Squirt."

"...Okay."

Avis was already drifting, but she didn't want to go to sleep. She had to stay awake until David took her down to her bedroom. He and Coby might talk about space some more, and who *knew* when they'd be back to talk to her again.

As it was, though, her brother and her new friend seemed determined to wait a very long time before speaking.

"Is she asleep now?" She heard Coby whisper, apparently sitting on the back of the bench above her.

"I think so. She *needs* to sleep, with the day she's had." Avis felt her brother's warm hand ruffle through her hair and brush it back out of her face again.

"She looks very peaceful."

"Mm."

"You're annoyed at something?"

"Of course I—Cobalt Mereday, what in all the *stars* were you thinking?" Her brother's voice had turned serious, in a tone she'd never heard before from him. From Pops, maybe, when she'd done something that had disappointed him and Mother—but *never* from David.

"Thinking?" A pause. "Your little sister has a *brilliant* imagination, for a human."

"Cobalt..."

"She could be an amazing explorer, or better! She doesn't need to be... squashed into a box like the rest of you."

"Cobalt."

"Do you have any idea how rare it is anymore to find a human that can click into a daydream like that without questioning it? She shines even brighter than Heather did when I was a kitten, and *awake*, too... I'd love to introduce her to Nida someday—Oh! And Entile Jade! They'll be *so* impressed with her space whales—"

"Cobalt!" Avis couldn't remember ever having heard David sound angry and afraid like that, all rolled into one horsely whispered word.

"*What*, Foxy?"

"Do you have *any* idea how much danger you could have put her in just now?"

"Danger? *Really*? What's so wrong about letting her have an imagination just for an evening? Or sharing a few moments of happiness with her so she can have a little *hope* in her to hold onto when we have to leave her here with your family." The Florivan sounded upset; hurt, even. "She probably won't remember any of it outside of her dreams anyway..."

If she hadn't been so tired, Avis might have asked them what was wrong. But she could only barely keep awake to listen—and she didn't even understand why or what the two of them were arguing about in the first place.

There was another long silence.

Finally, David let out a frustrated sigh. "Avis is a *human child*, Cobalt."

"I *had* noticed."

"And you were *flickering*."

"I—no. I'd have noticed... wait. Was I?"

"You *were*. Here, Cobalt. Planet-side. With my little sister in tow, and her so enthralled with you encouraging the sort of brain patterns that could ruin her chances in the real world... You had *her* flickering too."

"...Oh."

"Yeah."

"You're sure?"

"I *think* I know what that feels like, Cobalt."

"...How long?"

"Only five seconds or so, there at the end, but that's long enough."

Silence. A very long silence.

"I wasn't trying to harm her, David."

"I know." David sighed, but his tone stayed the same. "And you don't even have your earpiece in because we're planet-side. If something had happened... I don't want to think about not being able to call you back."

Another long silence.

"I'm sorry, David. I didn't mean to scare you, either."

"Just... don't go that far with her again, Coby. Please."

"That... *shouldn't* have happened in the first place. I'll have to talk to Nida about it... or Entile Ultramarine, when we see them tomorrow..." Coby trailed off with a sigh, then shifted back from their worried tone to a more formal one. "I'll do my best not to get carried away again, Navigator. I'm sorry."

"Thank you, Cobalt." David's voice returned to normal, now. "Come on, let's get the squirt down to her bed before my folks start looking for us."

"You mean for her? She's been out of their sight for a while now."

"You've *met* my family now, Coby. What do you think?"

"Ah."

Avis felt herself being carried downstairs and put into her bed. She did her best to pretend to wake up just before David and Coby left her there so they'd have to say goodnight. As near as she could tell, neither one caught on that she'd been awake and listening to their confusing argument.

As confusing as it was, though, she fell asleep happier than she'd been in a long time. Her brother was home, and his counterpart was wonderful. She couldn't have asked for a better pair of birthday presents.

✴ The End ✴

Characters Appearing in *Rooftops and Space Whales*

The following list of characters is divided by species and arranged in order of their appearance in the narrative. Only characters with significant "speaking roles" have been detailed here. All others present are listed as a group for the reader's reference; characters who are mentioned but do not appear are not included.

Florivans

COBALT MEREDAY

They/them. Also called "Coby." Junior Secondary Quantum Space Drive Engineer, MSS *Spirit*. Counterpart to **David Foxbury**. Adoptive older sibling of **Bernadette Venture**.

Humans

AVIS FOXBURY

She/her. Little sister of **David Foxbury**. Also called "Squirt."

DAVID FOXBURY

He/him. Junior Secondary Navigator, MSS *Spirit*. Older brother of **Avis Foxbury**, counterpart to **Cobalt Mereday**. Also called "Foxy."

RANDAL DELMONTE

He/him. Quartermaster's Assistant, MSS *Curiosity*. Also called "Del."

Others

SALZAR-NEWMAN'S BERNADETTE OF VENTURE

She/her. A sapient budgerigar with blue feathers. Also known as "Chirps." Adoptive little sister of **Cobalt Mereday**. Ensign in the Sol Coalition Defense Fleet and personal assistant to **Admiral Theodore Ruttiger**.

The Tragedy of Harold the Violet

★ A Strange Space™ Short Story ★

In honor of my various ancestors who also loved plants with soft fuzzy leaves and purple flowers.

There will always be the sort of human who names houseplants and talks to them. This is not something anyone sets out to learn about the species. It's more of a small, delightful fact that one discovers only upon meeting such a human and befriending them.

In the case of the Florivan known as Ocean Merlani Barker, it's a fact they know all too well. Their best friend in the whole of the galaxy, after all, happens to *be* such a human.

It was somewhat early on in Merlani's friendship with Teresa Vasquez when she first introduced them to her assortment of green "housemates." They'd never expected her small apartment to so closely resemble one of the greenhouses from Houston's nearby botanical gardens. Of course, they'd *also* never expected to be on a first-name basis with a collection of cacti and one particularly large spider plant.

At the time, Merlani was just beginning their second year at the Sol Central Space Service Academy, where they're working on their Advanced Geosciences and Exoplanetary Mineralogy degrees in addition to the QSD Engineering course all Florivan students take. Their new best friend, meanwhile, had been preparing to graduate as a dual Command and Tactical Flight student bound for service in the Defense Fleet. The two of them met through the Academy's Martial Arts Competition and Demonstration Team, and were fast friends almost immediately.

Two years later, and Theresa Vasquez is still on Earth with Merlani, now transferred over to the Astral Navigation program so she can add *that* to her rather long list of official certifications. Merlani couldn't have asked for a better or more interesting human to claim as their counterpart. They can't imagine anyone better suited to be the Navigator they'll spend the rest of their life working alongside to jump starships through the so-called "Quantum Space" shortcut their people have shared with humanity.

Their Navigator still has plants all throughout her apartment, of course. Likewise, she's still in the habit of talking to plants in general. Reese is always quick to inform Merlani when she's perceived an amusing opinion on whatever the two of them are discussing from some corner of her little domesticated jungle, too. It hadn't taken her long to be comfortable enough to show Merlani that side of her personality, even if she tends to conceal it from most people.

Normally, Merlani finds all of this to be rather endearing. Their Navigator's more well-developed imagination compared to other high-assessment-classed humans is one of her best qualities, as far as they're concerned. The fact that she often struggles to keep the names of other *humans* from getting mixed up in her brain only makes her houseplant-naming more amusing, since she never seems to forget the names of her plants.

At the moment, though, when their Navigator is standing in front of them excitedly presenting the latest houseplant she's acquired, Merlani has to wonder just a *tiny* bit about her sanity.

"See, Cinny?" The tall, deeply tan young woman asks, holding out the plant in question. She's still in her Academy uniform, even though she'd said she was going to the bedroom in the back of her apartment to change for their usual after-classes workout. That, it seems, was a ruse. "His leaves are *fuzzy*—and when he blooms, he'll have purple flowers!"

"Is that so?" Merlani twitches one of their large catlike ears in amusement to match the swishing motion of their long, tufted prehensile tail. Their lower two eyes trace the contours of the plant, while their third one remains focused on their Navigator's face. Her own dark pair of eyes are practically sparkling with excitement.

"Well, that will be a good addition to your windowsill, I suppose," Merlani says at last. "Assuming you can find a space for it, that is."

"Oh, he's not going to live *here*." She laughs brightly and shakes her head, making the long hair in her high-tied black ponytail swish from the motion. "I got him for you!"

"For... me?"

"Of course! I'd been thinking an African violet would be perfect to brighten up your room, so when I found this little guy the other night, I couldn't resist."

Merlani reluctantly accepts the black ceramic pot full of plant she's setting into their lower pair of hands. They turn all three of their eyes down at the violet they're now holding. After a moment, they cautiously run a silver-striped, deep blue-green finger from one of their upper hands over a leaf. It *is* surprisingly fuzzy, and not in an unpleasant way.

"I will concede that it is a nice plant. But really, Reese..." Merlani fixes her with a curious look of their third eye and gives her a light nudge with the soft silver tuft at the end of their tail. "*Why* are you giving me this? You know what happened to the last plant you left with me..."

"Well, yes, I remember." Reese pauses to plop down onto the couch beside Merlani. "Anyone could have forgotten that a cactus still needs to be watered, though! I'm sure Erin didn't blame you."

"I wouldn't know about that..." Merlani hesitates, still holding the plant and trying to think of a way to get their Navigator to take back custody of it. This is hardly the first time she's tried to entice them into being a plant person.

"Erin" was the name Reese had given the now-deceased cactus in question. Merlani is quite certain that if the cactus was *able* to blame them for its untimely demise, it would have—and rightly so. Its corpse had been sitting in their windowsill for almost a month, after all, before Reese came over and pointed out that it wasn't normal for a cactus to have shriveled up and turned grey.

"Don't worry!" Reese says, smiling in her most charmingly conspiratorial way. She leans over and sets her arm around Merlani's shoulders. "I've already warned Harold that you're still learning how to take care of plants."

This is a bit of an understatement on her part. Merlani has never been able to keep anything green alive for very long, no matter how hard they've tried. One of the human housemates they'd had in their first year at the Academy had gone so far as to christen them the "grim reaper of houseplants."

The fate that housemate's aloe vera plant had met at their hands was only part of his reasoning for the nickname. Merlani themself still maintains that if he'd not wanted the plant to be knocked off the balcony of their shared fifth-story flat in on-campus housing, he *shouldn't* have left it so close to the edge and right where Merlani's long prehensile tail might accidentally strike it when they tried to sit down in one of the chairs there. They don't have as much of an excuse for overwatering the collection of kitchen herbs he'd left in their care over winter break to the point of drowning, though.

"Harold?" Merlani asks, focusing their attention back on the plant in their hands instead of the memories of all of its unfortunate predecessors. They wonder if the plant is able to suspect how much danger its life is in. "Is that what you're calling it, then?"

"That's the name that suited him."

Merlani turns all three of their golden eyes back to meet their best friend's two earnest brown ones now and sighs. "It's a nice name for a victim, I suppose. How long does it take for one of these to dry out?"

"Harold isn't going to be your next victim!" Reese gives them a bit of a reassuring laugh, shaking her head again in that way that makes the dark, wavy hair in her long ponytail swish dramatically. "I had a friend set him up with those sensors they use in the botany labs. He'll *tell* you when he wants to be watered."

"You really thought of everything this time, didn't you?"

"I wanted to give you a better chance at keeping this one alive."

Merlani is very bad at saying no to their Navigator when she's trying to do something sweet—even though they're sure that the plant's best interests would be to stay as far away from them as possible. Reese is their best friend, after all, and her plant-keeping hobby is something they know she wants very much to share with them. It's endearing that she keeps trying like this.

"...Thank you, then. I'll try my best."

"I knew you'd like him." Reese reaches over and pats Merlani on the head, lightly ruffling the silver hair right behind their catlike ears—a welcome gesture of close affection and acceptance. Even when she's standing, she barely has to reach at all, considering that she's tall for a human and Merlani's short for a Florivan, so their ears normally barely pass the level of her elbow. "Come on, hand me your pocket-com and I'll help you set him up before we go to the athletic center."

"All right." Merlani finds themself smiling. They almost believe that Reese is right, and that this little plant's fate will be different from all the others.

Almost.

To anyone who knows Merlani's reputation with plants, it is utterly shocking that not only does Harold survive under their care for more than two weeks, but even seems to be *thriving*.

Merlani themself is the first to point out to any incredulous witnesses of this seeming miracle that any success should be attributed to the sensors in the little plant's pot rather than any influence of theirs. The system regularly reminds Merlani via text pings whenever the plant needs attention and is set to *continue* to remind them until they do something about it. Supposedly, the sensors pick up electrical and chemical signals from the plant itself to determine how it's "feeling." The tone of the messages is determined by that information.

When Merlani accidentally forgot to arrange for someone take care of Harold while they and Reese and all of their housemates were gone for a month to the Sub-Solar Central Training Grounds with the rest of the Nav/Quan department, the alerts had gotten downright *testy*. Harold only narrowly escaped the same fate as Erin the Cactus, then.

Somehow, though, there was just enough of the plant still clinging to life when Merlani returned that it revived. It had even started blooming again a few weeks later, although the tone of the messages had stayed rather curt for quite some time.

The most recent message flashes across one of the three holoscreen projections arrayed on Merlani's desk while they're in the middle of writing a term paper for their Advanced Crystallography class:

23:45, Monday:

```
  ~~~ Good evening, Ocean! ~~~

I know you are busy, but would you
mind watering me?

It's been a bit warm in your room
this week and my soil is drier than
I'd like.

Thank you!

~~~ Harold the Violet ~~~
```

Reese, being the amusingly imaginative human she is, had taken the liberty of programming the alerts to reflect the "personality" she perceived in the plant when she first installed the sensor system. Merlani can't help wondering, sometimes, if their Navigator's good luck with her own collection of plants is because she talks to them enough to be aware of their complaining even without technological assistance.

Dismissing the message, Merlani sighs and gets up from their desk to take the plant to the sink in their flat's common area so it won't keep pinging them to complain and distracting them.

All three of their human housemates are hanging out in the common area playing cards with the trio of Florivan littermates who share the flat's fifth room. Even if Kingfisher, Bunting, and Jay didn't live there, though, Merlani knows they would be over all the time. Condrey and the Maltby twins are their respective counterparts, after all. It would be odd if they *weren't* all thick as thieves.

With the lot of them now in their final year at the Academy, Merlani is already starting to wonder how they'll handle it being *quiet* again once they're alone in the flat like they were for their first summer on Earth. They know they'll miss the reassuring chaos of their current batch of housemates.

"Ocean!" calls Robin Maltby, the pale, freckle-dusted redhead waving broadly in Merlani's direction. They're the more energetic of the two siblings. "You've emerged from under your rocks! Come play with us!"

Merlani laughs. "I've only emerged because my warden demanded it, Robin. I'm going right back under my cozy rock pile as soon as this opinionated little green thing is satisfied."

"Oh, is your plant talking to you again, Cousin Ocean?" Bunting, the grey-blue Florivan perched on the back of the couch above Robin, twitches their ears curiously. Their tail swishes to match, accidentally tickling the young human's ear. Robin giggles and bats it away.

"Making demands is more like it." Merlani turns their lower eyes down to the plant in mock disgust.

"What's he demanding this time?" asks Condrey, leaning over on the armrest of the chair to get a better look at the plant.

"Water, apparently." Another loud message alert sounds from the open door to Merlani's room, where they'd left their pocket-com. It's unmistakably the bubbling tone Reese set for all of Harold's messages. "And it's being impatient with me."

Robin's twin brother, Richard, chuckles as he stands from his spot on the couch beside his sibling and stretches some apparent stiffness out of his limbs. He hands his cards to Jay, then makes a subtle gesture towards the flat's tiny kitchenette area. "Mind if I join you? I was starting to get a bit thirsty myself..."

Merlani rolls their third eye, although more from amusement than anything. "Sure, Richard, I'll water you too. Do I need to try to avoid your leaves?"

"I'll have you know I'm a self-watering sort of fellow," Richard tells them, in his most proper and serious tone. "The grim reaper of houseplants has no sway over me."

"That's good to know." Merlani laughs. "Jay would be upset if my powers affected you."

"I would!" calls Jay from the couch. "Wilting isn't good for Navigators, you know."

Merlani sets their plant down by the sink. Just as they turn on the water to fill Richard's glass and the watering can, another ping with Harold's tone sounds from their bedroom.

All of their housemates break down into giggles from across the common area.

"Well, Ocean," Richard quips, "I think he's *very* excited about the prospect of being watered..."

Merlani turns all three eyes over to the black ceramic pot and the mass of fuzzy leaves and purple flowers with a silent glare. They have half a mind to tell Harold that it is a *very* demanding little life form who should be more patient with them. They don't, though. Merlani has still yet to develop the habit of talking to plants themself—even though this one certainly seems to always have something to say to *them*.

✦

On an evening not long before the end of the spring term, Merlani is in the locker room with the rest of their teammates changing into their gym clothes. As usual, there's more banter and catching up going on than actually changing and preparing for their weekly Martial Arts Competition and Demonstration Team practice session.

"I still can't believe we're graduating before *you*, Vasquez." Beck Lavine, the light-skinned, sandy-haired martian leaning against the door frame outside one of the curtained changing alcoves laughs brightly. Lavine is always the first one dressed, but they can't resist hanging out and chatting as long as anyone else is left in the locker room.

From behind the alcove's curtain, Reese laughs in response. "What can I say? I owe Nav/Quan another year, thanks to a certain delightful geologist..."

Merlani shakes their head, focusing their attention on tying their black judogi belt correctly. Lavine and Martins, the young woman behind the other changing alcove's curtain who's practically inseparable from the martian, were both in their first year when Merlani joined the team. They're both graduating in a week now.

"Hey, I'm all for you having a reason to stick around, Vasquez!" Martins chimes in as she emerges from the changing alcove. As usual, the pale, freckle-covered young woman has all of her bright reddish, wavy hair pulled up into a rather messy bun. She bounds over to the bench by Merlani and shoves her uniform into the gym bag she'd left there, then gives them one of her usual energetic hugs. "You too, Barker—I'm going to miss trying to keep up with you and your crazy Florivan reflexes *so* much…"

Merlani gives their friend a squeeze in return. "You say it as if you'll never see me again. You're *family*, we'll wind up in the same place again sooner or later. And then we'll get to spar and you can show off for all of your new shipmates."

"Yeah…" Martins lets them go reluctantly, then shoves her gym bag into her open locker. "But it won't be the same."

"No," Merlani agrees, with a somewhat somber swish of their tail. "It won't… but 'see you later' is always better than 'goodbye.'"

"Is that another one of those bits of ancient Florivan wisdom that Jade made you memorize?" Reese asks, finally emerging from the changing alcove in her crisp white judogi. She casually tosses all of her gear into her locker.

"It's one of Dad's, actually." Merlani chuckles, now following their Navigator and their two friends out into the training room. "But Entile Jade *does* have a version too. Three or four of them, even."

"Oh?" Lavine takes their usual seat beside Martins at the front of the practice mat. "What's theirs?"

"Never deny the chance for paths to cross again, and carry the memories with joy until they do." The serene wind-chime-toned Florivan voice that answers isn't Merlani's—it belongs to the paler green-tinged blue figure who's just walked into the room with the team's coach. "That's my favorite one."

"Entile Jade!" Merlani leaves their extra sweater on the practice mat and scampers over to give the older Florivan a long-overdue hug. As usual, they hadn't known their entile was even in the system, much less coming to visit. "What in the *stars* are you doing here?"

"Well, now!" Entile Jade ruffles Merlani's hair affectionately and then holds out both of their left arms towards Reese, Lavine, and Martins, who are also coming over now to join in the welcoming hugs. "Did any of you really expect me to miss being here to celebrate and take far too many pictures of my human kittens in their adorable graduation outfits to send to the rest of the family? Not to mention that you all are going to be *competing* the week after! I couldn't resist rearranging my schedule so I could be here to cheer you on."

Merlani's three friends all share a laugh about that. All of them seem to finally have gotten used to Entile Jade's tendency to just *appear* without warning. The four other members of the team, though, have wide eyes. They're all freshmen, so this is the first time any of them have met the enigmatic Star-Keeper in person.

"Jade's going to be joining us for practice and helping me critique everyone's forms while they're visiting," says the team's coach, a tall, pale woman Merlani has always known as their Aunt Penny. She pauses to readjust one of the two poofy white ponytails at the base of her neck and sets her gym bag down. "And I believe you said you were up for giving my newer kiddos a taste of that fancy Star-Keeper's dancing you do?"

"After I see them in action!" Entile Jade laughs and takes a seat in the middle of the practice mat with Merlani and their friends. "You never know, Penny, I might want to borrow them someday..."

Amidst the laughing from the collection of humans Entile Jade has already adopted and the confused whispers some of the others are exchanging, Merlani catches a distinct melody sounding from their folded sweater. Their ears twitch in embarrassment as they fish the offending device out of the sweater's pocket with their tail so they can turn it off.

"*Again*, Cadet Ocean?" Aunt Penny raises an eyebrow and makes a point of lowering her specially-tinted wraparound glasses to fix Merlani with the most dramatic look she can muster. "Am I going to have to go give him a lecture about pinging you during my practices again?"

Ocean feels the deep blue warmth of a blush coloring their cheeks. "No, Colonel Albright," they say, since their aunt likes to keep up the formalities when she's acting as their instructor. "I just forgot to leave my pocket-com in my locker. I apologize for the disruption."

"Lucky for you, kiddo, we haven't started yet." Aunt Penny flashes them a reassuring smile. "Just turn the thing off so we don't have to listen to it all evening, will you?"

"Is this someone *I* need to find and lecture?" Merlani hears their entile whisper to Reese.

Merlani shakes their head. They know that tone; it's the one that says Entile Jade is offering to conspire with their Navigator if there's a person in their life who needs *more* than lecturing. The two of them are just as overprotective as the rest of Merlani's family, sometimes. It's endearing, but in this situation it's just one more layer of embarrassment.

Reese stifles a giggle. "Oh, no, but we'll introduce you later..."

★

After the usual post-practice waffles-for-dinner outing with the team, Merlani returns to their flat to take care of things. Reese and Entile Jade come with them.

"So, what was it he wanted this time, anyway?" Reese asks, while Merlani's housemates are distracted with greeting and catching up with Entile Jade.

"According to the messages? Water." Merlani taps the keypad to open their bedroom door. "But there was something weird about a 'great beast' taking a bite out of his leaf and 'meaning to do grevious harm' in the last message." They give their Navigator a pointed look. "Is that something you can translate?"

Reese shrugged. "Something nibbled him. Can't imagine what, though. It's not like you leave your window open or anything."

The answer streaks out of the room as the door slides open. A small, multicolored ball of fluff scampers out of Merlani's room and underneath the corner chair in the common area.

"There you are, Zunar!" Richard laughs, getting off the couch to coax the little creature out from its hiding place. "I was wondering where you'd gotten to. Have you been in Ocean's room this whole time?"

"Zunar?" Ocean asks, tilting their head curiously.

"She's Miss Fielding's," Richard explains, still with both hands and most of his attention under the chair. "I promised to watch her while her keeper is out of town this weekend."

"Ooh, Rebecca asked you for a favor?" Reese grins, sharing an unmistakable look of teasing delight with Robin as she goes over to steal Richard's vacant spot on the couch beside them.

"Rebecca left her *cat* with him!" Robin flashes the same grin. "I keep telling him that's quartermaster-speak for 'I trust you with my life and I like you, now ask me on a date already', but he doesn't believe me."

Richard makes no comment on this, although Merlani knows him well enough to guess that the barely audible sigh of resignation he lets out is probably accompanied by a rather dramatic eye roll. According to Robin and Reese, he and Rebecca Fielding are firmly in the "adorably awkward" stage of human courtship behavior.

"Zunar isn't much of a cat yet, though," Jay comments, going over to help their Navigator. They turn back to the group while they pointedly dangle the tuft of their tail under the edge of the chair to tempt the cat in question out. "She's more a fluffy little tornado with claws."

Merlani looks back into their room. The mess of blankets pulled out of their nest and clothes that have been tipped out of their laundry basket is bad enough. The broken flowerpot in the middle of the floor and associated pile of dirt and lightly nibbled plant is worse. "I can believe that, Jay. It *looks* like a natural disaster came through here..."

"Sorry, Ocean," says Richard, surveying the damage. He now has the tiny fluff of a cat recaptured and tucked neatly into the crook of his arm. It's purring contentedly, too, for whatever reason. "I'll help you clean it up—I still have no idea how Zunar even got into your room in the first place."

"Kittens do that, regardless of species." Entile Jade giggles softly, coming over and giving little Zunar's ears a light stroke. "I've always suspected that Earth cats had a touch of the Strange to them somewhere, you know."

"Maybe you can talk to this one and tell her to stay out of my room, then," Merlani quips. They go over to the mess where the unfortunate plant is sitting in the middle of the floor and start picking up the bits of its broken pot. "Reese? Come tell me if this counts for my record."

Reese stifles a laugh when she sees it. "No, I think you're good this time—we just need to get Harold a new pot to live in."

"Maybe something less fragile this time." Merlani shakes their head. "No wonder he was pinging me all evening."

"*This* is who you were going to introduce me to?" Entile Jade asks, now standing above Merlani and Reese. Their curious voice is accompanied by a swish of their tail that makes the little enameled bangles on it jingle brightly.

"Yep!" Reese holds the sensors she's been picking out of the dirt pile up to show them. "Harold uses these to remind Cinny that he needs water and things like that."

"Or to pester me at all hours for attention because *Reese* programmed the system and thinks it's a 'social plant' who needs fussing over." Merlani notes.

"Regular watering isn't fussing, Cinny. It's just basic care." Reese gives them a playful nudge.

"Harold." Entile Jade considers it a moment, then nods. "Well, it's nice to meet you then, Harold," they say, bending down and lightly patting one of the plant's fuzzy leaves. "I'm sorry it had to be under such unfortunate circumstances."

Somehow, Merlani is not surprised at all that their entile is *also* the sort of person who talks to plants. As far as they know, they themself are the only person in their family who's bad with plants in the first place. Their Entile River is an *agricultural* specialist, even.

"Here," says Jay, appearing with one of the big bowls from the flat's kitchenette. "You can put him in here until Richard and I can get you a replacement pot."

"Thanks, Jay." Merlani busies themself with scooping all of the loose dirt into the bowl. "Say, Reese? Can you set those sensors to tell Jay and Richard if the cat's gotten into my room so we won't have to clean Harold up again?"

"Sure! I can set it to ping them for emergencies once I reinstall the system in Harold's bowl." Reese transfers the plant into the bowl and sets about neatening the dirt around it.

"Here," says Richard, pulling out his pocket-com with his free hand, "Miss Fielding gave me Zunar's ID microchip code... I'll send it to you so you can set up a proximity alert, Vasquez."

"While you're at it, Teresa," Entile Jade chimes in, "do you think you could set it up so Harold can send *me* the odd message? I'd love to have pings from a plant to add to my list of things to blame if I need to get out of a meeting."

Reese laughs. "Sure, Jade. Why not?"

Merlani groans, although more teasingly than anything. "Stars save me from plant people... Harold's going to have a wider social circle than I do at this rate."

"Mew?" asks the little furry thing trying to wriggle out of Richard's arms.

"Oh, no," Merlani replies, standing and giving it their best narrowed glance. "This is *not* your playground anymore, Zunar. I don't care how cute you are..."

✦

A year later, Merlani is helping Reese pack up her apartment. After the graduation ceremonies tomorrow and their extended visit to her family's ranch afterward, the two of them will be heading off to their first posting on a working starship.

Merlani has already finished clearing out their small room on campus, not that they ever had much there. Florivans tend to travel light, after all. What belongings they cared to take with them are sitting in a neat pile near the door of Reese's sitting room.

"So, Steve and Agatha are coming with us. We'll leave the rest with my other things that are going into storage at the ranch."

"Your spiky friends don't want to come into space with us?" Merlani asks, gesturing with the silver tuft at the end of their long prehensile tail in the direction of the windowsill full of potted cactuses. All four of their hands are busy folding one of the bright striped blankets from Reese's couch.

"Not on this first run. Tía Luz said she'd look after them for me, thankfully, since we don't know yet how much room we'll have aboard *Ammonite*. I may pick one or two of them up from her the next time we come by Earth."

Merlani nods. The aunt in question is one of the agricultural specialists in Reese's family who run the ancestral horse ranch as a working 'Earth Cultural Heritage Historical Site.' She's also the person who passed the tendency to name and talk to plants on to Reese.

"But the new orchid and the... hungry one... get to come?" Merlani has been assured more than once that the vine their Navigator calls 'Agatha' only consumes insects that fall into its pitcher-shaped leaves. Somehow, though, the idea of living with a carnivorous plant is still a bit disturbing.

"Colonel Albright gave Agatha to me for good luck, remember?" Reese laughs. "*Naturally* I'm bringing her along."

"...Naturally." Merlani shakes their head. *Why* Aunt Penny, of all people, would think that carnivorous plants are 'lucky,' they still haven't figured out. They know her best as a no-nonsense former Defense Fleet darter pilot and martial artist. Granted, considering what all of the *other* former Fleet pilots they know are like, including their Dad, eccentricities like that tend to come with the territory.

"Besides," Reese says, grinning, "both of them are small enough that it'll be easy to set them up in our quarters. It just wouldn't be home without a plant or two to keep us company, now, would it?"

"Oh, I suppose not." Merlani matches her smile. If having some greenery in their shared living space makes their Navigator happy, then that's enough for them.

A ping from Merlani's pocket-com prevents them from further questioning the fates of Reese's collection of sharp plants. They flick out the device's holo-screen to read the message, thinking initially that it's something from one of their instructors.

It isn't.

"Say, Reese?"

"Yeah?" She looks up from the box she's packing.

Merlani stifles a laugh. "I forgot to ask you what I'm supposed to do about Harold."

"Oh! Harold's coming with us too, of course." Reese pauses and looks over to the pair of duffle bags and wheeled box containing Merlani's belongings. "Say, where is he, anyway? I thought you said you'd brought the last of your things with you and turned in your key-card already."

"...Apparently I left Harold sitting on the desk in my room. It just pinged to complain about the window shade being down."

"Cinny! No wonder he's pinging you!" Reese chuckles and gestures towards the door. "Go on, I'm sure someone will let you back in to get him."

As they walk back towards their former accommodation building for the last time to pick up the mislaid plant, Merlani has to wonder if Harold wouldn't be better off left at the ranch with Reese's cactuses where they won't be responsible for it anymore. In the two years since Reese gave them the little African violet, it's had no fewer than six near-death experiences. Thinking back on it, Merlani's surprised that it's still growing at all. They've never been able to keep a plant alive for so long before.

At the same time, Merlani knows that once the two of them have moved into their shared quarters aboard ESS *Ammonite*, Harold will most likely fall into Reese's care instead of theirs—meaning the little plant might stand some chance of long-term survival after all.

A baggage handling robot at the Lunar Orbital Space Station is facing a rather odd problem.

The robot knows its programming: scan arriving luggage transponders; move the object to the correct bag transfer belt. It's simple.

In this particular instance, though, when it scans the item in front of it, *two* transponders echo back instead of the usual one.

The first transponder is a standard code including the owner's name along with the other necessary information.

The second transponder is non-standard, and contains a vague yet urgent request which activates in response to the robot's scan.

This confuses the robot's programming, making it spend several minutes processing the situation.

Ultimately, because the second response specifies a request, the robot's algorithms deem it reasonable to prioritize and accommodate that.

The robot places the item in question precisely where it has requested to be placed without so much as a digital shrug and carries on with the rest of its work.

✦

"Harold's got a lot of personality, Cinny, but he could hardly have run away." Reese isn't doing a good job of hiding her amusement.

"Well, where is it, then?"

"You're *sure* you dropped him off at decontamination and baggage transfer with Steve and Agatha?"

Merlani sighs and flops down onto the couch in the sitting area between the two connected bedchambers of their new quarters. It has been a very long day getting to their new home aboard the starship *Ammonite*, even before this latest little problem cropped up.

"I promise, Reese. I put the transponder tag on just like I did for the rest of our bags. The last time I saw that plant, it was sitting right beside the other two."

"Weird." Reese shrugs and sits down next to them, patting one of their lower hands. "Well, I'm sure he's on the ship somewhere. We'll just have to ask the quartermaster to help us find him—I think I saw some things marked for the botany department being loaded with the other cargo on the shuttle we took to get here. Someone probably took Harold down to hydroponics by mistake or something like that."

"Maybe so..." Merlani looks around the room. "Before we go hunting for stray violets, you said something about unpacking and rearranging this place?"

"Yeah, I know most of the furniture's built-in, but I was thinking we could figure out a way to hang Agatha up on the wall by the viewport window-seat. That'd give us room on the open shelf she's sitting on now to get out some of those neat geodes of yours to arrange around Harold once he catches up with us..."

Just as Merlani and Reese have finished unpacking and head out to join *Ammonite*'s command team for a welcome-to-the-ship dinner, a series of pings sounds on Merlani's pocket-com.

"What's all that about?"

"I don't know. Thing finally synced up with the ship's relays, I guess." Merlani reads through the series of messages and then turns their third eye over to Reese sheepishly. "So, apparently something *has* happened to Harold."

"Oh?"

They pass her the pocket-com and let her read the messages for herself:

12:05, Saturday:

```
~~~ Copy of message sent in response
to   unknown   status   inquiry.   ~~~


Hello, new friend!

My name is Harold!

I  am  a  Saintpaulia  difficilis
belonging to Ensign O. M. Barker of
ESS Ammonite!
```

Ocean takes very good care of me. I only have to drop them two or three hints now before they remember to water me, too!

If it's not too much trouble, could you please move me somewhere where I can see the sun? It's a bit too shady where I'm sitting right now.

Thank you!

~~~ Harold the Violet ~~~

"New friend?" Reese asks, raising an eyebrow. "Who'd have been pinging his sensor-system's transponders?"

"I have no idea..." Merlani makes a vague gesture with one of their lower hands, even as they're setting their upper-left over their face to try to hold in their awkward giggles. "Just... keep reading. It gets odder."

12:10, Saturday:

~~~ Hello, Ocean! ~~~

The window here is very big and I am in the sunlight!

Thank you for taking such good care of me!

~~~   Harold   the   Violet   ~~~

13:30 Saturday:

~~~ Hello, Ocean? ~~~

I am not sure how I feel about being in microgravity.

My roots are confused, and I am
cold.

~~~ Harold the Violet ~~~

"Microgravity?" Reese looks back up to Merlani. "Why in the *stars*?—"

Another ping interrupts her.

"Is that another one from Harold?" Merlani asks, equally confused.

"No, it's not." Reese hands them back the pocket-com, wordlessly shaking her head in amazement.

17:30, Sunday:

~~~ Ensign Barker: ~~~

We regret to inform you that a
technological issue has resulted in
the misplacement of your property.

We are unable to recover your item
at this time.

We will be reviewing the programming
of our baggage handling robots in
light of this incident and updating
their protocols regarding non-
standard transponder auto-response
codes and station airlocks.

Our sincerest apologies,

~~~ Baggage department, Lunar
Orbital Station ~~~

"Well, that explains why we couldn't find Harold, at least." Merlani sighs lightly, putting the pocket-com away.
~~~

"I'm sorry, Reese—I really *did* do my best to keep him alive..."

"I know you did. Don't worry about it too much." Reese sets one of her warm and reassuring arms around Merlani's shoulder. After a moment, she nudges them with her other hand. "You know, Cinny, under-watering a cactus is one thing... so's knocking the odd plant off a balcony... or having a cat assassin take one out... but I don't think I've *ever* met someone who managed to have a houseplant lost out of an airlock."

Merlani turns all three of their eyes to her. "Does this mean you're not going to give me any more plants to accidentally kill, then?"

"I *think* it means I should warn the ship's botanists about you." Reese grins at them, making it clear by her tone that she's teasing now and isn't too terribly upset about what's happened to her ill-fated gift. "You know, before they find out the hard way that the only thing that will grow for you are crystals. Although I suppose if there are any weeds they happen to *want* to see meet a swift demise or plants that aren't cooperating with them, we can get you a nice long-handled sickle and a black robe and send you down to hydroponics..."

Reese's grin is infectious. Merlani can't help letting out a small laugh.

"...Fair enough, Reese, fair enough."

✶ The End ✶

Characters Appearing in *The Tragedy of Harold the Violet*

The following list of characters is divided by species and arranged in order of their appearance in the narrative. Only characters with significant "speaking roles" have been detailed here. All others present are listed as a group for the reader's reference; characters who are mentioned but do not appear are not included.

Florivans

Ocean Merlani Barker Hämäläinen

They/them. Also known as "Cinny". A cadet at the Sol Central Space Service Academy (Advanced Geosciences, QSD Engineering, Exoplanetary Mineralogy). Former survivor-smallest kitten. Counterpart to **Teresa Vasquez**. Child of **Ocean Marbree** and littermate of **Sky Miradyn** and **Storm Melbryl**. Adoptive child of **George Barker** and **Taimri Hämäläinen**. Nibling of **River Myrval** and adoptive nibling of **Jade Ilmi**, **Cerulean Mirawynd**, and **Elias Rudolph**. Adoptive grandchild and member of the household of **Elder Celadon**.

Kingfisher Relevi

They/them. A cadet at the Sol Central Space Service Academy (QSD Engineering, Chemistry). Littermate of **Bunting Renyl** and **Jay Reelim**.

Bunting Renyl

They/them. A cadet at the Sol Central Space Service Academy (QSD Engineering, Literature). Littermate of **Kingfisher Relevi** and **Jay Reelim**.

JAY REELIM

They/them. A cadet at the Sol Central Space Service Academy (QSD Engineering, Archaeology). Littermate of **Bunting Renyl** and **Kingfisher Relevi**.

JADE ILMI

They/them. Also known as "The Fleet's Phantom". A former survivor-smallest kitten. Star-Keeper and Agent of the Florivan Council of Elders. Child of **Elder Celadon.** Adoptive entile of **Ocean Merlani** and their littermates. Adoptive parent of **Teresa Vasquez, Antionette Martins, Beck Lavine**, and **Simon Katz**.

Humans

TERESA VASQUEZ

She/her. Also known as "Reese". A cadet at the Sol Central Space Service Academy (Astral Navigation, Command, Tactical Piloting). Counterpart to **Ocean Merlani**. Co-captain of the Martial Arts Competition and Demonstration team. Niece of **Esteban Vasquez**. Adoptive daughter of **Jade Ilmi**.

ANTON CONDREY

He/him. A cadet at the Sol Central Space Service Academy (Astral Navigation, formerly Engineering). Counterpart of **Kingfisher Relevi**.

RICHARD MALTBY

He/him. A cadet at the Sol Central Space Service Academy (Astral Navigation, formerly Astral Cartography). Twin brother of **Robin Maltby**. Counterpart of **Jay Reelim**.

Robin Maltby

They/them. A cadet at the Sol Central Space Service Academy (Astral Navigation, formerly Navigation Technology). Twin sibling of **Richard Maltby**. Counterpart of **Bunting Renyl**.

Beck Lavine

They/them. A cadet at the Sol Central Space Service Academy (Command). Member of the Martial Arts Competition and Demonstration team. Adoptive child of **Jade Ilmi**.

Antoinette Martins

She/her. A cadet at the Sol Central Space Service Academy (Security). Member of the Martial Arts Competition and Demonstration team. Adoptive daughter of **Jade Ilmi**.

Colonel Penny Albright

She/her. Lead Tactical Piloting instructor and assistant Security/Tactical instructor for Judo, Sol Central Space Service Academy. Head of the Academy's Martial Arts Competition and Demonstration team. Defense Fleet veteran and former 2nd Darter Squadron pilot. Adoptive aunt of **Ocean Merlani**. Member of the household of **Elder Celadon**.

Others

Harold

He/him. A *Saintpaulia difficilis* with purple flowers.

Zunar

She/her. A *Felis cattus* kitten training to be a starship's cat. The pet and coworker of **Rebecca Fielding**.

APPENDIX

ON COLONY STARS AND THE SOL COALITION

Sleeping Beauties is set at the onset of the Sol Coalition's First Contact Era, marking the moment at which humanity's long and storied friendship with the enigmatic Florivans began. In fact, the Sol Coalition itself owes its continued existance largely to the events of *Sleeping Beauties*.

More than two centuries before the starship LSS *Hulthemia* set out from Luyten's Star, the generation ships North, South, East, and West left Earth to found settlements at their respective Colony Star Systems: Luyten's Star, Kapteyn's Star, Teegarden's Star, and Proxima Centauri. At this time, humanity's spacefaring technology was limited to solar sails and arguably primitive ion and chemical propulsion engines. As such, each of these four great colonial ships took eighty years or more to reach her destination.

Each Colony Star was chosen specifically for its closeness to both Earth and the other Colony Stars, as well as the suitability of at least one of its known planets for human habitation. Every effort was made to ensure that the colonists would arrive with all of the supplies and experts they would require to establish a self-sufficient settlement. As generation ships, the initial crews of colonists were chosen both for their expertise and for their willingness to dedicate the lives of their grandchildren to settling the world they had chosen.

A notable exception among the colonists were the artisans and experts who traveled with the cargo of the generation ships. These people volunteered to become part of the colonies as well, but because the skills and specialist knowledge they carried were of a sort that could not easily be transmitted to a new generation during interstellar transit, they were put into cryogenic stasis for the duration of the voyage. Stasis technology was, at the time, still new and required too much dedication of a ship's energy resources to be used for more than a dozen or so people per generation ship.

After the founding of the Colony Stars and the expansion of the Proxima Centauri colony to the planets of its sister stars Alpha and Beta Centauri, the Sol Coalition itself was little more than a communication network built on promises from the different Colony Stars to remain a connected and united part of humanity. Messages between the Colony Stars and Earth were limited to the speed of light, thus taking anywhere between a year and over a decade to arrive at their recipients. There was no interstellar trade or transportation to speak of, but administrative and scientific communication kept the Colony Stars tied to their origin.

Upon *Hulthemia's* contact with the Florivans at Procyon and her subsequent return to Luyten's Star, everything changed. The technology humanity's new friends shared reconnected the Colony Stars with Sol on a level previously thought impossible. The Quantum Space Relay Network developed between the Florivan experts and technicians from Luyten's Star allowed for realtime communication between ships and star systems, and was quickly adapted for use across all of the Sol Coalition's territory.

Along with the Relay Network, the Florivan gift of the Quantum Space Drive was the center of the reconnection efforts. This technology was not without its dangers, particularly on account of the human sensitivity to the miasmas of Quantum Space, but it allowed for starships to travel between planets and stars far more rapidly. With a Florivan "jumper" running the Drive in tandem with their human Navigator, a starship could skip along through space like a stone thrown across a still lake, using the so-called Quantum Space Shortcut to travel beyond the limits of light speed and physical distance.

It was, therefore, the Navigators and their QSD Engineer counterparts who were at the center of reconnecting the disparate worlds of the Sol Coalition, as well as integrating Florivan and human societies as inextricably as they would become in later years. Henrietta Rose Lin, the starship *Hulthemia's* Artisan, and her Florivan counterpart Midnight Amaril were the first such pair. The Sol Coalition's historians would remember them primarily for their careers after the events of *Sleeping Beauties*, as the pair at the center of the development of the Quantum Space Drive for use on human starships, as the ones carrying *Hulthemia* between all of the Colony Stars on her grand mission to set up the Relay system and introduce humanity's new allies, and as the trainers of the first true generation of Nav/Quan teams.

The Human Visitor's Welcome Guide to City-on-the-River and Florivan Kittens

Welcome to the Florivan Sanctuary Planet at Procyon and City-on-the-River!

In the decades since the arrival of LSS *Hulthemia* and the initial contact between humans and Florivans, our peoples have become close allies. Needless to say, the Sol Coalition as we know it today would not exist without this friendship between our species. The Florivan gift of the Quantum Space Drive and the development of the associated Communications Relay system keeps all of our settled worlds connected and united as we continue to explore our little corner of the galaxy together.

As a visitor to the Sanctuary at Procyon, whether you have come for diplomatic or academic exchange purposes, on shore leave from a starship, or as a Navigator meeting your counterpart's family for the first time, you are among a lucky minority of humans who have had the opportunity to fully experience our home and culture. You may also have chanced to visit the Florivan Sanctuary quarter in North City on Luyten's Star Prime, and had a taste of what life is like among us before. Compared to City-on-the-River and the other settlements of the Sanctuary at Procyon, however, that is barely more than a handful of households.

Here at City-on-the-River, you are in the capitol of Florivan society. You will find yourself surrounded by your enigmatic, but remarkably friendly alien allies for the whole of your visit. At present, there is exactly one human who lives on this planet full-time.

NOTE: If you become homesick for interaction with a member of your own species during your visit, use the interactive map provided in Appendix A of your welcome data packet to find your way to the Bakery at the northwestern corner of the Council House Courtyard. City-on-the-River's resident human can usually be found there. This is also the only establishment on the planet liscensed to import and serve coffee, should you desire it.

The two defining landmarks of City-on-the-River are its namesake, the small river which runs through its center, and the Council House. The latter is home to the Florivan Council of Elders. This is the governing body for our entire society, and is composed of all of our Elders, who are the heads of individual households. Each of these Elders is also one of the somewhat rare reproductive members of our species, and therefore has authority over all of their progeny.

Please keep in mind, dear visitor, that when encountering an Elder, it is considered incredibly rude for humans to ask questions about the details of their anatomy and how, exactly, reproduction works for a genderless, asexual species. If there is a reason for you to be trusted with this information, an Elder will inform you voluntarily of the parts you need to know. Florivans are a private species by nature, and have valid and important reasons for keeping such information to ourselves.

As a human visitor to the Sanctuary at Procyon, you are here as the guest of one of the Elders' Households. The Elder hosting any given visitor will usually welcome them to Procyon personally. If you are a diplomatic visitor, you are the guest of the Council as a whole, and therefore the Eldest's Household. Otherwise, which Elder is responsible for you while you are visiting depends, usually, on the purpose of your visit. Academic exchange visitors typically are guests of an Elder with an interest in the same discipline, while Navigators and other members of a starship's crew are guests of the Elder to whose household the ship's Florivan Quantum Space Drive Engineer or "Jumper" belongs.

> *Note: Your host Elder's contact code is listed in Appendix B of your welcome data pack, along with the information for your local guide and your lodgings if you are staying overnight.*

As the heads of their respective households, Elders are responsible for not only caring for and raising their kittens, but also for coordinating the efforts and careers of their fully-grown offspring. An Elder's household may also include other relatives or adopted members whose parent has died. It is not uncommon, therefore, for an Elder to have an assortment of non-reproductive Florivans in their household who are older than the Elder themself. Most often, any living littermates of an Elder will also join their household at its establishment.

Since the first contact of humans and Florivans, it has also become somewhat common to find human members of Florivan households. Specifically, a tradition formed from time of the first human Navigator and Florivan Quantum Space Drive Engineer pairing wherein the parent of a Florivan who takes a human counterpart will adopt that human formally as a member of their household.

NOTE: *If you are a Navigator visiting the Sanctuary at Procyon for the first time, your counterpart has doubtless already explained all the details of this process to you. In that case, congratulations and welcome to the extended family shared by all Florivans!*

As a human guest of an Elder's Household, it is likely you will encounter some of the youngest members of our species. We refer to these as "kittens". The more time you spend in the company of Florivan Elders, or in City-on-the-River in general, the more likely you are to be befriended by a kitten or three.

Physically, Florivan kittens of all ages are miniatures of our adults, with the same distinctive cat-like ears, three eyes, four arms, and long prehensile tail which humans lack. They first emerge from the safety of their parent's "brood pouch" at roughly one year old, when their eyes have opened. At this time, they are half the size of an Earth chipmunk on average and covered completely in a soft coat of fluffy silver fur. If a creature matching this description makes contact with you and attempts to inspect you or your belongings, or climbs up onto your shoulder, please do not be alarmed. Kittens are, by nature, very curious about new people and things.

Kittens are usually encountered in litters of two to six, somewhere in the general vicinity of their parent or an adult relative. Younger kittens will typically stay closer to their guardians than older ones, although within a familiar and safe setting they may range further regardless of age. Littermates are closely bonded and tend to explore together, keeping within earshot of each other in most cases.

Over the first four to five years after opening their eyes, Florivan kittens grow to about the size of a North American grey squirrel. At this point in their development, they begin to lose their fur, first in patches around their ears and shoulders, and show their adult skin coloration. This is also the time at which a Florivan Elder will present their kittens formally to their people's Council of Elders and give them their public names. (For example, "Navy" or "Indigo.") Before this, kittens are called only by the given names chosen when their eyes first opened. (For example, "Irleeim," or "Taivin".) After their Council Naming, only close friends and family members will use a Florivan's given name. When interacting with Florivans, humans should use their public names unless otherwise instructed.

Over a few years after shedding the last of their fur, Florivan kittens go through some remarkable growth spurts. They ultimately reach a stage at which they are about the same size as a human toddler. After this point, they will continue to grow to their adult height at the same rate as a human child of a similar age.

While kittens highly intelligent at all ages and are able to communicate in a simplified, squeak-based version of the language all Florivans know by instinct, they only begin to pick up words in human-understandable language around the same time they lose their first patches of fur. If a kitten is attempting to communicate with you and does not have enough words to do so, it is recommended you seek out the nearest adult Florivan for translation. Usually, however, kittens are able to get their point across to an observant and patient human without too much difficulty.

As a guest of a Florivan Elder's Household and a visitor to City-on-the-River, you are likely to encounter kittens of all stages of development. While it should be noted that unaccompanied kittens are common in City-on-the-River, particularly in the area of the Council House, if you are approached by a kitten who is showing signs of distress or who expresses to you that they are lost, please assist them in returning to their parent if possible.

__Note:__ It is advised that if a parent, guardian, or relative is not nearby, you should accompany "lost" kittens who request your help to the Bakery at the northwestern corner of the Council House Courtyard as shown on the interactive map in Appendix A of your welcome data packet. The baker Indigo Taivin of the household of Elder Woad and their human counterpart, Monica Malarius, are official kitten guardian contacts of the Council and will be able to coordinate the reunion of the kittens in question with their respective parents.

You will find our people generally to be quite hospitable, and happy to share tea and food with you quite often during your visit. In particular, as a guest of an Elder's Household, you will likely be taking your meals with your local guide and other members of the household throughout your stay. It is customary and somewhat instinctive for Elders to ensure that those in their care remain healthy and well-fed. Do not be surprised if you are offered tea and snacks in most social settings, and more often than you might be accustomed to, depending on your own family's traditions. Also, please be aware that kittens, particularly younger ones, tend to assume that all adults around them are willing to share their snacks. If you need help establishing boundaries with any kittens who befreind you, consult your host Elder or local guide.

As humans are far more omnivorous on average than Florivans, you need not worry which of our foods are safe for you to eat. Our diet is largely composed of plant-based items grown around our Sanctuary planet such as fruits, vegetables, nuts, seeds, and roots, and will seem quite familiar to the average human visitor. Florivan cooks and bakers offer a wide variety of dishes made from these which you will find analogous to many of those common in human cultures. There are also many human recipies which have been adapted to Florivan tastes, particularly in the sphere of baked goods. If you have special dietary or medical requirements, please remember to discuss this with your host Elder so that accommodations may be made for your health and safety needs.

NOTE: Certain categories of common Earth-sourced human foods are either toxic or inedible to Florivans. Appendix C of your welcome data pack contains a full list of these, including which ones are restricted or banned from import to the Sanctuary. Particularly of note are products of the plants of the Coffea, Theobroma, and Capsicum genera, such as coffee, chocolate confections, and pepper sauces, all of which are highly toxic to us. In no case should any of these be given or made accessible to curious kittens.

On behalf of the Florivan Council of Elders, welcome to City-on-the-River! We hope that you enjoy your visit to our Sanctuary.

Addendum:

In light of recent events, the Eldest of the Council suggests that all human visitors keep the following facts in mind when interacting with Florivan kittens:

1. While we are an instinctively pacifist species, our kittens are also born with an innate understanding of their vulnerability to predatory animals and how to defend themselves and their littermates until an adult can intervene.

2. Certain kittens have more highly attuned defensive instincts than others and may act on those instincts if they perceive a threat to themselves or their littermates, or if they perceive an active attack on one of their littermates. Usually this takes the form of hissing or loud squeaking to intimidate the predatory animal and draw the attention of the nearest adult.

3. In extremely rare cases, this instinct-driven defensive behavior can extend to biting.

Therefore, it is recommended that visiting humans ask any kittens they encounter for their *consent* to be touched, petted, or picked up. This lessens the likelihood of causing distress to the kitten, and thus potentially triggering defensive instincts in their littermates.

The Eldest thanks you for your understanding in this matter.

On the Defense Fleet's Darter Squadrons

The Sol Coalition Defense Fleet's squadrons of darter pilots are either legendary for their bravery or infamous for their love of danger, depending upon whom one asks.

The technology for small, two-person craft capable of maneuvering both within a planetary atmosphere and in the zero-gravity environment of outer space was already in development prior to the beginning of humanity's involvement in the Novan War. At that time, the inherently pacifist Florivan Council of Elders was still restricting the use of their all-important Quantum Space Drive to civilian and Ranger Corps vessels only. Without the Drive to allow their ships to use the veiled dimension of Quantum Space as a shortcut around the physical distances between planets and stars, the Sol Coalition Defense Fleet was left to come up with other means of protecting the eight star systems in its charge.

The concept of short-range fighter craft serving as a mobile force which could be placed on individual inhabited worlds or space stations as a final line of defense against potential invaders was the Defense Fleet's best option at the time. The danger of invasion was primarily theoretical at the onset of Project SnailDarter's development, as the only alien species humanity had thus far encountered were the neighboring Sol-based Europans (who were unable to leave their moon of origin without assistance) and the charismatic and friendly Florivans who had become humanity's closest ally and begun a process of peaceful societal integration.

When humanity found itself suddenly in the middle of the ongoing war between the Novan Imperium's conquest force and the Prelvee and T'irsh-fel Alliance, the development of Project Snail Darter was sped up in order to provide a serviceable defensive and expeditionary force.

Notably, the representatives of both senior member species of the Alliance were reported to be "horrified, but thoroughly impressed" by the demonstrations held for them of the capabilities of the "darters" and their pilots in combat scenarios against long-range particle weapons and unmanned drones. While the Alliance's strategists were familiar with the live-piloted "strikers" used by the Novans to overwhelm their enemies with seemingly endless waves of disposable attack craft, neither species had ever *dreamed* of placing live pilots at the controls inside similar spacecraft themselves. The idea of a single human being responsible for operating an object operating at the very limits of what the laws of physics and understanding of human science would allow and sending them out to attack the enemy directly was as completely alien to them as humans themselves were. Nevertheless, the Alliance quickly recognized the value of the Defense Fleet's darters as a counter to the Novan Armada's striker forces.

Initial plans for the use of these unique small fighter craft centered around forming squadrons of darters to be stationed as the defense of individual inhabited worlds within the Sol Coalition's territory. Additionally, a number of these squadrons would be selected to serve as an expeditionary force on the Alliance's ships in nearby battle sectors. The so-called "defection" of the Florivan Elder Celadon Toreval and the arrival of their household as the Fleet's "Florivan Volunteer Corps" made several changes to the Alliance's core strategies possible. The newly formed squadrons of darters were instead posted on the Defense Fleet's brand-new QSD-equipped starships, where they could more easily be mobilized to defend the Sol Coalition's territory and aid the other members of the Alliance when possible.

The first nine darter squadrons were formed by the time the Fleet's ships were ready, and each was placed under the command of one of the veterans of the Project Snail Darter test pilot program. While eight of these squadrons were immediately assigned to starships, the 9th remained stationed at the Teegarden Shipyards to defend the base there and assist in the training of additional pilots.

At the time of *Aliens at a Tiki Bar*, there are a total of twenty-eight darter squadrons in service. Each is composed of sixteen pilots, divided into four "wing teams" during maneuvers. The wings of a squadron are subdivided into patrol pairs. Each wing is led by one of the squadron's most experienced pilots, with the "lead wing" being that of the squadron's commanding officer. A darter squadron also includes a number of maintenance technicians responsible for repairing and updating the darters as needed. Typically, there is one of these technicians assigned to each wing, with a "chief mechanic" overseeing all of them.

The Second Darter Squadron is a notable exception to this standard personnel arrangement. The Second began as a typical squadron, albeit as the only one with more than one former test pilot in its ranks. After its commanding officer and the majority of its members were lost along with SCV *Athene* during the first Battle of the Teegarden Expanse, the decision was made to allow the remaining three pilots to reform their unit as a single-wing squadron retaining their initial designation. At the time of *Aliens at a Tiki Bar*, the resulting smaller Second is assigned to SCV *Surnia* as an attachment to the ship's own recently-formed 18th Darter Squadron.

On Fleet Protocol and Florivan Kittens

A memo from the desk of Fleet Admiral Jennifer Marvin, for the information of the officers and crew of SCV Aegolius:

Most members of this ship's crew are, by now, familiar with a certain Florivan kitten associated with the Second Darter Squadron and SCV *Surnia*. Mirawynd has no doubt introduced themself to the majority of you since we picked up their squadron at the Mayview Outpost several weeks ago. Therefore, the general nature of Florivan kittens should come as no surprise to you; they are essentially silver-furred miniatures of the adults of their species, and both highly intelligent and curious.

As it is no longer classified information that *Aegolius'* Quantum Space Drive Engineer, Commander Celadon, also has their two youngest offspring aboard ship, please be advised of the following regarding the three Florivan kittens in question:

1. **Mirawynd is the largest of the three kittens.** They have bright blue patches of skin on their face, hands, and back. They are able to communicate with a number of simple words in Standard.

2. **Teryin and Tesnee are Commander Celadon's youngest kittens, and are now approximately a**

year old. They are each about the size of a young Earth chipmunk, and cannot communicate outside of their natural squeaks and trills.

3. **Ask the kittens directly for their consent to be touched before attempting to pick them up or pet them.** While the kittens will likely be the ones pestering you for attention, it is important that they be allowed to choose the level of interaction they have with others. Be advised that on rare occasions, a stressed kitten may bite to defend themself or their family members, even if the danger is only in the kitten's perception.

4. **If you find one of the kittens alone, they have likely become lost while exploring the ship.** Commander Celadon requests that in such a situation, you return Teryin and/or Tesnee to them, Lt. Hsu, or the Second Squadron's Petty Officer Rudolph directly. If this is not possible, these kittens may be delivered either to my office or to any member of the Second Squadron. Mirawynd should first be asked who they are supposed to be with, and then returned to the person in question if possible. If no members of their squadron are available, Mirawynd may also be delivered to my office.

5. **If the kittens approach you in the crew mess, you may choose to share food with them at your discretion.** Please ensure that any food you offer to the kittens is Florivan-safe. If the kittens show interest in food items which are not safe for Florivan

consumption, Commander Celadon asks that you inform the kittens directly in the following format: "This is [food item]. I cannot share [food item] with you because it is not safe for Florivans to eat and would make you sick." This is an important part of the kittens' education, and the Commander assures me that the kittens will respect such statements. (You may, however, consider softening such a statement by offering the kitten in question an alternative safe food item.)

6. **Florivan kittens are strongly affected by low temperatures.** If one of the kittens approaches you seeking warmth, Commander Celadon asks that you oblige them until you are able to return them to one of their stated guardians. If you find one of the kittens and they are chilled or otherwise unresponsive, inform Commander Celadon *immediately* and take the kitten either to them or to the Second Squadron's Petty Officer Rudolph directly.

7. **Florivan kittens are known to "borrow" items which they percieve as shiny or interesting.** If you suspect an item of yours has been borrowed, you may contact the guardians of the kitten you believe has borrowed it to arrange for its return. If you can, ask the kitten directly if they have seen your item and can find it and bring it to you. Mirawynd in particular is usually willing to return borrowed items if asked directly. According to Commander Celadon, kittens primarily borrow things if they

are curious about them, and learning the names of items and what they are used for is an important part of their education. They suggest that if one of the kittens shows interest in tools which you do not wish to have borrowed, you tell the kitten directly in the following format: "This is [item name]. It is a working thing, and needs to stay here where it lives." Alternatively, if they are showing interest in something dangerous, you are to inform the kitten in the following format: "This is [source of danger]. It is dangerous and could [simple, nongraphic statement of harm]. You need to leave it alone." (Commander Celadon assures me that the kitten will respect this, but also asks that the kitten be removed from the vicinity of the danger as soon as possible and returned to them directly so they can ensure the kitten understands.)

Those of you who require more thorough briefing regarding the care of Florivan kittens than this will be contacted directly by Commander Celadon. Be advised that I will *not* be tolerating any attempts to pry into the Commander's personal affairs in connection with their kittens. If you receive a direct request from one of the kittens' guardians to not interact with them, consider yourself under my orders to respect this. Likewise, if one of the kittens shows signs that they are not comfortable interacing with you such as hiding, running away, or hissing, leave the kitten be and do not press the matter.

More information regarding *Aegolius'* resident Florivan kittens will be issued as it is deemed necessary. Any questions or concerns on the matter may be directed to my office so that I may discuss them with Commander Celadon.

–J. Marvin, Admiral

ON FLORIVAN KITTENS

A memo from the desk of Elder Celadon Toreval of the Florivan Council of Elders, to be distributed to those personnel of the Alpha Centauri-New West Space Station with a need to know at the discretion of their human son-by-line-adoption, George Barker:

Greetings! If you are reading this, you have the distinction of being one of the wonderful humans with whom my adoptive grandkittens wish to associate closely. Please take it as a compliment on behalf of the kittens that they so favor you; it means that you have a "safe, warm, and interesting person" aura in their eyes.

Because my people are somewhat secretive regarding our reproductive matters (and for good reason, I assure you), humans are often confused when first encountering the youngest members of our species. I'm not surprised that you are, too, considering that your own young start off disturbingly helpless and remain that way for so long, but seem to more clearly resemble adults of your species.

Our way is different.

As you may know from interacting with the adults of my species, we do seem quite similar to you on the surface. That's part of why we chose to tie ourselves to you in the first place! Even if we're quite different in fact, our peoples still have enough in common when it comes to environmental needs and general form that we're wonderfully compatible as friends. It's convenient for both of us, really—I have spent time on Prelvee and T'irsh-fel ships, and while both species are delightful, their idea of pleasant temperatures and artificial gravity levels is uncomfortable to say the least.

Florivans are similar to humans, but our biology is drastically different. Most notably, we are on the whole genderless and asexual. I won't go into details with you on it, but trust me when I say that the few individuals among us who bear kittens are *unique* and the role we play in our species is important. What matters to your situation is the kittens themselves, regardless of where they came from.

The parent of these particular kittens, Ocean Marbree, was a member of my household due both to their service with the Defense Fleet and the death of their own parent during the Novan War. The kittens are now the legally adopted children of Ocean's former Navigator, George Barker, and are members of my household just as he is. To that end, it falls to *me* to explain a few things to you about Florivan kittens.

Since you're reading this, I assume you've met the two larger kittens, Storm Melbryl and Sky Miradyn. They're lovely little silver fuzzy things, aren't they? Kittens start off smaller than this! If you've had the delight of meeting their little survivor-smallest sibling, Merlani, you may have an idea of what I mean.

When Florivan kittens first open their eyes and leave the safety of their parent's brood pouch, they are usually about the size of an Earth chipmunk at the most. A miniature Florivan, truly, but so covered in silver fur from ears to tail that people often mistake them for members of a separate but related species. Kittens from the moment they open their eyes are highly intelligent and curious. You'll find they try to get into everything in their innate quest to learn more about the world, but are prone to getting chilled and constantly seek warm places and people to snuggle. (Little Merlani is at about this stage still; as a survivor-smallest kitten, their growth is a bit delayed compared to their siblings.)

Within three or four years, Florivan kittens grow to more of an Earth squirrel's size and begin to lose their fur. This happens in patches, starting with the kitten's ears, hands, and upper shoulders. As their later growth spurts hit, the bald patches grow until only the belly and tail remain fluffy. (This is about the stage Storm and Sky are at, as of my latest visit.) Kittens receive their public names at this stage, once they have lost large enough patches of fur for their skin coloration to be clearly seen.

Kittens also begin talking in human-intelligible standard around the same time they start to lose patches of fur. They do, however, already have much more developed minds from the beginning, even if it takes a while for their communication abilities to catch up. Kittens usually learn the names of the most important people in their lives before anything else. Over time, handfuls of words become proper sentences. Please note that the kittens understand far more than they are able to imitate, even at earlier stages of their development.

Kittens are also more likely to pick up words that are used around them often, so please mind your manners around Storm and Sky. The other members of the Council get upset with *me* when they get wind of my household's kittens cursing like sailors, don't you know?

Once all of a Florivan kitten's fur has shed off save for what becomes the hair on their head and the tuft at the end of their tail, they are usually around the size of a small cat. This typically happens by around six years from the time they open their eyes. Another rapid growth spurt around the same time takes them to 'human toddler' size, after which their development more closely resembles that of humans. Florivans are usually fully grown young adults by the age of fourteen or fifteen. (Thankfully, aside from the handful of us who are destined to become reproductive members of our species, Florivans do not have to endure anything like human puberty. Lucky us!)

Now, the other thing George has asked me to include in this memo is a note on why the kittens act like little magpies and try to "borrow" things from folks. Quite simply, it's an instinct even we don't know the full origin of. Kittens are drawn to "shiny" or interesting things, and tend to want to bring those things back to their family's nest for safekeeping. In my experience, this is also because the kitten wants to show the shiny thing they found to their parent and siblings, particularly so their parent will tell them more about what the shiny thing *is*.

If one of the kittens consistently is borrowing your shiny things, please take that as a compliment. They think you have good taste in shiny things, and would like to know more about them and what you do. If you consistently tell the kitten the name of the shiny things they've borrowed, it shouldn't be too much trouble to ask them to return it.

My Navigator has had quite a bit of success in the past with the kittens he's known by keeping small biscuits or dried fruits in one of his pockets to reward them with upon returning items. Notably, he even trained my nibling Cerulean to be his assistant when they were a kitten and retrieve tools for him while he was working! Cerulean has gone on to be quite the skilled mechanic as an adult, too.

That's about all I can think of that's particularly important to know about kittens, aside from the fact that they can get chilled easily when they're small and need to be given plenty of warm places to snuggle and adjust their body heat. If you've met the kittens, though, you've probably already noticed how sweet and cuddly they can be in general! I have it on good authority that kitten purring is good for alleviating human stress, too, so if you've been having a hard day and one of the kittens has shown up to check on you, perhaps you should take a break and pet or play with them for a while? It would do you good, I'm sure.

Thank you again for being one of the people I can count on to watch over my grandkittens and keep George informed of their whereabouts on the station as they grow and become more wide-ranging in their explorations. Should you have any questions, feel free to contact me. Likewise, if you happen to take pictures of the kittens being cute and kitten-like, you now have my contact codes. I love seeing what my grandkittens are up to and hearing about their adventures!

With much affection,

Elder Celadon Toreval

Lead QSD Officer, LSS *Starbright*

Fleet's Elder, Member of the Florivan Council of Elders

On Navigators and their Counterparts

The integration of Florivan society into that of humanity began with and centers around the so-called "Quantum Space Drive". This marvelous, yet highly secretive technology which allows starships to travel through the intradimensional shortcut of "Quantum Space" (called "the Strange" by the Florivans) to get around the inconvinences of physical distance between planets and stars was the first gift the Florivans shared with their human friends. The second gift, the Intersteller Relay Network, uses similar technology to send messages along the fringes of the veil and allow near-realtime communication.

While the technology was certainly not without risk, use of the Drive was crucial in the reconnecting and unifying of the seven star systems inhabited by humans: Sol, Kapteyn's Star, Luyten's Star, Teegarden's Star, and the the triad of Proxima Centauri and her sisters Alpha and Beta Centauri. Prior to first contact with the Florivans, only solar-sail powered generation ships carried humans between the stars and communication between inhabited worlds was similarly limited to the physical reality of the speed of light.

The resulting post-contact spacefaring society, commonly known as the Sol Coalition, still bears an eighth point in its emblem to represent the star system of Procyon, which had been home to the Sanctuary planet of the Florivans prior to its destruction at the end of the great Novan War. While the Florivans suffered the unfathomable loss of all but a small percentage of their population due to this disaster, some decades later at the time of *The View from a Distance*, signs are pointing to this endangered species slowly beginning to recover.

A majority of the Florivans who survived the Novan War were those who had made a compact with a human Astral Navigator counterpart to serve on the crew of a starship. This tradition of human-Florivan working pairs began at the same time as initial contact between the two species and the development of the system which allows the Quantum Space Drive to be safely used on human-crewed starships. With the Florivan half of the starship's Nav/Quan team sealed into the ship's Drive bay and all of the ship's viewports shuttered, a bubble of 'Normal space' can be maintained within the ship while the Drive is active. The Navigator provides their Florivan counterpart with landmarks and contextual information to keep them oriented as they direct the ship from one point to another. Small 'jumps' in and out of Quantum Space thus allow such a team to maneuver a starship in a matter of days or weeks across distances which would otherwise take years or even decades to cross with conventional spacecraft.

Every starship requires a Nav/Quan pair to function. By the time of *The View from a Distance*, the population of Florivans has begun to recover enough that it is once again becoming more common for a secondary pair, usually younger, to join the crew of a ship with an established team. While in the days before the Novan War, only a small percentage of adult Florivans had taken human counterparts, at this time, *every* young Florivan is expected to choose a Navigator for themself. This rule of the Florivan Council of Elders is just as much for the protection of their people as it is to allow as many starships as possible to have Nav/Quan teams. A Florivan's Navigator becomes a member of their family, essentially as a chosen sibling, and is seen as a lifelong protector and companion. From the human perspective, the relationship between a Navigator and their counterpart is viewed as equivalent to a chosen family member or platonic life-partner. Florivans are fiercely loyal to their counterparts, once chosen, and the humans who ultimately become Navigators are much the same.

While more than a few Florivans, historically, have chosen humans with no formal training in Astral Navigation, after the Novan War, a system was put in place to ensure that appropriately educated and screened candidates could be presented to young Florivans who were of an age to select their future Navigators. This is the system of the Central Space Service Academies. Each young Florivan, upon completion of their traditional QDE apprenticeship to an established Nav/Quan pair, signs to one of the several Academies for further study in their secondary subject and to take part in that Academy's advanced Nav/Quan training program. The Florivan cadets are then rotated with a cohort of Astral Navigator candidates who have been carefully selected based on their personalities, academic backgrounds, and tested aptitudes. A Florivan Cadet will remain in such a program until they have found a sutiable counterpart for themself, while human participants in the program are given one full academic year to see if they fit with any of the available Florivans. Nav Cadets who fail to be chosen after that period are released from the program, but carry a highly respected "Nav Certified" mark on their professional record going forward. (Such people are sought after for the crews of starships, as they are qualified to serve as stand-in Astral Navigators in the case of an emergency or the temporary incapacitation of a given Florivan's counterpart. It is also not unheard-of for a "Nav Certified" person to later be selected by an unpartnered Florivan for their counterpart long after both have graduated from their respective academic programs.)

On Florivans and their Names

At the time of *Fox in the Cave*, the enigmatic, genderless aliens known as the Florivans have been the friends and allies of humanity for roughly 150 years. A peaceful species with a strong tradition of exploration, it was only natural that the Florivans chose to ally themselves with the ever-curious humans who had begun to colonize other stars. Roughly humanoid in form with silver-striped blue skin, a second pair of arms below the first, a long tufted prehensile tail, catlike ears at the top of a head crowned with silver hair, and a third golden eye above the first two in the center of the forehead: it's easy to see them both as "human-like" and "entirely alien" all at once.

An important aspect of Florivan culture when compared with humanity is their relationship to the very human concepts of gender, sexuality, and romance. To put it bluntly, Florivans by nature have no concept of these things. They are, without exception, genderless, asexual, and aromantic, to use the most accurate human terms. (Florivans do, of course, find the vast diversity among their human friends fascinating! It's part of why they think humans are neat.)In light of their genderless nature,

Florivans are always referred to with singular "they/them" personal pronouns in English and whatever neutral equivalent is most appropriate in other human languages.

Florivan names consist of two parts: the 'public' name and the 'personal' name. The 'personal' or 'kitten-name' is given to a Florivan when they first open their eyes, while the 'public' name is chosen for them when they are old enough to be presented to the Council of Elders. Some kittens receive one or the other half of their name in honor of one of their ancestors or entiles, which has become more common since the end of the Novan War.

Personal names come from the ancestral Florivan language, and are largely untranslatable. All of the kittens in a litter will usually be given names with the same or similar initial sounds.

Public names are always words from human languages which connect somehow to the individual's coloring. Kittens, therefore, receive their public names once they have shed enough of their fur to show a large patch of a recognizable color. Elders will often carry a theme through the public names of their kittens such as different stones, plants, or a specific language of origin.

Florivans are most often addressed by their public names. Only Elders, family members, or the closest of friends will address or talk about a Florivan by their personal name, and then only in private. (Private, in this case, also extends to situations where only other Florivans or close friends of the family are present.)

On the Subject of Aptitude Classification and Martian Social Structure

In the time of *Rooftops and Space Whales*, the academic systems of the Sol Coalition's member worlds have been standardized for several centuries. The universal academic standards in use throughout the Sol Coalition's shared society allow for efficient and comprehensive education to be provided to all human children regardless of where and how they are being raised. In addition to a common core curriculum, the Sol Coalition's education system uses the highly renowned Martian Standard Academic Assessment and Aptitude Classification Matrix to ensure that all students are placed in appropriate learning environments and guided towards their best-suited careers.

The MSA³M was developed during the early years of permenant settlement at Mars, based on several decades of thorough research by a committee of experts in education, developmental psychology, and social anthropology. The focus of the Matrix itself is in categorizing the inherent aptitudes of a given individual, and therefore providing educators with an understanding of what areas of study require improvement or should be encouraged as a future career focus. While modifications have been made to the system to reflect developments in space travel and associated careers, there is little difference between how the MSA³M is used in the time of this story as when it was first developed.

Students are first assessed for their base aptitudes between the ages of five and seven. Passing this provisional assessment is a requirement for a student to advance from

Nursery to Primary schooling. Assessments are repeated yearly until the child has met the appropriate minimum requirements for advancement to the next stage of their schooling. The assessment for young children includes a set of interactive tests to check that they are adequately prepared for Primary school knowledge-wise, as well as an interview with a panel of highly-trained experts to assess the child's social skills and scholastic interests. Upon completing the assessment, the child is assigned their base aptitude letters and numerical rankings. These will be used and updated throughout the student's academic career to reflect their growth and learning potential.

Assessments are repeated for students at the point of their transition from Primary to Secondary schooling, and again at their graduation from Secondary school. The aptitude letters and numerical rankings given to students at the latter point are their permanent Final Classification, and will be used in higher education settings to determine the best course of study and career guidance for each individual.

The MSA^{3}M codes each student with a combination of letters and numbers to reflect their personal aptitudes and levels of potential competency. The competency ranking is numerical, on a scale from zero (unranked) to twelve (highest possible). The letter codes represent academic subjects or career skill aptitudes as follows:

- S - Sciences
- T - Technology
- E - Engineering
- Ed - Education
- M - Mathematics
- Med - Medicine
- L - Leadership
- D - Diplomacy

- H - Humanities

While a student's assessments will include a numerical ranking for each of the above areas, traditionally focus will be put upon their two top-ranked areas. These are referred to as the student's "Prime" Classifications, and are considered the best indicator of their ideal higher educational and career trajectory.

Additionally, although it is relatively rarely issued as a Prime Classification, the letter code "A" exists for students who show a marked aptitude for arts and/or traditional crafts. These students are typically guided towards the separate system of education for humanity's Artisans. If the student has suitably highly ranked aptitudes in other areas, they will be allowed to choose a related career path at the end of their Secondary schooling. So-called "Class A" students, for whom the A designation is their Primary Classification, are incredibly rare at the time of *Rooftops and Space Whales*, and invariably become the most talented of humanity's treasured Artisans.

While the majority of the Sol Coalition's settled worlds view the MSA³M's assessments as a loose guideline, it must be noted that the society of Mars itself takes matters of aptitude classification far more seriously. Particularly among the descendants of the two dozen Founding Families, but also among martians in general, one's standing in society is informed in part by one's Primary Classification code. Individuals with strong aptitudes for Sciences, Medicine, Leadership, Engineering, Mathematics, or Technology are celebrated both by their families and their greater community. Those with lower-ranked aptitudes or Primary Classifications towards other subjects are seen by some martian communities as less crucial for the functioning of society and, perhaps, less necessary overall. Among the Founding Families, it is not un-heard-of, even, for marriages to be arranged between the most "high classed" individuals in hopes of producing the most intelligent offspring possible. This practice is considered to be going a bit too far by most citizens of Mars outside these families, however.

ON THE ACADEMY NAV/QUAN PROGRAMS

At the point in time at which *The Tragedy of Harold the Violet* takes place, humanity and the Florivans have been close friends and allies for just over a century and a half. The spacefaring culture of the integrated Human/Florivan society of the Sol Coalition is dependent upon this relationship. Without a Florivan to run the all-important Quantum Space Drive, the ship is limited to solar sails and basic sub-light propulsion methods; without a human Navigator counterpart to direct them and keep them anchored to Normal space, the Florivan 'jumper' cannot run the Drive.

Before the Novan War, only a small percentage of Florivans had taken Navigators and begun to use their technology to jump human ships between the Coalition's inhabited worlds. The majority of them remained un-partnered either by choice or by chance and lived at their people's Sanctuary planet in the Procyon star system, with a far smaller group living at Luyten's Star with the human colony there at North City. With the utter destruction of the Sanctuary's planet at the hands of the Novan Armada towards the end of the War, however, the fragmentary population of Florivans was centered around the North City residents, the Defense Fleet's small group of Volunteers, and those Florivans who were already out in space with Navigator counterparts.

Soon after the end of the War, the surviving members of the Florivan Council of Elders came together to determine the future of their species. With only a meager five thousand or so adults left, and a mere twenty known reproductive individuals, two of whom were no longer able to bear kittens, the Council was hard pressed to ensure the safety of every remaining Florivan.

Of particular concern were the adolescent Florivans who were still in their apprenticeships on various starships and the orphan kittens whom the Defense Fleet had rescued during the disastrous Battle of Procyon. Where before, these young Florivans would likely return to their home planet to live with their parent's household and undergo training in their chosen career if they did not make a compact with a human Navigator and remain in space, now the majority of them were not only orphans, but the sole surviving members of their families. Florivans being a semi-eusocial species, this posed a distinct additional risk to their wellbeing.

In the end, the Elders decided that it would be best to work towards *every* Florivan taking a human counterpart of some kind in order to compensate for their scattering from their kin and to provide an additional layer of protection. They saw it best that the majority of their species would move out into the starship-jumping role, in order to prevent future losses of large portions of their population. They also put into place what would ultimately become the Academy Nav/Quan system in order to ensure that the younger generations of Florivans would be able both to find appropriate counterparts for themselves and to spend a few additional years after being released from their apprenticeship in the company of other Florivans and similarly-aged humans.

As it stands in Ocean Merlani's time, there is an Astral Navigation and Quantum Space Drive Engineering program at the most prominent Space Service Academy in each of the Coalition's inhabited star systems: Sol Central Space Service Academy at Earth, North City Exploration Technology Institute at Luyten's Star, the University of Teegarden-Millefleur at Teegarden's Star, Kapteyn Central Academy at Kapteyn's Star, West Memorial Academy of Sciences at Proxima Centauri, Alpha Centauri-New West Space Service Academy at Alpha Centauri, and Toliman Interstellar Space Service Institute at Beta Centauri. Each of these programs is theoretically under the jurisdiction of the individual Academy's administration, but the curriculum, appointment of instructors, selection of Astral Navigator student candidates, and core workings of the program are overseen by the Florivan Council of Elders. The lead Florivan instructor for each program reports directly to the Council and has the final say on the program's internal matters, although in most cases they share these duties equally with their Navigator, who serves as the lead instructor for the human half of the program.

Upon completion of their apprenticeship on a working starship, an adolescent Florivan will sign to one of the Academies. Usually, they are between the ages of fourteen and sixteen at this time, having begun their apprenticeship at ten or eleven. In most cases, all of the kittens from a litter will sign to the same Academy program. The apprenticeship stage is seen as the adolescent Florivan's time to grow into independence from their parent, and in the same way their Academy training is when they learn to be independent from their littermates. The transition from being constantly together with members of their family to being largely alone on a starship is softened by the introduction of human friend groups and ultimately the relationship formed with the young Florivan's chosen human counterpart.

The Florivan cadets in an Academy Nav/Quan program take a secondary course of study in their preferred career focus in addition to their main program studies. Each of them will remain in the program until they have both made their compact with a human counterpart and completed first two years of advanced paired training with that counterpart and then a two-year posting as an 'Assistant Secondary' Nav/Quan team on a working starship. Upon graduation, the pair will be recommended to a starship with an open Secondary position.

In order to introduce the young Florivans to a variety of potential human counterparts, the programs bring in new Astral Navigator prospects each year. These prospects will rotate through as training partners to the available Florivan students until either they are chosen as a Navigator, run out of Florivan students who can hear their voice over the intercom channels which reach into Quantum Space during a Transit cycle, or reach the end of the school year. The vast majority of Nav cadets wash out of the program at some point in this process, although those of them who do can be granted 'Nav Certified' status if their performance in the program meets certain criteria. (Nav Certified personnel are sought after on most starships, as they can fill in for an ill or incapacitated Navigator if needed. It is not uncommon for one of these trained people to encounter a Florivan later on in their career who will go on to make a Navigator's compact with them.)

The humans selected as Astral Navigator candidates are either recommended by working Nav/Quan officers, offered the opportunity to go through the application process by the Academy's Administration based on their assessment scores and career goals, or apply to the program directly. All potential Nav Cadets go through a series of further assessments, psychological screenings, background checks, and field trials in simulations with the program's Florivan instructors before being admitted to the program. This is partially in order to gauge the human student's aptitude for the Navigator's duties, and more crucially to ensure that humans with ill intentions or inclinations are removed as prospects before they have the chance to come in close contact with the young Florivans in the program's care.

Occasionally, a young Florivan will be set on making their compact with a specific human from outside their Academy's program. These humans are similarly screened and tested by the program's instructors, as well as the Elder of the Florivan's household. In most cases, such a human will be granted admission to the program even if they would not otherwise meet the Academy Administration's criteria.

Aside from the lifelong friendship the young Florivan forms with their human counterpart, the Academy Nav/Quan system also offers them the opportunity to form friendships with the other Navigator prospects and human students from their secondary studies and extracurricular activities. These friendship groups often carry on into the graduated Nav/Quan pair's career and create a network of support both on their eventual starship posting and throughout the Coalition's inhabited worlds. In addition to helping further compensate for the adult Florivan's separation from the tightly-knit extended family groups they naturally live in, this continues to cement the bond between Florivans and humanity as an integrated society and near symbiotic species.

On Character Identities and Pronouns

The stories contained in *Tales of the Navigators, Volume One* take place in a far future setting in which human society has long since reached the stage of accepting and celebrating all varieties of diversity. This is a sort of world that I, personally, would like to live in. I don't claim it to be a *perfect* setting, but I do take an optimistic view of our potential as a species.

Several of the human characters presented in this story would, in today's terms, likely identify with one or more communities under the LGBTQIA+ umbrella. While the narrative of this story did not call for the characters to specifically state which labels they would use, and I like to imagine that a lot of who they are can be inferred through their interactions, as a member of the LGBTQIA+ community *myself*, I'm aware of the importance of clear representation. Seeing characters like ourselves in stories where they are valued for who they are and able to live without being marginalized for their nature is, in my opinion, *powerful*, and a big part of my philosophy as a writer.

Please note that at the same time, it is impossible to represent an entire community in the form of one character. My characters are simply themselves, and while they draw on my own experiences and those of people I know, they are not meant to be "perfect" renditions of one thing or another. Just like every human, their various identities are *aspects* of them, rather than the entirety of their personality.

That all being said, in order of their appearance in *Tales of the Navigators, Volume One*, the following characters who feature in these stories would like to "come out" to you and share this aspect of their lives:

Henrietta Rose Lin would describe herself as asexual and aromantic.

Monica Malarius would describe herself as asexual and aromantic.

Admiral Jennifer Marvin would describe herself as asexual and aromantic.

Elias Rudolph would describe himself as homosexual/homoromantic. (In his words: "a man who happens to be attracted to other men." Rudy has never been all that interested in labels of any sort.)

Lt. Hsu Li would describe himself as pansexual and demi-romantic.

Abigail Ioane would describe herself as asexual and aromantic.

Anna Toussaint would describe herself as a sapphic-leaning bisexual.

CPO Thomas Sidney would describe himself as a heterosexual transgender man.

Ensign Theodore Ruttiger would describe himself as asexual and aromantic.

Dr. Reba Kiely would describe herself as "demi-attractional" (demi-sexual and demi-romantic).

Merek Fiala would describe himself as asexual and aromantic.

Teresa Vasquez would describe herself as bixexual and aromantic.

Robin Maltby would describe themself as genderless. (If asked how they identify, Robin usually responds with a noncommittal shrug and then changes the subject to something they find more interesting.)

Beck Lavine would describe themself as nonbinary and/or agender.

(Note: Please keep in mind that this is not an exhaustive list of the LGBTQIA+ characters who appear in these stories, any more than it is a full description of each of the characters in question. These are simply the folks who feature most prominently and asked me to clarify their identities.)

On behalf of all of my characters, humans and Florivans alike, I'd like to thank you, dear reader, for being accepting of them and respecting their preferred sets of pronouns.

I hope that we all will one day live in a world like the one these characters inhabit, in which a person can openly be themself without fear. I do believe it's possible for us to get there, too; every small step we make in the right direction matters.

—Katie Silverwings

Katie Silverwings is an award-winning author, artist, and glassblower, originally from Texas and now a nomadic creative spirit. She holds a BA in English and History from McMurry University in Abilene, Texas, as well as a BA (Hons.) in Glass from the University for the Creative Arts in the UK. Silverwings identifies as aromantic, asexual, and genderfae; "she/her", "they/them", and "fae/faer" pronouns are all welcome.

Long fascinated by nature and space, Silverwings' speculative fiction work centers around notions of optimistic futurism, friendship, found family, and adventurous journeys into the known and unknown. Her characters do most of the driving, and she does her best to keep up and negotiate pleasing stories with them.

Silverwings' two cats are commonly found staring over her shoulder while she's writing. The small cloud of dark matter with eyes likes to sit in her lap and interfere with typing, while the calico makes operatic editorial comments from across the room.

www.KatieSilverwings.com
ⓕ ⓘ @KatieSilverwings

MORE BOOKS
BY KATIE SILVERWINGS

Celadon

✦ A Strange Space™ Novel ✦

The Novan War has just begun. All that stands between Humanity and utter destruction are the ships of the Sol Coalition Defense Fleet.

The only problem? None of those ships are equipped with the all-important Quantum Space Drive which allows humanity to travel between planets and stars at a reasonable scale of time. The Drive needs Florivan QSD Engineers to run it, and Florivans are pacifists. Their Council of Elders has never allowed service on military vessels.

The Fleet can do little more than sit at the edges of the Coalition's seven member systems and *wait* for the Novans to attack.

Celadon Toreval is the Youngest of the Florivan Council of Elders. If anyone can come to Fleet Admiral Marvin's aid and help her save her people—and theirs—it's them.

Celadon, though, has their own reasons to get involved...

Warmth and Darkness

Admiral Jennifer Marvin used to think she'd seen everything the galaxy had to throw at her. That, though, was before she met the Florivan Elder Celadon Toreval. She can sum up this Quantum Space Drive Engineer and dear friend of hers in two words: *cryptic chaos*. Their preference for the company of the most troublesome humans they can possibly find in the Fleet's ranks doesn't make matters better.

These days, Admiral Marvin is just grateful that the galaxy occasionally sends her a sign that something unusual is about to upset her carefully laid plans. Whether she manages to see those signs in time to do anything about it, though, is always a gamble.

Join Admiral Marvin's crew aboard the starship SCV *Aegolius* as they face the next chapter in the tales of the Novan War, and find out what new adventure waits for them in the darkness.

Even in the depths of space, you can find warmth...

The Garden in the Darkness

Adventures happen when you least expect them.

In the time of the Novan War, the pilots of the 2nd Darter Squadron "Musketeers" are no strangers to peril. Even the little Florivan kitten who serves as their mascot has a tendency to get into trouble. When two of the Musketeers and their mascot find themselves stranded on a seemingly deserted mining colony, though, they find themselves in a situation none of their previous adventures could have prepared them for.

With no way to contact the rest of the Defense Fleet, they'll have to find their own way to repair their darters and get back to their starship. To make matters worse, enemy forces are lurking in the nearby asteroids.

The Mayview outpost was abandoned at the start of the War, but the Musketeers aren't alone here. Someone is watching them from behind the overgrown vines...

Feathered Friendship

✶ A Strange Space™ Novella ✶

Dr. Ariadne Salzar-Newman is *not* a mad scientist.

She *is* a scientist—a brilliant one at that—but she's hardly *mad*. If one asks MSS *Venture's* staff psychologist and QSD Engineer, the Florivan Elder Navy Irleeim, she's only "amusingly eccentric, with a bit more of a fascination with the Strange than is healthy for a human."

That fascination has her once again working with the dangerous miasmas of Quantum Space, in hopes of making travel through that veiled dimension safer for human starships. It's not particularly safe for a scientist, for sure. Still, having taken Navy's apprentice under her wing as a part-time assistant, she's safer than usual. Working with her is good for Cobalt Mereday, too, if only because her unique brand of oddity seems to be the only thing capable of helping them.

Even Dr. Salzar-Newman has no reason to suspect just how much of an effect this particular project will have on her family and her protégé, nor how far-reaching the consequences will be.

Little Bernadette is *not* an ordinary budgerigar...